OTHER STORIES IN THE
L.A. METRO SERIES

In a Heartbeat

RJ NOLAN

ACKNOWLEDGMENT

It has been a long and often bumpy road as I endeavored to complete this novel. If not for the support and assistance from a group of wonderful people I would not have completed the project. Thank you all.

As always to ETJ. Your love and support keep me going every day.

To Pam. You stuck with me through it all and I'm very grateful for your friendship. You told me things I needed to hear, even when I didn't want to hear them. Thank you.

To Jae, my critique partner. Thanks for catching all those danglers. Glad I could provide some humor along the way.

To Eleanore. Thank you for having faith in me, even when I had lost faith in myself. Your unflagging support means so much.

A special thank-you goes to my editor, Sandra Gerth, for making the editing process as stress-free as possible. It was a pleasure working with you.

Thanks to Glendon at Streetlight Graphics for creating a fantastic cover.

Thanks go to Day Peterson for editing and to Blu for proofreading.

And last, but certainly not least, a big thank-you to my publisher, Astrid. I appreciate your patience and understanding.

DEDICATION

To my sister, Gwenn.
No matter what separates us, be it time,
distance, or barriers of our own making, you
will always be in my heart. I miss you.

CHAPTER 1

Officer Sam McKenna strode across the street to the station house. Pausing for a moment before entering, she glanced at her navy blue uniform shirt and adjusted the bulletproof vest underneath, then settled her equipment belt more firmly around her hips. Satisfied with her appearance, she pulled open the door and stepped into the main lobby.

Long-ingrained habit made her scan the room.

At this time of the morning, things were fairly quiet. An overweight man paced the length of the bulletproof glass that boxed in the main desk area. The wooden chairs lining one side of the room were empty except for one forlorn-looking woman whose already pale face was given a sickly pallor by the industrial green paint on the walls. She kept glancing at the door through which prisoners were released, a sure sign that she'd been there before.

As Sam passed by the desk on her way to roll call, she waved at the duty sergeant, who was tied up on the phone.

"Hey, Sam. Wait up."

At the sound of Marina's voice, a smile tugged up the corners of Sam's mouth. Memories of their brief time together as lovers filled her mind. The passion had burned out fairly quickly, but they had ended up becoming good friends.

"What's up?" Sam asked as they made their way toward the room where roll call was held.

"Have you heard how many rookies we're going to get?"

Sam grimaced, not wanting to be the bearer of bad news. Marina had just qualified as an instructor for the Field Training Officer program, but with the limited number of rookies being assigned to their division wouldn't be training one this time around.

"Only two."

"Damn!" Marina smacked her hand against the doorframe as they entered roll call. "We need at least six."

"I know." Sam shook her head. "Budget constraints, resources spread thin, and all that crap."

Today would bring the new training assignments for the next eighteen weeks. As one of the senior FTOs, Sam would be assigned one of the incoming rookies.

"Come on. Let's grab a seat," she said. The rows of long tables and folding chairs in the briefing room were rapidly filling up.

Marina groused under her breath but slid into the chair next to Sam.

From her place in the back of the room, Sam scanned for the two rookies. They weren't hard to spot, even though she could only see them from behind. Where the veteran officers were all relaxed, joking and enjoying their breakfast as the briefing continued, the rookies sat stiffly, almost at attention.

As always, the sergeant left the introductions for the end. "One last thing before I let you go," he said. "We have two new rookies with us today, Brad Davidson and Kellie Matthews. Stand up, you two."

The rookies stood to face their fellow officers. Greetings and catcalls echoed through the room.

"Okay, everyone is dismissed," the sergeant said. "Howard, McKenna, come get your rookies."

As the other officers crowded out of the room, Sam made her way to the front to appraise the rookies.

Matthews was short, probably just making five feet four. But she was sturdily built, with well-muscled arms showing beneath the sleeves of her uniform shirt. Her long blond hair was done up in a tight French braid. Davidson, sporting a military-style haircut, personified the description of ordinary: brown eyes, brown hair, average build. Both had to be at least twenty-one, but they looked like kids to her. She shook her head. Thirty-three suddenly felt old.

Davidson was working hard at appearing relaxed, but his rapid blinking and the flickering of his gaze around the room gave him away. Matthews, on the other hand, wasn't even trying to hide her nerves. She still stood at attention, not daring to move a muscle.

Smothering a grin, Sam gently bumped her shoulder in passing and winked when scared green eyes met hers. "Relax before you strain something," she said, her voice pitched just for the woman's ears.

Matthews' rigid stance eased a little, but not much.

Sam propped her hip against a nearby table and glanced over at her fellow FTO. Howard was a know-it-all blowhard, who filled rookies' heads with a lot of outdated nonsense and was not a big fan of female police officers.

Assign her to me, she mentally willed the supervising sergeant.

"Officers Howard and McKenna are the FTOs you'll be working with for the next eighteen weeks. Matthews, you're assigned to Officer Howard. Davidson, you're with Officer McKenna," the sergeant said, pointing to each of them in turn.

Sam grimaced internally. *Damn.* She spared Matthews a sympathetic glance before turning to the rookie assigned to her.

His gaze roamed her body before finally making it to her face.

Not the way to make a good start with me, rookie. Sam straightened, watching his eyes widen when she easily matched his height, and pinned him in place with a withering glare.

He gulped and quickly averted his gaze.

"Let's go, Davidson." She turned and stalked out of the room, never looking back to see whether he was following.

It was going to be a long eighteen weeks.

CHAPTER 2

"Y ou should've seen Davidson's face after this little bit of nothing took him down," Sam said.

Laughter erupted from the women gathered in the back room at O'Grady's bar for their regular Friday night bullshit session.

"Yeah, but did a kick in the crotch cool his jets toward you?" Karen asked.

Sam snorted. "I wish. I still can't believe no one at the station clued him in." She shook her head. "I thought for sure Howard would. I finally just told Davidson that asking me out was a lost cause."

A bottle of beer appeared over her shoulder. Looking back, she grinned at the new arrival. "Hey, Marina. I didn't think you'd make it." She took the offered beer and set it down among the bottles and snack bowls that littered the table. "We were just getting ready to pack it in."

Marina greeted the other police officers at the table, then pulled a chair over and sat down next to Sam.

Waggling her eyebrows, Sam asked, "How was your vacation?"

"Good," Marina said with a soft smile.

Tilting her head, Sam peered at her friend. For a while, she had thought Marina was like her—out for a good time and leery of commitment. Marina had been the one to end their affair and suggest they just be friends, but her attitude had changed when she met Elizabeth a few months ago. Sam

5

quashed a brief surge of envy. *Face it. You don't do girlfriends. You proved that once again with Christy.*

Marina tousled Sam's hair. "I like the new look."

"Cut it out." Sam rubbed her hand through her freshly shorn locks, still not used to it. While she had always worn her hair short, it had never been to this extreme. She had seen the pixie haircut on a TV newswoman and on a whim decided to try it.

"She's going for the butch look, hoping to cool off her overeager rookie." Darcy smirked. "Or was it to try and attract some new women you haven't managed to bag yet?"

Sam shot her a dirty look. Talk about holding a grudge. Their falling out had been two years ago, and she'd apologized—twice.

Marina turned her back on Darcy. "So what happened with your rookie while I was gone?"

As Sam began to relate the story, the other women at the table said their good-byes. Soon, she and Marina were alone.

Marina winced and laughed when Sam got to the climax of her story. "Poor kid. Bet he never looks at a 'little lady' quite the same way again."

Sam joined her laughter, then sobered. "Better a kick in the crotch early on than something worse later because he thinks he's invincible. You know as well as I do, there's a fine line between confidence and arrogance. And this kid was on the wrong side of it." She blew out a breath and snagged her neglected beer.

"I hear you on that one." Marina grinned. "Maybe I should add that to my teaching techniques: if a rookie doesn't listen, deliver a swift kick to the crotch. It would work on men and women."

Laughing, Sam dropped her hands into her lap and covered her sex. "Youch! Talk about a motivational technique."

"Enough work talk. Are Kim and Jess going to be back from their honeymoon in time to come to our game next week? I want to ask them which island they liked best in Hawaii." Marina's expression grew soft, her eyes shining with emotion. "Elizabeth wants to go there for the Christmas holidays."

Sam smiled, still not quite believing that her big sister was married. Refusing to give in to the feelings of inadequacy that tugged at her, she focused on Marina, and being happy for her as well.

While she really was pleased that her friend had found someone special, that wasn't going to stop her from tweaking her. "Marina, it's barely summer. Isn't it a little early to be planning for Christmas? Geez, three months together, and you're pussy-whipped already."

Marina laughed and waggled her eyebrows. "Chica, you don't know the half of it. And it is so worth it!"

"They'll be back on Sunday. Kim is the one you want to talk to. She planned it all out. If it was up to Jess, they probably would have just stayed at home, so she could keep Kim all to herself." Sam grinned. *Not that I could blame her for that.*

"I always knew your sister was a smart woman."

An image of Jess, her face aglow with love as she stood beneath a rose-covered arbor with Kim, flashed through Sam's mind.

You've got that right.

CHAPTER 3

T his is so not fair." Davidson slapped the steering wheel. "After six weeks together, you finally let me drive, and what do we end up doing? Following an ambulance transporting a drunk with a cut on his head to Grandview. Come on, they're not even running lights and sirens."

He sounded just as Sam had when she'd been a rookie. "What have I told you? Most police work is routine and boring." Still, she couldn't resist nettling him. "What? You didn't get enough excitement in the bar?"

Davidson scowled. "You call that excitement? It wasn't even a bar fight. The guy just trashed the place because the bartender cut him off. He was passed out on the floor by the time we got there."

"So that's what you want? Some excitement?" In her almost nine years on the force, she'd had more than her share of excitement. She would take a nice, boring day any day, as would most experienced officers.

"Couldn't hurt. Our whole day is shot. We're gonna be stuck babysitting this guy for hours in the ER, then more time processing him at the station. What a waste. We could be out stopping actual crime."

"Haven't you ever heard the old Chinese proverb about that? You know, the one that says, 'Be careful what you wish for, you might get it.'"

His brow furrowed. "Huh? Isn't that the point of wishing for something?"

Sam shook her head. The kid still had an awful lot to learn.

Trying to distract herself from the guy's deafening snores, Sam surveyed the patient cubicle where they had been relegated to wait with their suspect. Her surroundings had not gotten any more interesting in the minutes since the last time she had done so. Three ugly gray walls, one dingy brown curtain, one wall cabinet, one IV stand, one—

With a loud snort, their suspect woke up and looked around blearily. When he tried to sit up, he realized he was cuffed to the gurney. "Let me go! I didn't do nothing." He jerked on the cuffs and drummed his feet against the gurney. "Let me go. Let me go."

Sam pressed her hand against his shoulder. "Settle down." She looked over at Davidson on the opposite side of the gurney and arched an eyebrow. *This the kind of excitement you were looking for?*

A panicked yell, followed by what sounded like falling equipment, from somewhere close by drew her attention.

It's an ER. People are hurt, and they yell. Still, Sam felt compelled to check it out. She peeked out from behind the curtain, just in time to see a man in a business suit drag a woman wearing a lab coat into the last cubicle and then whip the curtain closed.

"Someone call security," a woman in blue scrubs shouted.

Sam pulled open the curtain and stepped out. "I'm going to check this out." Davidson moved to follow her. "You stay with him."

"But—"

"Stay with him." Sam tapped the mike clipped to her shirt. "I'll call if I need backup."

She raced up to the staff milling around outside the cubicle where the man and woman had disappeared. "Everyone get back," she said quietly but firmly and herded the group away from the closed curtain. "Did any of you see a weapon?"

"No," one of the nurses said. "The guy just walked up to the nurses' station and grabbed Dr. Connolly."

The rest of the gathered staff nodded.

"Did he call her by name? Did she seem to recognize him?"

The assembled staff glanced at one another, but no one offered any information. The nurse who had spoken up the first time said, "I think she might have known him, but I'm not positive. He didn't say anything, just snatched her before anyone could react."

Sam kept her eye on the curtain but saw no sign of movement. It was deathly silent behind the curtain. What the hell was going on?

She quickly surveyed the area, motioned to one of the nurses, then pointed down the hallway at the single row of curtained rooms. "Quietly clear any patients from those cubicles. Get everyone back to the nurses' station. Stay there and wait for security." The last thing she wanted was a confrontation with innocent bystanders nearby.

As soon as the hospital employees had moved out of the way, she stepped up to the curtain and eased it aside.

The perp had the petite doctor pinned against the wall next to the gurney. He had one hand over her mouth and was tearing at her clothes with the other. She was fighting him for all she was worth.

The sight galvanized Sam into action. "Police! Stop. Take your hands off her."

The man backpedaled at her approach. In the close quarters, his feet got tangled in the IV stand. He grabbed the pole for support and then shoved it at Sam. "Fuck you! She's mine."

The IV pole banged into Sam, and the equipment attached to it snagged on her utility belt.

His hand dove into his suit coat pocket.

Weapon!

She struggled to free herself from the IV stand with one hand and reached for her gun with the other.

Time seemed to almost stand still. Each second ticked by as if it were a minute.

A small-caliber handgun cleared the man's coat pocket and zeroed in on the doctor before Sam could raise her weapon.

In a heartbeat, she was moving. Before even being aware of making the decision, she stepped directly into the line of fire.

The report of the gun was loud in the small room.

The doctor screamed.

A burning sensation spread across Sam's shoulder and down her arm. Despite the pain, she struggled to bring her weapon up.

"She's mine," he yelled and fired again.

Searing pain in her leg robbed Sam of breath, and she staggered. She felt herself going down but was powerless to stop it.

Arms wrapped around her waist from behind, but they weren't enough to stop her momentum.

The muzzle of the gun pointing directly at her filled her vision as she crumpled to the floor.

Pain lanced through her head, darkness following swiftly on its heels.

No! Dear God, please. No. Dr. Riley Connolly threw herself over the body of the downed officer.

"Police! Drop the weapon!"

Relief washed over her.

"She's mine!" Keith screamed again.

Boom! Boom! The sound of the shots reverberated in the room.

Riley flinched, expecting to feel the searing pain of a bullet in her back. When no pain came, she jerked her head up, ears still ringing.

A few feet away, Keith lay on the floor, half-sprawled against the wall. A lurid red smear trailed down the wall above him.

A police officer, his weapon still extended at arm's length, stood frozen in the entrance to the cubicle.

His gun tracked her movement as Riley eased herself up onto her knees. Shaken, she blurted out the first thing that came into her head. "I'm a doctor." She slowly raised her trembling hands so that he could see them.

His gaze slid over her torn scrub shirt, but his gun never wavered. "Don't move." He stepped over and checked Keith, then holstered his weapon. "He's dead," he said, his voice shaky.

Bile burned at the back of Riley's throat. Her professional instincts kicking in, she quickly assessed the location of Keith's wounds and realized he was undoubtedly correct. Her gaze darted to the fallen officer and the rapidly spreading pool of blood seeping out from under her, then back up to the policewoman's partner. "Please let me help her."

The sound of running feet heralded the arrival of hospital security.

"Wait. Stay back." The officer stepped forward and quickly secured Keith's gun and then his partner's weapon. Turning an agonized gaze on Riley, he said, "Save her. Please."

Riley nodded.

Two security guards peered into the room.

Riley raised her voice to be heard over the sound of excited voices in the hall. "Let the medical staff through. We've got two people down."

She reached for that place inside that allowed her to push away all emotion so that she could do her job. This wasn't the time to think about what had just happened—what this woman had done for her. She tugged her lab coat closed to cover the remnants of her ruined scrub shirt, the formerly pristine white stained by the officer's blood. After pulling a pair of gloves from her pocket and donning them, she moved quickly to evaluate the condition of the wounded officer.

Once she'd made sure her airway was intact, she moved on in her examination. She had seen the officer strike her head on the wall cabinet when she fell, so she checked the woman's pupils. They were equal and reactive. *Good.* Riley gave the head laceration a cursory glance. It could wait, and so could her shoulder.

The officer's pants were saturated with blood, and Riley hurriedly cut away the material. Blood pulsed from the thigh wound.

"We need to get her into a trauma room," she called out to the arriving medical personnel. "Move it, people, I've got an arterial bleeder here."

As they lifted the officer onto a gurney and rushed toward the trauma bay, Riley kept pressure on the damaged artery to tamponade the vessel.

The ER was in a state of pandemonium.

Riley remained the calm at the center of the storm, aware of nothing but the injured officer. Even as she worked to stop the bleeding, she was issuing orders for lab work, IVs, and blood.

The ER staff moved around her as if in a choreographed dance. The officer was quickly stripped of her gear and clothing. A nurse called out her vital signs. IVs were inserted, blood drawn, and she was attached to a monitor.

There it is! Riley slid a vascular clamp onto the damaged artery and temporarily occluded the blood vessel. "That's it. Let's get her to the OR." She grabbed the gurney and pulled it out of the room.

CHAPTER 4

As Jess McKenna neared the nurses' station, she frowned at the sight of Karen and Terrell, two of her residents, huddled together over the screen of his phone. She strode over. "Back to work."

The duo jumped at the sound of her voice.

"You both know there's no use of personal phones during working hours."

"I'm sorry, Dr. McKenna," Terrell said, his hand clenched tightly around the phone. "I was walking through the waiting room and saw a news flash on the TV that a police officer had been shot. I was trying to find out where in the city it happened."

Jess's stomach sank. *Don't let it be his brother.* She gave his shoulder a brief squeeze. "Go ahead and see what you can find out."

Though he was trying to hide it, she knew Terrell must be terrified. If the shooting had been in San Diego instead of LA, she would have been too. She sent up a prayer for her sister. *Stay safe, Sam.*

Terrell let out a whoop. "Thank God."

"What?" Jess asked.

"It couldn't have been Jerome. The shooting wasn't even in LA."

"What shooting?" Kim asked as she walked up to stand next to Jess.

Jess smiled at her wife. *My wife!* She still couldn't believe it. They had been back at work only three days, and she already wished they could go back to the beach in Hawaii where they had spent their honeymoon.

"Terrell saw a news bulletin about a police officer being shot, but it didn't happen in LA."

Terrell shut off his phone and stuck it in his pocket. "I know I shouldn't be happy, because it means someone else is going to get bad news, but I can't help it."

"That's perfectly understandable," Kim said. Her brow furrowed. "Was the shooting in California?"

"Yeah, San Diego."

Jess's insides turned to ice. *No. He's wrong. It was someplace else.* She reached for Kim's hand.

Scared blue eyes gazed back at her.

The phone on the counter began to trill stridently.

Penny answered. Her gaze flickered over to Jess, and her eyes went wide.

A dark premonition shrouded Jess's soul. *God, no! Please, not Sam.* She tightened her grip on Kim's hand as if it was her lifeline.

Penny held out the phone. Jess knew what she was going to say before she spoke. "Dr. McKenna, it's the police. They say it's an emergency."

Kim held Jess's hand in a crushing grip and refused to let go. This couldn't be happening. Everything around her faded into the background. It was just her and Jess and the phone call that could change their lives forever.

With her free hand, Jess touched Kim's face for just a moment. Swallowing heavily, Kim released Jess's hand.

Jess walked to the counter as if approaching the gallows and took the phone from Penny. "This is Dr. McKenna."

Kim clenched her hands so tightly that her nails bit into her palms.

Jess listened for a moment, then her knees buckled and she grasped the counter for support.

Kim rushed to her side, but Jess waved her off and quickly regained her composure. Pain stabbed Kim's heart at the rejection. *I thought we were past this.* She immediately berated herself. *This isn't about you and Jess. God. Sam.* A tear trailed down her face.

"Yes. I understand. Thank you," Jess said. "We'll be there as soon as we can."

The flat, emotionless tone of Jess's voice worried Kim, adding to the burning sensation in her stomach. *Please, God, just let her be alive. We can deal with anything else.*

Jess turned, her face a blank mask. As if she had heard Kim's prayer, she said, "She's alive."

Kim burst into tears. "Thank God." She threw herself into Jess's arms and clung to her. "Thank you, God."

Jess patted her back for a moment and then pulled away. Her eyes were dry. "We need to get to San Diego as quickly as we can."

"I'll call psych and get someone to cover for me. Give me five minutes." *Hang on, Sam. We'll be there soon.*

"Come on. Move already!" Jess glared through the windshield at the sea of cars. Traffic had slowed to a crawl as the heavy afternoon commute reached its peak. "Anything new?" She glanced at Kim.

"Nothing new since they released Sam's name and academy picture half an hour ago. Local and national stations keep repeating the same information," Kim huffed out a frustrated breath, "over and over again. She's still in surgery."

You're just torturing yourself, and Kim. As the head of the ER, Jess knew that neither the police nor the hospital would release any information about Sam's condition until the family arrived. But this was her sister. Even though she knew it was pointless, she couldn't help checking, in case even a speck of information was released. At the same time, a part of her dreaded what she might hear. *Sam could be dead and they would still say she was in surgery.* The icy hand of fear clutched her heart. *Don't even think that. Sam is alive. She has to be!*

"Should I try to reach Frank and Cheryl again?"

Jess's fear morphed into anger. "Why can't they just answer their fucking phones!" She slammed her hand against the steering wheel, causing the SUV to swerve. Quickly, she righted it and clenched the wheel with a white-knuckled grip. Why the hell did Frank have to pick now to go on vacation?

"Hey. Easy. We know they're hiking in Yosemite. They're probably still in an area with no cell service." Kim put her hand on Jess's shoulder.

Jess jerked away, then immediately regretted the reaction. She risked a look at Kim and wanted to smack herself in the head. *Idiot.* "I'm sorry." She gently took Kim's hand and placed it on her thigh, then laid her hand on top. "I don't mean to take it out on you. I know this is hard on you too. I'm just so..."

"I know, love." Kim pulled her hand from under Jess's and leaned across the console. She slid her hand into Jess's hair at the nape of her neck and softly stroked her neck. "We're doing everything we can. Aunt Edna is dealing with the cruise ship lines to contact your folks. The rangers are looking for your brother and Cheryl."

"I know. But what if..." Jess clenched her teeth so tightly her jaw ached. "I screwed up. I should've gotten a contact number when they called me at the hospital. I should have the phone numbers of Sam's police friends. I should've—"

"Jess. Stop this. Right now!"

Jess whipped her head to the side to stare at Kim. She had never heard her use such a commanding tone. Blue eyes that seemed to glow from within met her gaze, and she quickly turned her attention back to the road to escape the piercing look.

"Enough," Kim said, her tone much calmer. "We'll drive ourselves crazy with what-ifs and should haves." She squeezed Jess's thigh. "I'm scared too." She held up her phone and set it on the dash. "And this isn't helping. I could check every ten seconds, and it wouldn't change a thing. We need to have faith that Sam will be all right. That's what we need to focus on."

As usual, she was right. Consciously relaxing the tense set of her shoulders, Jess took a cleansing breath and then another. It took some time, but eventually some of the tension drained from her body. Smiling, she looked over at Kim, this time unafraid to meet her gaze. "I love you."

"I love you too, Jess. And we're going to get through this, like we always do—together."

Kim eyed the press people and their cameras as she and Jess rushed into the lobby of Grandview Medical Center. Jess had a firm grip on her hand but still wore the blank, emotionless look she had donned the second they stepped out of their SUV.

Jess tugged on her hand. "There's the information desk."

As Jess headed in that direction at a fast clip, Kim spotted a man wearing a press pass lurking near the info desk.

When he caught sight of Jess, he did a double take and moved within hearing range of the clerk manning the desk.

"Wait, Jess."

"What?" Jess slowed but didn't stop.

"Come with me." Kim pulled on her hand, trying to lead her away from the desk. For a moment, she did not think Jess would come.

Jess stopped. She glanced at the desk as if drawn to it, then back at Kim. After blowing out a breath, she allowed herself to be led away. "What's wrong?" she asked as soon as they stopped.

"There are reporters everywhere. See that one standing right in front of the info desk?"

Jess glanced over and nodded.

"You know what the press is like. If they hear you ask about Sam and say you're her sister, all hell will break loose."

"I don't care." Jess's expression hardened. "We have to find out where Sam is."

Kim heard what Jess didn't say. *And how Sam is.* She was as anxious to get to Sam as Jess was. The question was how to do that without alerting the ghouls from the press. Her gaze swept the lobby again. Standing off to the side, near the information desk, was a uniformed San Diego police officer, keeping a close eye on the desk, probably waiting for them.

CHAPTER 5

B right overhead lights reflected off the white tile of the surgeons' locker room, making Riley's tired eyes sting. A glance around confirmed she was alone. After finding her boss and a hospital lawyer waiting for her outside the OR, she wasn't in the mood to face anyone else. She stretched her aching back as she trudged over to her locker.

After stripping off her outer surgical gown, she froze and started to tremble when her ruined scrub shirt came into view. Memories of Keith's hands tearing at her clothes ambushed her. She again felt his body pinning her forcefully against the wall, his intent blatantly apparent against her belly. The soiled gown dropped from her suddenly nerveless fingers. She slid down the front of her locker and buried her face against her upraised knees. Unwanted tears dampened the fabric of her scrub pants.

The sound of the outer door opening made her lift her head and rub frantically at her tear-streaked face. She scrambled to her feet and spun toward her locker before anyone could witness her tears.

"Riley!" Denny called.

Not about to embarrass herself in front of her friend and fellow trauma surgeon, she fought back renewed tears.

Rapid footsteps sounded behind her.

Riley took a deep breath and turned to face him. His dark, bushy hair stood on end as if he had run his hands through it countless times. Worried brown eyes gazed at her. Before she could stop him, he pulled her into his arms. She stiffened, then forced herself to relax in his embrace. After a moment, she gently pushed him away.

"Are you all right? The nurses downstairs said you weren't hurt, but I needed to be sure."

With long practice, she pushed her emotions down and put a calm expression on her face. "I'm fine."

His gaze dropped to her scrub shirt, and his eyes widened. "He didn't...?"

Tugging her torn shirt back together, Riley said, "No."

"What happened, Riley? I thought you broke it off with Keith months ago. Why would he do something like this now?"

She really did not want to get into this with him. What was done was done. But she knew Denny wouldn't let it go.

"There's not much to tell. Keith wanted to keep dating. It wasn't bad at first. He kept asking me out, sending me flowers, that kind of thing, but then six weeks ago, things changed." Riley had no intention of telling Denny what had happened that set Keith off. "He followed me a few times, started calling at all hours, and vandalized my car."

"Damn it, Riley. Why didn't you say something?" Denny looked as if he wanted to shake her.

When he reached toward her, unexpected fear chased down Riley's spine. She took a hasty step backward and banged into her locker. Her hands clutched the front of her scrub shirt closed.

Denny held up his hands in a placating gesture and moved back.

"Sorry." This was Denny. He would never hurt her. "I guess I'm just kind of jumpy after...everything."

"I didn't mean to scare you. I should have realized." He jammed his hands into his lab coat pockets. "I wish you had told me Keith was bothering you. Maybe I could have helped."

She had learned early on to handle things on her own, so asking for help had never occurred to her. She crossed her arms over her chest and shrugged.

Denny raked his fingers through his hair. "What did Dwayne the Pain and the lawyer want? I saw them lurking outside the OR when they brought the officer out."

Riley grimaced. Her interactions with Dr. Dwayne McBain, the interim trauma center medical director, were aggravating on the best of days. After everything she had been through, she was physically and emotionally exhausted. Finding McBain outside the OR waiting to pounce had gotten on her last nerve. Not that she would ever give him the satisfaction of knowing that.

"You know McBain." She shrugged. "Nothing makes him happier than the chance to give one of *his* surgeons a hard time and remind them that he's in charge. I'll be so glad when Dr. Lin comes back and resumes his position. Anyway, McBain was ticked off that I operated on the police officer. According to him, I should have let someone else do the surgery."

When Denny shuffled his feet and didn't reply, she narrowed her eyes at him. "You think he was right?"

"Well...I can kind of see his point."

Anger seized Riley and dug its talons deep. "So I should have just hung back and done nothing? And watch the woman who saved me bleed out in front of me?"

Denny stared at her open-mouthed.

Riley wasn't sure who was more surprised by her outburst: she or Denny. *Get control of yourself.* She took a deep breath and then blew it out.

"I'm sorry. I know how hard this must be with everything that has happened. I shouldn't have questioned your judgment." He glanced away. "I heard about Keith."

"Keith made me miserable, and I wanted him out of my life...but not like this." A vivid flashback of the blood-smeared wall and Keith lying sprawled on the floor slammed into her. She pressed her hands to her stomach as a wave of nausea threatened to overwhelm her.

Denny wrapped his hands around her upper arms as her knees buckled. "Come on. You need to sit down." He guided her to a nearby bench, where he pulled her down next to him and wrapped an arm around her shoulders.

Riley shrugged off his arm and slid down the bench to put some distance between them. Although he meant well, she needed some space—physically and emotionally. "I need to change and get back to work. I have to check on my patient." She frowned when she realized she didn't even know her name. Rising to her feet, she pulled her shirt together. "If you'll excuse me."

"Wait." Denny jumped up. "When you get done, come over to the house. Carol will want to see you. If she wasn't confined to bed because of the baby—"

"You didn't call her, did you?" Carol's pregnancy was already difficult enough. Riley did not want to be the cause of any additional stress for her.

"Not yet. I was waiting until I got home," Denny said. "Thankfully, she's not the TV type, so I figured it would be safe to wait until I could be there with her."

"Don't tell her. I'm fine. It's over. Please don't upset her."

"You don't think she'll be more upset if I don't tell her? That's not the way it works when you love someone."

I wouldn't know. Riley pushed the pointless thought away. "Okay. Whatever you think is best." She edged away from him. "I really have to go. I need to check on my patient and see if her family has arrived." She did not relish that prospect at all. How could she face them, knowing she had almost gotten their loved one killed?

"All right. I'll go. Come over when you're done, okay?"

Although the last thing she wanted was to be around anyone, she didn't want to argue with him either. "Sure. I'll try."

As soon as he walked away, she headed for her locker, already pulling off the tattered scrub top.

The beeping of equipment, shuffling of feet as the nurses went about their duties, and the soft murmur of voices filled the recovery room.

Standing next to her patient's gurney, Riley used the computerized chart in her hands to learn the officer's name. *Samantha Ann McKenna.* She traced her finger over the name of the woman who had saved her life. If it weren't for her, she would be down in the morgue. Riley did not know how to come to terms with that, or if she ever would. *Stop it. Don't think about it. Do your job.*

She methodically checked the monitors, IVs, and finally, Samantha's dressings. Satisfied that all was as it should be, she entered all her post-op orders into the chart and then turned her attention to the woman herself and gazed down at her slack face.

The ghostly pallor of her skin almost matched the color of the pillowcase she rested on. A dark bruise was already forming at her temple. Sutures stood out starkly on her scalp where her short black hair had been shaved off.

With trembling fingers, Riley touched the unblemished side of Samantha's face. *Why did you do it?* That question had been running through her mind incessantly. It had not been an accident. Riley could see it in her mind's eye as if it were happening again—Samantha had stepped purposely into the line of fire. *Why? I'm nobody to you.*

"Dr. Connolly."

She started and glanced up to find Holly, one of the recovery room nurses, standing at the foot of the gurney with a curious look. Riley flushed when she realized she had the side of Samantha's face cupped in her hand, softly stroking her cheek with her thumb. She jerked her hand away as if burned.

"Yes. What is it?" she asked, her tone crisp and professional.

"Sorry to interrupt, but I thought you'd want to know that Officer McKenna's family is here."

"Thank you for letting me know."

Holly puttered with the equipment but kept glancing at Riley. Her lips were pressed together in a firm line. "Dr. McBain went out to talk to them," she finally blurted.

What? How dare he? In retrospect, Riley realized she should have figured he would do something like that. When he confronted her outside the OR, he had been furious about her doing the surgery and worried about the repercussions. Apparently, he had decided that she shouldn't have any contact with the family. She stared down at Samantha for a moment. Regardless of what McBain wanted, she had done the surgery and the woman was her patient. She could almost hear her uncle's voice. *Don't react. Act.*

"Thanks, Holly. Once Officer McKenna is ready to be released to the SICU, please make sure she's sent to radiology for her head CT before she's taken to the unit." After one last glance at Samantha, she spun on her heel and headed for the surgical waiting room to face the officer's family.

CHAPTER 6

Riley strode toward the double doors that restricted access to the ORs and recovery rooms.

This is just like meeting with any other patient's family. Be clear, concise, and keep things in layman's terms.

Normally, she didn't have to think twice about what to say to her patients' families. Then again, she had never before been the cause of the patient's injuries. Her mind on the meeting with the family, she reached blindly for the wall plate to open the swinging doors. Movement caught her eyes through the large windows inset in the doors, and she stopped just shy of pressing the door release. The normally quiet hallway on the other side of the doors was filled with people. What were so many people doing outside the OR?

A closer look provided the answer. Quite a number of the people were wearing press credentials.

Great. Just want I need. Not! One of the reporters spotted her and motioned for her to open the doors. Ignoring the gesture, she turned and took an alternate route to the fourth-floor waiting room that had been set aside for the police officers. While it could often get busy, the whole area was teeming with more people than usual. Was every reporter in the state there? She kept her head down as she approached the door to the waiting room.

When she found her way blocked by a pair of legs encased in dark blue trousers, she looked up.

"Excuse me," she said as she tried to step past the police officer.

The stern-faced officer did not budge from his post in front of the doorway. "Can I help you?"

Glancing past him, Riley tried to spot McBain. The room was filled with police officers, but her boss was nowhere in sight. Had he taken the family into the patient conference room?

"Ma'am?"

"Never mind." She turned to walk away.

"Wait." He took hold of her arm.

Riley flinched, and he immediately let go.

He glanced at her chest, then met her eyes. "Sorry, Dr. Connolly. Do you know anything about Sam, the officer who was shot? I mean Officer McKenna. There was another doctor here a little while ago. He told Sam's sister to come with him but didn't say anything about Sam's condition, so we were all wondering..."

Riley ground her teeth. McBain must have scared the family witless. The first words out of her mouth would have been, "She's in the recovery room." She gazed up into worried brown eyes. While she could not give him any details about Samantha's condition, she could at least ease his fears. "She's out of surgery and in the recovery room."

The officer let out a whoop. "Thank you." He turned and rushed into the waiting room.

A cheer erupted from the gathered police.

The noise attracted the attention of the press people lurking farther down the hall. Several of them made a beeline for the waiting room.

Using the commotion to her advantage, Riley made her exit.

Outside the patient conference room, she paused for a moment to compose herself. This wasn't about McBain. *Focus on the family.* She stepped into the room and quietly closed the door behind her. Her gaze swept the room.

Dr. McBain was sitting at the head of the table. Two women sat next to each other with their backs to her, one dark-haired, the other blond.

"That's no answer." The dark-haired woman rose from her chair like a tsunami rising from the ocean to loom over McBain. "You either know or you don't. Did you even do the surgery?" Her voice was flat, devoid of inflection. The only thing that gave away her true emotional state was the white-knuckled grip she had on the edge of the conference table.

The blonde stood and placed a comforting hand on her back.

"Now see here, young woman," McBain said.

Riley hated it when he used that pompous tone. "I performed the surgery on Officer McKenna," she said from her spot near the door. "I'll answer any questions you have."

At the sound of her voice, the woman who had questioned McBain spun around to face her. "Who are you?" Her silvery-blue eyes pinned Riley in place.

Riley tried hard not to stare. The woman's resemblance to her patient was uncanny. Was she Samantha's twin? It took her a second to find her voice.

McBain intervened before she could introduce herself. "I've got this under control. Return to your duties."

Riley froze for a moment. Her first instinct was to back down, but she forced herself to ignore that impulse and strode over to the table. Acting as if she had not heard him, she offered her hand to the woman who had to be Samantha's sister. "I'm Dr. Connolly."

"Dr. Jess McKenna. I'm Sam's sister." She released Riley's hand, and the blonde offered hers in its place. "This is my spouse, Dr. Kim Donovan."

Were they medical doctors? Plenty of PhDs used their title whenever possible. She shot a glance at McBain but couldn't get a clue from his expression other than that he was thoroughly pissed at her.

As if she had heard the question, Dr. McKenna said, "I'm chairman of the ER at L.A. Metro. My spouse is the ER psych attending at the same hospital."

That made things easier. Knowing how stressed both women must be, Riley got right to the point. "When I left your sister in the recovery room, she was in serious but stable condition. She has two gun—"

"Dr. Connolly." McBain stood. "I—"

"Quiet." Dr. McKenna glared at McBain. "If you can't be quiet, feel free to leave." She gripped the back of her chair so hard her knuckles blanched. "On second thought, I think it would be best if you did leave. Dr. Connolly will fill us in since she's the one who actually performed the surgery."

Riley kept her expression carefully neutral, although inside, she was smiling. It wasn't often McBain got put in his place. It served him right for coming in here and making them think he did the surgery.

McBain huffed, for a moment looking as if he was going to argue. Then his expression changed to what Riley thought of as his "politician face." "I'll leave you in Dr. Connolly's competent hands. I'm needed downstairs to make the press announcement. I'm sure you understand." He reached to clasp Dr. McKenna's hands, then seemed to think better of it. "If there is anything you need, just let the staff know. I just wanted to come by and assure you that your sister is receiving the highest quality care."

Riley bit the inside of her cheek to keep from reacting. She glanced over at Dr. McKenna just in time to see her expression darken.

McBain must have seen the look as well. Without another word, he made a hasty retreat.

Some of the tension left the room with him.

"I'm sorry you had to deal with him." Riley resisted the urge to sigh. "If you'll please have a seat, I'll go over everything I did and bring you up to date on Samantha's condition."

Kim kept a tight grip on Jess's hand as Dr. Connolly detailed the extent of Sam's injuries and what she had done to repair them. *My God. Twice. She was shot twice.*

"When can we see her?" Jess asked as soon as the doctor finished.

Dr. Connolly glanced at her watch. "She's probably still in radiology, getting her head CT. Let me call and check on her status."

Once she was busy on the phone, Kim turned in her seat, took Jess's face in her hands, and placed a soft kiss on her lips. "She's going to be okay. Sam's strong."

"She is." Jess put her hands over Kim's and smiled half-heartedly. "But I'll feel better after we've seen her."

"Me too."

They separated when Dr. Connolly approached the table. Jess gave Kim's hand one last squeeze.

"Good news," Dr. Connolly said. "Her head CT was clear. She's on her way to the SICU. It will take them a while to get her settled, then you can see her. I'll show you where the SICU waiting room is."

"Jess, we should let Marina and the rest of her fellow officers know she's out of surgery before we head to the SICU," Kim said.

Jess's brow furrowed. She glanced toward the door and then back at Kim, clearly torn.

Kim didn't blame her; she needed to see Sam too, but they had an obligation to the officers gathered in support of Sam.

Dr. Connolly cleared her throat. "I hope you don't mind, but when I stopped by the waiting room, looking for you, one of the officers asked, and I let them know that Samantha was out of surgery." She stuck her hands in her lab coat pockets. "I didn't give any details of her condition, just let them know that she was in recovery."

Kim smiled. "Thank you."

"Yes. Thank you," Jess said.

"All right, then," Dr. Connolly said. "If you'll follow me, I'll show you to the SICU waiting room."

Jess reached for Kim's hand as they neared Sam's room. Through the glass wall that fronted the room, she could just make out her sister's form in the bed, surrounded by equipment. The normal sights and sounds of the hospital that were part of Jess's daily life were suddenly foreign and threatening. No matter how much she tried to view this situation with a physician's eye, she couldn't.

She halted at the foot of the bed. *God. Sam.* Her normally strong, vibrant sister looked so pale, small, and helpless.

Kim sniffed.

Jess turned to see a tear track down her face. She pulled Kim close, and together they moved to stand near the head of the bed.

Jess took Sam's cold, limp hand and chafed it between her own much warmer ones. She leaned down and placed a kiss on Sam's forehead. "What have you done to yourself, kiddo?"

Kim laid her hand on top of Jess's. Tears ran freely down her face. "We're here. We love you."

Jess swallowed hard and shot a glance at Dr. Connolly, who had her gaze glued to Sam's chart, giving them at least the semblance of privacy.

To distract herself from the gut-wrenching emotions evoked by seeing Sam like this, Jess turned her attention to the equipment that surrounded her sister. She scanned the monitor readout, then the IV bags. Her stomach churned when she spotted the unit of blood hanging among the IV fluids. "How many units of blood has she had?"

Dr. Connolly looked up. "That's the second unit. I've ordered her hematocrit checked every hour for the next six hours, then I'll reevaluate the need for further transfusions."

"I'd like to see her chart," Jess said as she stepped away from the bed.

After hesitating for a moment, Dr. Connolly handed over the tablet and moved to stand next to Jess as she went over the chart.

Kim took Jess's place at the head of the bed and winced at the sight of the darkening bruises and sutures above her ear. She stroked Sam's cheek and then touched her hair, grimacing. "Why did they scalp her like that?"

"Excuse me?" Dr. Connolly frowned.

"Why did they cut all her hair off like that?"

Dr. Connolly stepped up next to Kim and peered down at Sam. She gently touched the bare area surrounding the sutures. "They needed to shave the area to be able to suture her scalp wound."

"I realize that," Kim said. "But why did they cut the rest of her hair so close to her scalp?" Of course, Sam had much bigger problems than her hair, but it raised Kim's ire, as it seemed an unnecessary indignity.

The conversation drew Jess's attention away from the chart. She moved to the opposite side of the bed. Scowling, she ran her fingers through Sam's hair. "They didn't need to do this for a scalp wound."

"No. Of course not." Dr. Connolly shook her head. "It was that short to start with."

"Oh. Sorry," Kim said, a bit embarrassed at overreacting. "She must have had it cut while we were gone on our honeymoon."

Dr. Connolly smiled. "Congratulations. I'm sorry you had to come back to something like this." She gazed down at Sam, her expression unreadable. "She is going to be okay," she said, her voice filled with determination.

"Excuse me." A nurse stuck her head in the room. "Dr. Connolly, there's a police detective here demanding to speak with you."

The doctor paled. It took her a moment to respond. "Thank you. I'll be right there."

Kim looked at the nurse and then at Dr. Connolly. Why did the police want to talk to her? And why did that make her so nervous?

Sam shifted and groaned.

Kim forgot all about the doctor's reaction.

"Samantha, can you open your eyes?" Dr. Connolly asked.

Sam's eyes fluttered open for a moment, then closed.

Dr. Connolly checked her over. "Everything looks fine. She'll be in and out of consciousness tonight. It's unlikely she'll know you're here..." Her voice trailed off, and a bright flush covered her cheeks. "Right. You're both familiar with patients coming out of anesthesia. Feel free to stay as long as you'd like. I'll let the nursing staff know they're to let you stay. If you have any further questions, have the nurse message me." She glanced at her watch. "I'll come by and check Samantha again before I leave for the night."

"Thank you," Jess said. "For everything,"

"Yes. Thank you," Kim said.

When Dr. Connolly was gone, they returned to Sam's bedside.

Sam's head moved back and forth on the pillow, and she whimpered.

"Sam, can you hear me? Open your eyes." Jess grasped her sister's hand. "Can you squeeze my fingers?"

Sam's fingers slowly curled around hers.

Jess grinned. "Come on, sis. Open your eyes."

A long groan was her immediate response, then slowly Sam's eyes blinked open.

"That's it. Good," Jess said.

Sam had a hard time focusing; her eyes kept drifting shut. When she tried to lift her head, her face contorted in pain.

"Easy. Don't try to move." Jess petted the unblemished side of Sam's face. "Just take it easy."

Kim moved closer and wrapped her hands around Jess's upper arm. Seeing Sam in such pain made her feel sick. "Hey, Sam, we're right here for you."

Sam tried to speak, then winced before trying again. "It hurts." Her eyes filled with tears.

Empathetic tears flooded Kim's and Jess's eyes.

"I know," Jess said, her voice choked with emotion. "I know it does. You just try to rest." She stroked Sam's face until her eyes closed and her breathing evened out.

Jess turned. "My God, Kim. What if we'd lost her?"

Kim pulled her into her arms. "We didn't lose her, and we're not going to!"

They clung to each other, their tears equal parts grief and relief. It was a catharsis, purging them of all the emotions they had kept pent up since receiving that fateful phone call.

CHAPTER 7

Denny slowed the car as they approached the physicians' parking lot at Grandview. "You don't need to do this. Let me take you back to my place. Maybe for once McBain is right. Take a couple of days off, and let this all die down."

"No. I told you." *Three times already.* "I'm not handing off Officer McKenna's care to anyone else." Riley gripped the armrest. "I appreciate you letting me stay with you last night so I could avoid the reporters swarming my condo building, and you coming to the police station with me this morning to give my statement, but I'm not going to let McBain or a bunch of reporters keep me from doing my job." *You should've dealt with this on your own. Like always.*

"But—"

"Denny, please, drop it." She rubbed her tight neck muscles. "I'm going to work." She blew out a breath. "Look, just take me back to your place. I'll pick up my car and come back on my own."

Denny threw his hands up. "No. Fine. You win." He pulled up to the security gate and shoved his key card into the slot. When the arm rose, he drove into the lot. As he pulled into a parking space, he shot her a glance. "What's gotten into you? When did you become so contrary?"

"Contrary?" Riley snorted. "Seriously...contrary? Does anyone still use that word?"

He turned off the engine, then unfastened his seatbelt before responding. "Yes. I just did," he said with a "so there" tone.

"Besides you, smart aleck." Riley undid her seatbelt. "Sounds like a word you'd see in..." She grinned. "Oh. You're buying children's books again."

Denny crossed his arms over his chest. "I'm—"

"Don't try to deny it." She patted his arm. "Don't worry. I won't tell Carol you're nesting again."

"I am not nesting!" He huffed. "There's nothing wrong with preparing for the arrival of my son. Or looking out for his future."

Riley struggled not to smirk at the outraged expression on his face. "Whatever you say, Denny. But according to Carol, if your boy came out of the womb able to read, he would still be eighteen by the time he read all the children's books you've bought."

"Okay. Maybe I got a little carried away. But you should see this book. It's really cute. This little boy wakes up and puts his clothes on inside out. And that's just the start. He's totally contrary." Denny's face lit up, and he gestured with his hands as he got into relating the story.

Laughter bubbled up and helped to lift some of the lingering stress from the interview with the police detective. "Thank you. I needed that."

"Always glad to help a friend," he said. "And I'm not nesting."

Riley grabbed his hand before he could poke her in the side. "Your secret is safe with me." She gave his hand a firm squeeze before releasing it. "I'm so happy for you and Carol. I can't wait to meet the little guy." She reached for the door handle. "We should head inside."

"Wait a sec."

She turned back around.

He arched an eyebrow. "Nice job of dodging my question."

Dang. Thought I'd pulled that one off. Riley blushed.

"What's gotten into you? And don't act like you don't know what I mean."

It was a valid question, but Riley wasn't sure she was ready to talk about it. Typically, she did take the path of least resistance. *Not anymore.* Despite what had happened with Keith, she was determined to keep the vow she had made on her birthday.

She met his gaze for a second, then looked away.

"Come on. We've been friends for years." He nudged her shoulder. "Talk to me."

Riley took a deep breath, mentally squaring her shoulders. "It's not just about McBain. I'm tired of trying to please everyone, no matter what it costs me. I have to do what's right for me."

Denny goggled at her. "I'll be damned." He grinned. "Good for you. It's long overdue."

Air left her lungs in a rush. "Really?"

"Are you kidding? I've been waiting since med school to hear you say that."

Riley smiled. "Thanks, Denny."

"Come on. Let's get inside. You have people to piss off."

"Denny!" Riley said, trying to sound outraged. But she couldn't help laughing.

The reassuring beep of the heart monitor was music to Riley's ears as she paged through Samantha's chart, going over her lab results and reading nursing notes. *She's going to be okay.* More relieved than she cared to admit, she sighed and glanced down at Samantha, momentarily startled to see blue eyes gazing back at her.

Riley set the chart down and moved to the head of the bed. "Good, you're awake. How are you feeling this morning?"

Samantha blinked several times. "My head hurts," she said, her voice a husky rasp.

"You hit your head pretty hard. You've got a mild concussion. Between that and the anesthesia, it's normal to have a headache. Just let the nurses know if it gets worse." Riley checked the suture line above Samantha's ear.

Samantha's brow furrowed, and she studied Riley intently. After a moment, her eyes widened. "I know you." She grasped Riley's arm in a surprisingly firm hold. "Did he hurt you?" She reared up off the pillow, then gasped. Her hand dropped from Riley's arm and shot down to her own leg.

"Easy. Take it easy." Riley's stomach churned as she stroked Samantha's shoulder, trying to soothe her pain. While she always empathized with her patients' pain, Samantha's unexpectedly affected her. *She's suffering because of you.*

"Let me take a look at your leg." She pulled the covers back, lifted Samantha's gown, and inspected the bandage. When she found no seepage, she gently peeled the dressing back. The two incision sites were red and indurated, but there was no sign of infection. She put the dressing back in place, then checked her popliteal and pedal pulses before covering Samantha back up. "I know you're in a lot of pain, but the incisions look good."

Samantha tried to lift her hands, but one was encumbered by an IV. She pressed her free hand to her temple and winced. "Can't think good. Head hurts." She shifted on the bed, emitting a soft cry.

"I'm sorry." Before Riley could stop herself, she reached out and stroked the side of Samantha's face. When she realized what she was doing, she shoved her hands into the pockets of her lab coat. "You've been badly hurt. You need to rest. Give your body time to heal." After checking the chart, she adjusted the IV infuser to give Samantha a dose of Demerol. "Sleep now. We can talk about everything when you're feeling better."

"Okay," Samantha murmured, her gaze already losing focus.

Even after she was sure Samantha was asleep, Riley remained at her bedside. She gazed down to find their hands clasped together. When had that happened? She pulled her hand away.

The sudden prickling of her senses made her look up.

A dark-haired woman stood in the doorway, watching her. "Is this Officer McKenna's room?"

"Yes. Can I help you?"

"I'm here to see Samantha McKenna," the woman said as she strode into the room without glancing at the bed or any of the equipment surrounding it.

Her manner immediately put Riley on alert. The woman's demeanor was not that of someone coming to see a loved one in the intensive care unit. Was she a reporter trying to sneak in? Riley hurried around the bed to intercept the woman before she could reach Samantha's bedside.

"I'm—" Riley caught herself before she gave her name. "I'm her physician. Are you a family member?"

"Lieutenant Weise, Internal Affairs. I'm here to speak to Officer McKenna." She sidestepped Riley.

Almost as bad as a reporter. Riley moved into the lieutenant's path. "She's sleeping."

Weise frowned. "When will she be awake?"

Riley herded her toward the door. "Not for several hours, at least. But even if she was awake, she's in no condition to be questioned. It would be detrimental to her recovery at this juncture."

Weise stopped just short of the doorway, her gaze fixed on Riley's ID badge. "Connolly," she muttered and stared at Riley for a moment before fishing her phone out of her suit coat pocket. A quick check on the phone made her frown. "You're Connolly? Riley Connolly?"

"Yes. I'm Dr. Connolly."

Weise's gaze went to Samantha; then she looked down her nose at Riley. "And you're taking care of Officer McKenna."

Oh great. Here we go. "Yes."

Weise's expression hardened. "Did you operate on her too?"

Riley bristled at the woman's tone. "Yes. I did."

"I see." She nodded as if having already made up her mind about Riley. "I see. Well, then I will need to speak to you as well." She gave Riley a stern look. "I have quite a few questions for you, Doctor."

"I gave a detailed statement this morning to the detective running the case, a Detective Shultz."

"I have questions of my own that you need to answer," Weise said, stepping close, crowding Riley.

The impulse rose up in Riley to do what she always did: meekly bow her head and go along. *No!* Riley stiffened her spine and met Weise's gaze head on. "I've cooperated and provided a full statement. Get what you need from Detective Shultz. I don't have anything else to say." She pointed to the door. "Please leave."

"I still need to speak to Officer McKenna. I'll just wait here until she wakes up."

"Officer McKenna is not up to speaking to anyone. You'll have to wait until she recovers enough to be transferred to the surgical progressive care unit."

Weise's chin jutted out. She brushed aside the jacket of her pantsuit and touched the gold shield clipped to her waistband. "This says I talk to her when I say."

Riley's hackles rose at the thought of this woman subjecting Samantha to a grilling like the one she had received that morning. "Officer McKenna is sedated. As her physician, I'm informing you that she is not physically or mentally able to answer questions at this time." She motioned toward the door. "Please leave. I won't have my patient disturbed." When Weise didn't move, Riley added, "Do I need to call security?"

Weise spun on her heel and stomped down the hall.

As soon as she was out of sight, Riley slumped against the doorframe.

"Dr. Connolly, is everything okay?"

Riley jumped.

"Sorry," Alicia, one of the SICU nurses, said. "Didn't mean to startle you."

"That's okay." Riley smiled at her. "Is Officer McKenna your patient today?"

"Yes."

"Did you see the woman who was just here, the brunette wearing the gray pantsuit?" Riley asked.

Alicia's brow furrowed. "The one that just blew down the hall?"

"That's her. Make sure she doesn't bother Officer McKenna. She's a police officer, not a family member. She's not to go into her room."

"No problem, Dr. Connolly. I'll let the other nurses know."

"Thanks." Riley turned to walk away.

"Oh, wait. I almost forgot," Alicia said. "Dr. McKenna left a message for you. She wanted to speak to you as soon as you came in. She seemed pretty adamant."

Oh no. They've already seen the news reports. "Thanks for letting me know." She forced herself to smile at the nurse and not let any of her trepidation about the coming encounter show.

As Riley approached the SICU waiting room, her nerves started to get the better of her. She should have told Samantha's family right away, before they heard it on TV, but she hadn't wanted to add to their stress. And if she was honest with herself, she had not wanted to face their reaction.

Two uniformed police officers looked over at her from their spot near the television.

Riley winced when she recognized her own face on the screen, with the word "update" underneath her picture. *Why can't they leave us alone?* She nodded in the officers' direction, then scanned the room for Dr. McKenna.

She and Dr. Donovan sat slumped on opposite ends of the couch in the far corner, both still wearing the clothes from the previous day.

"Good morning," Riley said as she approached. "I got your message that you wanted to speak to me."

Dr. McKenna rose, as did Dr. Donovan. The friendly smiles of yesterday were absent. Neither one spoke for several long, uncomfortable moments.

Riley squirmed under their scrutiny.

Dr. McKenna glanced over at the television, where Riley's picture was still plastered, then back at her. "Why didn't you tell us that you were the doctor Sam saved?"

This was the moment Riley had been dreading. She couldn't bring herself to look at either of them. "I'm sorry. I had no idea he would ever do anything like that. I kept thinking he'd get tired of me and move on. I'm so sorry Samantha got hurt."

"What! You knew the man that shot Sam?" Dr. McKenna shouted.

Riley's head jerked up.

Dr. McKenna glared down at her.

She chanced a glance at Dr. Donovan and was met with a wide-eyed stare. *They didn't know?* She looked back at the television. *But I thought...* It didn't matter. Blowing out a breath, she forced herself to meet their gazes. "Could we sit down and talk about this, please?"

"There is nothing to talk about," Dr. McKenna said. "All I want from you is to hear exactly how you got my sister shot." Her eyes blazed with anger.

"I'm sorry," Riley stammered. "I—"

"Jess, I know it's a shock...for me, too, but it's not like Dr. Connolly could control something like that." Dr. Donovan put her hand on her spouse's back.

Dr. McKenna glanced at her, then back at Riley. She crossed her arms over her chest. "I'm waiting."

As succinctly as possible, Riley explained the circumstances that had led up to the shooting. "I'm so sorry that Samantha got hurt. She saved my life, and I'll never forget that."

Dr. McKenna's rigid posture did not ease one bit. "I want another physician assigned to Sam's care."

Riley and Dr. Donovan gasped simultaneously.

"I'll contact Sam's primary care physician immediately," Dr. McKenna said. "She'll take over her post-op care."

"But I—"

"Jess. Wait," Dr. Donovan said.

Dr. McKenna's hand slashed out in negation. "It's not open to discussion. You saved her life." Her jaw clenched, and she seemed to have to force the words out. "Thank you. But I don't want you caring for her. You've done more than enough already."

Riley winced at the insinuation. This was worse than she had imagined. Her shoulders slumped. "I understand."

CHAPTER 8

Still half asleep, Sam turned onto her side. Pain lanced through her leg, bringing her to full alertness. She clutched her thigh and groaned.

A warm hand stroked her arm.

She opened her eyes and looked up.

Marina hovered over her with a concerned expression.

Quickly, Sam pulled her hands away from her leg and rolled onto her back. "Hey, when did you get here? You should have woken me."

Marina brushed her fingers over Sam's cheek. "Do you need a nurse? Is it time for your pain med?"

Ignoring the throbbing pain in her thigh, Sam said, "Nah. I'm fine." She pushed the button to raise the head of the bed. When she reached back to straighten her pillow, sharp pain stabbed her thigh again, and she clenched her jaw.

"Let me get that." Marina reached to adjust her pillow.

Sam waved her off. "I've got it."

Marina shook her head and scowled but didn't try to help.

Once Sam was situated, she smiled at her friend. "I'm glad you came."

"I'd have come to see you in the ICU if they would have let me. Hearing you're fine and seeing you are two different things." Tears glimmered at the corners of Marina's eyes. "I've been so worried."

"Nothing to worry about."

"Nothing!" Marina sputtered. "You've been—"

"I'm fine." Sam reached out and squeezed Marina's hand, working hard to keep her from realizing how much pain she was really in. "Don't worry about me. I'm—"

"Oh, Sam."

At the sound of her name, Sam peered past Marina toward the door. *What's she doing here?*

Christy, tears running down her cheeks, rushed to the bedside, brushed Marina aside, and threw herself into Sam's arms. "Thank God."

Sam bit back a groan as Christy pressed against her injured shoulder. "Take it easy." She wedged her good arm between them, trying to take off some of the pressure.

"You're hurting her," Marina said. She tugged on Christy's arm.

Christy straightened and pulled her arm from Marina's grasp. Her hand flew to her mouth. "I'm so sorry. Are you okay? I was just so relieved to see you. I've been sick with worry."

Sam suppressed a sigh. "It's okay. You didn't realize. Shoulder is a little sore."

Marina eyed her. "Maybe I should get the nurse."

Sam shot her a scowl. "No. I'm fine." Despite her words, shafts of pain were shooting down her leg with every beat of her heart, and now the added ache in her shoulder threatened to rob her of her composure. She fought down the pain as best she could and turned her attention to Christy. "I'm kind of tired now. I appreciate you coming by. Thanks."

Christy shook her head. "I'm not going anywhere. I know we've had our problems, but this changes everything. Once you're doing better, I'll take you home and make sure you have everything you need until you're fully recovered."

What? Sam glanced at Marina, who looked just as shocked. "Christy, we broke up—months ago. I'm not going home with you. We never lived together to start with." While she still cared about Christy, she couldn't give her what she wanted—a commitment.

Christy's expression crumbled. "I know that. But let me take care of you. You'll see how good it can be if we're together." Tears threatened to spill over. "I love you. Just give me a chance to show you."

Sam had a feeling this was about to turn ugly. Between trying to hide her pain and now this, she struggled for control. "Marina, would you mind giving us a few minutes?"

Marina looked as if she wasn't about to budge from her spot at the foot of the bed. She shot a glare at Christy, then met Sam's gaze. "You sure?"

"Positive."

"Okay." Marina cut her gaze toward Christy. "I'll be right outside." She gave Sam's blanket-covered toes a quick squeeze before leaving the room.

Sam straightened as upright as she could get and faced Christy. *So much for trying to let her down easy. Should have done this the first time.*

As if Christy knew what was about to happen, she clutched at Sam's hand. "Don't do this. Please. I love you."

Sam withdrew her hand and hardened her heart. "I'm not going home with you. Not now. Not ever. It's over, Christy." The pain pounding in her thigh made her voice harsher than she intended. "Please go," she said, softening her tone.

Tears ran in earnest down Christy's face. She turned and fled from the room.

Damn it. Sam threw her arm over her face, her own eyes stinging with tears. Once before, she had tried to be everything to one woman and failed— with tragic results. She should have known better than to try again and accepted that she just wasn't relationship material.

"Mi amiga." Marina stroked the arm Sam had over her face. "Are you all right?"

Shoving her emotion down, Sam lifted her arm and peered at her friend. "I'm a bitch."

"No, you're not. She's just not the right one for you. The right woman is out there; you just haven't met her yet."

Even if I did, I couldn't give her what she needed. After seeing how her sister Jess was with Kim, she had allowed herself to hope, but maybe she wasn't capable of that kind of love.

A nurse stepped into the room. "Are you ready for your pain medication?"

More than ready. "Sure."

Marina left the room while the nurse gave Sam an injection and then came back in. "I should get going and let you rest."

Sam knew from previous pain shots that she would start to get sleepy in just a few minutes. "Thanks again for coming."

Marina placed a soft kiss on Sam's forehead. "I'll see you tomorrow after work."

CHAPTER 9

When the elevator doors slid open on the floor that housed the progressive care unit, Riley peeked out and scanned the hallway before exiting the elevator. Assured the coast was clear, she headed for the nurses' station with a purposeful stride. *No sense upsetting the family—again.* A chance encounter with Dr. McKenna as Samantha was being transferred to the progressive care unit had garnered Riley a white-hot stare that should have singed her where she stood. Since that day, she had been quietly following Samantha's recovery but had tried to stay under the family's radar.

The nursing staff was busy with change-of-shift duties so, for the moment, the nurses' station was empty. Riley sat down at the computer workstation and called up Mrs. Gavin's chart, then read the latest entries. After being certain that her patient was stable, she accessed Samantha's chart and reviewed her progress.

A firm hand landing on her shoulder caused her to jump, and her heart rate spiked.

"How's she doing?" Denny asked.

She had been so engrossed in Samantha's chart that she hadn't heard him walk up behind her. She feigned a scowl. "You just took a month off my life."

He grinned unrepentantly. "Sorry. How's she doing?"

"Good." Riley smiled. "Really good." Just yesterday, she had seen Samantha in the hallway, using a walker, her sister hovering protectively at her side. The sight had filled her with a sense of profound relief. "She'll probably be ready to be released tomorrow or the next day."

"Have you talked to her yet?"

She sighed. "You know what happened with Dr. McKenna. She made it clear she doesn't want me anywhere near her sister."

Denny pulled over a chair and sat next to her. "When she was incapacitated, that was one thing. Her sister could speak for her then, but not now. And you wouldn't be talking to her as her physician, but as someone who shared a terrible experience. Shouldn't Officer McKenna be the one to decide whether or not she wants to talk to you?"

Riley shrugged. "What's the point? What's done is done." She stared unseeingly at the computer screen. One of her uncle's favorite homilies came to mind. *You can't unspill the milk.* "Nothing I could say would change anything."

"I know how much you're still bothered by what happened. Don't think I don't know that you've been checking on her several times a day. The guilt is not healthy." He cupped her chin and tilted her face up to look at him. "What happened is not your fault; it's Keith's. I bet Officer McKenna would tell you the same thing." He put his hand on her shoulder. "Talk to her. You need some closure about all of this."

"So, what? Now you're a psychiatrist?"

His hand dropped from her shoulder. "No. I'm your friend."

Remorse at the sharp words filled Riley. "I'm sorry, Denny. You didn't deserve that." She rubbed the back of her neck, trying to ease the suddenly tight muscles.

The sound of nearby laughter caught her attention.

She grimaced when she saw Dr. McKenna and Dr. Donovan approaching the desk. *Dang.*

Dr. McKenna glanced toward the nurses' station. Her steps faltered, and the smile dropped from her face.

Riley resisted the urge to pretend she had not seen them. She had every right to be there. "Good evening," she said, keeping her tone polite and professional.

"Good evening." Dr. Donovan offered a smile.

At a nudge from her spouse, Dr. McKenna nodded stiffly, then continued down the hall.

As soon as they were out of sight, Riley slumped in her chair. "See what I mean?"

Denny scowled. "I understand she's angry that her sister got hurt, and that she needs to blame someone, but that someone shouldn't be you." He held up his hand to keep her from interrupting. "That doesn't mean her sister feels the same way. Talk to Officer McKenna. Let her speak for herself."

Riley had seen that determined tilt of his chin plenty of times over the years. He wouldn't let this go. "I'll seriously consider talking to her." Hoping to lighten the mood, she held up three fingers. "Scout's honor."

Denny scoffed. "You were never a scout."

Laughing, she placed her hand over her heart. "I promise." She pushed her chair back. "I should get go—" Her phone buzzed. She pulled it off her waistband and glanced at the screen. An unexpected surge of apprehension struck, but she forced it away. *I can do this.*

Today was her first day covering the ER since the shooting. Up until now, it had been an uncommonly quiet day, and she hadn't gotten called to the ER trauma unit.

"Incoming trauma?" Denny asked.

Riley nodded.

"You okay going back into the ER? I could take it for you."

"I'm fine."

He stared into her eyes as if gauging her sincerity. *Never let anyone see you unsure.* Riley met his gaze and held it. "I'm perfectly fine. I have to go." She hurried away before he could object.

Sam shifted in the hospital bed, trying to get comfortable, but no matter which way she turned, her leg ached. She couldn't wait to get out of here. Her empty stomach growled, adding to her discontent. She eyed her dinner tray with distaste. The first two days out of the ICU, she had been hurting too much to care. But today, after the mush the hospital passed off as breakfast and lunch, she'd had enough. *Hurry up, you guys. I don't want to have to eat that.*

The door to her room swung open.

Finally. "Gimme," Sam said by way of greeting and held out her hands.

"Good to see you too, sis," Jess said. "I'm so glad that you're feeling better—and hungry."

Surprised by the catch in Jess's voice, Sam met her gaze. "Hey, come on. I'm getting stronger every day." She gave her sister's arm a firm squeeze.

"I know." Jess kissed her cheek.

Kim leaned in and gave Sam a kiss on the forehead and then handed over the bag she was carrying. "Sorry we took so long. Cheryl wanted to stop by the grocery store so there would be food in the apartment when you get home."

"More like Frank was worried there wouldn't be any good cookies," Jess said with a laugh. "You know our brother. He can't go a day without his junk food fix."

Sam nodded absently, engrossed in pulling the large takeout container free of the bag. After popping the lid open, she took a deep sniff and groaned. "Oh, yeah. One of my favorites—sesame chicken." She grabbed a piece of the sauce-covered chicken and popped it into her mouth. "Hot," she muttered, shaking her burning fingers.

Kim reached into the bag and pulled out a plastic fork.

Sam snatched it from her fingers. "Thanks. I'm starving."

Jess and Kim pulled chairs up next to the bed as Sam dug into her dinner.

"Did you see Dr. Warren?" Jess asked.

Sam nodded, held up one finger, and ate several more bites before answering. "She said I should be out of here tomorrow or the next day. I told her I'm ready to go tomorrow."

"No." Jess shook her head adamantly. "Not tomorrow. An extra day is warranted. You're only five days post-op."

Laying her hand on Jess's arm, Kim said, "I don't think the doctor would release her before she's ready."

Sam spoke up before her sister could utter the protest she saw forming. "There's nothing they're doing for me here that I can't do at home. Relax, Jess. She's been my doctor for a couple of years. I trust her. And Cheryl and Frank are going to stay with me." *Because you insisted.* "Most people don't go home and have a sister-in-law who's a registered nurse staying with them."

Jess scowled. "I still think—"

Kim leaned close to her and said something Sam couldn't hear.

Shaking her head, Jess said, "All right. Whatever she thinks is best."

The PA system came to life. "Attention. Visiting hours are over in five minutes."

"We better get going." Kim started gathering up the remains of Sam's dinner.

"Don't forget," Jess said. "Mom and Dad's ship is due to arrive in London tomorrow. With the time difference, that makes the web chat with them tomorrow morning, our time."

"I never thought I'd hear the words 'Mom' and 'web chat' in the same sentence." Sam laughed. "She hates computers."

"That was before she found herself stuck in the middle of the Atlantic Ocean when her daughter got hurt," Kim said. "It's a shame we weren't able to get the video link to work while they were still on board the ship, but at least they were able to talk to you. Not being able to be here with you has been really hard on your folks."

"I didn't have any luck on the phone, but maybe once Mom and Dad actually see me, I can convince them not to come home." She looked at Kim and put on her most beseeching look. "You could help me convince them. Please."

"Never going to happen, Sam," Kim said.

"But they've been planning this trans-Atlantic cruise and European vacation for two years. There's really no reason for them to be here." *And Jess hovering over my every move has been more than enough. I can't take Mom too.* "I'm fine."

"You're not fine," Jess said, her voice cracking with emotion. "But you will be." She patted Sam's leg. "And you know if Mom could've gotten off that ship, she would've been here long before now." She wagged her finger at Sam. "Save your breath. You're not going to convince her. There's no way on

God's green earth that Mom and Dad won't be on the first plane home."

Oh great. Mom and Jess. I'm doomed.

The PA sounded again. "Visiting hours are over."

"That's our cue," Kim said.

CHAPTER 10

Jess watched as Kim rummaged through Sam's freezer. Was this a preview of her future if they succeeded? She could already picture Kim, her belly swollen with their child, raiding the freezer in the middle of the night.

"Aha! I knew it would be here." Kim tugged the lid off the carton and then grabbed a spoon from a drawer. "Sam always has a stash of chocolate ice cream."

Jess laughed. "You two and your chocolate." She was much more interested in the gaping front of Kim's robe and the impressive amount of cleavage on display than she was in chocolate ice cream. "What do you say we take it back into the bedroom? I could think of a few places I'd like to lick it off you."

Kim's spoon froze halfway to her mouth. "Hmm..." Taking encouragement from Kim's glazed expression, Jess slipped her hand inside the robe. Soft, warm skin met her questing hand.

Kim glanced at the clock. "You're sure Frank and Cheryl won't be back any time soon?"

"Positive." Jess's hand dipped lower, and Kim groaned. "They were going to go to dinner and then a late movie. They know this is our last chance before Sam comes home and we have to head back to LA."

Setting the ice cream container down, Kim sighed and turned a pleading look on Jess. "You really think this way will make a difference? That we'll be successful this time?"

All thoughts of seduction gone, Jess pulled Kim into her arms. "I think it's worth a try. Freezing semen isn't supposed to affect it, but who knows, maybe it does. Using fresh might make all the difference." She gently stroked Kim's face. "We need to think positive." Her heart broke a little more as each month passed and they were faced with disappointment again. "I know we're all here together because something bad happened, but maybe something good will come out of it." Jess smiled. "I can't wait to hold our child in my arms."

Kim sniffed and then buried her face in Jess's neck. "I'm sorry I'm letting you down."

"You know that's not true." She kissed Kim's forehead. "Please look at me." When Kim lifted her head, Jess placed a soft kiss on her lips and then cradled her face between her palms. "We're in this together. And this time it *is* going to work."

Dashing away her tears, Kim offered a watery smile. "You really believe that?"

Jess's heart overflowed with love for this incredible woman, who had given her a life and a future she had never dared dream possible. "With all my heart." She gazed deeply into Kim's loving blue eyes, willing her to believe it.

Kim's smile could have lit a city. "I love you."

"I love you too." Jess grinned. "And think of how much fun it'll be to torture Sam by telling her I got you pregnant in her bed. Or better yet, that Frank donated in the guest bedroom."

Kim gasped. "You wouldn't."

Squeezing her tightly, Jess said, "You know I wouldn't. But you have to admit it's fun to imagine the outrage on her face."

Their laughter rang through the kitchen.

CHAPTER 11

Visiting hours long over, the surgical progressive care unit had settled into the subdued rhythm of the night shift. Nurses were going about their duties with quiet efficiency.

The ridged soles of Riley's shoes squeaked on the freshly waxed floor as she walked toward the nurses' station. She nodded a greeting to the maintenance woman.

A lone nurse staffed the desk.

Riley leaned against the counter and stretched her aching back. Her call to the ER had resulted in a two-hour surgery.

"Good evening, Susan."

"Hey, Dr. Connolly. Long night?"

"The usual. Has Mr. Robinson arrived yet?"

"Sure did. We got him all settled. He's in four-oh-two. Anything else I can do for you?" Susan smiled brightly and winked. "Anything at all."

Susan loved to make Riley blush and she didn't disappoint her.

Riley scowled, but there was no real heat to it. Although she liked the spunky nurse, she never responded to her flirting. "Could I get one of the tablets, please?" she asked, willing her blush to fade. It was one of the banes of having a fair complexion—even a slight blush was impossible to hide.

Susan laughed as she handed over the tablet. "You're too easy, Doc."

Shaking her head, Riley accepted the tablet. She had only taken a few steps away from the counter when Susan called out to her.

"Wait. I almost forgot."

Riley turned around.

"I know she's not your patient, but Officer McKenna asked to see you."

She does want to talk to me. Regardless of Denny's take on the matter, Riley hadn't really believed that Samantha would want anything to do with her. Her sister probably hadn't wasted any time informing her of Riley's prior involvement with Keith. *Then again, maybe she wants to tell you off for getting her shot.* Even as the thought crossed her mind, Riley realized she didn't actually believe it. The mental image of Samantha deliberately stepping into the line of fire came far too easily to mind.

"Dr. Connolly?"

Her eyes blinked open. She hadn't even been aware of closing them. *Get it together.*

Susan was staring at her.

"Okay." Riley nodded as if nothing had happened. "Thanks for letting me know." She turned and, making sure to keep her pace measured, went down the hallway to check in on Mr. Robinson.

After checking on her patient, Riley went back toward the nurses' station, thoughts of Samantha dominating her mind. It was late, so she was probably sleeping. Maybe it would be better to wait until the next day. Riley stopped and looked around in confusion. While she had been busy trying to convince herself she shouldn't see Samantha, her wayward feet had delivered her right to her door.

The door was propped open.

Unable to resist, Riley stepped into the doorway and peered inside. The room's overhead lights were off. Faint light from outside the window bathed the room in mottled shadows. The only other illumination came from the light strip above the bed. Samantha's head was turned toward the window, so all Riley could see was the back of her head.

Leave her be. She needs her rest. It's late. Letting out a soft sigh, Riley turned to go.

"I'm awake."

Riley jumped and turned back but hesitated to enter the room. "Sorry. I didn't mean to disturb you."

"You didn't." Samantha used the bedside control to raise the head of the bed into an upright position. She winced when she tried to pull her pillow into a more comfortable spot.

Riley was beside the bed before she was even cognizant of making the decision to enter the room. "Here. Let me."

Samantha tried to wave her help off.

Riley ignored her. She could see that she was hurting. She adjusted the pillow behind Samantha's back. "Better?"

"Yes." Samantha smiled. "Thank you."

Even in the muted light, Riley was struck by the silvery-blue color of her eyes. The bruises and bare patch of scalp over her ear did little to diminish her striking good looks. When Riley realized she was staring, her cheeks went hot. She brushed a hand over her face, willing the blush to fade.

"I appreciate you granting my request to see you," Samantha said. "I know we haven't been formally introduced." She held out her hand. "Sam McKenna."

Sam, not Samantha. Being given the privilege of using Samantha's nickname lessened some of Riley's unease. Her hand was engulfed in Sam's much larger one. She caught herself before she used her title, reminding herself that she wasn't Sam's doctor. "Riley Connolly."

Sam fidgeted with her blanket. "Thanks again for seeing me. I...umm... I just needed to see for myself that you're really okay. You are okay?"

"I'm fine. I didn't get hurt." *Unlike you.* Now that she was face to face with Sam, Riley struggled with what to say. I'm sorry didn't even begin to cover it.

An awkward silence descended.

Riley's eyes lit on Sam's bedmate, and she smiled. The teddy bear was outfitted as a police officer, complete with uniform, hat, and utility belt. "Who's your friend?"

"This is Izzy." Smiling, Sam pulled the teddy bear into her lap and stroked the silky-looking brown fur on its face. "A friend gave her to me to keep me company."

Riley had noticed all the flowers, balloons, and cards scattered throughout the room, glad that Sam had so many people who cared for her. For her part, Denny and Carol had been very supportive. Unlike the single call from her uncle that had consisted of: You weren't hurt. Good. Don't talk to the press. *This isn't about you. It's about Sam.*

Guilt flooded Riley. *Tell her what you came here to say, and then leave her alone. Her sister was right about one thing. You've already done more than enough to her.* "It will never make up for what happened, but..." Tears prickled at the corners of her eyes. "I just... I wanted you to know how sorry I am that you got hurt." She wrung her hands. "If it wasn't for me, you wouldn't be in that bed."

"Hey. No." Sam reached out and touched the sleeve of her lab coat. "It was Talbert's doing, not yours. Drugs do terrible things to people."

What! Shock rendered Riley momentarily speechless. *Drugs?* "I don't understand. What do drugs have to do with this?"

"My captain brought me up to speed on the details of the case. Cocaine was found in Talbert's system. And at his condo."

My God. Drugs. How could I not have known that? Riley's hip pressed against the mattress as she leaned in and rested her hand on Sam's arm. "I swear to you. I didn't know."

"I believe you. Apparently no one suspected. Happens more often than people realize. On the outside, everything looks normal. It's frequently someone in a high-pressure job. Starts out as an occasional thing, and before they know it, things spiral out of control."

"Maybe if I'd done things differently." Riley sighed. "Let him down easier or...something." *Like being more careful that he didn't see a woman kissing me.* Even though she knew Sam's sister was gay, she didn't feel comfortable sharing that tidbit of information.

Sam covered Riley's hand where it rested on her arm. "You can't think like that. If there is one thing I know for sure, it's that you can't be the sole source of other people's happiness. Don't do that to yourself."

Riley stared at her, surprised by the passion in her voice. *Maybe she's right.* She was reminded of the vow she'd made to herself. *Remember Patrice.* But it was hard to let go of the guilt. Sam had suffered because of her.

A yawn caught Riley by surprise.

As if it were contagious, Sam stifled a yawn.

"I'm sorry. I should go." Riley realized she still had hold of Sam's arm. She flushed and withdrew her hand. "It's late. You need your rest."

Sam caught her sleeve and took Riley's hand in hers. "Please. Don't go."

Mesmerizing blue eyes held her captive, and she found herself nodding.

Silence reigned for several moments.

Riley looked down at their joined hands. A soothing warmth permeated her palm. She knew she should pull away but couldn't bring herself to do it. There was something she wanted to ask Sam, yet she still hesitated. She would never admit this, not even to Denny, but if anyone could understand without judgment, it would be Sam. She gazed into Sam's warm blue eyes, and the decision was easy. "Can I ask you something?"

"Sure," Sam said.

"Do you have bad dreams?"

Sam looked away, then tugged Izzy closer with her free hand.

For a moment, Riley didn't think she was going to answer.

"Sometimes," Sam finally said. She ran her thumb over the back of Riley's hand. "What about you?"

Riley swallowed heavily and nodded. "Yes. I—"

The buzzing of her phone interrupted.

"Sorry." Riley glanced at the screen. She didn't want to, but she had no choice. "I've got to go."

Sam tightened her grip on Riley's hand. "Will you come back tomorrow? We can talk about...things."

After being on-call all night, the last thing Riley would want to do was hang around tomorrow. She started to tell Sam that, but one look at her hopeful expression made the words catch in her throat.

"I'll come by in the morning, after I get done with morning rounds."

Sam smiled and released her hand. "Okay."

With a quick wave, Riley made her exit. Feeling surprisingly lighthearted, she headed for the ER.

CHAPTER 12

Pain shot down Sam's leg. Her hands tightened on the handles of her crutches. Sweat dampened the back of her T-shirt after just one lap down the hall. *That's pathetic.*

A large hand tightened around her bicep, steadying her. "You don't be pushing too hard now."

"Too hard?" Sam stopped for a moment to catch her breath and looked over at her nurse. "I feel like an old lady with a walker."

"That was yesterday. Today you're only middle-aged. You're coming up in the world."

Sam growled.

Rasheed laughed, making the beads in his dreadlocks click. "Slow and steady, that's the ticket."

Footsteps sounded behind them.

"Sounds like good advice to me."

Sam smiled at the sound of Riley's voice. She turned and got her first good look at Riley in the light of day. *Wow. She's short.* The night before, she had noticed that Riley was very petite, but now, standing next to her, Sam realized just how small she was. She had to be all of five-feet-nothing and couldn't weight more than a hundred pounds—soaking wet. Coppery red hair fringed her heart-shaped face. Vibrant green eyes and a clear, creamy complexion with a healthy smattering of freckles completed the package.

"Good morning," Riley said.

"Hi. I..." Sam gazed down into Riley's eyes and lost her train of thought.

Rasheed cleared his throat. "Are we still walking here?"

A blush colored Riley's face, making her freckles stand out.

She's cute. Realizing she was staring and had an audience, Sam felt her own face heat. "I'm ready to go back to my room."

Riley followed along as Sam made her slow, painful way back to her room.

Sam tried not to think about how weak she looked with Rasheed hovering close to her side.

He helped her settle back into bed and then left.

She beckoned to Riley, who had stopped outside the door. "Come on in."

Riley approached the bed. "You're up and about early this morning."

"I'm hoping to convince Dr. Warren that I'm ready to get out of here. I figured getting up and walking was the best way to do that."

A smile lit Riley's face. "I'm glad you're doing so well." Her gazed darted away. "I...umm," she shuffled her feet, "I've been following your progress."

Why would she...? Oh. Of course she would. Riley's demeanor and apology the night before now made perfect sense. Sam wished that she could convince her there was nothing to feel guilty about. She tugged on Riley's sleeve until she looked up and their gazes met. "I meant what I said last night. You have no reason to feel guilty. I—"

"Hey, Sam. Ready to face the folks?" Jess asked as she stepped into the room.

Damn. Sam had totally forgotten about the video chat set for this morning. After their interrupted conversation last night, she wanted a chance to talk more in-depth with Riley about the experience they had shared. *No help for it now.*

Jess moved to stand on the opposite side of the bed.

Sam smiled. "Jess, I want you to meet—"

"We've met." Jess's eyes narrowed at Riley. "What are you doing here?"

Riley ducked her head and took a step away from the bed. "I'll go," she said in a subdued tone.

What? "No. Wait. You don't have to leave." Sam's gaze darted back and forth between Riley and Jess, then settled on her sister. "I asked Riley to come. Now, what's going on, Jess?" *And why are you acting like a jerk?* "What do you mean, you've already met her? When?"

Jess shot a glare Riley's way. "After she did your surgery."

Sam whipped her head around to stare at Riley. "You did my surgery?"

Riley straightened and met Sam's gaze directly. "Yes. I did."

Shaking her head, Sam tried to wrap her mind around the surprising revelation. *After everything she'd been through, she saved me.* She reached for Riley's hand and captured it between both of hers. "Thank you. You saved my life."

"It was the least she could do after she almost got you killed," Jess muttered.

Sam glared at her. "What the hell's the matter with you? It's not like Riley had any control over what happened."

Jess crossed her arms over her chest.

A glance at Riley's guilt-stricken face made Sam's anger flare white-hot. She rounded on her sister. "So I guess I should've just stood back and watched him rape her while I waited for backup to arrive—just in case he had a weapon. Is that what you would've wanted me to do?"

The air left Jess's lungs in an audible huff as if someone had sucker-punched her. "No. I... Oh, God. I didn't know." She turned remorse-filled eyes on Riley. "I'm so sorry. All I've been able to think about was how badly Sam was hurt." She raked her fingers through her hair. "Every time I looked at you, I was reminded that I almost lost my sister. I didn't let myself think about what you'd been through."

Anger drained from Sam. She realized she still had Riley's hand clasped firmly between hers. "It wasn't your fault. Okay?"

Riley nodded, tugged her hand free, and faced Jess. "I understand your anger. My fault or not, I'm connected to you almost losing someone you love. I'm sure you wish you'd never met me." She held up a hand to keep Sam from interrupting. "Believe me when I tell you, I will never forget what your sister did for me. I think it would be best if we all moved on with our separate lives and put this behind us." Tears glimmered in her eyes as she gently touched Sam's cheek. "Thank you for saving me. I wish you all the best in the world. Good-bye."

Sam could only stare in shock as Riley Connolly walked out of her room and her life.

CHAPTER 13

Sunlight filtered through the plethora of plants and created dappled shadows on the flagstone beneath Sam's feet. The sound of water gurgling over nearby rocks added to the tranquility of the setting. It was hard to believe there was a bustling hospital complex right outside these walls. She had stumbled across the hidden courtyard earlier in the week. Her gaze wandered over her surroundings. Orchids, in full bloom, filled the area where she was sitting. Stag horn ferns hung from the wall behind her. A giant bird of paradise provided the shade. The centerpiece of the space was a life-size bronze statue of a little girl, with a butterfly perched on the palm of her outstretched hand.

Sam leaned back against the bench and stretched out her legs. An hour of physical therapy had left her thigh throbbing like a bad tooth. She sighed and closed her eyes, allowing the earthy scents and sound of the water to wash away the pain.

The sound of a door clanking shut disturbed her reprieve. This was the first time anyone had come into the courtyard while she was there. She opened her eyes and straightened from her slumped position on the bench. Peering through the nearby foliage, she tried to spot the newcomer, but didn't see anyone. *I was sure I heard the door close. Oh well, time to head home anyway.*

Sam grabbed her cane and used it to lever herself off the bench. Her leg always felt weakest right after her sessions. As she made her way toward the door, a bright spot of white off to her left caught her attention. There was someone here.

A woman in a white lab coat sat with her back to Sam on a bench beneath a towering banana plant.

A glimpse of the woman's red hair stopped Sam in her tracks. It couldn't be. She had thought often of Riley Connolly in the weeks since her discharge, wishing she had gotten a chance to talk to her again. On her way to and from her rehab appointments, she had found herself scanning the corridors in hopes of spotting Riley. *Forget it. It's not her. She probably doesn't even come to this part of the hospital complex.*

Sam took two more steps toward the door, then stopped again. If there was even a slim chance it might be Riley, she couldn't let it go. She limped over to where the woman was sitting. Her heart pounded at the sight of the slight figure on the bench. Was it really her? "Excuse me," she said softly.

The woman turned.

Bright green eyes captured Sam and held her in place.

She smiled down at Riley as it took her a moment to find her voice. "Hi."

"What are you doing here?" Riley asked.

Sam's elation fled at Riley's tone. "I'm sorry I disturbed you." *She already made it clear she didn't want any further contact with you.* Her shoulders slumped, and she turned away.

"Wait." Riley rose from the bench. "You just caught me by surprise. Not many people know about this place."

Sam rested her cane against her leg. "I found it by accident when I was looking for a shortcut back to the parking lot." She swept one arm wide. "I found this instead."

"One of the trauma team nurses told me about it. It's a great place to escape to for a little while when I can't leave the hospital grounds."

And now Sam had intruded on her sanctuary. "Well, I'll leave you in peace, then."

Riley took a step closer. "You don't have to go."

Gazing down at her, Sam searched her face. "Are you sure?"

"Yes. Please." Riley sat down and motioned toward the other end of the bench. "Have a seat."

Sam lowered herself onto the indicated seat and tried to subtly stretch out her injured leg, not wanting to remind Riley of her injuries. She had hoped to run into Riley, but now that she had, everything she wanted to say had fled her mind.

An awkward silence settled around them.

Come on. Say something. Sam blurted out the first thing that popped into her head. "Izzy says hi."

Riley smiled. "Oh, she does, huh?"

Grinning, Sam nodded. "Yep. And she asks about you too." The unexpected sound of Riley's lighthearted laughter filled her with pleasure.

Riley's expression sobered. "How are you doing?"

"I'm fine," Sam said.

Riley's gaze slid over her, then lingered for a moment on her thigh. "Could we try that again? How is your recovery progressing?"

Sam didn't want to talk about her injuries. Riley's face had assumed the guilt-ridden expression she had worn when she'd visited Sam's hospital room. Sam wanted to see her smile and laugh again. "Really, I'm fine."

"Really, you're not."

Sam grimaced at the narrow-eyed stare Riley sent her way. *Called you on that one.*

"The truth." Riley laid her hand on Sam's arm for a moment before withdrawing it. "Please."

No fair! "Okay." She pulled up the sleeve of her T-shirt and bared her shoulder. "It's almost healed."

Riley scooted closer and skimmed her fingertips over the yellowing bruises and scabbed-over graze mark on Sam's shoulder. "Does it still hurt?"

Goosebumps erupted in the wake of Riley's touch. Sam tugged down her shirtsleeve. "It aches a little sometimes."

"And your leg?"

How much do I tell her? One look into Riley's eyes answered that question. *The whole truth.* Sam sighed. "My leg has quite a way to go before it's back to being fully functional, but it is getting better. I just got the go-ahead this week to start driving again. I started physical therapy two weeks ago. I've got at least another six to eight weeks of PT."

Riley gently touched Sam's knee, then quickly withdrew. "Are you still in a lot of pain?"

"It does hurt, especially after my therapy sessions." Sam shrugged. "But that's to be expected."

"I'm so sorry—"

"Don't! You have nothing to be sorry for." Sam put on her stern cop face. "I mean it. No more apologies."

Riley ducked her head and gave a vague nod.

"Riley." Sam softened her expression and tone when Riley looked up. "Promise me. No more apologies. Please."

"Okay." Riley offered a halfhearted smile. "I promise."

Sam smiled. "Good. For a minute there I thought I was going to have to bring Izzy here to get tough with you."

Riley burst out laughing.

That's what I want to see more of. Sam laughed, and she felt her own spirits lighten. She hated to turn the conversation serious again but remembered that Riley had previously asked her about bad dreams. "Enough about me. How are you doing?"

Riley took a sudden interest in the large leaves of the nearby banana plant. "I'm fine. Remember, I wasn't hurt."

Oh no, you don't. Not all injuries are physical, and you know it. She wasn't about to let Riley get away with minimizing her own trauma. "Could we try that again?" Sam asked, mirroring Riley's earlier question. "How are you coping? Any more bad dreams?"

Riley's brow furrowed, and she looked as if she wasn't going to answer. She met Sam's eyes and then blew out a breath. "Sometimes," she said, so low that Sam could barely hear her.

"I'm sorry—"

"Ah! No apologies," Riley said. "That goes both ways."

Sam smiled. "Right. Fair's fair." She hesitated, then gave Riley's shoulder a light squeeze. "I just want you to know if you ever need to talk, I'm here."

"I appreciate that, Sam, but there's really nothing to talk about."

Sam might have believed her if Riley hadn't avoided making eye contact. Her stomach picked that moment to remind her that she hadn't eaten since breakfast. Would Riley be willing to go to lunch with her? She looked down at her baggy workout pants and sweat-stained T-shirt. Her rumpled appearance was a sharp contrast to Riley's pristine white lab coat and pressed green scrubs. Maybe not.

The phone clipped to Riley's scrubs buzzed, taking the option out of Sam's hands.

Riley glanced at the screen. "Excuse me. I need to answer this." She slid open a small keyboard and typed out a message. When she was finished, she stood. "I need to get back to work."

Sam tried to stand without her cane and faltered. Her leg had stiffened.

Riley leaped forward and wrapped her arm around Sam's waist to steady her. "Okay now?"

Heat flooded Sam's face. "I'm fine," she said, her tone much sharper than she intended.

Riley instantly released her and stepped back.

Good going, jackass. Sam touched Riley's sleeve. "Thank you. It gets a little stiff when I sit." She resisted the urge to rub her aching thigh and reached for her cane. "Well, I've taken enough of your time."

"I'm glad I got a chance to see you again."

Sam smiled down at her. "Me too." Now that the time had come, she wasn't willing to see Riley walk out of her life again. "Maybe if you have time, we could have lunch some afternoon after my therapy." She tugged self-consciously at her sweat-stained shirt. "I promise to dress better."

Riley hesitated.

Think of something. Quick. She grinned to herself. "I'll bring Izzy. She'll be so disappointed she didn't get to see you today."

Shaking her head, Riley laughed. "Well, I would hate to disappoint Izzy. But I can't promise a specific time. I never know when I'll be free."

All right! Sam didn't care when they got together; she was just happy Riley had agreed.

Riley's phone sounded again. She gave the screen a quick glance. "I have to go." With a quick wave, she strode toward the door.

It wasn't until the door swung shut behind her that Sam realized she didn't have any way to contact her directly. *Damn it.* She limped toward the door, her good mood having departed along with Riley.

CHAPTER 14

"Just one more," Tony said.

Sam propped herself up on her elbows and shot him a glare. "That's what you said last time. That's what you always say. What is that...like a stock phrase in the physical therapist's handbook?"

Tony laughed. "But I really mean it this time."

She growled and glanced at the curtain surrounding the treatment table to make sure it was closed. Other patients and therapists were talking on the other side of the curtain, but at least no one but Tony could see how weak she was. Teeth clenched, she struggled to raise her injured leg.

"That's it. Just a little higher. Great."

Her leg shook as she lowered it. A sharp pain shafted through her thigh. "Damn it," she muttered under her breath. She grabbed her thigh and attempted to rub away the pain.

Tony tried to brush her hands aside. "Let me."

"I've got it."

"Sam." He shook his head as he urged her to move her hands. "This is my job. Let me do it."

She gave in and removed her hands.

He pushed up the leg of her shorts and massaged her cramped muscles, carefully avoiding her healing incisions. "Good job, by the way."

Sam snorted. "That was pathetic." She winced when he hit a particularly tender spot.

"Sorry," Tony said. "I know it's frustrating, but you need to be patient. You only started your therapy two weeks ago." He turned her leg from side to side. "There's a lot of muscle damage here. It's going to take time, but I promise you, you will get back full function of your leg."

That's what Sam kept telling herself, but she couldn't help worrying. She stared at the red scars marring her thigh. *I couldn't catch a perp who was on crutches and half-blind.* Blowing out a breath, she flopped back onto the therapy table. The ringtone of her cell phone made her jump.

Tony gave her a disapproving look.

She was supposed to shut the phone off during therapy but had forgotten. She pulled her phone out of her pocket and was just about to send the call to voice mail when she noticed the caller. She couldn't hold back her smile. "I need to take this."

"We still need to put some ice on this."

"Okay, I'll make it quick." Her thumb was already hovering over the soft button on the screen.

Tony frowned but nodded. "Okay. I'll get the ice packs." He pulled aside the curtain around her table and disappeared.

Sam stabbed the screen to connect the call. "Hello, Riley." She was greeted by silence. *Damn, did I miss her?* "Riley?"

"Yes. Hi. I umm...hope you don't mind me calling you. I realized after I left on Wednesday, I hadn't given you my phone number. Your number was in your records."

"I'm glad you called." The thought that Riley might have intentionally avoided giving her any contact information had stopped Sam from trying to reach Riley through official channels. Aware that Tony would be back at any moment, Sam quickly said, "Do you have time for lunch today?"

"Yes. That's why I called. I was hoping you'd have therapy today at the same time you did before."

Sam smiled at the prospect of seeing her again. "That's where I am now. Give me a chance to finish here, get cleaned up and changed, and I can meet you for lunch. Say, in about an hour?"

Riley hesitated. Papers rustled. "Maybe we could make it another time? I only have an hour, right now."

Disappointment dimmed Sam's mood. She glanced down at her sweat-stained T-shirt and shorts. It wasn't as if Riley hadn't seen her like that before. "If you won't be embarrassed by being seen with me while I'm rumpled and sweaty, I can meet you now."

"That's not a problem," Riley said. "Meet me in the arboretum, and I'll bring lunch. What would you like?"

"You don't have to do that. I'll meet you in the hospital cafeteria." Was Riley embarrassed to be seen with her and just didn't want to admit it? Sam didn't know her well enough to gauge from her tone of voice.

"There's no reason for you to walk all the way over here. The arboretum is closer to where you are."

Okay, it wasn't her scruffy appearance. Sam frowned. *Does she really think I'm so weak that I can't even make it over to the hospital's cafeteria?* "I can—"

Tony stepped back into the treatment area with a thick towel over his shoulder and two ice packs in his hands. He set the ice wraps down, then made a wind-it-up motion with his hand.

There was no time to discuss it further, and Sam didn't want to waste what little time free time Riley had. "Okay. The arboretum it is. Umm..." She glanced at Tony's frowning face. "You know better than I do what's available. Just go ahead and pick out something for me."

"All right," Riley said. "I'll get our lunch and meet you in the arboretum."

"Okay. Bye." Sam ended the call and met Tony's scowling gaze. "I have to go."

"All your therapy is important, Sam."

"I know. And I appreciate all you're doing, but this is a special circumstance. I'll put ice on it when I get home if you want."

"No. It's fine." Tony shook his finger at her. "Just don't make a habit of cutting sessions short."

"I won't." Sam pulled on her sweatpants, snagged her cane, and headed for the arboretum as quickly as her leg would allow.

Riley juggled the tray as she tried to open the arboretum door at the same time. After managing to get inside without spilling anything, she scanned the area for Sam. A smile tugged at the corners of her lips when she spotted her.

Sam was sitting with her arms along the back of the bench, her long legs stretched out in front of her and her face turned up to the sun. From where she stood, Riley couldn't tell whether Sam's eyes were closed or not.

"Hi, Sam," she said as she approached the bench.

Sam's eyes popped open, and she greeted Riley with a bright smile. "Hey." She began to stand.

Riley waved her to stay seated.

Sam stood anyway, and then reached for the tray.

"I've got it," Riley said. "Relax."

A frown marred Sam's face. "I'm not helpless."

"No. You're not. You're hurt. There's a big difference." Riley narrowed her eyes when Sam remained standing. *So stubborn.* Despite their short acquaintance, Riley knew that Sam was bothered by looking less than strong and independent. *I'd blame it on her being a cop, but since I feel the same way, I can hardly give her too hard a time.* "Just this once, humor me." She met Sam's gaze and smiled. "Please."

Muttering something that sounded like "no fair," Sam sat down.

Riley set the cafeteria tray on the bench between them. "I wasn't sure what you'd like." She handed Sam a bottle of water. "Hope that's okay."

"It's good." Sam opened the bottle and downed a good portion of the water. "Thanks. That hit the spot. What else have you got? I'm starving."

Riley laughed. "I figured you might be. They have the best fresh sushi here. I always splurge and get that when I'm really hungry." She slid the tray with the sushi toward Sam. "I brought you a few things: a sake nigiri, a four-piece tekkanaki roll, and a temaki."

"What are you having?" Sam asked.

Riley nabbed a small container off the tray and popped the lid open. "A sprout salad with a great raisin vinaigrette dressing."

Sam eyed the contents of the small tray for several moments.

"Is there something wrong?" Riley glanced down at the six pieces of sushi. "I know it's a lot of food, but I wanted to make sure you didn't go hungry. Just eat what you want." She frowned as a thought occurred to her. *Dang!* Maybe she didn't like sushi. "Would you rather have something else instead? I can go get whatever you want." Riley set down her salad.

"No. This is fine. Relax and enjoy your lunch." Sam picked up the sake nigiri and popped it into her mouth.

"You sure?" As Sam chewed the sushi, Riley studied her face for any signs of distaste.

"I'm sure." Sam picked up a piece of the tekkanaki roll. "It's fine. Thanks." She finished off her sushi before Riley was done with her salad.

I guess she was hungry. Riley picked up the small, foil-covered fruit cup she had chosen as a spur-of-the-moment indulgence for herself. "Would you like some fruit?"

"No. You go ahead. I'm good."

Riley smiled and slid the fruit cup and a plastic spoon into her lab coat pocket. "I'll save it for later, then."

Silence reigned for several minutes and began to feel uncomfortable.

This wasn't turning out as Riley had hoped. After seeming to connect the last time they'd met, today they had gone back to acting like the virtual strangers they actually were. Neither one seemed to know what to say. "I should probably get going."

Sam started and glanced at her watch. "Oh. I was hoping we might have a little time to visit."

Riley glanced at her own watch. "Well, I guess I could stay a little longer." Searching for something to say, she smiled as a familiar topic occurred to her. "So, how's Izzy? I thought she was going to come with you today."

Sam grinned, and the discomfort between them popped like a bad gas bubble. "Izzy's great. She just has an aversion to Tony, my physical therapist."

"Ah. You're working with Tony. He's pretty tough, but he's good."

Sam scowled. "He's a slave driver," she grumbled, just loud enough for Riley to hear.

Riley laughed. "I know. If I never hear the words, 'just one more' again, it will be too soon."

"Ah. His favorite phrase."

"One of them. Don't forget his ever popular, 'it's good pain.'"

"Oh great." Sam grimaced. "Haven't heard that one yet. Something to look forward to."

That was stupid. Now she's going to be worried. "That was just me. It might be different for you."

"So how did you end up in Tony's clutches? If you don't mind me asking."

Heat rose up to tint Riley's cheeks. "Umm..." It had not been one of her better moments.

"It's okay. You don't have to tell me. None of my business anyway."

Riley didn't miss the sudden distance in Sam's voice. She was surprised how bad it made her feel. "No. It's fine to ask. It's just embarrassing." She fiddled with the tray that sat between them. "I injured my shoulder."

"And?" Sam leaned back against the bench and rolled her hand in a "go ahead" motion. "Get to the embarrassing part."

Why did you even bring this up? Riley met Sam's gaze and saw nothing but humor sparkling in her eyes. *Lighten up. You're turning into Uncle Rielly.* "Okay. But no laughing."

"No way am I promising that," Sam said with a grin.

Riley mock-scowled, making Sam laugh outright. "I'd just come home from a very long shift. Exhausted, I fell asleep on my couch. I'm not sure what woke me up, but I was still kind of groggy, and it was pretty dark in the living room." She turned on the bench to face Sam more fully and drew one leg up under herself. "Anyway, I rolled over and happened to glance at the back cushion of the couch. A humongous spider, this big," she made a circle with her hands the size of a small plate, "was perched right there, barely two feet from my face." She shuddered. "I hate spiders."

Sam grinned. "Wow, that big, huh? Must have been some amazing super spider."

"Who's telling this story?" Riley asked.

Sam snickered. "Sorry, go ahead."

"I screamed and grabbed for the first thing I could reach, which turned out to be a big, thick coffee table book. I swung it at the blasted thing. Must have swung harder than I thought." Riley's face and ears went hot. "But it was a big spider!"

Sam's shoulders shook with repressed laughter. "Got it. Really big spider."

"Anyway, the book hit the cushion and then bounced back at me, and the momentum knocked me right off the couch. I bashed my shoulder on the coffee table on the way to the floor."

"Ow." Sam grabbed her own shoulder. "That must have smarted." Sympathy showed in her vivid blue eyes. "I'm sorry you got hurt."

Riley rubbed the shoulder she had injured. "Still aches occasionally, but otherwise it's fine."

Laugh lines appeared at the corner of Sam's eyes. "I do have one question for you."

Riley narrowed her eyes. "What?"

"Did you get the big, mean spider?"

"No! I searched for its squished body but never found it. For weeks afterward, every time I sat on the couch, I just knew the dang thing was lurking somewhere, just waiting to jump out at me. And I couldn't even swing a big book at it, 'cause I couldn't pick it up with one hand."

Sam burst out laughing.

"I told you it was embarrassing," Riley muttered.

"I can just picture you swinging this huge book at this little bitty spider." Sam mimed swinging a book. "Whack. Whack."

"I'm telling you it was huge. Biggest thing I've ever seen. Probably a mutant."

Sam wiped tears of laughter from her eyes. "So you don't have anyone at home to protect you from vicious, mutant spiders?"

That almost sounds like a pick-up line. Riley gazed at her, wondering about her intention. Sam had this little half smirk on her face that Riley couldn't interpret, and her eyes seemed to twinkle with some repressed emotion. *What's the likelihood she and her sister both are gay? She's straight. And has no idea you're not.* "No, just me...and my big book."

Sam threw her head back and laughed.

The beeping of Riley's watch alarm broke the moment. She glanced at her watch in surprise. It was later than she thought. "Now I do have to go."

The smile dropped off Sam's face. "Oh. Okay."

Riley stood and picked up the tray with the trash from their lunch.

"I can take that back," Sam said.

"That's okay. I'm heading in that direction."

They walked to the door in silence, and Sam held it open for Riley. "Thanks for lunch."

Riley gazed up at her and smiled. "You're very welcome." After a shaky start, their time together had turned out to be a lot of fun, even though she'd told the embarrassing story on herself. "Maybe we could do it again sometime."

A bright smile lit Sam's face. "I'd really like that."

Riley fished in the pocket of her lab coat and pulled out a small notebook. She wrote down her personal cell phone number and handed it to Sam. "You've got therapy on Monday, right?" When Sam nodded, Riley continued, "I'm the primary in the trauma unit all week, so I can't promise I'll be available, but call me when you're done with therapy, and maybe we can grab a quick lunch."

"Sounds like a plan. See you then." Sam waved and headed down the hall.

Riley watched until she had limped out of sight, then went back to work.

CHAPTER 15

Sam leaned back against the wall outside the physical therapy department and scrolled through the contact list in her phone. "Third time's the charm." Her two previous attempts to connect with Riley had failed. On Monday, every call had gone straight to voice mail. On Wednesday, Riley had answered but was called away for an emergency before they could make plans to meet. Sam crossed her fingers and touched the screen. The phone rang: once, twice, three times. *Bummer.* The phone rang a fourth time, and Sam expected to hear the click as it switched over to voice mail. *No sense leaving a message. If she's busy, she's busy.*

"Hello, Sam."

Sam started at the sound of Riley instead of the recording she'd been expecting. "Hey. Glad I caught you. How's it going?"

"It's been a crazy week. Just when I think I've seen it all, people find new ways to hurt themselves... and others. I've lost track of how many hours I've spent in the OR."

Hearing the fatigue in Riley's voice, Sam pushed aside her disappointment but couldn't rid herself of the worry that followed in its wake. She glanced down at the bag sitting near her feet. It would have to wait. "I understand if you're too tired to meet for lunch. Maybe next week?"

"Actually, you caught me on the way to the cafeteria. I'm free right now. Don't know how long the lull will last, but I need to get something to eat while I can."

While Sam had great respect for the importance of Riley's work, she was still concerned about the long hours. "I'm done with therapy."

Muted voices and the clatter of what sounded like the banging of plates and trays filtered through from Riley's end of the phone.

"Give me a few minutes to get over there, and I'll join you in the cafeteria."

"Let's meet in the arboretum instead."

Not this again. Stifling her irritation, Sam said, "I can walk over to the cafeteria."

"I'm sure you can." Riley hesitated, then continued, "To tell you the truth, I could really use some peace and quiet."

"Are you sure I wouldn't be intruding?"

"You're not. I wouldn't have answered my phone if I didn't want to see you."

Sam smiled, surprised at how relieved she was by the simple reassurance. "I'd like to see you too. I have a surprise for you."

Dead silence answered her.

"Riley? You still there?"

"Yes. So what can I get you for lunch?"

Sam grimaced. *No sushi.* "Could you grab me a club sandwich, a bag of chips, and a bottle of water? Oh, and a chocolate cookie or a piece of chocolate cake. Anything chocolate."

"I can do that," Riley said. "I'll see you in a few."

A grin split Sam's face as she disconnected the call and picked up the bag at her feet. "I can't wait to see the look on her face."

Sam stepped into the courtyard that housed the hidden sanctuary and let the tranquil atmosphere wash over her. She smiled at the now familiar bronze statue of the little girl, arm upraised, a butterfly resting on her palm. Spotting a flash of white through the foliage, she headed in that direction as quickly as her leg would allow.

"You got here fast," Sam said as she brushed a large banana leaf out of the way.

The white-coated woman on the bench glanced up at her with a frown.

"Oh. Excuse me." Sam backpedaled and left the stranger in peace. It was the first time she had seen anyone else in the arboretum.

The sound of the door opening drew her attention back to the entrance. *Ah. There she is.* She limped toward Riley. "Hey. Glad you could make it."

"Hi, Sam. Not to be rude, but I need to eat before I get called again." Riley moved toward the corner where Sam had just encountered the stranger.

She put a hand on Riley's lab coat covered arm. "Our usual spot is taken."

"No problem. Come on." Riley led them to the opposite corner of the arboretum. Pushing aside the leaves of a giant bird of paradise, she revealed two benches facing each other.

Between them was another life-size bronze stature that appeared to be the same girl as in the main courtyard. She was kneeling amidst a riot of brightly colored live flowers. Bronze butterflies covered her lap, and exquisitely detailed wings sprouted from her back.

"I really didn't think of it when I saw the first statue, but I wonder who the little girl is," Sam said.

"That's Sissy." Riley pointed to a small brass plaque. "Her parents had this arboretum built and also donated the money to expand the children's wing of the hospital."

Sam checked out the plaque. *In memory of our angel, Sissy Flowers.* A lump formed in her throat. "That's so sad."

"It is." A shadow passed over Riley's face. "I can only imagine the anguish it would cause a parent to lose their child."

This was not how she wanted to spend what time they had together. She had hoped to make Riley laugh.

Sam joined Riley, propped her cane against the bench, and set the bag at her feet. As unobtrusively as she could, she pushed a fuzzy ear back into the bag. She plucked the sandwich off the tray Riley had put down between them. "Thanks for the sandwich." She pulled some money from the pocket of her sweatpants and offered it to Riley, who shook her head.

"My treat."

"But you paid last time." Sam offered the bills again.

"It's the least I can do. Now let's eat."

Sam was already coming to recognize that stubborn tilt of Riley's chin. "Thank you."

"You're—" Riley's stomach growled. She flushed and placed her hand over her belly. "Excuse me. I haven't had a chance to get anything to eat since late last night." She grabbed a small container, popped it open, and dug into her lunch.

Another salad? After not eating all day? This one looked a little more substantial than the last, but not by much. Shaking her head, Sam concentrated on her own lunch. *Now you know how she stays so slim.*

Riley finished off her salad. "That hit the spot."

"Would you like to share my cookie?" Sam pulled the wrapping off her chocolate fudge cookie, broke it into two pieces, and held out half.

Riley stared at the cookie as if she was considering the offer, then shook her head. "No, thank you."

"You sure?" Sam waggled the cookie enticingly.

"I'm sure. You go ahead."

Your loss. Sam polished off the cookie in no time, brushed the crumbs off of her T-shirt, and wiped her hands on a napkin. She wanted to give Riley her gift before she got called away. When she picked up the bag, she made sure that the contents were not visible. "Before you have to go, I have a surprise for you."

Riley eyed the large bag.

Sam turned to block Riley's view of the bag as she reached inside. Gift in hand, she turned back toward Riley and held it up.

Delighted laughter burst from Riley. "You brought Izzy for a visit." She reached for the teddy bear.

Sam grinned. "This isn't Izzy."

Riley dropped her hands in mid-reach and looked more closely at the bear. While dressed the same as Izzy in a police uniform with hat and utility belt, this bear was different, its fur much lighter than Izzy's dark sable.

"She's Izzy's sister," Sam's brow furrowed for a second, "or if you prefer, her brother."

"Oh. You have two of them."

"Huh? No. Riley, I got her for you." Her smile wavered. "If you want her..."

Riley's gazed darted between Sam and the bear. She couldn't remember the last time someone had given her a gift. And certainly not anything like this. Emotion flooded her throat, and it took her a moment to find her voice. "Of course I want her."

When she took the teddy bear from her hands, Sam's smile returned, brighter than before.

Riley stroked the bear's soft, silky fur. "What's her name?"

"I don't know. She's yours. You need to give her a name."

Riley studied the bear. *What should I name you?* Her eyes lit on something purple sticking out of the bear's utility belt. *A flashlight?* It looked as if it had been an addition to the bear's attire. She tugged the item free and realized it was a mini-mag light. "What's this for?"

A little half smirk appeared on Sam's face. "Well, this bear is meant to be your protector. What good would she be without a bright light to scare away huge, mutant spiders? Or at least provide you with some light so you can whack them."

Riley guffawed, then slapped her hand over her mouth. *Aunt Margaret would faint dead away hearing you bray like that.* She pushed away the intrusive thought. She was having too much fun to care.

Sam met her gaze and held it for just a moment. "She's also good at keeping bad dreams at bay," she said, the humor gone from her voice.

Unexpectedly moved by the care apparent on Sam's face, Riley felt tears prickle at the corner of her eyes. She hid her face in the bear's soft fur until she had regained her composure. Hugging the bear to her chest, she looked up at Sam. "Thank you."

"You're welcome. Once you give her a name, maybe we can set her and Izzy up on a play date sometime?"

Riley laughed. *What an unexpected surprise you're turning out to be.* "How about if we adults go out to dinner sometime?" She shocked herself with the spontaneous invitation. Then she reminded herself of the as yet unfulfilled promise, made months ago, to start enjoying her life. Maybe Sam was just the person to help her do that. Judging by the look on Sam's face, Riley wasn't the only one surprised.

"I'd like that. A lot," Sam said. "When?"

Suddenly nervous, Riley stroked the bear to give herself something to do with her hands. Although she had issued the invitation, it was a big step for her to allow someone into her private life. "I'm covering in-house this weekend. It would have to be next week when I'm on back-up call."

"That's fine with me." Sam smiled. "You tell me when and where, and I'll be there."

"I know a great place that has really fresh sushi," Riley said.

Sam's mouth twisted for just a second. "Ah…"

I knew it. "You don't even like sushi—do you? Why didn't you say anything last week?"

Two spots of red stained Sam's cheeks. "I like it okay as an occasional thing."

Riley arched an eyebrow. "Oh. You mean like once every five years?"

"Maybe once a year," Sam muttered, her blush deepening. "But it was fine. Really. You were nice enough to bring lunch. And I didn't say what I wanted."

"I'm sorry. I should have realized that sushi isn't everyone's thing." *At least she was flexible enough to eat it. You couldn't even accept half a cookie.*

Self-disgust rose up in Riley at her inability to overcome a lifetime of restrictions. She poked Sam in the shoulder. "Next time say something. Okay?"

Looking chagrined, Sam nodded. "Um... So how about Ita—" She shook her head. "Chinese food? Do you like Chinese food?"

"Chinese would be great." The buzz of Riley's phone sounded loud amidst the quiet setting. "Sorry." She pulled the phone off her belt and checked the display. "I've got to go."

Sam stood with the help of her cane and picked up the tray. "I'll take this back," she said, in a firm, don't-argue-with-me tone.

Riley narrowed her eyes but forced herself not to protest. "Okay."

"Oh. I wasn't thinking about you going back to work." Sam snagged the now empty bag from the bench. "I can keep the bear until we meet for dinner."

Riley's arm instinctively tightened around her bear. *You gave her to me. I'm not giving her up.* "No. That's okay. I'll take her with me. She'll just have to go back into the bag for a little while until I can put her in my office." *And hopefully no one will notice her.*

That settled, they headed for the door.

"Thanks again," Riley said, hefting the bag in her hand as they stepped out into the hall. "See you later."

"You're welcome. See you."

Several steps down the hallway, Riley remembered their dinner plans and turned back toward Sam. "I'll call you later, and we can plan when to meet for dinner."

Sam waved in acknowledgement and sent Riley on her way with a bright smile.

CHAPTER 16

A short rap on her office door jolted Riley's attention from her paperwork. The door swung open before she could get up.

Claire strode into the room. "Hi, Riley. How's it going?"

Riley bit back a groan. If Claire was here, it meant one thing: she wanted something. Usually, Riley wouldn't care, but tonight she had plans. "Fine. Just catching up on the never-ending paperwork before I head out."

Claire had befriended her when she'd joined the staff, or so Riley had thought at the time, thrilled that there was another female trauma surgeon on staff. For once, Uncle Rielly had been right. He had always harped on the fact that colleagues were never truly your friends.

Claire sauntered over and sat on the edge of the desk. "I've been so busy, I just haven't had time for anything. John's been traveling, and Sherry... Well, you know how teenagers are. Everything's a crisis."

Riley glanced at her watch. *Enough with the buildup. What do you want?* She needed to get home so she could shower and change before meeting Sam for dinner.

Shifting against the desk in the growing silence, Claire said, "I need you to cover for me in-house tonight."

"Sorry. I can't do that. I have plans."

Claire's mouth dropped open.

That's right. I'm not going to be a pushover anymore. This had been part of the vow she had made to herself a few months ago. Up until now, she hadn't managed to keep that promise, but now she would. She pushed away the twinge of guilt. She really did have plans.

"I'll cover for you next month," Claire said.

That's what she always said, but she never actually did. Riley shook her head. "Sorry."

"But I promised Sherry a week ago I'd be at her play. She'll be heartbroken."

Her temper flared. So Claire had known about it all that time, but only bothered to ask her now? The guilt Riley felt at disappointing a child, even one as spoiled as Sherry, melted away. "Sorry. I have plans."

Claire's expression darkened. "You could change them."

Riley rose and faced her. "If you had let me know sooner, maybe I could have. But at the last minute, no, I can't change them."

"So you won't do it?" Claire's brow lowered; her eyes bore into Riley. "You'll make me disappoint my daughter and break her heart?"

Riley struggled to remain firm. "Sorry. No. I have plans." She motioned toward the door. "Now if you'll excuse me, I need to finish up here."

In a huff, Claire stomped to the door, opened it, and then turned back to Riley. "Wasn't the woman I saw you with in the arboretum last week the cop that got shot a few weeks ago?"

Riley nodded.

"That's right." Claire's head bobbed. "You did her surgery—didn't you?"

The sly look on Claire's face sent alarm bells ringing in Riley's head. What was she up to?

"Ah...if I remember correctly, there were a number of people who weren't too happy about that. I'm sure some of them would be interested in learning about your little rendezvous."

Are you threatening me? Riley's hackles rose. "I'm sure there are. Just like I'm sure there are a few people who would be interested in hearing about some of the things you do, Claire."

Claire's eyes went wide, and her mouth worked, but no sound emerged.

Never saw that one coming, did you? I'm through being afraid of what you might think of me.

Clair stepped out of the office and quietly closed the door behind her.

CHAPTER 17

Peering through the windshield, Sam scanned the parking lot. *Would have helped if you'd asked her what kind of car she drives.*

A sleek Jaguar coupe pulled into the lot. The overhead lights sparkled off its slate-blue paint.

Sam whistled. "Nice wheels."

The driver pulled the coupe into the only remaining spot along the back wall of the crowded city parking lot.

That can't be Riley. Can it? Sam opened her door and stepped out, watching the driver's side door of the Jaguar.

It opened, and Riley climbed out.

Sam glanced down at her Dodge Challenger, then back at Riley's gleaming Jaguar. She could only dream of owning a car like that. Leaning back inside her car, she grabbed her cane from behind the driver's seat. She tossed a glare at the cane, then sighed. When she turned around, she spotted a bedraggled man approaching Riley from behind. *Son of a bitch!* She slammed her car door.

Riley whirled around.

The man's voice drifted over, but Sam couldn't make out his words. Her incision burned as she forced herself into a fast pace. Pain shot down her thigh. Gritting her teeth, she forged on. She was still several feet way when the man's words became clear.

"Gimme a dollar. Gimme a dollar. Gimme a dollar." He had Riley trapped between her car and the one next to hers. The fronts of the cars were situated against the short concrete wall surrounding the lot. He was blocking her only way out.

"Hey," Sam called. "Leave her alone."

The panhandler jerked around and faced her. His hair and chest-length beard were filthy and matted, his face so covered in grime, she wasn't sure of his age. The unfocused look in his eyes made her heart rate speed up and sent her senses onto high alert. She had dealt with this type of street person before. He was like a bomb—primed to go off, but you never knew what would set it off.

Sam stopped at the rear of Riley's car so the man had a clear exit. She kept her free hand in plain view and leaned on her cane, in hopes that he wouldn't view it as a weapon. She spared a quick glance at Riley, silently praying she'd be still. Avoiding eye contact with the man, she said, "No money. Be on your way."

"Gimme a dollar. Gimme a dollar," the man continued to chant.

"No money. There's a mission not far from here, over on Kettner. They'll give you something to eat."

The man ignored her and turned back to Riley, still blocking her escape. "Gimme a dollar."

Illuminated by a nearby streetlight, Riley's pale, scared face was clearly visible. She shook her head. "No money." Her voice trembled.

"Gimme a dollar," the panhandler said, his tone turning strident.

Great. We had to run into a nut when I'm gimping around. No help for it now. Sam straightened, her hand tightening on the cane. "No. No money. Now leave." She kept her voice calm, but firm. "I'm a police officer. Don't—"

The man screamed as he whipped around, his eyes gone wild. He flailed his arms. "Police brutality! Police brutality!" He lunged toward Sam. "I've got witnesses."

"Riley! Get out of here!" Sam grabbed for his arm, praying her injured leg would hold.

He jerked back out of her reach and swung wildly.

Ducking back, Sam easily avoided the blow. "Calm down. Just walk away." She grasped her cane in the center of its length, prepared to use it as a weapon if need be.

The man spun around and launched a back kick at her.

She tried to dodge, but her injured leg couldn't take the strain. The kick landed on her injured thigh, sending her to the ground. She fell to her hands and knees on the asphalt, losing her cane in the process. Pain seared through her leg. *Fuck!*

As the man loomed over her, she flashed back to that moment in the ER when Keith shot her. She tensed for the next blow, even as she grabbed for her cane.

The man howled as if the devil himself were attacking him.

"Get away from her!"

Sam's head whipped up at the sound of Riley's voice.

Riley sprayed the man with a canister in her hand, apparently for the second time.

Catching a whiff of pepper spray, Sam's nose wrinkled.

The man ran from the parking lot, pawing at his face and bouncing off cars as he went.

Riley crouched down in front of Sam. "How badly are you hurt?"

Sam gazed into Riley's concerned face, amazed at her courage. "I'm fine."

Giving her a dubious look, Riley said, "Can you stand if I help you?"

"I can get up on my own." Sam picked up her cane. Leaning heavily on it, she regained her feet. Now that the excitement was over, embarrassment was starting to set in. *That's twice she's saved your sorry ass.* "Are you all right?"

"You're worried about me?" Riley shook her head. "You're something else. I'm not the one Karate Joe just used his kung fu moves on." She made a chopping motion with her hand.

Sam burst out laughing; then all the things that could have gone wrong flashed through her mind, and she sobered. "You should have run when I told you to."

Riley stared at her open-mouthed. "You're already hurt because of me. No way was I going to run away while some guy kicked the hell out of you." She huffed, thrusting out her chest. "Despite recent evidence to the contrary, I'm not helpless."

"I know you're not helpless. But this is what I do. It's my job."

"Not when you're hurt. Not because of me."

Sam was set back on her heels by the vehemence in her voice. "Riley."

Riley's hand slashed sideways in negation. "This isn't about me. I saw that kick land. How bad is it—really?" When Sam hesitated, she gave her "the look."

Sam blew out a breath. *She's got you pegged.* She rested her butt against Riley's car to take some of the stress off her leg. "I managed to avoid the full force of the blow. Damn leg just didn't appreciate the sudden moves." She rubbed her leg and tried not to wince. "I'm sure it will bruise, but that's all."

"We need to get you to the ER and have that leg checked," Riley said. "We can call the police from the ER and report this."

Sam shook her head. "I'm fine." Despite the throbbing in her thigh, there was no way she was going to the ER. She was already embarrassed enough. "I'm sorry about all this." She scanned the area, though she was confident the perp was long gone. "I'll contact the precinct tomorrow and let them know to keep an eye out for this guy. As far as dinner goes, it's up to you. If you want, we can just call it a night?" She wasn't sure she could walk to the restaurant, but if Riley still wanted to have dinner with her, she was sure going to try.

"There's nothing to be sorry for, but we should skip the restaurant," Riley said. "You need to get your leg taken care of. Tell you what, I'll buy you some takeout—after you get seen in the ER."

"No. I'm—"

Riley held up her hand. "Stop. There's no way you're not hurting. And don't think I haven't noticed how you're leaning against the car to keep the weight off that leg."

Busted. Sam pushed away from the car. The moment she put her full weight on her leg, she flinched. *Damn, that smarts.* "Honestly, I don't need the ER." She checked the front of her jeans for blood. There wasn't any. "I'm sure it's just bruised."

"Okay, here's the deal. You go to the ER and have your leg checked out, or you come over to my place for a while until we make sure it is just a bruise and doesn't get any worse. I'll order some Chinese takeout."

"You don't need to go to all that trouble. I'm fine."

Taking a step closer, Riley scowled up at her. Green fire sparked in her eyes. "The ER or my place. Pick."

Whoa. She may be small, but she's got that whole, 'don't mess with me, I'm in charge' thing down. Sam grinned. *I like that.* The thought caught her by surprise. "Okay. Fine. Your place."

CHAPTER 18

Sam followed Riley's Jag to a large, twelve-story brick building. *She lives here?* She'd driven past the high-rise and admired the stunning waterfront views, but living in the building was a pipe dream. The condos were priced way out of her league.

Riley stopped her car in front of the building.

Sam pulled in behind her.

A uniformed attendant approached and opened her door for Riley, who stepped out and handed him the keys. Together, they approached Sam's car.

Sam opened her own door and got out.

Riley smiled. "If you give Stewart your keys, he'll take care of your car."

Valet parking at condos? Sam eyed the man for a moment, then handed over her car keys.

Riley motioned toward the front entrance, allowing Sam to set the pace.

Though Sam's leg had stiffened in just the short ride, she tried not to limp as they walked toward the door.

A uniformed attendant opened the large glass doors for them.

As they stepped inside, Sam stopped for a moment to take in her surroundings. The lobby was immense, like a foyer in a very expensive hotel. The crystal chandelier hanging from the cathedral ceiling threw prisms of light around the room. A grouping of leather chairs rested on an expansive oriental rug that protected the gleaming hardwood floor. Living in this place probably cost a fortune.

Being a trauma surgeon must pay even better than she thought.

Another uniformed man stepped out from behind a massive desk. "Good evening, Dr. Connolly."

Geez, how many of these guys are there?

Frowning, the guard swept his gaze over Sam. "Do you need some assistance with your... guest?" His tone suggested he'd be more than happy to toss her out on her ass at the slightest indication from Riley.

It wasn't hard to figure out what the man's problem was. Sam glanced down at her dirt-stained jeans and scuffed shoes. Compared to Riley's pressed slacks and beautifully tailored blouse, she must look like some bum. She put on her cop face and met the guard's gaze head-on. Scruffy or not, she had every right to be here.

Riley's gaze dropped to the floor for a moment, then her body stiffened. "That won't be necessary."

Taken aback by her tone, Sam looked over at her. *Oh! She's pissed.*

Riley's stare pinned the man in place. "This is Officer Samantha McKenna of the San Diego Police Department. See to it that she is added to the permanent guest list and issued a parking pass."

"Yes, Dr. Connolly. Right away," the guard said in a subdued voice.

Sam resisted the childish impulse to smirk at him as Riley motioned her toward the elevator.

Sam followed Riley into her condo. *Wow!* The first thing that caught her attention was the floor-to-ceiling windows that provided a panoramic view of the bay. It was readily apparent that Riley lived a much different life than her own decidedly middle-class one.

Riley took off her shoes, placed them on a mat right inside the door, and slipped on a pair of soft-soled house shoes.

After setting her cane on the floor, Sam bent to tug at the laces of her shoes. She winced as pain stabbed her thigh.

"You don't have to do that," Riley said.

Sam glanced at the spotless inlaid tile entryway. Ignoring Riley's demurral, she pulled off her shoes. "No problem."

"Go ahead into the living room and make yourself comfortable. I'll gather what I need to take care of your leg." Riley disappeared deeper into the condo.

Sam resisted the urge to chase after her. The rubber tip of her cane squeaked on the highly polished hardwood floor as she gingerly made her way into the living room in her stocking feet.

A modernistic pristine white leather sofa faced the windows. She eyed the dirt staining her jeans and looked around for someplace else to sit.

The only other seat in the living area was a chair made of tubular steel and leather straps. Sam wasn't sure she would be able to get out of the chair if she sat down. Glass and metal furnishings dominated the cold, stark room. All of the pieces had unusual shapes and angles, and none of them looked comfortable or functional. A large abstract painting that consisted of slashes and trailing drips of red pigment hung on the far wall. *Looks like it belongs in a slasher movie, after the bad guy cut loose.* The whole room appeared as if it had been lifted straight from the pages of a modern design magazine. It wasn't at all the type of place she had pictured Riley living.

Banging, coming for what Sam assumed must be the kitchen, distracted her from the quest for someplace safe to sit. *What's she doing?* She walked over to the floor-to-ceiling windows and let the view ease some of her discomfort with her surroundings. Lights aglow, the harbor was laid out before her like a many-faceted jewel.

"You need to get off that leg and ice it down."

Sam started at the sound of Riley's voice.

Riley laid out the items she was carrying on the coffee table and motioned toward the sofa. "Take off your pants and stretch out on the couch."

In another time and place, Sam would have jumped on the provocative comment. *Not with her.* Even if Riley were gay, she didn't seem to be a no-strings-attached type of woman.

"Come on." Riley held out a folded bed sheet. "I've got ice for your leg, but it won't do you any good through your jeans."

She can't seriously expect me to drop my pants. Sam looked back and forth between Riley and the couch but made no move to comply.

Riley's brow furrowed. "I brought you a sheet to cover up with."

Gazing down at everything spread out on the coffee table, Sam shook her head. "There's no need for all this. It's nothing—"

"It wasn't nothing!" Riley's eyes sparked with intensity; then her expression crumbled. "That panhandler could've really hurt you."

Riley turned away, but not before Sam thought she had seen tears in her eyes. Riley dropped onto the couch and buried her face in her hands.

What the hell? This wasn't the strong, spunky woman who had pepper-sprayed her attacker. Heedless of her dirty jeans, Sam sat down next to her. "Hey. It's okay. It's just a bruise."

Riley brushed at her tears, then looked up with a guilt-ridden expression. "Your sister was right."

"What are you talking about?"

"I should've stayed away from you. All I ever do is get you hurt."

"What! That's ridiculous. What happened tonight wasn't your fault. If it was anyone's fault, then it was mine. I chose to meet at an unattended parking lot with no security." If she'd known what kind of car Riley drove, she'd have picked a secure lot.

Riley shook her head. "This wasn't a good idea."

Sam wasn't sure what *this* Riley was referring to: meeting for dinner, bringing her home, or having anything to do with her at all. Although they had not spent a lot of time together, the thought that Riley might want to walk out of her life forever sent an inexplicably strong surge of regret through her heart. *I'm not giving up that easy.*

Sam pushed off the sofa and stood. She unbuckled her belt and then unfastened her pants.

"What are you doing?" Riley asked.

"Proving to you that he didn't really hurt me." Sam pushed her jeans down, baring her thigh.

Riley scooted closer and gently skated her fingers over the fist-sized bruise above Sam's knee.

"See? Just a bruise."

Gazing at Sam's thigh, Riley moved her fingers higher to the reddened scars marring the pale skin. She lightly traced the healing flesh and peered up at Sam though half-lidded eyes. "What about these?"

Goosebumps erupted in the wake of Riley's touch. Sam resisted the urge to pull away. "They're fine too." She stepped back and reached for her pants.

"Wait. Please put the ice on it. Just for a little while."

Sam sighed, powerless to resist the entreaty in Riley's voice. "Okay."

"Dinner should be here in thirty minutes," Riley said.

Sam shifted, trying to find a comfortable position on the hard sofa. She couldn't help wondering why anyone would buy a piece of furniture like that. Riley had insisted she stretch out her legs on the couch while icing her thigh. Sam laughed to herself. *If Marina could see you now—in a woman's apartment, on her couch, with your pants off, and all you get out of it is a frozen thigh.*

Riley tugged over the tubular steel-and-leather chair and sank into it with ease.

The silence stretched out, eventually becoming uncomfortable.

Where's Izzy when I need her? The thought of the bear reminded Sam just where she was sitting. Allowing a half smirk to appear, she twisted and turned as if she were inspecting the couch.

Riley scowled, but there was no hiding the sparkle in her eyes. "What?"

Oh. She's on to you already. "Is it safe to sit here? Or do I need a big..." Sam drew out the word, "...book?"

"Very funny." Riley's eyes went wide. "Oh. No. It's back. There." She pointed over Sam's shoulder.

Sam jumped, whipping her head around before she could stifle the reaction.

"Gotcha." Riley burst out laughing.

Sam was relieved to see the last trace of guilt leave Riley's face. "Okay. I deserved that."

"Oh no. You're not getting off that easily. You owe me an embarrassing story in return."

"I owe you, huh?"

"Absolutely."

Sam bit her lip. *You've already seen me at my weakest.*

Riley's brilliant green eyes twinkled as she leaned forward in her chair. "Please."

Damn. No fair. Why do I have such a hard time saying no to this woman? "Okay." Considering Riley's petite size, Sam figured she'd get a laugh out of a woman not much bigger than she was taking Davidson down. She grinned just thinking about it. "A month or so ago—"

"Hold it. I said an embarrassing story about you, not about someone else."

What the...? "How did you know the story wasn't about—"

"No stalling. Story, please."

Sam couldn't resist the eager anticipation on Riley's face. After adjusting the ice on her thigh, she settled in to tell her story. "I was just a rookie. I'd only been on the force a few weeks when some of the female officers from different precincts got together and invited the women rookies out. Sort of a welcome-to-the-club thing." It had actually been a gathering of lesbian officers, but now wasn't the best time to bring that up since she was lying on Riley's couch with her pants off. "We went to a local barbecue restaurant."

"Get to the embarrassing part," Riley said.

Remembering she had said the same thing to Riley, Sam laughed. "Hold your horses. I'm getting there. Who's telling this story?"

"Sorry. You were saying?"

"This particular place is an old Victorian home they converted to a restaurant. So there are lots of small dining rooms instead of one big one. We walked through several rooms. As I came around the corner into the last room, I got distracted." She left out exactly what had distracted her since she'd been staring at the ass of the woman in front of her. "I didn't see the old man sitting just inside the doorway until it was too late. I ran right into him. Before I could grab him, he collapsed on the floor. I felt terrible, but I didn't start to panic until I realized he wasn't moving."

Riley's eyes went wide.

"There I was, a newly minted police officer, sworn to protect, and what's the first thing I do— knock down some helpless old man. I dropped to my knees next to him, then shouted for someone call nine-one-one." She shook her head at the memory. "I rolled him onto his back, all ready to save the day and do CPR if necessary... And it was a damn mannequin."

Riley's face twitched as she struggled not to laugh. She finally lost the battle, and gales of laughter poured forth.

"It was a really realistic mannequin." Sam crossed her arms over her chest, working hard to keep a straight face. "Could've been in a movie it was so real." It hadn't been funny at the time, but now, years later, she could laugh about it.

Clutching her sides, Riley continued to laugh.

Sam gave up the fight and joined her laughter. "Was that embarrassing enough for you?"

Riley wiped tears from her eyes. "Perfect."

"More shrimp lo mein?" Riley asked.

"No. I'm good. Thanks."

"How about some more tea? Or would you rather have water now?" Riley jumped up from her chair.

How the heck does she get out of that contraption like that? "I'm fine. Relax. Please." Riley had been catering to her every need since getting her situated on the couch. "You've gone to more than enough trouble. I'm not hurt. I can take care of myself."

Riley flushed and ducked her head. "I know. I just..." She began to gather up the remains of their dinner.

After making sure the sheet was securely wrapped around her hips, Sam swung her legs off the couch and reached for her jeans. "Let me help you."

"I've got it." Riley grabbed the containers and fled into the kitchen.

Taking the opportunity to get dressed without having to bare her injured thigh to Riley again, Sam quickly pulled on her jeans. After a rocky start, the evening had turned out to be all that she had hoped for. They had eaten and laughed together. It helped ease Sam's worries about the lingering effects the attack and shooting had on Riley.

Riley stifled a yawn as she came back into the room.

Sam glanced at her watch. It was later than she'd thought. She knew Riley had worked a twelve-hour shift before meeting her for dinner. "I should get out of your hair and let you get some rest. Thanks for dinner." She gestured toward the discarded sheet. "And for taking such good care of me."

"My pleasure."

"So when can we do this again?" Sam laughed. "Minus the whole Karate Joe thing."

The smile dropped from Riley's face, and her eyes went dark. "I'm so sorry about you getting hurt. I—"

"No. I'm sorry." Sam rested her hand gently on Riley's shoulder. The muscles were stiff under her hand. *Good going, twit. You and your big mouth.* "I shouldn't have joked about that. It truly wasn't your fault. Let it go."

Looking skeptical, Riley nodded.

"You've fed me three times now. I really would like to buy you dinner. You pick the place." Sam smiled down at her. "What do you say?"

"I'll have to see what my schedule looks like." Riley broke eye contact and looked down. "I'll...I'll call you."

"Okay." Sam worked to hide her disappointment. Regardless of her words, Riley's body language told a different story. As Sam limped to the door, she wondered whether she would ever hear from her again.

CHAPTER 19

Sam shook out her arms, then picked up the dumbbell. "Just one more." *Now I sound like Tony.* As she started her reps, her gaze lit on the phone lying on the end table. *Forget her.* She went back to her workout.

Despite her best intentions, she found herself glancing at the phone, willing it to ring. *It's been a week. She's not going to call.* Sam wasn't sure why she felt compelled to pursue a friendship with Riley. It wasn't as if Riley was the first person she had ever saved, although she was the only person she had taken a bullet for. *What do you care anyway?* But she did care, no matter how much she tried to convince herself otherwise. It hurt that Riley had just written her off. The dumbbell banged against her thigh. *Dammit.*

Sam grabbed the phone and limped into her bedroom, where she chucked it toward the bed, then cursed when it bounced onto the floor. *Screw it.* She nabbed her mp3 player, jammed the earbuds in place, and cranked up the volume. After returning to the living room, she resumed her workout. The pulsing beat of the music drove everything else from her mind.

Her sweat-soaked T-shirt clung to her torso; her arm and shoulder muscles burned. After shaking out her arms, she dropped onto the couch to catch her breath and grimaced when pain shot down her leg. Her head dropped back against the cushion, and she lost herself in the music, enjoying the rush of endorphins coursing through her system.

What was that? Sam lifted her head but couldn't hear anything except the pounding beat of the music. She glanced at the clock, surprised to see how much time had passed. In the next break between songs, she again thought she heard a noise. She pulled the earbuds out and was assaulted with sound of another type.

Bang! Bang! Something slammed against her front door. "McKenna, open this fucking door before I kick it in."

What the...? Marina? Sam jerked open the door. "What the hell are—?"

Marina, still dressed in her uniform and gear, rushed forward and grabbed her in a crushing bear hug.

The breath whooshed from Sam's lungs. "What's wrong?" She tried to squirm out of the viselike hold.

Marina released her and stepped back. "Thank God." Tears glimmered at the corners of her eyes.

"Get in here and tell me why the hell you're trying to knock down my front door."

Marina surveyed the room. "Why didn't you answer your phone?"

"I was working out. I didn't hear it."

"For three hours?"

"Of course not. I was listening to music." Sam dangled one of the earbuds between her fingers.

Marina eyed the free weights and strength bands lying on the floor. "Are you even supposed to be working out?"

"Therapist didn't say I couldn't. I was just working my arms. Now, what's going on?"

"Your car's in the lot. When you didn't answer your phone, I freaked out a little." A blush dusted Marina's cheeks. She scrubbed her hands over her face, then flopped down onto the couch. "Guess I overreacted. It's just that since you got shot, I've been worried..." She shook her head sharply as if unwilling to give voice to her fears.

Sam eased herself down on the couch close to her. "You've been worried about what? I don't understand. You haven't mentioned anything bothering you, then you show up here like a raging bull when I don't answer the phone for a couple of hours? What's this all about?"

Marina cupped Sam's face in her hand, her thumb softly stroking her cheek.

Sam smiled and leaned into the familiar touch. "Tell me what's got you so upset."

"You've been different since you got hurt. I mean that's expected, but..." Marina blew out a breath. "You haven't been to a single Friday night bull session since you got home. You haven't been by the station. You haven't come to watch any of our softball games." She held up her hand to keep Sam from interrupting. "It's not just that. I've asked you quite a few times to go out with me, and you've turned me down every time. You're distancing yourself from everyone." Her dark eyes bore into Sam's. "That worries me."

Guilt stabbed at Sam. She had been avoiding people from work. She hadn't stopped to think that Marina, of all people, might feel shut out. "Look, I'm sorry. It's just... I've been focusing on my therapy and trying to get back into shape. I just haven't felt like socializing." *Except with Riley.* Sam snorted to herself. *Who doesn't want anything to do with you.* It was hard to miss the irony in that.

"See, that's just what I mean," Marina said.

Sam jumped, startled from her thoughts. "What?"

"I'm sitting right here, and you just disappeared inside yourself."

Meeting Marina's gaze, Sam smiled. "I'm here. I'm fine."

Marina stared deeply into her eyes as if searching for something. "I hope so."

"That still doesn't explain why you were threatening to kick my door down."

Ducking her head, Marina said, "I thought you were falling into a depression, and when I couldn't reach you, I was afraid you'd..." Tears glimmering in her eyes, she looked away.

It took Sam a minute to get it. Shock ripped through her. "I would never—"

"That's what I thought about Ray!" Pain twisted Marina's face.

Jesus. Ray. It all suddenly made sense. The anniversary of Ray's death was this week. She wasn't sure Marina would ever truly recover from finding her older brother after he shot himself with his service pistol. Despite the tragedy, she had still gone on to become a police officer. *Just like you did after Leslie.* Sam ruthlessly slammed the door shut on those wrenching memories. She wrapped her arms around Marina and pulled her close. "I swear to you, the thought has never crossed my mind."

Marina buried her face against Sam's neck. "Promise me."

"I promise. It wasn't what you thought. I'm not depressed." Sam sighed and after hesitating for a second, added, "I didn't want everyone to see me while I was gimping around."

Marina squeezed Sam's waist, then pulled back. "No one would think any less of you. Jesus! You took a bullet to keep that woman from getting killed." She poked Sam in the side. "It's not like you let yourself go to pot and got fat and lazy or something."

"Hey. Watch it." Sam put on her best pitiful expression. "I'm hurt."

"Oh. Poor baby." Marina stood and offered Sam her hand. "Now get your butt off that couch and go take a shower. It's Friday night, everyone will be at O'Grady's."

"Not tonight. I'm beat. How about we go to lunch tomorrow or dinner?"

"Good idea. But tonight we're going to O'Grady's."

Sam allowed Marina to pull her off the couch.

"Go take a shower. You stink. I'll wait for you, then we'll head to my place so I can shower and change."

"You could join me." Sam stepped close, their breasts almost touching. During their time together, they had shared more than a few steamy showers. Dropping her voice to a husky purr, she said, "Wash my back for me?"

Marina gasped like a guppy out of water.

Gotcha! Sam burst out laughing. She knew there was no way in hell Marina would accept. She was devoted to Elisabeth. That didn't make tweaking her friend any less fun.

Marina muttered something under her breath. Scowling, she pointed toward the bedroom. "Go."

"You don't have to wait. I'll meet you at O'Grady's."

Marina searched her face. "You promise?"

"I promise." Maybe this was just what she needed.

CHAPTER 20

A noise startled Riley awake. "Ow." She rubbed at the crick in her neck.

A knock sounded on her office door.

Too tired to get up, she called out, "Come in."

The door swung open, and Denny stepped inside. "Good afternoon. How're you do—?" He pointed at her head.

Riley felt around and pulled off a sticky note that had stuck to her hair. Heat crept up her neck. "What're you doing here, besides giving me a hard time? Shouldn't you be with your wife and newborn son?"

"That's what I came to tell you. Carol got released this morning. We spent some time with Jeremy, then I took her home and got her all settled." Denny grinned. "Jeremy's off the respirator and breathing great on his own." He leaned against the corner of her desk. "I'm back to take over the rest of my shift and patients."

"That's great news." It had been touch and go for Carol and the premature baby for several days. "I can finish out your shift tonight. Stay with Carol or in the NICU with Jeremy. I've got this covered."

He shook his head "After being in-house six days straight with your own shifts and mine, you can't tell me you're not exhausted. I don't think I've seen you asleep at your desk since you were a fellow."

"It wasn't that bad. I was happy to help out."

"Go home, Riley. Get some sleep. I'll spend time with Jeremy if things stay quiet."

The offer was tempting. It felt as if she hadn't had a moment to herself all week. "Are you sure?"

Denny smiled. "Positive. Now go." He pulled her from the chair and gave her a one-armed hug. "We're both really grateful for all you've done this week."

"You're welcome. Give Carol and Jeremy my love."

Riley tugged her pillow closer. Her stomach rumbled. She glanced at the clock on her bedside table and groaned. It was just after seven. *I need sleep.* But her body wasn't cooperating. As she rolled back over, she caught sight of the latest addition to her bedroom. She smiled at Annie sitting on top of her dresser, keeping watch over her.

Seeing the bear turned her thoughts to Sam. Despite what had happened, she had thoroughly enjoyed their time together last Friday. She couldn't remember when she had last laughed so freely. She wanted to call her, but she was torn. The homeless man's attack had shaken her. Not the attack itself so much, but the fact that Sam had been injured trying to protect her. Riley had gone over and over the incident, sure there was something she could have done. Why hadn't she pepper-sprayed him sooner?

She shoved back the covers, got out of bed, then stopped for a moment to stroke Annie's silky fur before going to the kitchen. After making a cup of herbal tea, she retreated to the living room and gazed out the floor-to-ceiling window. The view of the boats in the harbor at night always soothed her.

The peaceful moment was broken by her growling stomach. She couldn't remember the last time she'd eaten, but the fridge was empty, and she didn't relish going food shopping. There were numerous takeout menus in the drawer, but nothing appealed to her. *Be honest with yourself. You know what you want to do.* But she wondered if she should. Even after being injured trying to protect her, Sam still invited her out. If Sam was willing to take a chance, why shouldn't she?

Riley marched into the bedroom to get her phone before her courage failed her. She plopped down on the side of the bed and gazed up at Annie. *I can do this.*

She listened to the phone ringing, her tension rising with each unanswered ring. When the call went to voice mail, she deflated like a pierced balloon. An automatic smile tugged at the corners of her lips at the sound of Sam's voice. As the beep sounded, an unpleasant thought intruded. What if Sam had changed her mind once she'd had time to think about it? Or what if her sister found out about Sam getting hurt again? Doubts assailed Riley. She sighed and ended the call without leaving a message.

CHAPTER 21

Sam smiled at the feel of warm breasts pressed against her back. A slim arm wrapped around her waist for a moment, then a small hand captured her breast and squeezed. Her lover's nimble fingers rolled Sam's nipple, making her groan. She tugged the petite hand off her breast and guided it down between her legs, whimpering as her lover began to stroke her clit. *Yeah. Just like that.*

An insistent sound jolted Sam awake. The dream vanished like a wisp of smoke on the wind, just when it was getting good. Rolling onto her back, she growled at the lingering pulse of arousal. *I'm gonna kill whoever's calling.*

She scanned the bedside table, but her phone wasn't in its accustomed place. Another ring helped her pinpoint its location. *How the heck...?* Then she remembered her fit of pique the night before, when the phone had ended up on the floor. She scrambled out of bed and made a grab for her phone, trying to catch the call before it went to voice mail. She glanced at the screen as she stabbed the connect. "What do you want, Marina?"

"Good morning to you too, sunshine."

"I was sleeping." Sam glanced at the bedside clock. "What's so earth-shattering you needed to call at eight in the morning after keeping me out till midnight?"

"I wanted to invite you to lunch. I just talked to my mãe. There's a big helping of your favorite empadão waiting for you. Oh, and she said to tell you my pai made bolo de nozes."

Sam's stomach rumbled at the thought of the chicken pie and thick-layered walnut cake. Marina had introduced her to a number of traditional Portuguese foods at her parents' restaurant. "What time do we eat?"

Marina laughed. "I thought that might change your grumpy mood. Want me to pick you up?"

"I'll meet you there." Sam thought she heard someone else's voice in the background. "Bring Elisabeth with you."

"Are you sure?"

Sam sighed at the hesitancy in her friend's voice. "Marina, we've had this conversation. I'm happy for you. And glad Elisabeth doesn't mind you hanging out with me. Bring her."

"You're the best."

"I'll see you both at two."

"Later," Marina said.

After ending the call, Sam checked her missed calls. She stared at the name she never expected to see again. *Riley! And I missed her. Damn it.* Should she call her now? She glanced at the clock. After waiting so long to hear from Riley, she could barely resist the temptation to call her back immediately.

Then again, Riley sure hadn't been in a hurry to call her. She forced herself to set the phone down. *A shower and breakfast, then maybe I'll call.*

Her anger washed away by her shower, she contemplated things she hadn't previously considered. What if Riley wasn't ignoring her? Maybe something happened at work. *You should've called her and checked. Some job you're doing looking out for her.*

Sam grabbed her phone. Her foot tapped as the phone rang several times.

"Hi, Sam."

An automatic smile bloomed at the sound of Riley's voice. "Hey. How are you doing? Is everything okay?"

"I'm good. I'm sorry it took me so long to get back to you. Work was crazy this week. I ended up not only covering my own shifts, but a friend's as well."

"Sorry I missed your call." *'Cause I had a tantrum and tossed my phone.* Guilt tinged Sam for doubting Riley. With the way things had ended between them the previous Friday, it had been hard not to.

"I was wondering..." Riley cleared her throat. "Are you still interested in going to lunch? I'm free today."

Ah. Damn. Sam wanted to say yes, then call and cancel on Marina. If it had been any other time, she would have done just that, but with the anniversary of Marina's brother's death this week, she just couldn't.

"Sam? You still there?"

She started, pulled from her thoughts. "Yeah. Sorry. I'd like to meet you. It's just that I've already made plans today, and I really can't get out of them."

"Maybe some other time," Riley said, her tone dispirited.

"How about tomorrow?" Sam crossed her fingers. "I'd really like to take you to lunch."

"I'm free. Where would you like to go?"

Sam smiled. "I promised you could pick the place."

"Do you like seafood? The cooked kind."

Picturing the smile on Riley's face, Sam grinned. "Yes. I like cooked seafood. Where did you have in mind?"

"What about *The Landing*? They have a very nice Sunday brunch."

Nice and expensive. Sam shrugged. *You did say she could pick.* "Sure. What time?"

"Twelve-thirty?"

"That sounds good. I'll meet you there."

"See you then," Riley said before hanging up.

While eagerly anticipating seeing Riley tomorrow, Sam had one pressing problem. *The Landing* was an upscale eatery located right next to the yacht club. What was she going to wear? One thing was sure—blue jeans were not going to cut it.

CHAPTER 22

After circling several times, looking for a spot nearby, Sam gave in and pulled up in front of the restaurant.

A uniformed attendant opened her car door and offered his hand. "Ma'am."

Sam waved off his assistance. She handed over her keys, then reached into the backseat and got her cane. She had wanted to leave it at home, but her leg had other ideas. When she had gone to the bar with Marina, she hadn't taken the cane, and she was still paying the price for that. Sam was reminded of one of her dad's favorite sayings: Pride goeth before the fall. *In my case, it will be literally.*

Sam brushed at the hanger crease on her Dockers. The tip of her cane came down on a stray rock, and she stumbled. *Damn.* The sound of running feet made her head whip up. *Riley. That figures.*

Riley wrapped her hands around Sam's bicep. "Are you all right?"

"I'm fine." *Why does she always have to see me looking weak?*

"Then let's go inside." Smiling, Riley kept her hand on Sam's elbow. Her coppery-red hair gleamed like a newly minted penny. The bright sunshine made her green eyes appear as if they were lit from within. She was dressed in beautifully tailored charcoal-gray slacks that hugged her slim hips and a dark jade short-sleeved sweater set. *Too bad she's straight.* Sam froze for an instant. *Whoa! Where did that come from?* Her gaze swept Riley. *She's not your type.* Sam preferred her women beautiful and on the voluptuous side. Riley was neither. She was cute, but not a classic beauty. And her figure was boyish to say the least. But there was still something Sam found very appealing about her.

Riley's grip tightened on her arm. "Is something wrong? Are you hurting?"

Sam shrugged away the unusual feeling. "Just thinking about all the great food. I'm starving."

"Me too." Riley released her arm and led the way to the tuxedoed maître d'.

"Good day, Dr. Connolly. Will your aunt and uncle be joining you today?"

He knew her by name. It once again made Sam aware that they lived very different lives. She couldn't image frequenting a restaurant this expensive often enough to become known by the maître d'.

"Not today, Edward." Riley slipped her hand around Sam's elbow. "It will just be the two of us."

The maître d' looked at Sam as if gauging her net worth.

She resisted the urge to straighten the collar of her knit polo shirt and pinned him in place with a hard stare.

His gaze dropped to the open reservations book on the podium.

Riley seemed oblivious to his perusal.

Maybe Sam was overly sensitive because she felt so out of place. The dining room was crowded with men in sport coats accompanied by women wearing dresses or expensive-looking dress slacks and blouses. A harpist on a raised platform near the back wall filled the room with the soft strains of her orchestral harp, muting the sounds of conversation and the clink of silverware. This would have not been Sam's choice of establishment for a relaxing Sunday meal.

"I see you reserved a window table," Edward said.

"Something special, please." Riley took Edward's hand for a moment.

The movement was so smooth, Sam almost missed it. *Wonder how much she passed him?*

"This way, please," Edward said.

Giving Sam's arm a quick squeeze before releasing her, Riley followed in his wake.

The panoramic view of the bay drew Sam's attention as they approached their table. *Very nice.* The table was draped with a pristine white tablecloth and set with linen napkins, stemware, and shining silverware. In the center of the table, a vase of freshly cut flowers provided a splash of color.

Edward pulled out a chair for Riley, then placed the napkin in her lap once she was seated.

While Sam would have preferred to seat herself, she waited her turn, not wanting to embarrass Riley. She drew the line at having the napkin placed in her lap.

Edward sniffed and placed the napkin on her outstretched palm. "Your server will be right with you. Enjoy your meal," he said, then made his exit.

Sam took a moment to enjoy the delectable scents filling the air. There were several food stations, each with a wide selection of choices. She looked to see what Riley had chosen to start with. *The salads. Of course, what else?* Sam had more meaty fare in mind. If she had to pony up fifty bucks each, she'd enjoy as many things as possible. She headed for the server slicing the prime rib.

Her plate filled to overflowing with a multitude of goodies, she returned to their table.

Riley was already seated. One side of her plate held raw vegetables and fresh fruit, the other side, a small portion of a vegetable dish and a piece of grilled fish.

Riley glanced at Sam's plate.

She flushed, then pushed the uncomfortable feeling aside. Just because Riley barely ate enough to sustain a small child didn't mean she had to.

The server arrived with the mimosas they had ordered before going to get their food.

Surprised she drinks.

"I'm glad you found some things you like."

Was that a dig? Sam stared at Riley. If anything, she looked a bit nervous. *Now you're being ridiculous.* Riley had never put her down or commented on what she ate. "Everything looked great. I had a hard time deciding. I guess I got carried away."

Riley smiled. "Enjoy yourself. The food here is wonderful. They're known for their lobster bisque. You should try it." She speared a piece of mango and nibbled at it.

Then why hadn't she taken any? Sam turned her attention to her own meal.

Conversation lagged as they focused on their food. The sound of the harp wafted over the table, filling the silence between them.

Finally, Riley pushed her empty plate away and patted her belly as if she had eaten a huge feast. "They do have the best food here."

"It was good. I'm glad we were able to get together."

Leaning forward in her chair, Riley met Sam's gaze. "I wanted to apologize again for not calling you sooner. As I mentioned on the phone, things have been crazy. A couple I've known for years were expecting their first child. Carol had a complication with her pregnancy and required an emergency C-section six weeks before she was due. Her husband Denny and I work together. I covered all his shifts and call so that he could be with Carol and their son." A shadow passed across her face. "It was touch and go for a few days, for mother and son. Between Denny's shifts and mine, plus call, I just didn't have a moment to myself."

"No need to apologize. Things like that come up unexpectedly." Sam felt doubly bad that she had not called Riley to check on her. Even if she hadn't reached her, at least Riley would have known she was concerned. "Are they okay now?"

A bright smile lit Riley's face. "Thanks for asking. They're both doing great. Carol's home, and Jeremy's getting stronger every day."

"That's great." Sam patted Riley's hand where it rested on the table. "I wanted to explain about turning you down yesterday." The sudden impulse surprised her since she wasn't one to offer reasons for her decisions. But the dispirited sound of Riley's voice when she said she had plans made her wonder if she somehow expected to be disappointed.

"You don't have to do that. I understand you already had plans."

"It's okay. I want to." Sam shifted in her seat and tried to stretch out her injured leg. "A friend I work with had invited me to her parents' restaurant for lunch. Normally, I would've rescheduled with her so we could meet. I know your time off is limited with your workload and call." She paused when she caught sight of the look on Riley's face. *What's so surprising about that?* "But this was a bad week for her and her family. It's the anniversary of her older brother's death."

Riley's smile dimmed. "Oh. I'm so sorry to hear that."

Sam nodded. "It's been ten years, but in the case of a sudden, unexpected death of a young person, I don't think it ever really gets easier. Ray was only twenty-five."

"No. You never get over losing a family member like that," Riley said, her voice going hoarse.

Sam got the distinct impression that Riley was speaking from personal experience and wondered who she had lost. While she was curious, she didn't want to ask something so personal. "Speaking of family, the maître d' mentioned an aunt and uncle. Do they live here in San Diego?"

Riley's lips puckered as if she'd tasted something sour. "No."

It seemed clear that she wanted to add, "Thank, God" to that "no." Apparently, the aunt and uncle weren't a good topic of conversation, but Sam couldn't resist trying again. "Any family in San Diego?"

"No. Just me."

Sam waited, hoping Riley would elaborate.

She didn't.

The server approached the table. "Would you ladies care for another mimosa?"

"Not for me," Riley said.

Sam waved him off. Unwilling to give up, she decided to try a different tactic. "My siblings and parents all live in California, but not here. How about yours?"

Riley hesitated and for a moment, it appeared as if she wasn't going to answer. Then she sighed and crossed her arms over her chest. "I don't have any siblings. My aunt and uncle live in LA." Dark shadows took up residence in her eyes. "My parents died in a car accident when I was a child."

"Oh. I'm sorry. I had no idea." *God.* No wonder she was so hesitant to talk about her family.

"It's okay. It was a long time ago." Regardless of Riley's words, her expression made it clear that she still strongly felt the loss of her parents.

"It's not okay." A lump formed in Sam's throat. Repressed tears stung her eyes. While she might bitch about her mother, just the thought of losing her was enough to make the food in her stomach feel as if it had turned to lead. The thought of losing both her parents as a child was unfathomable. "It doesn't matter how long it's been, it obviously hurts you. And I'm sorry about that."

Despite being in the middle of a restaurant, she wanted to wrap Riley in her arms and soothe away the pain in her eyes. The strength of the impulse took her aback. She settled for reaching across the table and clasping both her hands around Riley's much smaller one. "I'm so sorry for your loss."

Tears overflowed Riley's eyes and ran freely down her face.

"Oh, Riley." Sam released her hand, intending to go to her side.

Riley's gaze darted to the people seated nearby. "I'm sorry. Excuse me." She bolted from the table.

Sam's jaw dropped as she watched her retreat across the room. *What just happened?* As she rose to follow, she noticed the disapproving stares from a couple at the next table over. She stared them down until they looked away, then went after Riley.

Riley forced herself to walk at a normal pace, keeping her face averted to hide her tears. As she pushed open the door to the ladies' room, her aunt's voice echoed in her mind. *You should*

be ashamed of yourself, Riley Connolly. Stop that vulgar display this instant. She had been a child at the time, but she could still feel the harsh grip of her aunt's hand around her arm as she dragged her into the restaurant's ladies' room for crying. Her parents had been gone only a week, and she had not yet learned her aunt's cardinal rule: Never cry or display any other strong emotion in public. Her aunt considered it an unpardonable sin and an embarrassment to her and Uncle Rielly.

Riley blew out a relieved breath when she realized the anteroom was empty. She dropped onto a sofa in the back corner of the lounge and brushed at her tear-streaked face. She had never again shed a tear in public—until today, but seeing the open compassion on Sam's face had been her undoing.

"Riley, are you all right?"

She jumped but refused to look up. "I'm sorry."

Sam joined her on the sofa. "For what? You didn't do anything wrong."

"Just bawled like a baby in the middle of a restaurant," she muttered. She forced herself to look up and met Sam's gaze. "I'm sorry for embarrassing you like that."

"You didn't embarrass me."

"But the people sitting around us were—"

Sam snorted. "Like I give a damn about what some stuffed shirt thinks. There's no reason to be embarrassed by honest emotion. It makes me want to cry just thinking about losing my mother, and I'm a grown woman."

Emotion tightened Riley's throat. Renewed tears threatening to fall, she looked away.

Sam slid across the sofa cushion, closing the distance between them. "Hey." She gently turned Riley's face toward her. "You love your parents and you miss them. I would think it was strange if that didn't make you sad."

Her tears flowed again.

Wrapping an arm around Riley's shoulders, Sam urged her closer.

Riley rarely permitted herself to accept, or even expect, comfort of any kind. It was a lesson she had learned well. Yet an unexpected sense of peace stole over her as she took in Sam's scent and warmth. She allowed herself to relax against Sam and then gave her tears full rein.

Sam's hand trailed softly up and down her arm.

The impulse to wrap her arms around her and snuggle into her embrace washed over Riley. Struggling against the instinctive move, she pulled away. "I'm sorry." She brushed at her tears.

Sam shook her head. "No more apologies. Okay? If you need to cry, you cry. My shoulder's always available."

Gazing into Sam's caring silvery-blue eyes, Riley smiled. *You're an amazing woman.* "Okay."

"Good. Now dry your tears, then we'll go back out and have our dessert," Sam said.

"Dessert, huh?" Riley laughed, feeling surprisingly lighthearted despite the emotional upheaval. "I suppose it's going to involve chocolate?"

"Oh, you've got that right." Sam grinned. "Maybe I'll even share."

With you, maybe I can even eat it. Riley rose from the couch and held out her hand. With Sam's warm hand wrapped firmly around hers, Riley smiled up at her. "Let's go."

CHAPTER 23

R iley. Hold up," Denny called.

Not now. The temptation to pretend she had not heard him was strong. *Don't be like that. You've hardly seen him.* She stopped, allowing him to catch up. "Hey. How's Jeremy doing?"

A brilliant smile took up residence on his face. "Growing like the proverbial weed. Only seven ounces to go before we can take him home."

"That's wonderful news." She patted his shoulder. "I'm so happy for you and Carol."

"Thanks. Got time to head to the NICU with me? I'll officially introduce you to my son."

Riley glanced at her watch. If she didn't hurry, she was going to miss Sam. "Um... I stopped by the NICU last week and peeked in on him. Let's wait until you get him home and I can see Carol too."

"Sure. Come on, we'll grab some lunch and catch up. I haven't seen much of you the last two weeks, except in passing. I've stopped by your office several times to invite you to lunch. Where've you been hiding?"

Not hiding. Just with Sam. "Nowhere." Feeling the heat rise up in her cheeks, she lamented her fair coloring. It made the faintest blush impossible to hide.

"Really?" Denny stared as if trying to read her thoughts.

Riley glanced at her watch again. "I have to go."

He caught her arm before she could walk away. "Something coming in I should know about?"

"No. I'm meeting a friend for lunch, if I haven't already missed her."

"Anyone I know?"

"Denny."

"You can't blame me for being curious. I've never known you to have a friend show up during the workday."

Riley curbed her impatience. Denny was her friend, and he was right, this was very unusual behavior for her. "Remember the police officer, Samantha McKenna? She's here undergoing physical therapy."

His eyes went wide. "Oh. When did you run into her? So you're friends now?"

She glanced at her watch again and groaned. "I really have to go, Denny."

"But I thought you said—"

Waving off his questions, Riley said, "I'll talk to you later." She headed down the hall at a fast clip.

When she spotted Sam standing with Tony outside the physical therapy department, she slowed her headlong pace. Not wanting to interrupt, she stopped a short distance away and leaned against the wall.

Just the sight of Sam brought a smile to her face. *She's not just beautiful on the inside.* Until recently, she hadn't allowed herself to appreciate how physically attractive Sam was. A sweat-dampened T-shirt clung to her body, highlighting broad shoulders, shapely breasts, and a flat stomach. Baggy sweatpants hid what Riley knew were trim hips and muscled thighs. Sam's once super short hair had grown shaggy and covered any trace of the scalp injury. The bruises that had marred her face were long gone. Although Riley was too far away to see them, she had no trouble calling to mind the unique shade of Sam's striking eyes.

Sam threw back her head and laughed at something Tony said. Her laughter echoed down the hall.

She's beautiful. And straight. A moment's regret at what could never be dimmed Riley's good mood. *Even if she was gay, she would never be interested in someone like you. Enjoy her friendship.* When Tony disappeared back into the physical therapy department, Riley pushed off the wall and moved toward Sam.

"Hey, Riley. I didn't expect to see you today."

"Conference ended earlier than I thought. I figured I'd try and catch you and see if you wanted to grab some lunch."

Sam's smile brightened. "That'd be great."

As they started down the hall, Riley noticed something was missing. "Where's your cane?"

Footsteps sounded behind them.

"Tony said I don't need it anymore," Sam said.

"No, I didn't."

They both jumped at the sound of Tony's voice, then turned to face him.

He held Sam's cane in his hands. "What I said was: you don't need it if you're walking on flat surfaces, but if you're going to be on uneven terrain or climbing stairs, take it with you just in case."

Riley arched an eyebrow at her.

Sam flushed.

As if just noticing Riley, Tony smiled and turned his attention to her. "Hey, Dr. Connolly. How's your shoulder doing?"

"Good, thanks to you."

He cast a sidelong glance at Sam, then grinned. "So you know this big troublemaker, huh?"

"Troublemaker?" Sam crossed her arms over her chest. "I'm the perfect patient."

Riley smiled up at her before asking Tony, "What's she been up to?"

"We should get going." Sam edged away from Tony.

Riley narrowed her eyes. What else didn't Sam want her to find out? As much as Riley wanted to question Tony about Sam's progress, she knew she couldn't. Sam wasn't her patient—and she was glad about it.

Tony grinned at Sam with a "gotcha" expression. "She's a very compliant patient." He held out her cane. "Mostly."

Scowling, Sam took it from him. "One more week."

"We'll see," Tony said.

A tech stuck his head out of the doorway and called to Tony.

"I'll see you on Monday," he said, pointing at Sam. "Good to see you again, Dr. Connolly."

"You too, Tony," Riley said. She waved as he went back to work.

"Sorry he held us up. Let's get our lunch," Sam said.

Riley followed her toward the cafeteria, but her thoughts were no longer on lunch. "You've only got one more week of therapy?"

"Yeah. I've reached the point where I can do the rest of the rehab on my own." Sam grimaced. "Or at least I will be if I can complete whatever torture test Tony comes up with next Friday."

"Oh. I'm really happy for you." While Riley was thrilled that Sam was doing so well, she was going to miss having lunch with her several times a week.

"Thanks. I have to admit when I started therapy seven weeks ago and could barely lift my leg, I was doubtful about Tony's promise that he would get me back up to speed. But now," Sam twirled her cane, "I can't wait to get back to work."

The blood drained from Riley's face. Her steps faltered. *No. It's too soon.* The mere thought of Sam returning to work made her insides clench. *What if...?* She shook her head, unwilling to even finish the thought.

Sam stopped. "What's wrong?" She grasped Riley's elbow and steered her over to the side of the hallway. "You're white as a ghost. When was the last time you ate anything?"

Reaching inside for that place where she pushed her emotions to be able to work, Riley forced a neutral expression onto her face. "Sorry. I'm fine. Just thinking about a patient."

Sam searched her eyes. "You sure?"

Unable to hold her gaze, Riley glanced away. "Yes. Let's get some lunch before I get called." As if the words summoned the deed, her phone buzzed. She pulled it off her belt, glanced at the screen, then at Sam. "I have to take this." The trauma fellow wouldn't be contacting her unless there was a major problem. She moved out of earshot. "What's going on, Ken?"

"I've got a problem with Mr. Gardner, the amputation from yesterday. There's no pulse in his left leg. Doppler showed no flow in the femoral. Looks like we're dealing with an embolic femoral occlusion."

"Have you called vascular surgery?"

"Yes. They should be here any minute."

"I'll be right there." Riley shoved her phone back into its holder as she hurried over to Sam. "I'm sorry. I've got to run."

"I understand. Go." Sam tugged at the sleeve of Riley's lab coat. "Just promise me you'll get something to eat after you're done."

Warmed by the concern, Riley smiled. "I promise." She gave Sam's hand a quick squeeze, then rushed off down the hall.

CHAPTER 24

Sam drummed her hands on the steering wheel as she watched the entrance to the parking lot. She'd been pleasantly surprised when Riley called and suggested dinner to make up for their aborted lunch earlier in the day. After the fiasco at the public parking lot in the Gaslamp Quarter, this time Sam had picked a Chinese restaurant close to her apartment that had its own small parking lot. When she spotted Riley's sleek Jag entering the lot, she got out of her car, waved, and did a quick scan of the surrounding area to make sure no one was lurking nearby.

Riley pulled into the spot next to Sam's Challenger.

Sam hurried over and opened the car door. "Hi. Hope you didn't have any trouble finding the place."

"Nope." Riley accepted Sam's outstretched hand and allowed her to assist her from the low-slung car. "Just typed the name into my navigation system." She glanced around. "I don't think I've ever been in this part of North Park."

I bet you haven't. It was a working-class neighborhood with restaurants that catered to that clientele. *Maybe I should have picked someplace more upscale.* There wasn't any valet parking or a maître d' waiting inside to greet them. She shoved her hands into the pockets of her jeans. "I...um, I hope this is okay. I know it's probably not what you're used to." Everything about Riley screamed money—from her car and her condo, right down to the expensive dress slacks and silk blouses she always wore.

Riley's brow furrowed. "Do you really think I care about how expensive a place is?" She took a big step back as if distancing herself from Sam. "Have I done anything to give you the impression that I'm some kind of snob?"

Sam flinched at the hurt in Riley's voice. "No. It's just..." Her gaze swept Riley's car, then over to her own vehicle. The Jag stood out like a shining jewel amidst pebbles in the parking lot filled with run-of-the-mill cars. She shrugged, not sure what to say.

Riley stepped close to the Challenger and ran her fingers lightly across the rear quarter panel. "It may not look like the classic car with the same name that my dad worked on, but he would have loved your car. He would've much rather restored a muscle car than a sleek sports car any day."

"Your dad worked on cars?" Sam couldn't keep the incredulity from her voice. She had figured Riley's father had been a doctor or lawyer or some other type of white-collar professional.

"He restored classic cars for a living. Started out working as a mechanic in a Ford garage during the day and restoring cars at night and on the weekends. Once the quality of his work became well known, he opened his own classic restoration shop. Even when he had full-time employees to work on the cars, you could almost always find him in the garage working right alongside them. When I was a little girl, I used to go to the shop every weekend. I loved working on the cars with him." Riley smiled, her face glowing with the warm remembrance.

Wow. Sam tried to imagine Riley as a grease-stained child, working on a car. The image just wouldn't form. She bit her tongue to keep from asking: so what happened?

"I probably had pretty much the same middle-class upbringing that you did." Riley leaned against Sam's car and sighed heavily. "At least until I went to live with my aunt and uncle." She inclined her chin toward her Jag. "My uncle presented me with the car when I finished my trauma surgery fellowship." Her gaze dropped. "It's actually not what I would have picked for myself."

"I'm sorry. I shouldn't have assumed anything."

Riley shook her head. "I can understand you thinking otherwise. It's okay."

"No. It's not." Sam arched an eyebrow. "You know what they say about making assumptions."

It took Riley a moment, then she laughed. "Well, in that case, I'll let it go. If," she laid her hand on Sam's arm, "we have the dinner you promised. I'm starving."

You always say that, but you hardly eat anything. "You'll have lots of choices. They serve Chinese and Japanese dishes."

"Both? Isn't that a little unusual?"

"Yeah. The story goes that Mei and Takumi, the original owners, couldn't come to an agreement on which type of restaurant to open. Mei was Chinese, and Takumi was Japanese. Takumi insisted it be Japanese, but I guess Mei was a pretty feisty woman and wouldn't give in. Apparently at the time, it was a big family scandal. So this," Sam motioned toward the restaurant, "is what they ended up with. It's now a third-generation run family business. Oh, I almost forgot, they also have a small sushi bar."

Riley's eyes lit up.

Of course she'd go for the sushi. Sam hid her distaste. "Come on. I promised to feed you." Feeling more confident of her choice, she led Riley across the parking lot to the restaurant. As they stepped up onto the sidewalk, she halted. There was something she needed to make clear. "Remember, I'm paying this time. For both of us."

The last time they had met outside the hospital and gone to brunch, Riley had insisted on going Dutch. When Riley started to protest, Sam sent her a sharp look.

Riley smiled. "Okay."

It wasn't until they reached the entrance that Sam realized she had her hand resting comfortably on the small of Riley's back. She looked at her hand as if it belonged to someone else. *When did I do that?* She chanced a look at Riley to gauge her reaction.

Riley met her gaze with a warm smile.

Sam lost herself for a moment in Riley's vibrant green eyes. A strong urge to reach out and touch her cheek and see if it was as soft as it looked jolted Sam back to reality. *What's going on with you? You don't mess with straight women.* The realization of what she had almost done brought a flush to her face, and she wrenched her gaze away. Opening the door gave her an excuse to take her hand from Riley's back. She held open the door for Riley, then followed her inside.

"Officer Sam, to what do we owe the pleasure of seeing you twice in one week?" Mary stepped out from behind the cash register and gave her a quick hug.

She had given up asking the proprietor to call her Sam a long time ago. "I wanted to introduce a friend to your excellent food." She inclined her head toward Riley and glanced around the small, packed restaurant. They were doing a booming Friday night business. She hoped it wouldn't be a long wait. The restaurant didn't accept reservations. "Could we get a booth if you have one?"

Mary smiled and gave a half bow. "For you, of course. One moment."

It was only moments before Mary returned, led them to the far side of the restaurant, and motioned them to a large booth.

Sam caught Riley's arm before she could slide into the booth. "We can't take the family booth, Mary."

Mary crossed her arms over her chest. "I insist. It's the least we can do." She pointed at the booth. "You're adopted family. You sit."

Sam glanced down into Mary's dark, determined eyes. It had been a major battle to convince Mary that if she didn't let her pay for her meals, she would stop coming in. She could bend about this. She bowed slightly. "Thank you."

"You're very welcome." Mary waited until they were seated, then offered menus. "I'll get you some tea."

"So if you don't mind me asking, how did you get adopted by the family?" Riley asked as their petite hostess walked away. The more she learned about Sam, the more intrigued she became. Sam was proving to be a very special, caring woman.

Sam fiddled with her menu. Finally, she blew out a breath. "When they opened this location two years ago, I stopped by right away. I love Chinese food, and I live not too far from here." She set her menu down. "Anyway, I got to know the owners—Mary, who you just met, and her husband, Kento. About six months after they moved in, they started having some trouble with the local gangbangers scaring off customers, demanding money, and vandalizing the place at night. So I started coming in once a week after work in uniform. I'd also drive by the place on my way home from work and after I'd been out for the evening. Rousted some of the bangers a couple of times and let them know I was keeping an eye on them. Just made my presence known."

Riley's hands tightened around the menu as her mind filled with images of Sam confronting the gang members on her own.

"Riley? Are you okay? You're pale as a sheet all the sudden." Sam's warm hand wrapped around her ice-cold one clutching the menu. "Did you eat earlier like you promised?"

Shaking away the disturbing images, Riley met Sam's concerned gaze and forced a smile. "I'm fine. It was really nice of you to do that for them."

Sam shrugged. "It's not a big deal. The food's great. I'd come in once a week even if there hadn't been a problem. I don't expect anything in return, but they insist I'm part of the family."

Might not be a big deal to you, but I bet it means a lot to them. Riley opened her menu. "So, what's your favorite dish?"

Without hesitation, Sam said, "The Kung Pao chicken. I love spicy food."

"I do too." Riley perused the menu's many choices. Unable to decide, she looked up, and her gaze strayed to the small sushi bar along the wall opposite them. From what she could see, the selections looked varied and fresh. "Would you mind if I gave the sushi a try?"

"Of course not," Sam said, even managing not to grimace. "Go ahead and order whatever you want."

Riley smiled. Knowing what she did now, she was still amazed that Sam had eaten the sushi she'd brought for their first lunch.

Once their food was served, Riley used her chopsticks to pick up a rice pad with the tako held in place by a thin strip of nori. The sharp bite of wasabi mixed with the sweet aroma of the tako filled her senses. "This is really excellent." She popped the delectable piece into her mouth. "We're going to have to come back here again. This puts the place I usually go to shame."

"Really?" Sam tipped her head and regarded her as if trying to judge her sincerity.

"I'm not just saying that." She reached for another piece. "This is outstanding."

Sam smiled. "I'm glad you like it."

"Are you sure you don't want to try a piece? You don't know what you're missing."

"I'll pass." Sam's lips twitched. "No offense, but I prefer my food without little suckers all over it."

"It doesn't have suckers on it."

Sam eyed the octopus as if she expected it to crawl off Riley's plate at any moment. "It did before he cut it up."

Riley laughed at the look on Sam's face. "Okay." She ate the last piece of tako, savoring the taste. "You're safe. It's gone."

Sam mock-scowled. "Very funny." She reached across the table and briefly pressed Riley's hand. "Seriously, I'm glad you're enjoying it. My Kung Pao chicken is good too." She turned her plate so the remaining portion on it was within Riley's reach. "Want to try a bite?"

The enticing aroma of chicken and red peppers wafted across the table. Temptation to try the spicy dish warred with years of her aunt's ingrained rules. Offering Sam a piece of sushi had pushed the boundary of propriety; actually taking food from someone's plate, in public no less, was just not done. *Those are her rules, not yours.* Mentally stiffening her spine, she helped herself to a bite from Sam's plate. The mingled flavors of the dish erupted on her taste buds, and she hummed with pleasure. A brief flash of heat followed. "Oh wow. That's good."

"Have another bite."

Riley wiped her fork on a napkin. She peered at Sam, then down at the plate.

Sam pushed it a little closer. "You know you want to."

It was easier the second time. "Okay, just one more." She scooped another forkful of chicken and hot peppers. Relishing the taste, she resisted the urge to take another bite. "On second thought, maybe I'll order that next time."

"I'll guess we'll just have to come back more than once."

"I'd like that a lot." Riley's heart lifted. She had wondered if their time together would come to an end now that Sam was finished with therapy. The thought had bothered her more than she cared to admit. What had started out as concern motivated by guilt had turned into the beginnings of a friendship. She met Sam's gaze. "I'm going to miss our lunches." She snagged a piece of sushi from the assortment in front of her.

Sam's smile dimmed. "Me too." She brightened. "But maybe if my partner and I get stuck babysitting someone in the ER, I can stop by and say hi."

The mention of Sam returning to work chased away Riley's appetite. Her chopsticks clattered onto the table.

"What's wrong?"

"Nothing. It's—"

"Don't do that," Sam said. "Something's bothering you all the sudden."

Riley ducked her head, struggling with her emotions.

"Please tell me." Sam reached across the table and placed a gentle finger underneath Riley's chin, urging her to look up.

One look into Sam's concerned face, and Riley couldn't deny her. "I just... It seems kind of soon for you to be returning to work. You're barely out of rehab and just stopped using a cane today. What if...?" She couldn't bring herself to voice her fears. The image of Sam's blood seeping into the floor and covering her hands as she worked to save her rose far too easily in her mind.

"What if what?" Sam's brow furrowed. "Oh." She took Riley's hands in hers. "You don't need to worry about me. I'll be fine."

Riley pulled her hands free and clenched them together in her lap. Tears stung the back of her eyes. "How can you say that after what happened?"

"Hey." Sam slid out of her side of the booth and over into Riley's. She lightly wrapped an arm around her shoulders. "That was a fluke. I've been on the force almost nine years. That's the first time I've had more than a few scrapes or bruises."

Riley gazed up at Sam, staring deeply into her eyes. *Is she telling the truth?*

As if Sam had heard the question, she said, "I swear."

"I just..." *Get yourself together. You're making a fool of yourself.* The urge to bolt was strong, but the need to accept the comfort Sam was offering was stronger. She leaned against Sam and rested her head on her chest for a moment. Pulling away, she blew out a breath. "I'm sorry. That's twice I've embarrassed you in public. It's a wonder you want to be seen with me." She glanced at several nearby tables, but no one was paying them the least bit of attention.

"I told you before. I'm not embarrassed." Sam gave her a one-armed hug. "I appreciate your concern, but please don't worry. I'm not ready to go back to full duty yet. I'll be on desk duty."

Relief washed over Riley.

"But even when I do go back to the streets, I promise you have nothing to worry about." Sam grinned. "I'm good at what I do." Her expression turned serious. "And I'm always careful."

I don't doubt that, but you'll never convince me not to worry. Not after what I've seen.

"Is everything all right?" Mary asked as she approached their table.

Riley flushed and resisted the impulse to hide her face against Sam's shoulder. *If Aunt Margaret could see me, she would be having a stroke about now.*

Sam gave her shoulder a squeeze and returned to her own side of the booth. "Yeah. Can we get some more tea? And please bring some more of those," she glanced at Riley, "what did you call them, tako?"

"No. That's okay; you don't have to do that. I've had enough."

Sam waved away her protest. "Those tako sushi things."

Mary bowed, then hurried away before Riley could lodge any further protests.

Neither spoke as they waited for Mary. When she brought the tea and sushi, they busied themselves with their interrupted meal.

Riley willingly let the topic of Sam's return to work drop.

Finally, Sam pushed away her empty plate and fiddled with her fork for a moment. "I was wondering. If you're off this weekend, would you like to go see a movie or something?"

Thrilled at the prospect of spending time together, Riley smiled. "That would be—" Then she remembered, and her shoulders slumped. "I wish I could, but I have to go to LA."

Sam looked as disappointed as Riley felt.

She didn't want Sam to think she was making excuses not to see her. "One of the philanthropic endeavors my aunt is involved with is having a charity gala that provides art school scholarships to underprivileged students. It's a yearly event, and I'm expected to attend."

"Sounds like a worthy cause."

While it was a good cause, Riley always felt if they would just give the money they spent on the gala to the art schools, it would provide even more scholarships. "It is. I'm just not a fan of all the pretentious posturing that goes on at these things. My aunt and uncle love it." She shook her head and laughed. "They actually are the snobs you thought I was."

Sam flushed.

"I've been going to these galas since I was a twelve, but believe me, it's not my idea of a fun evening."

Sam leaned forward. "What is your idea of a fun evening?"

Riley spread her hands wide, encompassing both of them. "This has been fun."

Smile lines appeared at the corner of Sam's eyes. "What else?"

"Well...honestly, other than going to the gym at my condo or an occasional dinner out, I spend all my time working." Heat crept up Riley's neck at how pathetic that sounded.

That admission seemed to stymie Sam for a moment. "Okay. How about this? What's something you remember enjoying as a child that you haven't done in years?"

It had been a long time since she had allowed free rein to the memories of her time with her parents. She had spoken about her parents more to Sam in the last two weeks than she had anyone in years. Her aunt and uncle had strongly discouraged her from speaking of the past, insisting that she move on with her new life with them. She racked her brain, trying to remember her life before her aunt had attempted to shape Riley in her own image. She smiled as the memories filled her mind. "Going to a baseball game. I haven't been to a game since my folks died."

Sam's expression fell. "The Padres' last game of the season is this weekend."

Riley tried not to let her disappointment show. "Maybe next year."

Sam hesitated, then seemed to come to a decision. "Does it have to be a professional baseball game?"

"I guess not. What did you have in mind?"

"I belong to a women's softball league. My team is mostly made up of cops from various precincts. Our final game of the season is next Saturday. I can't play, but we could still go to the game. What do you think? Would you be interested in going with me?"

It was Riley's turn to hesitate. Was she ready to face Sam's fellow officers and friends? "Are you sure I'd be welcome?"

"Why wouldn't you be?"

Riley ducked her head. "I'm the one who almost got you killed."

"Riley," Sam blew out an exasperated breath, "we've been over this. You did no such thing. None of my fellow officers would blame the victim for what a perpetrator did."

Pushing away the guilt, Riley smiled. "Then yes. I'd like to go to your game."

"Good. Maybe we could go out to eat afterward?"

"We could always come back here."

Mary returned to the table. The small bill tray she set down had two fortune cookies on it.

Sam stared at the tray, then scowled. "Mary," she said, an edge to her voice.

Riley realized there was no bill on the tray.

Looking guilty, Mary reached into the pocket of her apron and pulled out the bill.

"Thank you," Sam said.

Mary gave a slight bow, then turned to Riley. "I hope you enjoyed your meal. Please come back."

"It was wonderful. Thank you." She smiled at Sam. "And I'll definitely be back."

Another customer called Mary away.

Sam picked up the tray. "Choose your fortune."

Riley's hand hovered over the cookies. She reached for the one nearest her, then changed her mind and selected the other one. She removed the cellophane, broke open the cookie, and pulled out her fortune.

"What's it say?" Sam asked.

Riley looked down at the slip of paper and then read it aloud. "A pleasant surprise is in store for you."

"Oh. Lucky you." Sam opened her cookie and read her fortune. "A beauty is a woman you notice, a charmer is a woman who notices you."

I should've gotten that one. "Oh well. Guess they can't all be relevant."

Sam's lips twitched as if she was repressing a smile, but she didn't comment.

"Anyway, thank you for dinner," Riley said. "Maybe we can catch lunch together next week."

"You're welcome. And that would be great."

As they slid from the booth and prepared to leave, Sam stopped and stared down at her for a moment.

Riley checked her clothing to make sure she hadn't spilled anything on herself. She didn't see anything.

It seemed as if Sam wanted to say something, but she pressed her lips together and remained silent.

Together they walked out to the parking lot and stopped by Riley's car.

"About the softball game next Saturday," Sam said. "How about I pick you up?"

"Sure," Riley said. "What time?"

"I'll come get you at two. Game's at three, so that should give us plenty of time to get to Poway. Um... one other thing. The ball field gets kind of dusty, and the wooden bleachers there are kind of old." Sam cleared her throat. "It's just that your clothes are really nice, and I wouldn't want to see them get messed up." She glanced away and shuffled her feet before meeting Riley's eyes.

Riley looked at her clothes. A little dirt wouldn't hurt them. What was Sam getting at?

"Well, um...you might want to wear something else, maybe jeans and sneakers or something like that."

Oh. Riley glanced at Sam's clothes. She had not really thought about it, but now she realized that compared to most of the customers dressed similar to Sam in a casual shirt and jeans, she had probably stuck out like a sore thumb in her linen blouse and tailored dress slacks.

"Sure I can do that." *As soon as I call Paula and get her to shop for a pair of jeans.* She hoped her personal shopper didn't faint dead away when she told her what she wanted.

CHAPTER 25

Sam's anxiety rose as the elevator hummed toward Riley's tenth-floor condo. She barely resisted the urge to pace as if confined to a cage, which was what the elevator felt like at the moment. *I hope I don't end up regretting this.* The more she thought about it, the more unsure she became about taking Riley to the game. Her friends could be a boisterous, rowdy bunch, and she was willing to bet Riley wasn't used to that kind of behavior. Then, there were all the questions her bringing Riley to the game was sure to garner since she had never shown up at a game with a woman. The elevator doors slid open.

Sam dragged her feet as she made her way to Riley's door. *I should've canceled at lunch on Friday.* But Riley had been so excited about going to the game, Sam hadn't had the heart to disappoint her. She rapped lightly on the front door, knowing Riley was waiting for her. The guard at the front desk had insisted on calling Riley before allowing her access to the elevator.

The door opened immediately. "Hi, Sam." Riley eyed Sam's jersey. "You're not playing—right?"

"I wish. Just supporting my team, even if I can't play."

Riley smiled. "Just let me grab my keys, and I'll be right with you."

"Okay." Sam's gaze dropped to Riley's denim-clad ass as she walked away. Her libido pinged in Riley's direction. *Knock it off.* She raked her hands through her hair. *I just need to get laid. It's been too long.*

When Riley returned, Sam took a closer look at her clothes. They looked new—too new. Toned arms showed below the short sleeves of a deep green V-neck knit shirt, and form-fitting, dark blue jeans accentuated Riley's boyish physique. Her shoes looked like some type of designer sneakers, without a mark on them.

Crap. She bought new stuff because of what I said about her clothes. Should have kept my big mouth shut. It hadn't occurred to her that Riley might not own a pair of jeans or at least something that wasn't dress slacks. She just hadn't wanted her to ruin her good clothes.

Riley ran her hands down the front of her jeans. "Is something wrong with what I'm wearing?"

"What?" Sam flushed. "No. You just look different than I've seen you before."

A frown creased Riley's brow.

"But good," Sam added quickly.

Riley crossed her arms. Her lips pressed into a thin line, she glanced down at her clothes.

"We should get going." Sam tugged at the hem of her jersey. "It can be crowded at the games, and I want to get a good seat."

Riley nodded, followed Sam into the hall, and locked the door.

An awkward silence accompanied them as they rode the elevator to the ground floor.

Sam racked her brain for something to say while they walked the short distance to her car. She had told the valet she would be right back and not to park it.

Sam tipped the valet and nudged him out of the way before he could open the car door for Riley. She opened the door, bowed at the waist, then offered her hand. "Your carriage awaits, my lady." She got the smile she was hoping for. After closing Riley's door, she went around to the driver's side and slid into the car. "Ready to watch some softball?"

Riley offered a tentative smile. "Sure," she said, sounding anything but.

Sam started the car. "Well, like in professional sports, I think you always enjoy a game more if you know the players. So let me tell you a little about my team and the games we've won and lost so far."

"I'd like that." Riley's smile seemed much more genuine this time.

"I pulled my brand-new jersey out of the dryer, and one of the numbers was gone. Instead of my name and the number ten, now I have McKenna and a big zero on my back."

Picturing the look on Sam's face at seeing her jersey, Riley laughed. "What did you do?"

"What could I do? It was the only jersey I had and the game started in less than an hour. I figured I was never going to hear the end of it." Sam tapped her blinker and turned into the sports center. "Thankfully, my friend Marina came to the rescue. She had a roll of duct tape in her truck. Taped a number one on the back of my jersey."

After the awkward start to the day, things were looking up. Sam had spent the drive regaling her with stories about her team and her experiences playing softball.

Sam hunted for a spot in the crowded parking lot.

Riley gazed out the car window. "I know you said it gets crowded, but I didn't expect this many people."

"The kids' leagues play in the morning, then afterward, the adults. Our league uses one field, and the men's league uses the other three, so it does get busy."

"There's a spot." Riley pointed to the next row over.

"Thanks." Sam made her way to the space and parked. "I should probably warn you, some of the women can get a little rowdy and mouthy. Just ignore them."

"I don't lead that sheltered a life." Riley turned in her seat, then arched an eyebrow at Sam. "I do work in the ER, you know. I've seen and heard plenty."

Sam flushed. "I know. I just...I just want you to have a good time."

"And I'm sure I will. Now, come on. Let's go. I don't want to miss the opening pitch."

The bright sun warmed Riley's skin. She tilted her face up to the cloudless sky. The smell of freshly cut grass scented the air. "Couldn't ask for a nicer day."

"We're lucky this year. It's not supposed to get above seventy-six. Last year, it hit ninety-one during our final game."

"It's dangerous to be playing in that heat."

"Yeah. The officials stopped all the games for two hours when the heat peaked," Sam said.

Excited voices rang out from behind them. It sounded as if a stampede were headed their way. They were engulfed by a herd of girls dressed in softball uniforms. "We won. We won," one of the girls shouted. Laughing, they raced away.

"Slow it down!" Sam hollered after them.

Was I ever that carefree? Riley shook her head. *Maybe I should take a lesson from those girls. Seize the day.*

As they approached the fence surrounding the ball field, the cement sidewalk changed to a gravel pathway.

Riley caught Sam's arm before she stepped onto the gravel. "Wait. You don't have your cane. Tony said you need it on uneven surfaces."

"Tony has a big mouth."

"Is it in your car? I can go back and get it."

Sam's lips pressed into a thin line as she gazed toward the backstop on the baseball diamond. "No. I don't need it."

Riley followed her line of sight and saw several women wearing the same softball jersey as Sam. *She doesn't want her co-workers to see her with a cane.* Riley understood where Sam was coming from. She wouldn't want to look weak in front of her co-workers either. "Okay then, let's go grab a seat."

Sam's eyebrows arched over the top of her sunglasses.

Riley smothered a smile. *She's knows me too well.* As they stepped onto the gravel, she asked, "Would you mind if I hold your arm? I don't want to take a chance of losing my balance on the gravel and twisting my ankle."

Sam pushed back the brim of her baseball cap and tugged down her sunglasses. Silvery-blue eyes glowered at her.

Not the least bit daunted, Riley met her gaze and gave her most innocent smile. "Please."

Sam muttered what sounded like, "I should've known," then offered her arm.

Riley stepped close and slipped her hand around Sam's arm. "Thank you."

Tugging her ball cap into place, Sam snorted. She guided Riley toward the bleachers.

When they reached the fence that separated the players from the fans, a brunette wearing a jersey that matched Sam's came running up. "McKenna!" She raised her voice. "Hey. McKenna's back!"

Riley released Sam and stepped aside. *She hasn't been to a game since she got hurt?*

Sam was quickly surrounded by her teammates.

"About time you showed up," the stocky woman said. "Must be nice not having to work."

A beautiful Latina threw her arm around Sam's shoulders. "Yeah. Just sitting around on your ass while the rest of us take up the slack."

Smiling, Riley leaned against the nearby fence. Insults flew back and forth. Not one woman mentioned Sam's injuries. To some, it might have seemed callous, but Riley understood; it was no different than the sometimes dark humor shared among the ER staff. Riley had eyes only for Sam as she bantered with her friends. This was a confident, boisterous side of Sam she had never seen.

"Are you going to flap your lips all day, or are we going to play some ball?" a voice yelled from the vicinity of the players' bench.

"Come on. You can strategize with Coach," the brunette who had called everyone over said and tugged on Sam's arm.

Sam shook her head. "I brought a friend to the game." She pointed in Riley's direction. "I'm going to sit with her."

The group fell silent, and all eyes turned toward Riley, who straightened, trying not to show how uncomfortable she was at finding herself the center of attention.

Sam extricated herself from her friends and went over to Riley.

Most of the women filed back toward the players' bench, but several followed Sam.

She moved close to Riley's side but didn't touch her. "These are my teammates." She pointed to each woman in turn. "Karen, Ann, Marina, and Diane. Everyone, this is my friend Riley."

"Hello," Riley said, trying not to squirm under the scrutiny of the women. She could see the questioning looks going back and forth between them. Did any of them recognize her from the news reports?

"Hey, Riley. Nice to meet you," Marina said and stuck out her hand.

Riley shook hands with her, then the other women followed suit.

An awkward silence filled the space around them.

"Any time, ladies. I'm not getting any younger." A middle-aged, black woman poked her head around the fence. "Welcome back, McKenna."

"Thanks, Coach."

Riley smiled. *That must be Louise.* Sam had spoken of the retired police officer with great affection. Louise was not only their coach; she also owned the bar that sponsored the team.

"Gotta go." Karen snapped her fingers. "Oh. Hey, Sam. You going to join us after the game at the bar?"

Sam never said anything about going to a bar!

Sam shot a quick look at Riley. "We'll think about it." Grinning, she pulled Karen's cap down over her eyes. "Depends on if you win."

"Of course we're going to win," Ann said. She pulled off her cap and raked her hand though her short, bleach-blond hair.

"You've got that right," Diane said.

"See you after the game," Karen called as they headed for the players' bench.

Marina doubled back. She glanced at Riley, then faced Sam. "Kerry's out with a wrenched knee."

Sam frowned. "Who's taking my spot?"

"We're short-teamed with you, Darlene, and now Kerry out."

"Marina," Sam said, a warning tone to her voice. "Who has my spot?"

Marina winced, then looked away. "Darcy."

Sam's frown turned to an outright scowl. She took several steps toward the field before stopping and turning back.

What was wrong with Darcy playing shortstop? Although it had been a long time since she'd played in a softball league as a child, Riley was pretty sure it was common for players to switch positions as the team needed. Yet it seemed as if Sam was barely restraining herself from charging out onto the field to take her place at shortstop.

Marina looked pointedly at Riley. "Be nice."

"Yeah. Fine." Sam crossed her arms over her chest, then muttered something under her breath.

Riley didn't catch what Sam said, but the grimace on Marina's face made it clear that she had.

"Later," Marina said. She jogged away.

Standing silently, Sam stared toward the players' bench. After several long moments, she blew out a breath and then looked down at Riley. "Sorry about that." She smiled, but it looked forced.

"You okay?"

"Yeah. It's just that Darcy... " Sam shook her head. "Never mind. Long story. Let's grab a seat."

So much for a having a pleasant surprise coming soon. Never trust a fortune cookie.

Riley winced as Darcy once again flubbed the ball. The fans around her booed. Several less than complimentary comments were shouted. Darcy had the wiry build and speed of a runner but seemed to lack the agility required to play shortstop.

Sam's scowl grew more ominous with each passing inning.

If this keeps up, it's going to be a really long game. While she empathized with Sam, Riley was still disappointed with the unexpected turn her day with Sam had taken.

The opposing team had found the weak spot and was exploiting it. Thanks to Darcy's errors, Sam's team was down two runs. And they had yet to score.

Riley held her breath as the next batter sent the ball straight at Darcy.

Diane raced toward Darcy and snagged the ball before she could touch it, then rifled it to Marina at first base, ending the inning.

A cheer went up in the stands.

Yes! Riley brushed her damp hair out of her face.

The next three batters for Sam's team went down one right after the other. In what seemed like only minutes, the team was back on the field.

"All right," Sam said. "About time. Put her back where she belongs." She hadn't said much during the first three innings, other than to mutter insults at Darcy's play and urge on her team when they were at bat.

It took Riley a minute to figure out what Sam was talking about. The coach had moved Darcy to centerfield. Diane had taken over at shortstop, and a player Riley didn't know was covering second base.

Unused to being outside in such heat for an extended period, Riley was starting to feel the effects of the sun. She pressed her face against her sleeve to blot some of the perspiration from her face. With her light, freckled complexion, she tended to burn rather than tan. Her arms were already starting to turn pink. She cursed herself for forgetting sunscreen and a hat. If she wasn't careful, she'd look like a lobster by the end of the day.

"Here, put this on." Sam held out her baseball cap.

Riley jumped. She hadn't thought Sam was paying any attention to her. "That's okay. I'm fine."

Sam ignored her and plopped the hat on her head. It dropped down over her ears. Laughing, Sam pulled it off and adjusted the band, then offered it again. "Take it. You're getting burnt."

"What about you?"

"I'm used to the sun." Sam held out her arm. Sun-bleached hair stood out against her golden tan.

"Okay. Thanks." Riley settled the ball cap on her head.

Sam turned in her seat and called out, "Hey, Janie. Can I bum your sunscreen?"

A redhead sitting three rows above them said, "Sure."

"Thanks."

A tube of sunscreen was passed hand to hand through the crowd until it reached Sam. "Janie always has sunscreen for her kids." She handed the tube to Riley.

Oh great. Now Sam thought she was a little kid who needed looking after. Riley applied the sunscreen liberally before sending it back to its owner. She waved to Janie in thanks.

While they had been involved with the sunscreen, Sam's team had returned the favor and retired the other team's batters in order.

"Now that's more like it," Sam said, a smile lighting her face for the first time since the game started.

Riley's smile mirrored Sam's. *Hope Sam's team can catch up.* But win or lose, she just wanted to enjoy her time with Sam.

"Yeah." Sam stamped her feet. "Go, Diane!"

Riley clapped and added her voice to the cheering crowd as Diane headed for second base.

Sam grinned at Riley's enthusiasm. *You're lucky she has any left.* Her smile faded. She knew she'd overreacted earlier, but she had already felt that she was letting her team down by not being able to play. Having Darcy, who never missed a chance to take a dig at her, replace her was like having salt rubbed into the wound. *That's still no reason to ruin Riley's day.* Ashamed of her behavior, she vowed to make the rest of the game fun for Riley.

The next batter approached the plate.

"Rhonda will bring Diane home," Sam said. "She's our strongest hitter."

Riley smiled. "I still can't get over how fast they pitch. I was expecting a nice, slow, arcing toss."

"Yeah. That's what we played when I was in high school. Most of the women's leagues are still slow-pitch, but there are fast-pitch leagues like this one as well." Sam laughed. "These pitchers can blow that ball past you before you know what happened."

The whump of the ball against the bat drew their attention back to the field.

The crowd leaped to their feet as the ball sailed deep into left field. A chant rose up. "Go. Go. Go."

The ball easily cleared the back fence.

Sam whooped. "Home run!"

"All right!" Riley grabbed Sam's arm and jumped up and down.

"I told you." Sam wrapped an arm around Riley's shoulders and gave her a quick hug. She caught the curious stares from several of the other players' spouses and let her arm drop. *Watch it. You know how fast rumors get started and spread.* She didn't want anyone thinking that Riley was her latest conquest.

A collective groan issued from the fans when Marina hit an infield fly that was easily caught, ending the inning with a tied score.

"There're three innings left," Riley said, in an apparent attempt to cheer Sam up.

The next two innings flew past, with neither team managing to score. The opposing team was preparing to take the field for the seventh and final inning.

"What happens if no one scores here?" Riley asked. "Does the game end in a tie?"

"No. It'll go into extra innings." Sam rubbed her hands up and down her denim-clad thighs. "Are you getting tired or too hot?"

"No. I just wondered what the rules were." Riley finished off the last of her water.

Sam wished she could see Riley's eyes. "You sure?"

Riley put her hand on Sam's forearm and smiled. "I'm fine. This is really fun. Thanks for asking me."

Sam's earlier guilt melted away under the brightness of Riley's smile. She laid her hand on top of Riley's. "I'm glad."

"Batter up!" the umpire yelled.

"Here we go," Sam said.

In short order, Sam's team had two runners on base with one out remaining. Marina was the next batter.

Sam cupped her hands around her mouth. "Hey, Sarzedas! Don't screw this up. Bring them home."

Marina shot her a thinly veiled, one-fingered salute as she made her way to the plate.

Sam laughed. "Now watch. If you get Marina's Latin temper up, that just eggs her on."

Marina swung at the first pitch and connected. The ball shot through the sweet spot between the shortstop and the third baseman. The center and left fielder chased after the fast-moving ball as the two runners raced around the bases.

The crowd was on their feet cheering. "Marina. Marina. Marina."

Both runners scored.

A powerful throw by the outfielder held Marina at third base.

Sam's team now led by two runs.

"See, I told you," Sam said.

Riley rubbed her hands together and grinned. "We've got them on the run now."

Sam smiled at the use of "we."

The next batter went down in flames, leaving Marina stranded at third.

"Oh no."

"That's okay." Sam patted Riley's arm. "The team can hold them. Just three outs, and it's all over." It wasn't anywhere near as certain as she made it sound, but she didn't want to put a damper on Riley's enjoyment.

"Come on, Karen. Strike her out," Sam hollered. "Strike!"

"Strike. Strike." The bleachers vibrated as the fans stamped their feet in time with the call.

Gripping the edge of her seat, Riley leaned forward and added her voice to the crowd's.

The ball flew from Karen's hand.

"Strike one!" the umpire called.

Again the ball blazed from Karen's hand.

"Strike two!"

The rising excitement swirled around Riley as if it were a living thing. *This is it. Last out.*

Karen wound up and let the next pitch fly.

The batter caught a piece of the pitch.

The ball drilled straight for Karen as if laser-guided. It struck her, and she dropped to the ground.

A collective gasp escaped the crowd.

Oh my God.

Sam jumped to her feet. "I've got to get down there." She plunged down the bleacher steps. At the bottom, she stumbled and grabbed the fence for balance, then took off running toward her fallen teammate.

Riley gasped. *Sam!* She raced down the steps after her.

By the time she reached the field, the other players had gathered around Karen. Riley pushed her way into the group. "Let me through. I'm a doctor."

Some of the women shifted out of the way, but several continued to impede her progress.

"I'm a doctor. Let me help her." Riley called on the voice she used in the ER to break through the hubbub that surrounded a trauma. "Move aside. Now!"

The remaining women parted in front of her.

Karen was flanked by Sam, kneeling on one side, and their coach on the other.

Riley dropped to her knees in the dirt next to Sam. "How is she?"

"Who are you?" the coach asked.

Sam spoke up before she could. "This is my friend Riley. She's a doctor. She'll make sure Karen's okay."

Riley pulled off her sunglasses and looked down at Karen, who was flat on her back in the dirt. She was conscious and had her hand cupped around her right shoulder. "Hi. Remember me from earlier?"

Karen nodded.

"Okay. I'm going to check you out." Aware of all the watching eyes, Riley glanced up at the coach. "It would be better if everyone gave us some room."

The coach stood. "You heard the doc. She's got it covered. Everyone back to the bench."

Sam remained next to Karen, her eyes filled with concern.

Riley gave her an encouraging smile. Worry that Sam had injured herself nagged at her, but she pushed it aside and focused solely on Karen, shutting out everything else. "Where did you get hit?"

"My glove took the brunt of it, but the deflected ball clipped my shoulder."

"Did you hit your head when you fell?"

"No." Karen started to sit up. "I'm fine. I can get up."

Riley put a restraining hand on her chest. "Not just yet." She ran her hands over Karen's shoulder, then across her collarbone. "Can you move your arm?"

"Yeah." She grimaced, and her jaw muscles clenched as she moved her arm.

"Okay. Good." Riley checked the range of motion of Karen's arm, then palpated down her chest from her collarbone to the top of her breast. "Any tenderness?"

Karen shook her head.

"All right. I want you to sit up. Slowly."

Sam slipped her arm around Karen's back and helped her to a sitting position.

"Any dizziness?" Riley asked.

"Nope." Karen stretched her shoulders and tried unsuccessfully to hide a wince. "I'm fine."

She sounds just like Sam. "You need to follow up with your doctor."

"It's no big deal," Karen said. "It just stung for a minute. I can still pitch."

Riley's temper flared. *What is it with cops and not admitting they're hurt?* "You are not fine. You're done for today." Her gaze bored into Karen's startled brown eyes. "And you will follow up with your doctor and have x-rays taken of your shoulder and chest to make sure there are no fractures. In the meantime, you need to ice it down."

"Um...sure, Doc, whatever you say," Karen stammered.

Riley glanced at Sam and found her grinning. She shot her a look that wiped the look right off her face. "Are you all right?"

"Fine. I swear," Sam quickly added.

Karen grinned and started to say something. A squelching look from Riley made her snap her mouth shut.

"Okay. Sam, would you help her stand?"

As Karen got to her feet, a cheer went up from both teams and the fans.

Karen smiled and waved with her uninjured arm as Sam and Riley walked her back to the bench.

The team gathered around the coach.

"What's the verdict?" Coach asked.

Karen settled on the bench. "Ball clipped my shoulder pretty good." She sighed. "Nothing's broken. Some ice, and I'll be fine." Her gaze flitted to Riley, then back to the coach. "But I'm done for today, and I need to follow up with my doctor."

"Good idea." Coach patted Karen's uninjured shoulder. "I'm glad you're okay." She pulled off her ball cap, raked a hand through her hair, and turned back to face her team. "All right, then. With both our backup pitchers out of commission, that's it. I'll let the officials know we forfeit."

The team groaned.

Riley's heart went out to the women.

"Wait, Coach," Sam said. "I can take her place."

"No!" Riley blurted before she could stop herself. "Sam, you can't."

The air around them went still as if the whole team was holding their breath, waiting for Sam's reaction.

Sam's expression turned thunder-cloud dark. She glared at Riley from beneath lowered eyebrows.

Riley refused to flinch. She couldn't stand by and watch Sam get hurt—again. Sorrow filled her heart. She hoped this wouldn't cost her Sam's friendship.

Sam loomed over Riley as she went toe to toe with her, gazing deeply into her eyes.

Please understand. I can't bear the thought of seeing you hurt. Riley longed to say the words, but wouldn't in front of Sam's teammates.

Sam blew out a breath, her stormy expression lightening. "I can do this," she said, her voice surprisingly gentle. "There's just one out left. I'll be all right." She turned to the coach. "Put me in. I'm still on the roster as a reserve pitcher."

The coach's gaze bounced between Sam and Riley. "I don't know. If the doc thinks you shouldn't..."

"I can do this, Riley."

Every fiber of Riley's being objected to what Sam wanted her to agree to, but she knew she had to. She wouldn't betray the trust shining in Sam's eyes.

"Forget it," a snide voice cut in. "Her little friend won't let her play with the big girls."

Riley whipped around to see who had spoken. It only took a second to recognize the smirking player.

"Shut the hell up, Darcy," Marina said.

Darcy flipped her off. "We don't need her. I'll pitch."

Muttering angrily, Marina and Diane stalked toward her.

"Knock it off. All of you," Coach said. "Or I'll pull you, and we will forfeit."

Riley turned her back on Darcy. She put her hand on Sam's arm and smiled up at her. "Go win this thing."

"You heard the doc," Coach said. "Get your butts out there and win."

The team cheered. Several of the women grinned and slapped Riley on the back before taking their positions on the field.

Sam smiled and tugged her sunglasses down from where they rested on top of her head. She clasped Riley's hand before joining her teammates.

Riley followed the coach over to the players' bench. She wanted to keep an eye on Karen and make sure the injury wasn't worse than she let on. And she needed to be close-by while Sam pitched.

A woman jogged up and handed Riley an Ace wrap and a plastic bag filled with ice.

She put the ice on Karen's shoulder and carefully secured it in place. Her gaze repeatedly strayed to the pitcher's mound, where Sam was throwing several warm-up pitches.

Karen patted Riley's arm. "Don't worry. Sam's a good pitcher. She can close this out."

Riley nodded. She wasn't worried about the game, but she didn't feel comfortable saying that to Karen.

"Play ball," the umpire called.

Forcing herself to sit next to Karen instead of pacing as she wanted to, Riley put on a calm expression.

Sam wound up for the first pitch and then let it fly.

"Ball," the umpire called.

"That's okay," Karen said. "She'll get the next one."

Riley smiled when Sam's head turned in her direction before the next pitch. She held her breath.

"Strike."

Yes! Come on, Sam. Riley watched closely as Sam wound up again. Was her leg holding up?

"Strike."

"One more, Sam," Karen hollered. "One more."

The batter laid into the pitch and drove the ball between second and third base. She took off and made it safely to first.

The coach jumped up and paced the fence line.

Riley wished she could join her.

The next few minutes passed as if they were an hour as the next batter took a full count.

Clutching the bench so hard her knuckles stood out in sharp relief, Riley waited for the decisive pitch. At that point, she didn't care what happened; she just wanted Sam off the pitcher's mound after having seen her injured leg falter with that last strike.

Sam wound up and released the ball.

The whump of the ball hitting the bat sounded overly loud to Riley. *No!* She leaped to her feet.

The opposing team's fans jumped up and cheered as the ball sailed deep into center field.

Taking off at a dead run, Darcy raced toward the back fence and launched herself into the air at the last possible moment.

The ball and Darcy landed in the tall hedges surrounding the ball field.

Fans on both sides of the field went silent.

Darcy pulled herself free of the clinging bush. She held her glove aloft triumphantly, the ball tucked in the web of her mitt.

"You're out!" the umpire called to the batter.

Sam's teammates and their fans erupted. Shouted congratulations and laughter filled the air.

Karen bounced up from the bench. "We won! We won!"

Riley tried to share their enthusiasm, but she had eyes for only Sam as she made her way in from the mound. As Sam approached with Marina and Ann, Riley hung back. She resisted the urge to run to Sam and make sure she was okay, knowing Sam wouldn't appreciate such a display of concern in front of her teammates.

Perspiration dripped down Sam's flushed face. Her jersey, soaked with sweat in several places, clung to her chest. The tense set of her jaw bespoke her pain.

I knew she shouldn't have pitched. But she had, and there was no sense in saying, "I told you so."

The rest of the team arrived with Darcy riding high on the shoulders of two of the women.

The coach called the team together. "Good job, ladies. First round of drinks are on me."

Riley suppressed a groan. She had forgotten all about going to the bar after the game.

"And the second round's on me," Sam said, to the cheers of her teammates.

Is she out of her mind? Riley bit her lip to keep from protesting. Sam didn't look as if she should be going anywhere but home.

The players grabbed their gear and headed for their cars.

"See you guys at the bar," Diane called to Sam.

Sam smiled and waved, then made her way over to Riley. "Don't worry. If you don't want to go, that's okay. I'll take you home."

Riley hesitated and searched Sam's face, trying to figure out whether she wanted her to go. Then she remembered her vow earlier to seize the day. "I'd like to go with you, if it's okay with you?"

"Of course it is." Sam offered her arm. "Let's go."

CHAPTER 26

The sun had set and the warm temperatures had fled by the time Sam and Riley approached the entrance to the bar. Riley rubbed her hands over her bare arms and wished she could wipe away her nervousness as easily.

"Cold?" Sam asked.

"Just a little. I'll be fine once we're inside." She put a hand on Sam's arm to stop her from opening the door. "Are you sure your leg is okay? We can still beg off."

"It's sore," Sam ran her hand along her thigh, "but it's all right. Icing it on the drive here was a good idea."

Wow. Didn't even hesitate to admit her leg was bothering her this time. Riley wasn't sure if that meant the pain was really bad, or if Sam had finally gotten to the point where she didn't feel the need to be evasive.

Sam gazed down into Riley's eyes. "Are you sure you don't mind coming to the bar? If beer and burgers aren't your thing, we can go somewhere else."

Riley studied Sam's body language. She didn't see any of the telltale signs of prevarication. Still, she couldn't help wondering if Sam was more concerned about her interacting with Sam's friends than she was about the food offered at the bar. Squaring her shoulders, she turned to face Sam. "I really enjoyed the game. I appreciate you taking me. But if you're not comfortable with me socializing with your friends, it's okay. Just be honest with me. I can take a cab home. I don't mind."

"No!" The word burst from Sam. "That's not it at all." She stuffed her hands into her pockets. "It's just that when everyone starts drinking, things can get a little rowdy."

Riley blew out an exasperated breath. "I thought I'd made it clear that I'm not some delicate flower that needs to be sheltered."

Sam's gaze dropped to the ground. "I know that."

"I'll admit I haven't been in a bar recently." *Okay, not since college, but she doesn't need to know that.* "Still, I've been around my share of rowdy, celebrating people." She poked Sam in the belly to make her look up. "Relax." She stood tall— or as tall as she was able to with Sam topping her by almost a foot. "I'm a big girl."

Sam's eyes twinkled and a little half smirk made an appearance.

"Don't even consider saying whatever you're thinking." Riley attempted a menacing growl. "Remember, I'm a doctor, and I know just where to hurt you."

Laughter burst from Sam, then she gazed into Riley's eyes. Her laughter cut off mid-chortle. "All right, then." She couldn't seem to tame her grin. "Don't say I didn't warn you. Let's go get a beer and a burger." She pulled the door open and held it for Riley.

Riley scanned the tavern as they entered the main room. It was packed with a fairly equal mix of men and women. A young man scurried along behind the bar, gathering the plates and beer glasses that were abandoned along its surface. Laughter and catcalls erupted from a group huddled around the flat-screen TV in the corner.

Sam waved at the coach, who was working behind the bar.

Oh. That's right. She owns the place.

Coach motioned them toward the end of the bar.

"Hey, Coach. What's up?"

"Season's over, Sam."

"Right."

Coach smiled at Riley. "I didn't get the chance on the field, but I wanted to thank you for taking care of Karen."

"You're welcome. I was happy to help."

"We were never formally introduced. I'm Louise." She stretched her arm across the bar.

"Riley," she said as they shook hands.

"Nice to meet you." Louise's gaze swept Riley, then she arched an eyebrow at Sam.

Tension seemed to suddenly radiate from Sam. "Um... We should head into the back."

Glancing back and forth between them, Riley felt as if she was missing part of the conversation.

"Hang on a sec." Louise drew up two beers, set them on the bar, and nudged one toward Riley. "Thanks again for helping out. Hope to see you around."

Riley fished in her pocket for some money.

Louise waved it off. "First round's on me."

Riley smiled and nodded her thanks.

Sam grabbed her beer. "I'll settle up with you later for whatever I owe for the second round."

A customer farther down the bar called for Louise.

She held up one finger toward the customer. "Not a problem. I trust—"

The customer hollered again, his tone demanding.

"Stuff a sock in it," Louise yelled back. "One more word out of you and you're done for the night." She turned back to Sam and Riley. "Go ahead into the back. I'll join you if things quiet down out here."

Beer in hand, Riley followed Sam to a door on the opposite side of the bar.

"Louise lets us use the back room for our get-togethers," Sam said. "It's nothing fancy, just a few tables, but it gives us some privacy. And we don't disrupt the folks in the bar." She pulled open the door.

The smell of beer, beef, and sweaty women wafted from the small room. Raucous laughter filled the air.

You said you were ready for this. Don't wuss out now.

"Sam. Over here," a voice called over the clamor. Marina waved from the long wooden table closest to the back wall.

As Riley followed Sam over to the table, she scanned the gathering. At least she wasn't the only one not wearing a team jersey.

Two empty chairs were waiting for them on Marina's side of the table. Sam slid into the chair closest to Marina and motioned Riley into the other one.

Marina leaned past Sam and smiled. "Glad you could join us." She shot a look at Sam that Riley couldn't read, then poked Sam in the side.

"What?" Sam said.

"Forget it." Marina turned to Riley. "You've already met Diane, Ann, and Karen." She pointed to each in turn and then continued on down the table. "That's Donna and Barb." The women waved. "The bruiser on the end down there is Rhonda."

Riley glanced at Rhonda. Bruiser was an appropriate appellation. Her shoulders were broad, with big, muscled biceps showing past her tight uniform jersey. Her thick neck rivaled those of most men. While she appeared to be about Sam's height, she outweighed her by at least fifty pounds. And from the look of her, all of it was muscle.

"Hey!" Rhonda wagged a finger at Marina. "Watch it. Or I'll come over there and kick your skinny Latina ass."

"Better yet, just tell Leo what she called you," Sam said.

Laughter broke out around the table.

Rhonda hooted. "Oh. Great idea."

Marina winced, then elbowed Sam. "Thanks a lot." She pushed a pitcher of beer closer to Rhonda. "I was referring to your prowess as a hitter. That was an impressive home run."

"Nice save there, Marina," Ann said.

Sam leaned close to Riley. "Leo is Rhonda's husband and Marina's partner. And he makes Rhonda look little. They're both weightlifters."

"Are they all police officers?" Riley asked.

"Marina and Leo are," Sam said. "Rhonda's a firefighter."

Riley could easily picture Rhonda carrying someone from a burning building. She smiled at the spirited banter going back and forth, though she couldn't imagine any of her colleagues speaking to each other in such a manner.

A chant erupted from another table. "Darcy. Darcy. Darcy." Beer mugs slammed against the table.

Darcy chugged directly from a pitcher of beer as her teammates egged her on.

"We're never going to hear the end of how she saved the game," Karen said.

"She's got every right to celebrate," Sam said. "That was a great catch, and it did win the game."

You're a good sport. While there was obviously no love lost between Sam and Darcy, she was still giving credit where credit was due.

Talk turned from the game to food, and Diane and Barb offered to take everyone's order to the bar.

As soon as they had left, Karen got up and took Diane's chair, bringing her opposite Riley.

"How's your shoulder?" Riley had noticed that Karen picked up her beer mug with her left hand.

"Got me good." Karen tugged down the collar of her jersey to display the edge of a large bruise like a warrior baring a battle wound. "But it's okay," she added quickly when Riley frowned.

"Talk about someone who's going to get their ass kicked," Marina said. "Wait until Pam gets a look at that."

Everyone laughed except Karen. She blanched.

Riley looked at Sam, hoping she'd fill in the blank.

Sam hesitated just long enough for it to be noticeable. "She's Karen's girlfriend."

Why wouldn't she want to tell me that? Is she worried how I'll react to her friend being gay? Riley didn't miss the irony in that but had no intention of outing herself in front of Sam's friends.

Karen darted a glance at Sam, then smiled at Riley. "So, Doc, what's your specialty?"

Riley resisted the urge to look at Sam. As far as she knew, none of the women had recognized her, and she really didn't want to give them any information that would make the connection to Sam and the shooting. She was sure Sam wouldn't want that either. "Please, it's Riley, and I'm a surgeon."

"A surgeon. Interesting. So how did you and Sam meet?"

Sam's hand tightened around the handle of her beer mug. "What is this, Karen, twenty questions?"

"Just being friendly," Karen said.

Riley wasn't buying the innocent act for a moment. *Just being nosy is what you mean.* "It's fine. I don't mind." This was nothing compared to the overly personal questions she fielded at the events she went to with her aunt and uncle.

While she focused her attention on Karen, she was well aware that everyone at the table seemed very interested in the conversation. It was pretty clear that Sam had never mentioned Riley to her friends. "We met in the hospital where I work. There's this really beautiful arboretum in the hospital complex where I like to go for lunch. I ran into Sam there after her physical therapy session a few weeks ago. We got to talking..." Riley shrugged. "And here I am." She chanced a glance at Sam.

The tense set of Sam's jaw loosened, and she smiled.

Diane returned to the table and shooed Karen out of her seat. She set a pitcher of beer on the table. "Heads up, Sam. Incoming."

Darcy strutted over, or at least she tried. It looked more like a stagger. She stopped at the end of the table and stared down at Sam with red-rimmed eyes. "Well. Well. If it isn't the returning hero." Darcy snickered. "Weren't much of a hero today— were you?" She leaned on the table and belched.

The smell of sour sweat and beer made Riley's nose wrinkle. Her gaze bounced back and forth between Sam and Darcy.

Sam's jaw muscles flexed. "You made a great catch. Congratulations."

Hearing the tension in Sam's voice, Riley wanted to cover her hand with her own but didn't dare.

"You can shove your congratulations. I want to hear you admit I..." Darcy stabbed a finger at her own chest, "...saved your screw-up." She teetered backward and then regained her balance. "Me."

"Go back to your own table, Darcy," Marina said.

"Fuck you, Marina." Darcy smirked. "Oh wait. That's right. That's Sam's job."

Riley gasped. *What?* Her head whipped around to Sam.

Sam looked as stunned as Riley felt. Then, like a fast-moving storm, her face clouded over.

Darcy threw back her head and laughed. "Shame on you, McKenna. You didn't tell your little friend about your fuck-buddy."

Riley's gaze darted to Marina.

Two bright spots of color stained Marina's cheeks despite her darker complexion.

The muscles in Sam's neck stood out in sharp relief. "Get out of here, Darcy." She gripped the edge of the table with white-knuckled intensity.

The air around them crackled with repressed violence.

Riley's heart pounded. She felt as if she were trapped between two raging bulls just waiting for the signal to charge.

Darcy's gaze raked her. "You must really be hard up, McKenna. Now you're going after the boys."

"Leave my friend out of this." Sam's voice held the whip of command.

"Friend?" Darcy sneered. "Don't you mean your latest fuck toy?"

"Shut your mouth." Sam bolted from her seat, sending her chair crashing to the floor. "Or I'll shut it for you." Her arm shot out toward Darcy.

No! Riley shoved her chair back and sprang up between them. "Sam. Don't." She grabbed Sam's arm. It was like latching on to a granite statue.

Darcy stumbled back out of Sam's reach.

Diane and Ann jumped from their chairs and converged on Darcy. Diane grabbed her arms and jerked them behind her back. "That's enough out of you."

Darcy struggled to free herself. "Get off me." She locked gazes with Riley. "Don't say I didn't warn you. Don't trust her. You're just the latest in a long line of women she's fucked. Once McKenna gets tired of you, she'll kick you to the curb, just like she did them. You're nothing special."

Two women from Darcy's table rushed over and took control of her. "Sorry," one of them said. They hustled her out of the room.

Riley could feel the waves of anger radiating off Sam and hear the harsh cadence of her breathing. She let go of her arm. *You did it again. You should've let Sam handle Darcy.*

The reaction had been instinctive. She wouldn't stand by and see Sam get into a fight while protecting her. Chancing a glance at Sam, she winced at the anger that still blazed across her face. Riley slumped into her chair and then looked around the table. Everyone avoided her gaze, except Rhonda, who gave her a rueful smile.

"Don't listen to her. Darcy is a mean drunk."

Sam righted her chair but didn't sit down. She put her hand on Marina's shoulder. "I'm sorry, mi amiga."

"Not your fault," Marina said.

Sam pulled out her wallet and handed several bills to Marina. "Pay for our food. And tell Louise I'll settle up with her on Monday."

Marina nodded.

"Come on, Riley," Sam said. "Let's get out of here."

Riley stared at her. She had so many questions. Was anything Darcy had said true? Was Sam gay? From the look on Sam's face, Riley didn't think she would be getting any answers today.

"Wait, Sam." Karen stood and came around the table. "Don't go. Darcy's an ass. We all know that. Stay and eat." She put a hand on Sam's arm.

Stone-faced, Sam stared down at the hand on her arm until Karen pulled it back.

Karen turned to Riley. "It was nice to meet you. Sorry about Darcy. She's a real bitch when she drinks." She offered her left hand. "Thanks again for checking out my shoulder. I promise I'll get it looked at."

Riley took Karen's hand and smiled. "I was happy to help." *Should I offer to stay?* Her gaze darted to Sam. Her eyes were silver, and a muscle in her cheek twitched. *Guess not.* She waved at the women, then followed Sam toward the door. Keenly aware of all the eyes on them, she held her head high.

Sam slid into the driver's seat and slammed the door. *Unbelievable. She outed me.* While her fury at Darcy raged, a portion of her anger was at herself. *I should've told Riley before now.* Sam wasn't quite sure why she hadn't; she had never been one to hide her sexual orientation. She shook her head as the rest of what Darcy had said reverberated through her head. The thought of how Riley and Marina had been treated made Sam's anger flare anew. *That fucking bitch!* Her hands gripped the steering wheel so tightly it creaked. *Get control of yourself and deal with this.*

Sam glanced over at Riley to find her staring out the passenger side window. She could only see her face in profile, but there was no mistaking the slump of her shoulders. "I'm really sorry about what happened." *And that you had to find out like this.*

Riley turned to face her, her expression unreadable.

"I should've said something before. I just..." Sam shrugged. Was this the end of their friendship?

Usually, she was quick to write off anyone who wasn't comfortable with her sexuality. But the thought that Riley might not want her in her life anymore filled her with an unexpected tension. "I...ah...hope this doesn't change things. I mean, you knowing I'm gay."

"Sam—"

"I should've told you up front." Sam focused on a spot beyond the windshield; she didn't want to see the disapproval on Riley's face if she rejected her. "It was just with everything—" Soft fingers pressed against her lips, stopping her mid-ramble.

"I'm gay too, Sam."

What? Gay? Sam stared open-mouthed at Riley. It took her several moments to regain her composure. When she did, she blurted out the first thing that came to mind, "How can you be gay? You had a boyfriend." She winced as soon as the words left her mouth.

"And no gay woman has ever had a boyfriend?"

"I just mean... I thought... You're really gay?" She barely managed to keep from adding, "Are you sure?"

Riley nodded. "It's a long story about Keith. But yes, I'm gay." Then, as if she had heard the unspoken question, she added, "Yes. I'm sure."

Sam flushed and scrubbed her hands over her face. A million questions were running through her head, but one thing kept repeating itself over and over: *she's gay!* Why that bit of information sparked such a strong reaction she wasn't willing to contemplate at the moment. "We need to talk."

Riley put her hand on Sam's arm. "I'll tell you what. I'll trade you my long story about Keith for your story about Darcy."

Sam scowled at the mention of Darcy. *She deserves an explanation after what Darcy said to her.* "Okay. Deal."

"Good. Your place or mine?"

What! The blush that had just begun to fade roared back. *She didn't mean it like that.* But everything that Sam had assumed about Riley had changed with her admission. It was going to take some getting used to.

Riley laughed. "Do you want to talk at your place or mine? I'm not really up to going to a restaurant."

"Okay." A brief flash of Riley's sterile condo passed through Sam's mind, making the decision for her. "My place, then. How about Chinese? The place we went to before is near my apartment and has takeout."

"Sounds like a plan."

"Would you grab the takeout menu in the glove box, please? They're fast. If we call now, it'll be ready by the time we get there."

Riley opened the glove box and rummaged for the menu. "Maybe we could get a bottle of wine too?"

"Chinese and wine. You've got it." Sam started the car, then glanced at Riley from under half-lidded eyes. *She's gay.* Shaking her head, she put the car in gear and proceeded out of the parking lot. The evening had certainly taken an unexpected turn.

CHAPTER 27

Sam put the key into the lock of her apartment door but didn't turn it. "My place is nothing fancy." She blew out a breath as she unlocked the door. "But it's home."

If she isn't comfortable with me here, why didn't she just pick my place when I gave her the choice? Riley wasn't sure whether she should be insulted.

"I really hadn't planned on having anyone over." Sam pushed the door open. "Don't mind the mess."

Riley followed her inside and glanced around the apartment. In sharp contrast to her condo, Sam's living room had a comfortable, lived-in look with a book and several magazines on the coffee table, a pair of cross trainers on the floor near the couch, and a very large dog bed in the corner. *She never mentioned having a dog.* Riley tensed, listening for any indication that a dog was present.

Sam took their food into what Riley assumed was the kitchen. She returned with two plates and set them on the small dinette table adjacent to the kitchen. "I'm going to grab a quick shower before we eat." Sam's nose wrinkled. "I stink. It'll just take me a few minutes. Can I get you something to drink?"

"I'm fine. Thanks."

"Okay. Make yourself at home. I'll be right back." Sam strode toward the hallway.

"Uh, Sam," Riley said before she disappeared from sight.

Sam stopped and turned back.

"Will your dog be okay with me here?"

"Dog?"

Riley pointed toward the dog bed.

"Oh. I don't have a dog. That's for Jess's dog, Thor, when he visits." Sam's brow furrowed. "You don't like dogs?"

"I do in theory. My folks were going to get me a dog for my tenth birthday, but then... Well, you know what happened with them. My aunt dislikes animals of any kind, so I've never been around dogs."

"Well, then I'll have to introduce you to Thor. He's a great dog."

"Is he friendly?"

That little half smirk that Riley was becoming wary of made an appearance. "Oh, yeah. He's just a big baby."

What wasn't she saying? Riley mentally shrugged. It didn't matter. Knowing the way Jess felt about her, the chances of her ever meeting Jess's dog were slim to none. "Get your shower."

"Okay. I'll be quick." Sam motioned toward the couch. "Have a seat."

Riley settled on the couch and sighed as she sank into the overstuffed cushions.

Instead of heading down the hall, Sam once again went into the kitchen and returned with a small plate and a bottle of water. Handing Riley the plate with an eggroll on it, she said, "I know you must be hungry. This will tide you over while I grab a shower." She set the water down on the coffee table. "If you need to use the bathroom, it's the first door on your left in the hall."

"Thanks." Alone in the living room, Riley nibbled on the eggroll and checked out her surroundings. The loveseat and couch sat catty-corner to each other. She slid her hand over the soft fabric of the sofa. A big screen television hung on the far wall. The stand below it held additional electronic equipment. She spotted two framed photographs on an end table. She set her eggroll down and leaned over the arm of the couch to get a better look.

One was a wedding photograph of Kim and Jess taken beneath a rose-covered arbor. The other couple in the photo with them was older. *Must be Sam's parents.* Riley sighed wistfully at the bright smiles on their faces. *They must be amazing people to accept having not one but two gay daughters.* Her aunt and uncle were not going to take her coming out well.

She shoved the thought away and looked at the next photograph. Sam's parents were in this photo as well. The other couple, a dark-haired man and a petite brunette woman, were at their own wedding, under the same rose-covered arbor. The younger man in the photo was a masculine version of Sam and Jess. *That has to be Sam's brother, Frank.*

It was clear that all three siblings had gotten their looks from their tall, broad-shouldered father. Although his hair was salt and pepper in the photo, Riley was willing to bet it had once been as dark as Sam's. Her mother was blond and had striking blue eyes, the same shade as her children's. An unexpected stab of envy struck as Riley wondered how it must have been to grow up with such loving parents and siblings.

She looked up at the sound of Sam's approach. She had changed into clean jeans and a dark blue tank top that brought out the blue of her eyes. Her hair, wet from the shower, was combed back away from her face. *She's beautiful. And gay. I guess that fortune cookie wasn't wrong after all.*

"Come on," Sam said. "Let's eat."

Riley pushed her plate away. *I can't believe how much I ate.*

"Get enough to eat?" Sam asked.

"More than enough. The Kung Pao chicken was excellent." Riley smiled. "Guess I worked up a big appetite being out in all that fresh air."

"Would you like some dessert? I've got chocolate ice cream or German chocolate cake."

Of course dessert is chocolate. Riley smothered a smile. *Why am I not surprised?* "No thanks. I'm stuffed. But you go ahead."

"I'm good. Maybe later." Sam stood and starting clearing the table.

Riley pushed back her chair and picked up her plate. "Let me help."

"Okay. Why don't you pour us some wine and take it into the living room while I clean up?" Sam had opened a bottle of wine, but they had both opted for water with dinner to rehydrate.

"Sure. I can do that."

Sam took care of the dishes, then joined Riley in the living room, settling on the opposite end of the sofa. She picked up her wineglass and fiddled with it for a moment before taking a sip. "I wanted to apologize again for how you were treated at the bar." A scowl marred her face. "I'm really sorry."

"That wasn't your fault. Darcy came over to our table and went off on you. You tried to be a good sport. You didn't do or say anything to her."

"No. Not tonight. But we have a history."

Darcy was her lover too? Riley wondered just how much of what Darcy had said was true. *How many exes does Sam have?* "She's an ex?"

"Definitely not. That's actually part of her problem with me."

Riley frowned. "How so?"

Sam grimaced. "Okay. I'm going to have to go back a number of years first. Darcy and I went to the police academy at the same time. The academy was my life back then, and I was totally focused and driven." A shadow passed over her face.

That wasn't a good memory. How bad could this be?

"Don't really know why, but right from the start Darcy and I competed at everything." Sam shrugged. "Always tried to one-up each other in every class, especially during any physical training. And I always came out on top."

"That's what she has against you? You bested her at the academy?" Riley picked up her wineglass and took a sip. She breathed a sigh of relief. From the look on Sam's face, she had expected something much worse.

"Part of it." Sam raked her fingers through her hair. "The rest didn't happen until after the academy. Three years ago, Darcy left the Sacramento PD and came to San Diego. First time Darcy and I ran into each other, we decided we had just been dumb kids at the academy and to let bygones be bygones. Everything was fine until the first time she asked me out and I turned her down. I guess at first she thought I turned her down because I was with someone. I didn't." She shifted on the couch. "Darcy just wasn't the type of woman I usually went for," Sam looked away, "at the time."

You mean someone scrawny and flat-chested, like me. Riley crossed her arms over her chest. After seeing the beautiful and voluptuous Marina, it was clear what type of woman Sam favored.

"Over the course of the next few months, she asked me out a couple more times. I turned her down every time." Sam took a healthy drink of her wine. "It all came to a head two years ago, after our final softball game of the season. We won and were at O'Grady's celebrating. I...ah...I had more to drink than I should have." A flush tinted her face. "Kind of like Darcy did tonight. Anyway, she came on pretty strong, wouldn't keep her hands to herself. I was irritated that she just wasn't getting it and was tired of telling her no. Like I said, I was drinking." Her gaze darted away. "I blew her off in front of everyone. Pushed her away and told her I was interested in women. I wasn't into boys."

Riley grimaced. The remark hit a little too close to home. She had a hard time imagining Sam doing something like that. *Guess you don't know her as well as you thought.*

"I know. It was a lousy thing to do. I wish I'd kept my big mouth shut. I felt really bad and apologized the next day. I even tried again a few days later, figuring she just needed time to cool off, but the damage had been done. From then on, Darcy has never missed a chance to take a dig at me or try to make me look bad." Sam met Riley's gaze. "So, in a way, what happened tonight was my fault. Darcy sniped at you to get back at me." She slid down the couch, closer to Riley, but didn't touch her.

Riley reached out and patted her arm. "We all say things that we regret later."

Sam sighed. "I am really sorry you got caught in the crossfire like that."

"You don't owe me an apology." Riley squeezed Sam's arm. "No matter what you said in the past, it doesn't excuse what Darcy did tonight. You made a mistake, and you apologized. It's her problem now if she won't accept it."

Still, she couldn't help being a little disappointed in Sam. The tiny part of her that still clung to the belief in such things saw Sam as her guardian angel. Now her angel's luster was a bit tarnished. *Just wait until you tell her why you dated Keith. See what she thinks of you after that.*

"Would you like some more wine?" Sam asked.

"No thanks. One glass is my limit."

An expression Riley couldn't read passed across Sam's face. Did she think that was a jab at her? "I'm a real lightweight when it comes to alcohol. Always have been. I could use some more water, though."

Sam smiled. "Sure thing. Be right back." She picked up their glasses and headed into the kitchen.

Sam set the wineglasses on the counter. *Hope I don't look like too big a jerk in her eyes after that confession.* The thought that she had disappointed Riley bothered her more than she cared to admit. She grabbed them each a bottle of water and returned to the living room.

Sam handed Riley the water and then sat down on the opposite end of the couch. She pulled her knee up onto the couch and turned to face Riley more fully. "Well, that was the sorry saga of me being a big jerk. Will you tell me about Keith? Please."

"Okay." Riley took her time opening her water and then took several sips.

Maybe talking about him reminds her too much of the shooting? Sam was just about to tell her never mind, when Riley broke the silence.

"Against my better judgment, I let myself get talked into going to a Halloween party last year. That's where I met Keith." She snorted. "That should have sent up a huge red warning flag right there. Halloween parties are always a bad idea."

Sam wanted to ask what was wrong with Halloween parties but didn't want to interrupt Riley's story.

"He asked me out, and I turned him down. That would've been the end of it, but I called him a month later and asked him to accompany me to a Christmas charity event in LA." Riley scrubbed her hands over her face. "If I'd known how it would all turn out…"

"So you didn't know you were gay then? This is something new?"

"No. I knew. I've known since medical school. It's…" Riley rubbed her neck, "…complicated."

She's still in the closet? After all this time? Up until now, Sam had been impressed with Riley's strength and her feisty manner. The revelation that Riley was hiding such an important part of who she was bothered her.

"Let me explain," Riley said.

Sam gazed at Riley's forlorn expression. *Don't judge. She has her reasons.* Memories of Leslie filled Sam's mind. *Haven't you learned your lesson?* She forced the painful remembrances away. "Go ahead."

"So much has changed in the last several months. I need to explain a few things first." Riley took a deep breath as if preparing to jump into the deep end. "The one thing I remember most about my parents was how important family was to them. My dad was estranged from his family for many years for following his own dream, but he never gave up trying to reconcile with them. That's why I was named Riley—after my father's brother. I was ten when my Aunt Margaret and Uncle Rielly took me in. They didn't have any children, and my aunt didn't want any." She remained silent for several moments. Her expression dimmed as if unpleasant memories gripped her.

And she never let you forget it, did she?

"But even after all the years of conflict with my dad, they still opened their home to me. I've done my best over the years to live up to their expectations and make them proud of me." Shadows darkened Riley's eyes. "But no matter how hard I've tried, it's never been enough."

"I'm sorry." *What kind of people are they? How could they not be proud?* Sam longed to say those words but kept quiet.

"Keith was just the latest failed attempt to make them happy, regardless of what it cost me." Riley ducked her head. "I know, by now I should have outgrown the impulse, but it's difficult."

"Hey," Sam said, drawing Riley's gaze back to her own. "I understand. I still struggle sometimes with wanting to please my mother."

"It's not just that." Riley chugged her water. " Honestly, I wanted to get my aunt off my back." She grimaced. "Several times throughout the year, I'm expected to attend charity events with my aunt and uncle—and an appropriate escort. In the past, when I didn't have one, my aunt set me up with someone she and my uncle considered worthwhile. When I showed up on Thanksgiving by myself, my aunt was furious. A couple of weeks before the annual Christmas gala, she called to make sure I had an acceptable escort. I didn't want them setting me up—again." Riley scowled.

"So you decided to ask Keith?"

Riley nodded. "I didn't want to ask anyone at work, and I really don't know anyone except the people I work with. After the event, I continued to go out with him. Just often enough that when my aunt asked, I could honestly say I was dating." Her hands dropped to her thighs, and she kneaded the material of her jeans. "I should've just told them the truth and faced the consequences." Tears glistened at the corner of her eyes. "Then you wouldn't have paid the price for my deception."

Sam slid closer and put her hand on Riley's shoulder. "You couldn't have known what would happen."

Riley bolted from the couch. "Hiding who I am almost got you killed. If I'd never gotten involved with Keith, you wouldn't have gotten hurt."

Sam reached for Riley's hand. "Riley—"

"You need to know the truth." She shoved her hands into her pockets. "Keith was stalking me, but what you don't know is that he saw a woman kissing me. That's what set him off. That's why he came into the ER that day, determined to take what I wouldn't willingly give him."

Huh? Oh. She never slept with him. Sam blinked. "You were dating a woman and Keith at the same time?"

"No. Not at the same time." Riley crammed her hands deeper into her pockets. "I told you this was complicated. I just..." She paced in the small area next to the couch.

Sam watched helplessly. "Take your time." She patted the cushion next to her. "Come sit down."

Riley hesitated, then plopped down next to Sam. "Could I have some more water?"

"Sure." As Sam stood, her thigh cramped. She winced and grabbed her leg. *Damn it.*

"You did hurt yourself pitching." Riley got up and stood close to Sam.

"No. It's just stiff from sitting. I'll be fine. I just need to move around a little bit."

"Let me take a look, make sure everything's okay."

Shaking her head, Sam took a step back. "It's fine. I checked when I took my shower." The very thought of Riley's fingers gliding over her bare thigh caused an unexpectedly strong spark of arousal. "I'd tell you if I wasn't okay."

Riley gazed deeply into Sam's eyes as if searching for something.

"Trust me," Sam said.

"I do," Riley said without a trace of hesitation.

Sam smiled. "I'll get the water." She went into the kitchen, grabbed two bottles of water, then returned to the living room. After handing Riley a bottle, she sat down next to her on the couch. "Tell me the rest. Please."

Riley sighed. "Okay. I broke it off with Keith at the end of April. He kept pushing to escalate our relationship beyond friendship. I just couldn't," she met Sam's gaze, "I wouldn't do that. Not again."

So Riley had slept with a man, and apparently, it hadn't been a good experience. *But what about a woman?* Sam was still trying to come to terms with the fact that Riley was gay. "What made you decide to start dating women?"

"I've been with a woman before, in med school."

"But then—?"

Riley shook her head. "Another long story."

Sam quirked an eyebrow. "And?" She had so many questions.

"That I'll tell you about another day," Riley said.

Curiosity raged, but no matter how much she wanted to, Sam resisted the urge to question Riley. *Now is not the time.* At least now she knew that Riley had been with a woman. She didn't know why that was so important to her—it just was.

"Like I said, I've spent my life trying to live up to my aunt and uncle's expectations. I couldn't be who I really was, so I buried myself in my work and took satisfaction in that."

"What changed?"

"Sounds cliché, but I had an epiphany on my thirty-fifth birthday." Riley took a sip of water.

"And what caused that?"

Tears filled Riley's eyes. She set her water on the end table. "A thirty-six-year-old woman died on my birthday."

Sam put her hand on Riley's knee. "That's terrible." It reminded Sam of what Riley had to deal with every day as a trauma surgeon. *That's a heavy burden to carry.*

Riley brushed at her tears. "She wasn't even my patient. I was at the SICU nurses' station, checking on my patient before I went home, when a commotion broke out in another patient's room. The mother of the patient apparently decided it was the appropriate time to tell her dying daughter what a disappointment she had always been."

"My God. What's wrong with people? How could she do that to her daughter?"

Riley put her hand on top of Sam's as if seeking support. "People often react irrationally to guilt and fear."

Like how Jess treated you after I got hurt. "You're right. I've seen that at work too."

"After the mother stormed away, I went into the patient's room. I'm not sure why; I just felt compelled. The patient, Patrice, had end-stage ovarian cancer. As if that wasn't bad enough, she was in the SICU because she had been in an auto accident a few days before. She suffered a ruptured spleen, and it had to be removed. The surgeon wanted to go back in because she was still bleeding inside. Patrice refused." Her voice faltered.

Sam cradled Riley's small hand between both of hers. "She knew she was dying."

"Yes. And she didn't want to suffer through another operation. I guess that was the final straw for her mother. According to Patrice, nothing she had ever done had been the right thing in her mother's eyes."

"Knowing her daughter was dying...that must have been so hard on her mother," Sam said. "But still, no matter what had been between them before, how could her mother squander even one remaining second with her daughter instead of telling her how much she meant to her?"

After she had been shot, her mother had wrapped her in her arms and held on tight, telling her over and over how much she loved her. For days afterward, her mother hugged her every chance she got.

Riley shook her head. "I'll never understand it. As I listened to Patrice talk about how she had never measured up to her mother's expectations, I realized Patrice could have been talking about me and my relationship with my aunt and uncle. She said her one regret was spending so much time and energy trying to please her mother instead of living her own life and doing what made her happy." She swallowed heavily. "I stayed with her all day and listened to her stories. I kept hoping her mother would come back." Tears trickled down her face. "She never did. Patrice died late that evening with no one there but me."

Oh, Riley. Sam wrapped her arm around Riley's shoulders and drew her close. "I'm so sorry you went through that."

Riley pulled away and brushed at her tears. "Don't be sorry for me. I still have a chance to change. Be sorry for Patrice. I made a vow to myself that night. Things were going to be different; I was going to live my life my way from then on."

"I am sorry about what happened to Patrice," Sam said and put her hand on Riley's shoulder. "But I'm also sorry that your aunt and uncle never told you how very special you are. You're a strong, competent woman. Your parents would be very proud of you."

Riley smiled through her tears. "I hope so."

"I know so." Sam squeezed Riley's shoulder. "I didn't mean to interrupt what you were telling me, but that needed to be said."

"Thanks." Riley blotted her tears on her shirtsleeve before continuing with her story. "During this time, Keith was trying to get me to come back to him, sending me flowers and asking me out. I kept telling him no. What happened with Patrice had stiffened my resolve to do what was right for me." She picked up the bottle and sipped her water. "That's when things started getting worse. Keith stopped asking to reconcile and began to demand it. Despite what was happening with him, I asked a woman I'd met in the gym at my condo out on a date. We went out a few times." Riley smiled. "It was nice."

Sam couldn't help but be impressed by Riley's strength and bravery, even if had almost gotten her killed. Under the circumstances, it would have been so easy to just retreat and continue to hide who she was.

Riley's smile dimmed. "Things continued to escalate with Keith. I started getting hang-up phone calls at all hours from unknown numbers, and my car was vandalized. I knew in my gut it was Keith, but I couldn't prove it. I spotted him a few times hanging around the doctors' parking lot at work when I was leaving, but he never approached me."

"Why didn't you call the police?" Sam knew from the police report that Riley hadn't reported the vandalism or Keith stalking her.

"I didn't want to make a huge deal out of it." Riley shrugged. "What could they have done—really?"

Sam scowled. In reality, there wasn't much the police could have done. Even with proof, they could have charged him with a misdemeanor at best and recommended a restraining order. A piece of paper would not have stopped someone like Keith.

"I honestly thought I could handle it on my own, that he'd eventually get tired of it all and move on." Riley trailed her fingers along Sam's injured thigh. "But I was wrong."

Goosebumps erupted in the wake of her touch. "You couldn't have known." Sam covered Riley's hand with her own and gave it a brief squeeze. "So that's how Keith saw you with a woman—he was following you."

"Yes. It happened in a parking lot outside a restaurant. Blair kissed me goodnight, and suddenly Keith was there, screaming like a maniac, ranting about how I'd made a laughingstock of him by leaving him for a woman. Blair pulled out a can of pepper spray and threatened to spray him and call the police. He took off."

I bet that's why she had pepper spray with her the night we ran into the homeless guy in the parking lot.

Riley blew out a shaky breath. "The calls suddenly stopped, and I hoped that was the end of it, that he'd leave me alone." She shook her head, and her bottom lip quivered. "He showed up in the ER three days later. That's my one regret. If I'd just had the courage to stand up to my aunt and uncle and be true to who I am," tears trailed down her cheeks, "you would never have gotten hurt."

Tightness grew in Sam's chest. "Please don't cry. Come here." She opened her arms. The tightness in her chest eased when Riley readily accepted the offer. Sam tugged Riley against her. A bone-deep need to keep Riley safe and ease her pain filled her. "Thank you for telling me, but it doesn't matter why you dated Keith or why you chose to break it off. This is on him. He was involved with drugs, and you know how drugs mess with a person's head, especially cocaine."

A memory of that day flashed through Sam's mind. Riley was pressed against the wall with Keith tearing at her clothes. "Even knowing that I was going to get shot, I would do it all again—in a heartbeat."

Riley pressed her face against Sam's chest. "He had his hand over my mouth, whispering in my ear." Tremors shook her slender frame. "He kept saying how he was going to...going to fuck me, then blow my brains out." Her tears broke loose in a torrent.

Oh my God. Has she been holding that inside all this time? "You're safe. I'll never let anyone hurt you again." The vow surprised her. She knew from hard experience that she couldn't protect Riley every second, but she was damn well going to try. She stroked Riley's back and murmured soothingly to her. "That's it. Let it all out. Let it go. Once and for all."

Riley's arm tightened around Sam's waist.

Sam placed a tender kiss on the top of her head.

Riley pulled back and looked up. Her eyes were red-rimmed and her face blotchy from crying. "I'm sorr—"

Sam pressed her finger against Riley's soft lips. "No. No apologies. I told you, my shoulder is always available."

"Thank you." Riley pulled a tissue from her pocket and wiped her tear-streaked face. "I can't tell you how much that means to me." A yawn seemed to catch her by surprise, and she quickly covered her mouth with her hand.

Glancing at her watch, Sam frowned. "It's after eleven. I didn't mean to keep you out so late. Are you working tomorrow?"

"I wish. My aunt and uncle are coming down to go to lunch. How about you? Do you have plans?"

"I haven't seen Kim and Jess in a few weeks. Kim's been under the weather. I'm going to LA to see them."

"Oh." Riley's shoulders slumped.

Was she going to ask me to go with her to lunch?

Riley's smile looked a bit forced. "I hope Kim feels better." A second yawn struck.

As if it were contagious, Sam yawned too. "I should get you home. It's been a long day." She eased herself off the couch, then offered her hand to Riley.

Riley allowed herself to be pulled off the couch and then grasped Sam's other hand as well. "Despite the drama," Riley ducked her head for a moment, "and the tears, I really had a good time today." She squeezed Sam's hands. "I can't thank you enough. For everything."

"You're welcome." Sam lost herself in Riley's expressive green eyes. Giving in to the impulse, she leaned down and placed a soft kiss on Riley's forehead. "Let's get you home."

CHAPTER 28

Riley pulled off the blue sweater and tossed it toward the other clothes strewn across the bed. *It doesn't matter what I wear. They're not going to take this well.* After her talk with Sam, she was determined to finally tell her aunt and uncle who she really was—no matter what the consequences. She had tossed and turned the night before, plagued by nightmares of the shooting, a stark reminder that hiding had already cost too many people too much.

A glance at the clock made her frown. Her aunt and uncle were due within the hour. She grabbed her favorite deep green shirt and slipped it on, then pulled on a pair of dove-gray slacks. As satisfied with her attire as she was going to get, she set about cleaning up her bedroom.

The sound of the front door closing echoed through the quiet condo.

Her heart shot into overdrive. *I'm not ready.* She paced next to her bed. Maybe she should have talked to Sam and asked if she had any ideas on the best way to handle this.

"I'll be right out," Riley called. After grabbing the last of the clothes off the bed, she put them in the walk-in closet. As she came out of the closet, she felt a presence in the room.

Aunt Margaret was standing next to her dresser, one of Annie's furry ears twisted between her fingers, holding her out at arm's length as if the bear were dirty or smelly. "What is this?"

Riley snatched Annie from her aunt's hand and cradled the bear against her chest. "A friend gave her to me."

"You never were very skilled at choosing your friends." The corners of Aunt Margaret's mouth twitched. "That thing is hardly an appropriate accessory for your bedroom. If you must keep it, the closet seems a fitting place for it. I'd have thought you'd finally outgrown such childishness by now."

A long-forgotten memory surfaced of her aunt holding another teddy bear by its furry ear. *Bernie.* Riley's ragged, much-loved teddy bear had been taken from her only days after she had gone to live with her aunt and uncle. She could still remember the disdain in her aunt's voice.

"You're much too old to be clinging to such childish things."

Riley's grip tightened on Annie. *Not again.* She fought against years of giving in to her aunt's wishes. If she couldn't stand up to her about something as simple as a bear, how did she expect to tell them who she really was? She stepped past her aunt and carefully placed Annie back on her dresser. "I liked her just where she was."

"Riley." Her aunt's tone held a clear warning.

"Maybe you're right. The dresser isn't the best place for her." Riley picked up Annie.

Aunt Margaret nodded like a queen granting her approval to a loyal subject.

Fueled by the memory of her childhood bear, Riley refused to back down. Still holding Annie, she marched over to her bed. "She would be much more comfortable on my bed." She fluffed the pillow shams, then propped Annie up among the pillows. "Much better." She straightened and met her aunt's shocked gaze.

If her aunt's masklike face were still capable of producing a frown, it would have been ominous. Hazel eyes narrowed as she eyed Riley. "You've gained weight." It wasn't a question; it was an accusation.

Riley barely stopped herself from running her hand over her stomach. With Sam, she didn't feel as if she had to monitor every bite. While she had gained a pound, there was no way her aunt could tell. Realizing what her aunt was trying to do, she stiffened her resolve. *Don't let her do this to you anymore. You don't want to end up like her.*

Her gaze swept over her aunt. She had clearly lost weight. Bird-thin arms showed below the sleeves of her stylish dress. She had passed waif-thin and moved on to gaunt. At sixty-eight, every part of her aunt that could be nipped, tucked, or injected had been—numerous times.

"I suppose this is due to the bad influence of your new friend?" Aunt Margaret asked. "Where did you meet this person?"

"Margaret, what's taking so long?"

Relief washed over Riley at the sound of her uncle's voice. "We'll be right there, Uncle Rielly." She slipped past her aunt and out into the hallway. Her relief was short-lived. *Out of the badger's cave and into the lion's den.*

"Good afternoon," Riley said as she approached the couch.

Uncle Rielly nodded and glanced at his watch as he stood.

That's when Riley realized her aunt had not followed her out of the bedroom. Before she could turn back around, the click of Aunt Margaret's heels sounded on the wood floor as she entered the living room.

It's now or never. Riley took a deep breath. "I have something important I need tell you before we leave for the restaurant."

"Whatever it is, you can tell us at the restaurant," Aunt Margaret said. "I don't want to be late for our reservation."

Uncle Rielly and Aunt Margaret started toward the door.

"No," Riley said. "Now."

They turned in unison to face her.

Uncle Rielly's brow lowered. "You heard your aunt. Let's go."

This was not starting out well, so Riley played the card she knew would get a response. "This is a family matter that should not be discussed in public." As she expected, they returned to the living room without a word.

"Please sit down."

They sat on the couch. Uncle Rielly glanced at his watch. "Fine. What is so important?"

Riley gazed down into their faces. She tried, as she had since she had been a child, to feel anything more than gratitude and a sense of obligation for them, but the emotions just wouldn't come. The final realization that she was never going to please them settled around her heart. She would never be happy until she claimed her life for herself.

"If you have something to say, say it." Uncle Rielly's voice cut through her thoughts.

Riley's anxiety closed her throat for a moment. She pushed through the fear. *Just say it.* She met her uncle's gaze. "I'm gay."

He stared at her, his face an unreadable mask.

Riley glanced down at Aunt Margaret. Two bright spot of color stood out on her heavily made-up cheeks. Her mouth worked like a fish out of water.

"That is unacceptable. I will not permit it." Judgment pronounced, Uncle Rielly rose from the couch and gave her a hard stare. "Do not ever mention it again." He turned his back and walked away. "Come along, Margaret."

Aunt Margaret scurried after him.

Riley's temper flared. *He thinks he can just tell me not to be gay?* She forced her anger down. *Be calm and firm. Use his own methods. Don't react—act.*

"It doesn't matter if you find it acceptable or not," she said to his forbidding back. "I'm gay. I won't hide who I am anymore—not for anyone."

He spun on his heel and stormed back to her. "You will not defy me on this."

Riley took an involuntarily step back, fear shafting through her at the blazing anger on his face. It was totally at odds with the behavior of the cold, emotionless man she had grown up around. An image of Sam flashed through her mind. Drawing strength from it, Riley refused to be cowed. "This is who I am. Who I've always been. You can't make it go away by refusing to acknowledge it." She met his angry stare head-on. "I'm gay. Nothing you say will change that."

The large veins on Uncle Rielly's temples began to pulse. His apoplectic rage robbed him of speech.

"Your parents would be so ashamed of you," Aunt Margaret said.

Riley glared at her. *Leave my parents out of this.* She forced herself to reply calmly. "You're wrong. My parents would be proud of me. They always encouraged me to be myself and be true to my feelings."

Aunt Margaret sneered. "Liberal claptrap from your mother most likely. I'm sure she manipulated your father into believing that tripe." She got right in Riley's face. "If it wasn't for that white-trash little slut he married, your father could have made something of himself. Instead, he ended up working as a common mechanic. If he had stayed in Los Angeles with his family, where he belonged, he would still be alive."

Searing anger blindsided Riley. Her hands fisted at her sides. "My father loved my mother and would've done anything for her. He wouldn't have wanted the empty life that you and Uncle Rielly have with your pretentious friends and your sanctimonious posturing. He married my mother because he loved her. Not because of her money." She jerked her head toward her uncle. "Like he did."

Riley's head whipped back from the force of her aunt's slap. She pressed her fingers to her lip; they came away bloody. *She actually hit me.* Her aunt's weapon of choice had always been words. In all the years she had lived with them, neither her aunt nor uncle had ever physically struck her.

"Don't you dare speak to us like that. Your uncle and I did everything for you—took you in, raised you as our own—and this is the thanks we get?" An ugly sneer twisted her aunt's lips. "You think I wanted to give up my life for the likes of you? I never wanted you. Never!"

Acid burned in Riley's stomach. She had always known her aunt had not been pleased about taking her in, but to hear it put so bluntly...

"Blood tells in the end. You are the same white trash as your mother." Aunt Margaret drew her hand back to strike again.

Uncle Rielly grabbed her arm before Riley could. "That's enough, Margaret." His cold, distant demeanor was once more firmly in place. Flat, emotionless eyes gazed down at Riley. "You think hard about what you are doing. If you persist with this, I will disown you. I won't have you shame me or the family name. Drop this foolishness. Now."

This was it. The moment Riley had dreaded since first realizing she was gay. She gathered her courage around her like a protective blanket. "I can't do that. This is who I am. I'm gay."

"So be it," Uncle Rielly said as if accepting a criminal's plea. "I expect you to be out of the condo within the hour."

"What are you talking about? I own this condo."

The cold smile that appeared on Uncle Rielly's face sent alarm bells ringing.

"No. You don't. I own this condo." His gaze swept the room before coming to rest on her. "And everything in it."

Riley gasped, feeling as if she had taken a blow to the solar plexus. That was all she was to him—a possession. Her gaze darted to her aunt, who looked as shocked as Riley felt.

"But I bought it from you last year. I've been paying the mortgage."

"You've been paying rent," Uncle Rielly said.

Riley remembered agreeing to delay the transfer of ownership for six months due to tax issues, but that had been a year ago. With Uncle Rielly holding her power of attorney, the accountant who handled her bills would not have questioned her change of heart about going through with the sale. No matter how busy she was, she should have never let him talk her into giving him that kind of control over her finances. But he was her uncle, and she had trusted him. The only saving grace was that it was a limited POA, or there was no knowing what else he would have done. She stared at the man she thought she knew. "Why did you stop the sale and not tell me?"

"I was starting to see the signs," Uncle Rielly said. "It was only a matter of time before you once again succumbed to your low-class nature."

What was he talking about? Then it hit her. He had known about Linda. *But how? We were so careful.*

"Reconsider your actions," he said. "I'm giving you one last chance. Apologize and never mention this again."

Riley either buckled under to his demands and allowed him to control the rest of her life—or walked away. She glanced at her aunt.

Aunt Margaret stared back, her face filled with contempt.

All those years. Tears stung the back of Riley's eyes. *All those years I spent trying to please them. It was all for nothing.* She turned her gaze upward for a moment. *I tried, Mom and Dad. I really tried.* She faced her uncle and aunt, refusing to let them see her tears. "I'll have my personal things out of the condo within the hour."

CHAPTER 29

Riley slumped into the chair next to a large window overlooking the hotel parking lot. She felt her temper rekindle at the thought of what her aunt had done to Annie. She hugged the bear to her chest. After her aunt and uncle had left, she had found Annie on the floor of the closet. Her gaze drifted over to the items lying on the hotel room bed. *My whole life reduced to two suitcases, a laptop bag, and some plastic garbage bags.*

In the end, it had taken her more than an hour to pack, but by the time her aunt and uncle had returned from the restaurant, she had the last of her personal items out of the condo. Other than to demand the keys to the condo, her uncle had not spoken to her. He'd taken the keys, turned his back, and walked away. Her aunt had not even bothered to accompany him inside. They had cast her off as easily as a pair of worn shoes.

The tears she had refused to shed in front of them finally broke loose. She buried her face in Annie's soft fur and sobbed.

The ringtone of her cellphone sounded loud in the quiet room. She swiped at her tear-streaked face, flinching when she bumped her split lip, and she grabbed the phone with her other hand. *Sam.* Her thumb hesitated over the connect button. She didn't want to drag her into this mess, but she knew Sam wouldn't see it that way. She could almost hear Sam's voice. *My shoulder is always available.*

Riley touched the screen, connecting the call. "Hi, Sam. How's it going?" She tried to make her voice sound as normal as possible.

"What's wrong? Are you okay? What happened at lunch?"

While Riley was a bit taken aback at the stress in Sam's voice, at the same time, she was deeply touched by Sam's concern. "I'm okay. Things didn't go very well with my aunt and uncle today." That was the understatement of the year. Renewed tears choked her voice. "I told them I was gay."

"Are they still there? Are you safe?"

Riley touched her split lip. "They're gone. I'm all right." She didn't want to burden Sam with her problems, yet, an unexpected longing to be held in Sam's strong arms filled her. She sighed. "Just a little worse for wear. My aunt decided to express her displeasure by slapping me in the face."

"That bitch. I'll—" Sam growled. A door slammed. "I'll be there as quickly as I can. Don't open the door to anyone until I get there."

"Wait," Riley said before Sam could end the call. "I'm not at ho—the condo." Her voice broke. Unwilling to explain over the phone, she blew out a breath. "I'm not at the condo. I'm in a hotel." She gave Sam her location and room number, grateful when Sam didn't ask any questions. "You really don't have to do this, Sam. I don't want you to cut short your time with Kim and Jess."

"I'll be there in ten minutes—tops." Sam's voice was resolute, leaving no room for argument. She hung up before Riley could respond.

Ten minutes? She's back from LA already? Riley stared at her phone, considering whether she should call Sam back and tell her she didn't need to come. *Who are you kidding? You know you want her here.* She tossed the phone onto the bed, then hurried to the bathroom to wash her tear-streaked face before Sam arrived.

Sam broke a land-speed record covering the distance to Riley's hotel. She tossed her keys to the valet and bolted for the hotel entrance.

The sound of Riley's voice when she answered the phone had flashed Sam back to that fateful call so many years ago. *It's not like that. Riley said she was fine.* Just the thought of Riley's aunt hitting her made Sam's temples pound. She took several deep breaths. The last thing Riley needed right now was more anger.

She rapped on Riley's door. "Riley. It's Sam. Let me in, please."

The door swung open. Riley offered a watery-eyed smile, then winced.

Sam's resolve to remain calm evaporated with one look at Riley's bruised face and puffy split lip. *That fucking bitch!* Her gaze swept Riley, looking for any additional signs of injury. She didn't see any. She forced her hands to unclench. Her fingers trembled as she reached out to put a hand on Riley's shoulder.

Tears began to trickle down Riley's face.

The sight of them broke through Sam's anger. *Oh, Riley.* One long step and she wrapped her arms around Riley, drawing her close.

Riley stiffened for an instant, then slumped against Sam as her tears began to flow. Clutching at Sam's shirt, she buried her face against Sam's chest.

"Easy. I've got you." Without releasing her firm hold on Riley, Sam used her foot to shut the hotel room door and murmured to her as she guided her into the hotel room. A quick glance around found nowhere they could sit together, except the bed. Sam moved them over to the foot of the bed.

Riley allowed herself to be tugged down and buried her face against Sam's chest again.

As she stroked her fingers through Riley's silky hair, a million questions whirled through Sam's mind, the biggest one being why Riley was in a hotel room instead of her condo. When she spotted the suitcases and garbage bags on the bed, more questions were added to the litany already ricocheting through her head. She put her questions aside and concentrated on comforting Riley any way she could.

Finally, Riley sniffed and pushed out of Sam's arms. She dashed the tears from her face. "I'm sorry. I—"

"Stop right there. We've been through this before. No apologizing for honest emotion, remember?"

Riley grimaced. "Ow." Her hand went to her lip. "I know, but you must be getting sick of me crying all over you all the time." She scooted sideways, putting some distance between them.

"It's hardly all the time." Sam slid across the bed, closing the gap between them, then gently brushed her finger over Riley's bruised cheek. "You need to get some ice on this and on your lip. Are you hurt anywhere else?" She barely resisted the urge to run her hands over Riley to check for herself.

"No. I'm fine." Riley laid a hand on Sam's arm. "She just slapped me the one time. She was about to do it again, but my uncle stopped her."

Sam covered Riley's hand for a moment, then pushed off the bed and stood. "I'll get some ice for you."

"I iced it before I left the condo and again when I got here. It's okay."

Sam scowled as she sat back down on the bed. "No, it's not okay. I don't care who she is, that bitch hurt you."

Fresh tears glimmered at the corners of Riley's eyes.

Sam knifed her fingers through her hair and forced herself to calm down. "Feel up to telling me what happened?" She swept her gaze across the bags on the bed. "And how you ended up here?"

Riley jumped up and began to pace. "Let's see." Words burst from her. "I found out that my aunt has always hated me."

Sam gasped. *That can't be true—can it?*

"That my uncle has known all along that I was gay." Riley's voice got louder with every word. She stopped and faced Sam. "And that, of course, gave him the right to not only betray me, but to throw me out of the condo I stupidly thought I owned."

What? Sam gripped the bedspread so hard that her fingers ached. Her head spun with each new revelation. She swallowed the barrage of questions that wanted to burst forth.

"Then there was the whole disowning me thing." Riley's face twisted. "Not that that's any big loss." As quickly as her anger appeared, it dissipated. Tears flooded her eyes. "Damn it." She spun away, turning her back on Sam. "Damn them both! They never loved me."

Sam sat frozen, struggling with her own rage. Riley's tears once again broke through the red haze clouding Sam's thoughts. She stepped up behind Riley and placed her hands on her shaking shoulders. Sam gently turned her around and gazed down into pain-filled green eyes.

Riley's lower lip quivered.

Gently cradling Riley's face in her palms, Sam leaned down and placed a lingering kiss on her forehead. "I'm so sorry." The impulse to kiss away Riley's tears was overwhelming. She brushed a butterfly-soft kiss across the bruise on Riley's cheek.

Riley rose up on her toes and pressed her body against Sam.

Without any conscious direction from Sam, her arms enfolded Riley and drew her even closer. She bit back a groan at the feel of Riley's body molded to hers.

Riley's hands came up to clutch Sam's shirt-covered chest for just a moment before her body went taut. Wide green eyes met Sam's. Ducking her head and mumbling a hasty excuse, Riley pulled away and fled to the bathroom.

Good going. Like she didn't have enough stress already today. You totally freaked her out. Sam's shoulders slumped.

Gripping the bathroom counter with white-knuckled intensity, Riley struggled to regain her composure. Embarrassment warred with anger. She had blubbered all over Sam like some little girl who needed her to make it all better. She gritted her teeth and faced her reflection in the mirror. Puffy, red-rimmed eyes glared back at her. *What's the matter with you?* She hadn't been that little girl for a very long time, and she'd never been this needy and pathetic. She grabbed a washcloth off the shelf and soaked it in cold water, then pressed it against her swollen eyes. Groaning, she remembered what else she had almost done. Had she really been about to kiss Sam? As Sam's soft lips brushed her cheek, she had lost all rational thought. *She was trying to comfort you, not make a pass. Idiot.*

Riley threw the washcloth aside. Could this day get any more screwed up? Rubbing her aching temples, she blew out a breath. She couldn't hide in here all night. *You're a grown woman. Act like it. Go out and face Sam.*

She quietly opened the bathroom door and peered out. Sam was standing by the windows with her back to Riley. Stepping out, she said, "Hey, Sam. Sorry about my meltdown."

Sam turned to face her. "You're handling all this better than I would."

"I doubt that." Riley smiled when she spotted Annie safely cradled in Sam's arms as she herself had been. For a moment, she envied the bear. "I see you're making friends with my girl."

Sam stroked the bear's soft fur. "Yeah, but she's a little upset with me 'cause I don't know her name."

Riley crossed the room to stand next to Sam. She ran a finger over Annie's furry face. "Her name is Annie."

A smile lit Sam's face. "Hey, my middle name is Ann."

"I know." Heat crept up Riley's neck. She hadn't meant to admit that. Glancing up at Sam, she was surprised to see a pink tint on her cheeks. "She's a good protector. Like someone else I know."

Sam's expression fell. "I wasn't much good to you today," she muttered and frowned. "I can't help but feel responsible for what happened with your aunt and uncle."

"What? No, Sam. It—"

"Wait. Hear me out." Sam's arms tightened around Annie. "I know you still feel guilty about me getting injured. Maybe you thought telling them was some kind of atonement for what happened."

Riley shook her head. "You're wrong. While I will probably always carry some guilt about what happened to you, this wasn't about you. It was about me." She thumped her own chest with her fist. "It was long past time for me to claim my own life." A life that had been turned upside-down in just a matter of hours. Groaning, she slumped into a nearby chair and rubbed her aching temples.

"What's wrong?" Sam knelt down next to her.

"It just hit me...everything I need to do. I have to find a place to live, contact my accountant, find a lawyer, just to name a few. To top it all off, I've got to do all that while I work twelve-hour days and cover on-call." Her hands clamped onto the arms of the chair. "Damn you, Uncle Rielly. I don't need this."

Sam took Riley's hand and intertwined their fingers. "I'm here for you. Not to tell you what to do, but as your friend, to support you in any way you need." She hesitated, then added, "If you want me."

Riley's hand tightened on Sam's. "Of course I want you." She felt her ears heat when she realized how that sounded. *It's true, but that's not what she meant. She would never be interested in you like that.*

"Then you have me." Sam smiled. "Me and Annie."

Tugging Annie from Sam's grasp, Riley smiled. She wrapped one arm around the bear, hugging it to her chest as she wished she had the courage to hug Sam. "I'm lucky to have you both."

Sam stood with groan and slid into an upholstered chair across from Riley.

"How's your leg?" Some friend she was. She'd been so caught up in her own drama that she hadn't even thought about Sam.

"It's fine. Just a little stiff." Sam ducked her head, then ran her hands up and down her thighs.

A bit worried by Sam's suddenly tentative body language, Riley asked, "You sure?"

"Yeah." Sam took a deep breath and looked up. "Umm...listen. I have a solution to one of your problems." Her hands kneaded the material of her jeans. "Come stay with me until you find a place of your own."

Shock rendered Riley momentarily speechless. *You are one special woman.* "Oh, Sam, I can't impose on you like that. You've done more than enough just by being here and letting me cry all over you."

"It wouldn't be an imposition. I have a guest room." Sam leaned forward in her chair. "Come on, say yes. I haven't had a roommate in years. It would be nice to have someone to come home to." A blush tinted Sam's cheeks. "I mean, just until you find a place of your own."

As Riley surveyed the sterile hotel room with her belongings stuffed in trash bags, her shoulders slumped. The thought of coming back here after a long day at the hospital was disheartening. The memory of how comfortable she had felt at Sam's apartment filled her with longing. Was Sam just offering because she felt sorry for her? Gazing into Sam's eyes, she saw nothing but an honest attempt to help. *Can I really do this?* Sam wasn't the only one who had not had a roommate in years. The opportunity to spend more time with Sam wasn't lost on her.

It's really your life now. Do what you want. With that little pep talk, Riley stood and held out her hand. "All right. If you're sure." She smiled at Sam's quick nod. "Let's do it."

Grinning, Sam stood and captured Riley's hand in hers. "Roommates, it is."

An unexpected wave of sadness washed over Riley at the thought that roommates were all they were destined to be.

CHAPTER 30

After dowsing the lights, Riley eased open the guest room door and peered out. The nightlight Sam had left burning in the bathroom threw a soft patch of light into the hall. She glanced toward Sam's room. The door was open, the room beyond a dark void. Stepping out into the hall, she tightened her grip around the flashlight she had borrowed from Annie's utility belt. Once she was sure she was clear and the light wouldn't shine into Sam's room, she turned on the small flashlight but kept her hand cupped around the end to mute the glow and tiptoed toward the front door. A floorboard creaked under her stocking feet, making her cringe. When she reached the front door, she breathed a quiet sigh of relief.

"Good morning."

Clutching her chest, Riley spun around. The beam from her flashlight danced crazily around the dark room.

The light in the kitchen turned on. Sam stood framed in the kitchen doorway, the light from the kitchen streaming around her.

Riley shut off the flashlight, hoping that Sam couldn't see the blush she was sporting at having been caught sneaking around like a burglar. "I was trying not to wake you. I know it's really early."

"No problem." Cradling a cup in her hands, Sam rubbed one bare foot over the other. "I was up." She turned on the light over the dinette table.

The sudden illumination made Riley blink. What was Sam doing up at five a.m.? Then it hit her. "Today's your first day back at work, right?"

"Yeah. Not real work, just administrative stuff." Sam found her coffee cup suddenly interesting. "No big deal."

Regardless of Sam's words, the thought of her returning to work was enough to make Riley's pulse spike. "Still, it's been what...almost twelve weeks? I'm sure it has got to be a little stressful."

Sam shrugged. "Want a cup of coffee before you take off?"

It stung that Sam didn't want or need her moral support. "That would be great. Thanks."

"Have a seat, and I'll grab you a cup. Black, right?"

"That's right. Thanks."

Sam disappeared into the kitchen.

Riley slid into a chair at the small dinette table adjacent to the kitchen.

When Sam returned, she leaned over to place the coffee on the table.

Riley's gaze was drawn to Sam's T-shirt, which stretched tight over her broad shoulders and clung to firm breasts. The sudden kick of her libido caught Riley off guard. *None of that.* She forced her gaze down to her coffee.

"How's the lip this morning?"

Riley looked up. "Not too bad. A little sore."

Sam frowned and lifted a finger to gently stroke across Riley's bruised cheek.

A pleasant tingle followed her touch.

"These are going to bring lots of questions at work. You ready to face all that?"

So she doesn't want to talk about how going back to work makes her feel, but wants me to? "It's no big deal," Riley said, echoing Sam's earlier words. While she appreciated Sam's support, she was becoming uncomfortable with it always being one way—Sam supporting her.

Sam's brow furrowed. "But—"

"I've always tried to keep my professional life separate from my personal one." Which had been easy, since she didn't have a personal life. "This is no different. I'll cover up the bruises and go to work like always."

Sam stared at Riley, her lips pressed into a thin line. "That won't cover up what happened. What your aunt did to you. That has to affect you."

"No, it doesn't cover up what happened." Riley met her gaze head on. "But neither does blithely saying it's no big deal going back to work for the first time—no matter what you're doing—after you were shot in the line of duty."

Sam's usually expressive blue eyes turned a flat, hard silver, then she looked away.

What are you doing? Why are you pushing her? Riley put her hand on Sam's arm. The muscles were tense under her fingertips.

Sam barely resisted the urge to pull away from Riley's gentle touch. While she found it aggravating, she respected Riley for calling her on her evasion. Still, she hesitated, struggling against the need to look strong. *This is Riley. She has already seen you at your weakest.*

"I'm sorry," Riley said. She let go of Sam's arm and clasped her hands together in her lap. "I'm projecting my own fears about you going back to work onto you."

"You don't have anything to be concerned about. I'm going to be on desk duty." Sam huffed with enough force to stir her shaggy bangs. "But I am a little worried about going back to work. Not about getting physically cleared, but I have to meet with the department psychologist as many times as he recommends before he'll clear me to return to full duty."

Riley's brow furrowed. "Is there some reason you think you won't get cleared?"

"No." Sam's hand tightened around her coffee cup. "I just hate the whole 'tell me how that makes you feel and let's talk about your feelings' crap."

"I can understand that. Not my favorite thing either." Riley stroked Sam's arm, peering deep into her eyes. "Are you still having nightmares?"

Sam started. She did still occasionally have a nightmare about that fateful day, but of late, the nature of her dreams had morphed. In her nightmares, she didn't arrive in time to stop Keith from hurting Riley, but Riley didn't need to know that. Sam nodded reluctantly. "Not like I used to, though." She searched Riley's eyes. "Are you?"

Riley looked down. "Sometimes," she said, so softly that Sam had to strain to hear her. She shook her head roughly as if trying to clear it of bad memories. "Back to the department psychologist." Her gaze locked with Sam's, and she squeezed her arm. "Just be your honest, straight-forward self, and I'm positive you'll be fine."

Sam picked up her neglected coffee and grinned. "Well, the straight part isn't going to work for me."

Riley smiled, then winced as the movement tugged at her lip. "Me either. I'm not going to hide who I am anymore." Her eyes sparked with determination. "I do plan on coming out at work, but it will be on my terms, not because I'm forced to."

"I can respect that."

"Guess I did make a mistake. I shouldn't have been so quick to leave behind all the makeup my aunt kept pushing at me." Riley's hands tightened on her cup. "Instead of covering up my unsightly freckles she disliked so much, I could've used it to cover the bruises she caused."

Sam growled. "I'd like to give that bitch some matching bruises of her own."

Riley shook her head. "While I appreciate the sentiment—"

"I know." Sam scowled. "I wouldn't, no matter how tempting it might be, but it doesn't keep me from wanting to. What she did to you really pisses me off." She smiled and captured Riley's hand. "Besides, I like your freckles."

Riley stared into Sam's eyes as if trying to judge her sincerity.

"They give you a unique appearance." Sam itched to run her fingers across Riley's silky soft, freckled cheek.

Riley snorted, then flinched. Her hand went to her lip. "Yeah, unique as in freaky spotted-looking."

"No." Sam leaned closer. "Unique as in cute and appealing."

A bright red flush crept over Riley's face, making her freckles stand out. She rubbed her hands over her cheeks as if willing the blush to fade. "So, umm... anyway, back to the bruises. I should get going. I need to stop by the drugstore."

"Hang on. I'll be right back." Sam had been in the process of making herself a bagel when she'd heard Riley moving around in the living room. She hustled into the kitchen, pulled the bagel from the toaster, slathered it with strawberry cream cheese, and returned to the dinette. "Have something to eat before you go. I know you've got a long day ahead of you." She pushed the plate with the bagel into the center of the table.

Riley shook her head. "You go ahead. I'll grab something at the hospital."

Sam nabbed half of the cream-cheese-covered bagel and took a big bite, then nudged the plate with the remaining half closer to Riley.

Riley's gaze darted down to the bagel, then back to Sam.

Sam hadn't been around Riley long before she realized she had issues with food, no doubt thanks to her bitch of an aunt. Sam racked her brain to come up with anything else in her kitchen that Riley might find acceptable.

Before she had a chance to offer an alternative, Riley reached for the bagel and took a small bite. "This is good. I can't remember the last time I had cream cheese." She took a second, larger bite. "Much better than the dry toast I usually have. Thanks."

Score one for Riley.

A comfortable silence prevailed as they enjoyed their first meal as roommates.

CHAPTER 31

After pushing her bangs out of her eyes, Sam read the numbers on the box, then cross-checked them against her clipboard. *I need a haircut.*

"About time you did some work." Marina stood with her hands on her hips at the end of the row of shelves.

Sam straightened and pressed a hand to her aching back. "Bite me."

Marina threw back her head and laughed. "Only in your dreams." Dodging boxes, she made her way to where Sam stood and wrapped her in a one-armed hug. "It's great to see you back, mi amiga, no matter what you're doing."

Sam pulled away, disgruntled with the reminder of the shooting that had relegated her to desk work. "Sorry I missed you this morning." By the time she had finished with the department psychologist, Mariana was already out on patrol.

"Yeah. Must be nice to stroll in whenever you get around to it."

"Marina." Sam shoved her shoulder. "Aside from harassing me, was there something you wanted?"

"You almost done here?"

Sam scowled. "As done as I'm going to get for today."

"Great. Let's hit O'Grady's. I'll buy you a beer."

Sam hated to turn her down, but she wanted to go home and move all her stuff out of the guest room before Riley got off work. Last night Riley had been so physically and emotionally exhausted they had just left her stuff in the suitcases and garbage bags until Sam could clear some space for her. She hesitated, not ready to tell Marina that Riley was temporarily living with her.

Marina's brow furrowed, then as if a light had gone on she grinned. "Got a hot date with your little doc, huh?"

Sam shook her head. "It's not like that. We're just friends."

"Right." Marina burst out laughing. "Come on, one drink." She nudged Sam. "You can wait an hour to jump her bones."

"I mean it. We're just friends. Nothing else."

Marina smirked. "Yet."

"No." Sam's jaw clenched. *What do you expect? She knows how you work.* "No," she repeated, wanting to be clear. "Not ever. All we will ever be is friends."

Despite her growing attraction to Riley, she would never pursue her. Riley deserved someone who could love her and be a true partner to her. Sam knew she couldn't be that woman. Her failed attempt at a relationship with Christy had driven home what she had learned long ago.

Marina stared at her for a moment, as if she had never seen her before, then shook her head. "Then what's the problem? Come out with me for a beer." She edged closer and lowered her voice. "It was supposed to be a surprise. I talked to a bunch of our squad today, and we're going to meet at O'Grady's tonight. A little impromptu welcome back for you."

Torn between wanting to be there for Riley and not wanting to disappoint Marina, Sam glanced at her watch. She didn't expect Riley to get to the apartment until after seven, so she had enough time to grab a quick beer and pick up some takeout for Riley on the way home. "You're buying, right?"

"I knew you wouldn't turn down a free beer." Marina tugged on Sam's arm. "Let's go."

"Hey, Sam." Marina's partner, Leo, was waiting for them outside the property room. "About time you got your ass back to work."

Sam grinned. "Yeah. You guys are helpless without me."

Leo growled. "I'll show you helpless." He wrapped his arms around her and lifted her feet off the floor.

Sam laughed. "Put me down, you big gorilla."

"Don't scare us like that again, or I'll have to kick your ass," Leo said close to her ear before releasing her.

Sam caught sight of Brad Davidson lurking farther down the hall. "You two go ahead. I'll meet you at O'Grady's."

Marina glanced down the hall and nodded. "Okay. See you there."

As Marina and Leo walked away, Sam went to talk to Davidson. Aside from a brief meeting in her hospital room only days after the shooting, she hadn't had any contact with the young rookie who had saved her and Riley. Wiese from Internal Affairs had barged into her hospital room and demanded Davidson leave and that there be no further contact between them until the investigation of the shooting was complete. Marina had been keeping track of what was going on with Davidson for her. Although he had been cleared in the shooting, the rookie had struggled with the decision of whether to stay on the force.

"Hey, Davidson," Sam said as she strode up to him. "Glad to see you decided to stick around." She clasped his shoulder. *If it wasn't for him, Riley and I would both be dead.* "You did good. Really good."

"Thanks." His expression grew serious, and he reached for Sam's hand.

Unexpected tears prickled behind her eyes. She shook away the rising emotions. Before Davidson could take her hand, she pulled it back and popped him in the arm. "Yeah, you did good, but don't let it go to your head."

Davidson smiled. "I won't."

"A bunch of us are heading for O'Grady's. Join us and I'll buy you a beer."

"You sure, Officer McKenna?" He shoved his hands in his pockets. "Despite what happened, I know I'm still just a rookie."

"No. Not anymore." Sam adamantly shook her head. "You've more than proven yourself. I would gladly ride with you any time. And call me Sam."

A grin lit his face. "Really?"

"Yeah." She narrowed her eyes at him. "But I still don't date guys."

He laughed and held his hands up in surrender. "Right. Got it."

CHAPTER 32

S am opened one side of the sliding closet doors in the guest room. She stared at the space she kept clear for Kim and Jess when they visited, then eyed the suitcases and garbage bags on the floor. It was never going to fit, unless she emptied out the other side. Sam hesitated. "Can I do this?" she muttered.

She had already cleaned out the chest of drawers and cleared a space for Riley's laptop on the desk in the corner. Surprisingly, that hadn't bothered her, but emptying out the closet was a lot bigger. Whenever Christy had pushed to move in, the mere thought of her invading Sam's space had made her feel smothered.

It's not the same thing. Riley wasn't her girlfriend; maybe that was why it felt different. The thought of Riley brought an instant smile to her face. She wanted her to feel at home, even if it was only for a couple of weeks.

Decision made, she slid open the far-side closet door. Camping and sports equipment tumbled out onto the floor. *Where am I going to put all this crap?* A glance at her watch made her curse under her breath. It was a little past eight, so Riley would be home any moment. Pushing her bangs out of her face, she started gathering up the sporting equipment spread out at her feet.

Thirty minutes later, she surveyed the newly cleared space. *Almost done.* Having saved the tent for last, she hefted the cumbersome bag onto her shoulder. A sudden prickling of her senses made her turn toward the door.

Riley was standing in the doorway of the guest room. In dress slacks and a tailored blouse, she looked much the same as she had that morning, only now she had a bad case of hat-hair, probably from spending time in the OR.

"What are you doing?" Riley asked.

"Just clearing out some gear so there's room for your stuff. I emptied the dresser for you too."

Stepping into the room, Riley shook her head. "You didn't have to do all this. I don't want to put you out."

"I wanted to." Sam let the tent drop to the floor and then moved closer to Riley. "I want you to feel at home here." The smile that blossomed on Riley's face caused Sam's heart to do a strange flip in her chest.

"Thank you." Riley took hold of Sam's hands and gazed up into her eyes. "You'll never know how much this means to me."

Drawn in by the emotions swirling in Riley's vivid green eyes, Sam barely resisted the urge to tug her into her arms. She took a step back, out of temptation range, then glanced at her watch. It was almost nine. *She must be beat.* While she didn't want Riley to feel as if she was keeping tabs on her, she couldn't help worrying. "Did you have time to eat today?"

"It was a crazy day. I spent most of the shift in the OR and the recovery room." Riley looked away and shuffled her feet. "I did manage to grab a protein shake around lunchtime and a second one after the last case."

Sam frowned. "That's no substitute for a meal. I've got—"

"I'm fine. I'll grab something on the way to work tomorrow. You've already done too much for me. You don't need to feed me too." Riley grabbed one of her suitcases and hefted it onto the bed. "I'm going to work on getting some of this unpacked."

"Riley, you just worked a fourteen-hour shift. You must be hungry."

As if on cue, Riley's stomach growled—loudly. A bright flush washed over her cheeks.

"Come on." Sam tugged on her arm. "You can unpack later. I picked up some takeout on the way home. There's plenty left." *Especially since I got it for you.* Sam chose not to admit that since Riley seemed uncomfortable with being cared for. *Well, I'm going to change that.*

Sam sat cross-legged on the bed with Annie in her lap and watched Riley put her things away.

After making short work of her dinner, Riley started right in on unpacking her stuff. She moved methodically about the room and quickly emptied both suitcases, then pulled a picture frame from her laptop case and hugged it to her chest for a moment. With an audible sigh, she slipped it back into the bag.

"Hey. You don't have to do that," Sam said.

Riley jumped as if she had forgotten Sam was there.

"Put your picture out."

Riley peered at Sam from beneath half-lidded eyes. "I know this is only temporary. I don't want you to think I'm settling in or anything."

"Riley, this is your room. For however long you want it."

Sam froze as the import of what she had said sunk in. *It's true.* It struck her as strange that she had no qualms whatsoever about Riley invading her home. She never would have believed that she'd give a woman an open-ended offer to life with her. She gazed over at Riley. *Then again, I've never met anyone quite like Riley.*

Sam turned and settled Annie against the pillows at the head of the bed. She smiled at Riley. "Put your picture out and anything else of your stuff you want."

Not that Riley had much. Apparently, that awful furniture in the condo belonged to her aunt and uncle.

Riley pulled the picture from the laptop case, then crossed to where Sam was perched on the side of the bed. She gently rubbed her fingers over the glass before setting it on the bedside table. "This is the only thing I have left of my parents." Deep sadness filled her eyes. "My aunt and uncle hauled me off to LA just days after my parents died. I didn't find out until a few months later that they had an estate service come in and clear out our house and dispose of everything. Pictures, mementos—everything."

A lump formed in Sam's throat, choking off any words of comfort.

Riley scrubbed her hands across her face as if she could wipe away the painful memories. "At least I still have this." She touched the edge of the picture frame.

Her heart aching for Riley, Sam looked at the picture.

Her parents flanked a young Riley, who couldn't have been more than eight or nine. She was holding up a trophy of some sort and had the biggest grin on her face. Her parents were beaming at her.

"What was the trophy for?"

"Believe it or not, the high jump. Our local rec center held a kind of junior summer Olympics." Riley laughed. "I might be short, but my dad swore I had springs in my feet."

Sam thought of all Riley had lost at such a young age. *And she still made a success of herself, despite her bitch of an aunt and uncle.* Her respect and admiration for Riley grew. "I'm glad they're out of your life," Sam muttered before she had a chance to censor herself.

"What!"

Sam's gaze darted to the picture and then back to Riley. "Not your folks. God, no." She shook her head vehemently. "Your aunt and uncle. I'm glad they're out of your life."

Riley sank onto the bed next to her. "Me too."

A yawn escaped before Sam could stifle it.

"I'm sorry. It must've been a long day for you too." Riley frowned. "You went to all this trouble getting things ready for me, and I didn't even ask how your first day back at work went."

Sam stood. "It was fine."

"Sam." Riley shot her a narrow-eyed glare.

Like there was any chance you were going to get away with that with her.

Huffing out an exaggerated breath, Sam plopped down on the bed. When Riley touched her arm and smiled at her, Sam lost herself for a moment in Riley's mesmerizing green eyes. *Focus, McKenna.*

"The department shrink wasn't too bad. He asked a lot of questions but didn't push." Sam raked her hand through her shaggy hair. "I'm stuck working in the property room—which sucks. I'd much rather be on the front desk where I'd at least have some contact with people." *Or better yet on the streets.*

Riley's hand tightened on Sam's arm as if she had heard the unspoken words, then she pulled away. "Well, I'm glad the psychologist worked out okay. Just be patient."

Sam scowled. "I'm trying."

Truth was, she was sick of not being able to do her job. It felt as if she had lost an important part of herself. As far as she was concerned, the sooner she was back on the street, the better. Knowing how Riley had previously reacted to her wanting to return to the streets, she kept those thoughts to herself.

Yawning, she stood. "Well, I should let you get some rest. I know you probably have another long day tomorrow."

Riley stretched. "Barring anything major happening, this week should be fairly easy. I just work twelve on, twelve off, plus back-up call."

She considers that easy? Amazing. Sam moved to the door with Riley trailing in her wake. She stepped out into the hall and turned back to face Riley. "I'll see you in the morning."

Riley smiled, then beckoned for Sam to lean down.

Sam quirked an eyebrow but did as requested.

"Thank you." Riley placed a soft kiss on her cheek. "Thank you for everything."

Her cheek tingling, Sam froze. Her gaze went to Riley's soft lips, and the urge to feel them pressed against her own surged through her. *Don't even go there.* She straightened to her full height and settled for cupping Riley's cheek in her palm. "You're very welcome. Goodnight." As she turned to walk away, she sighed. If only things could be different.

CHAPTER 33

Sam parked in Kim and Jess's driveway, but her thoughts were back in San Diego. Just as she and Riley were leaving to look at prospective apartments, Riley's friend Denny had called. His infant son had been hospitalized, so he needed Riley to cover for him. Sam pulled her phone out of its holder. Should she call and see how Riley was doing? She stared at the phone, then shook her head. *Nah. I probably shouldn't bother her while she's working.*

At the front door, she rapped lightly and waited for the booming bark that always announced her arrival. It never came. *Strange.* The large wrought-iron gate that restricted access to Kim and Jess's driveway had been open when Sam arrived. The gate also acted as the final link of the property's perimeter fencing, so if the gate was open, Thor was not outside. The front door was unlocked so she opened it and stepped into the foyer. "Jess. Kim," she called out. She walked into the living room, then opened her mouth to call again.

Rapid footsteps sounded. "Shhh!" Jess appeared in the archway that separated the living room from the family room. "Quiet!"

Sam's greeting died on her lips. When Jess beckoned her, she followed her into the family room.

Once there, Jess said, "Sorry. Kim's sleeping and I didn't want you to wake her."

At ten in the morning? That wasn't like Kim at all. She and Jess were both early risers. "She's still not feeling well?"

Last Sunday, Kim had begged off going out to eat and then called an early end to Sam's visit. "This has been going on for quite a while now." Frowning, she gripped Jess's arm. "Is there something wrong you're not telling me?" Jess had a tendency to be overprotective of her since the shooting.

Jess patted Sam's hand where it rested on her arm. "She's—"

"I'm fine." Kim stood in the doorway of the family room with Thor by her side.

Sam's anxiety ratcheted up another notch when Thor wagged his tail but didn't budge from Kim's side. He always made a beeline for her whenever she visited. Sam swept her gaze over Kim. She didn't look any better than she had last week. If anything, the dark smudges beneath her eyes appeared more distinct.

Before Jess could move, Sam crossed the room to Kim and pulled her into a hug. "Please tell me what's going on. I know something's wrong."

Kim glanced over Sam's shoulder, slipped from her arms, and went to Jess. Thor trailed after her.

Jess met her with open arms, then placed a soft kiss on her lips. She said something to Kim that Sam couldn't hear.

Kim nodded.

A band tightened around Sam's chest. "You guys are freaking me out."

"It's nothing bad," Kim said as she settled on the couch. "Come sit down." She patted Thor, and he flopped down at her feet.

If I need to sit down first, it sure as hell isn't good. "Tell me." She rounded the end of the couch and stood looking down at Kim and Jess, increasingly bad possibilities racing through her mind.

A beautiful smile curved Kim's lips. She glanced at Jess, then up at Sam. "I'm pregnant."

When her breath left her lungs with a whoosh, Sam was grateful for the close proximity of the couch. She sank down next to Kim. "Wow. Pregnant. I didn't know you were trying to start a family. Congratulations." She knew she was grinning like a fool, but her smile couldn't be any bigger than Jess's. "When are you due?"

"Around the end of April. We've been waiting until the end of my first trimester before telling anyone. That was this week."

Sam did some quick mental calculations. "Oh. You got pregnant on your honeymoon. That's really romantic."

Jess's face twitched.

Kim elbowed her in the ribs.

What's that about?

"Yeah, around that time," Jess said. "We haven't really told anyone yet. So we'd appreciate it if you didn't say anything until we get a chance to tell the folks."

"No problem." Sam shook her head, trying to wrap her mind around the fact that Kim and Jess were having a child. *Wonder who the sperm donor was?* Although her curiosity was raging, she resisted asking. She rubbed Kim's shoulder. "I'm sorry you've been so miserable. But I can't begin to tell you how thrilled I am for both of you."

Kim shared a look with Jess. When she received a nod, she reached for Sam's hand and clasped it between both of hers. "Jess and I would like you to be the baby's godmother."

Sam gulped. *Whoa. That's a huge commitment.* Thoughts of her failed relationships paraded through her mind. *I can't even keep a girlfriend. Could I be there for a child?* Her gaze darted between her sister and Kim. "Are you sure you want me?"

Kim squeezed Sam's hands. "We couldn't be more certain."

Jess nodded. "No question in my mind. But you don't have to answer right now—just think about it."

Sam's gaze dropped to Kim's belly. There was no sign of her pregnancy yet. She pictured the tiny baby nestled safely inside. *That's going to be my niece or nephew.* Sam was humbled by the fact that Kim and Jess would trust her with something so precious. Her thoughts turned to Riley. Tears stung the backs of her eyes. A soul-deep resolve filled her. *I'll never let this child down.* She looked into Kim's shining blue eyes and smiled, then met Jess's gaze. "I'd be honored to be your child's godmother."

Jess smiled as Kim ate the last bite of the cheese omelet she had made for her. It was the first meal Kim had managed to finish in several days. Now if she could just keep it down...

Turning her attention to her sister, she asked, "How did your first week at the station go?"

"Okay, I guess." Sam scowled and added a second helping of freshly sliced cantaloupe to her plate. "But I hate working in the property room. I can't wait to get back out on the streets."

Jess gripped the edge of the dining room table as she struggled to control her expression. She glanced over at Kim in time to see her face drain of what little color it had.

Sam set the plate of cantaloupe on the table with a thump. "Not you guys too. You know this is what I do."

"Come on, Sam," Jess said. "Can you blame us?" The thought of Sam back on the street and in the line of fire—literally— made the omelet she'd just eaten sit like a lead ball in her stomach.

"It was a fluke." Sam tossed her napkin on the table. "In the nine years I've been on the force, I've never got more than a few scrapes and bruises."

"We almost lost you." The fear churning in her gut made Jess's voice crack.

"It's over. I'm fine. I'm a cop." Sam pushed her plate away, shoved her chair back, and stood. "I like it, and I'm damn good at it."

Jess crossed her arms over her chest. *You almost got killed.*

"We're not saying you shouldn't go back to work." Kim tilted her chin toward Jess. "Are we, Jess?"

Truth was, that was exactly what Jess wanted, but she knew that wasn't fair to Sam. This was about her fear, not Sam's job. Before the shooting, she had been able to rationalize the danger of Sam's job and push those thoughts to the back of her mind. Now, she would never forget the sight of Sam looking so small and fragile lying in that hospital bed. With a sigh, she slowly shook her head.

Kim urged Sam back into her chair. "Just cut us a little slack, okay?" She frowned. "What did you mean by us too? Does the department psychologist have a problem with you returning to regular duty?"

"No. Nothing like that." She fiddled with her juice glass. "It's Riley. Every time I mention returning to full duty, she looks like she's going to pass out."

Jess didn't blame her. She didn't even want to imagine what it had been like to witness the shooting. Not to mention what Riley herself had gone through in the assault.

"And you're surprised by that?" Kim asked.

"I guess not." Sam rubbed the back of her neck. "But she knows I'm fully recovered. And I've assured her I'm always careful."

Kim entwined her fingers with Jess's, then patted Sam's arm with the other hand. "Just give her some time. Give all of us some time. Okay?"

"Yeah. All right." Sam nabbed a piece of cantaloupe off her plate and took a bite. "I'm just concerned about Riley. She's got a lot going on right now. She doesn't need to be worrying about me."

Jess didn't understand her sister's growing friendship with Riley. She had thought that Riley would be the last person Sam would want to be around, if for no other reason than the traumatic memories associated with their shared experience. Clearly, that had not been the case.

"Anything we can help with?" She had promised herself that she would do everything she could to be supportive of Sam. It also gave her a chance to make up for the way she had acted toward Riley immediately after the shooting.

Sam hesitated, then seemed to come to a decision. "Maybe. She needs a lawyer. Do either of you know a good lawyer here in LA?"

Looking at Kim, Jess said, "Maybe Alan?"

"Good idea." Kim turned to Sam. "Remember Alan, from the foster home where Jess and I donate our time?"

Sam nodded. "Right. I met him when we went with the older kids to Magic Mountain."

"That's him," Kim said. "Well, he limits his legal work to the foster home and whatever the kids need, but he's active in the community. I'm sure he can recommend someone to Riley."

"Great." Sam raked her hands through her hair. "That would be one less thing she has to contend with."

"Has something happened?" Kim asked.

Again Sam hesitated. She took a sip of her pomegranate juice. "I didn't say anything last weekend because I didn't know how Riley planned to handle things, but now..." Her gaze shifted between them as if she was trying to anticipate their reaction. "I found out last weekend that Riley's gay."

She's what? Jess shot Kim a look, expecting her to be as shocked as she was.

A smile tugged at the corners of Kim's lips.

"Seriously...You knew?" Jess asked.

Kim's eyes twinkled. "I suspected."

"No way," Sam said, looking just as stunned as Jess felt.

Laughing, Kim reached out and patted Sam's hand, then Jess's. "I can't help it if both of you have bum gaydar."

Sam pushed her shaggy bangs out of her face. "Got to get that sucker fixed," she muttered.

Jess snorted. "Yeah. Let me know when you find a repair woman. Mine's never worked worth a damn."

"You said 'found out.' Riley didn't tell—" Kim's hand went to her belly. Her face pale, she began to deep-breathe.

Oh damn. Jess bolted from her chair and stood next to Kim. "That's it. Deep breaths. Slow and easy." She stroked Kim's hair, hating that she could only stand by and watch Kim suffer through these bouts of morning sickness without being able to do anything to alleviate it.

"Is there anything I can do?" Sam asked in a subdued voice.

Jess shook her head, her gaze never leaving Kim.

After a few minutes, Kim's tense posture eased, and she laid her head against Jess's belly.

Jess placed a soft kiss on her forehead. "Okay now?"

"I'm good," Kim said.

"Let's get you into the family room so you can put your feet up."

Sam stood when Kim did. "I'll clean up."

"Thanks, Sam." Jess wrapped her arm around Kim and led her away.

When Jess lifted the covers and slipped carefully into the bed, Kim rolled onto her back. A nasty bout of nausea had struck after dinner, and she had retired early. "I'm awake." The glow of the nightlight in the bathroom cast a pale pool of light on the bed.

Jess froze for a moment, then shifted closer. "I'm sorry I woke you. How are you feeling?"

"You didn't. I woke up a little while ago." Kim brushed her sleep-tousled hair out of her face. "This pregnancy-induced exhaustion is getting old. I feel like I'm eight years old and can't stay up with the adults." Tears pooled in the corners of her eyes. *Not to mention the whole crying every other minute thing.*

Jess rolled onto her side, then scooted over until the length of her body was pressed against Kim. She lifted her head and placed a soft kiss on Kim's lips. "You need the rest." She slipped her hand under the hem of Kim's gown and pushed it up until she could rest her hand on Kim's lower abdomen.

Kim smiled as Jess began to gently stroke her belly.

244

"I know it's easy for me to say, but it will get better. I promise." Jess kissed her again. "But right now, our little one needs you to get lots of rest."

The soft, rhythmic strokes of Jess's hand across her bare belly soothed Kim, and her eyes fluttered closed. She resisted the encroaching sleep. "Were you able to convince Sam to stay?"

Jess started as if she had been about to fall asleep as well. "What?"

"Did Sam stay?"

"No." Jess's hand stilled on Kim's abdomen. "She was determined to go home."

Considering all the things Sam had told them, Kim wasn't that surprised. "I understand her wanting to be there in case Riley needs her."

Jess pulled away and flopped onto her back. "I've never understood Sam wanting to be friends with Riley. I figured once she was done with her therapy, they would drift apart and return to their own lives. Then tonight she springs on us that she let Riley move into her apartment." She scrubbed her hands over her face. "That's not like Sam. And it's got me worried. You know how she used to rant about Christy wanting to move in."

Kim nodded. "I can actually understand them being friends. But I'm still pretty shocked she let Riley move in." She shrugged. "Then again, Riley's not her girlfriend."

"Still, Sam hasn't had a roommate since college. While she was in the police academy, she lived in a crappy hole-in-the-wall place by herself rather than sharing a better place with a roommate."

That fit what Kim knew of Sam. When they first met, Sam had seemed more emotionally open than her sister, but as Kim had gotten to know her, she realized that was not the case. In her own way,

Sam was as emotionally guarded as Jess had ever been. What Kim didn't know was why.

Kim leaned on her elbow and rested her head on her hand. She wished she could see Jess's eyes, but the dim lighting prevented it. "What's got you worried? It's not like Riley is leeching off of Sam."

"I just can't help wondering if Sam has some, 'I saved her, I'm responsible for her' kind of complex going." Jess fisted her pillow. "It just isn't like her to do something like this."

Kim thought back to Sam's body language and tone of voice as she talked about Riley, especially when she told them Riley was gay. She had never seen Sam's face light up as it did when she talked about Riley. "It might have started out like that, but I don't think that's the case anymore. I think Sam has real feelings for Riley."

"I know they're friends—"

"No, Jess. I mean romantic feelings."

Jess jerked into a sitting position. "No. You're wrong."

"Maybe I am. But I don't think so. What would be so wrong if she did?"

Sagging back onto the bed, Jess huffed. "Nothing."

Oh, that was really believable. "Jess." Kim nudged her in the ribs. "What's wrong with Riley? We don't even really know her."

"We know enough."

Kim sighed. She'd thought Jess had gotten past this. "What happened to Sam wasn't Riley's fault."

"I don't blame Riley for what happened. She was as much a victim as Sam." Jess rolled onto her side to face Kim. "It's just..." She blew out a breath. "Why Riley? I'm already worried sick about what might happen when Sam goes back to full duty. Every time she talks about Riley, it reminds me of the shooting, and that it's not an unsubstantiated fear. There's a very real, very concrete possibility that Sam could get hurt again." Her voice hitched. "And she might not be so lucky the next time."

"I'm afraid for her too, but you can't let the what-ifs rule your life." Kim rubbed Jess's shoulder. "You're not being fair to Riley. None of those things have anything to do with her as a person."

She lifted her arm and urged Jess to rest against her side with her head on Kim's shoulder. She stroked Jess's hair. "When I came to LA Metro, one of the first things I heard about was their tough-as-nails ER chief, and I wondered what I had gotten myself into. After my experience with Anna, could you blame me?"

"No." Jess placed a kiss on her chest.

"Then I met you. The attraction was immediate, but I was determined to fight it. I mean, another emotionally guarded, hard-ass ER chief, that was the last thing I needed in my life."

Jess sighed heavily as if she realized where this was going.

"I couldn't have been more wrong." Kim tightened her arm around Jess's back, pulling her closer. "Turns out, you were exactly what I needed."

Jess raised her head and kissed her. As she broke the kiss, a shaft of moonlight pierced a gap in the drapes and caught her eyes, making them seem to glow from within. "I love you. You're the best thing that ever happened to me."

"I love you too." Kim tenderly cupped Jess's cheek in her hand. "Despite how they met, who's to say that Riley won't turn out to be the best thing that has ever happened to Sam?"

Jess reclaimed her spot against Kim's shoulder. "Are you sure about Sam's feelings?"

"Judging by Sam's reactions and how she spoke of Riley, she cares about her deeply. And she was thrilled with the knowledge that Riley is gay." Kim hugged her close. "Of course, there's no knowing if Riley feels the same about Sam. She might see her as just a friend."

Jess stiffened. "Why wouldn't Riley be interested? Sam has a lot to offer someone."

Kim laughed to herself. *Ah. Big sister Jess makes an appearance.* "She might very well. Without seeing them together, I have no way of knowing."

Although Jess remained silent, Kim swore she could hear the gears turning in her head.

"I've got it." Jess rose up on an elbow and gazed down at Kim. "Halloween's just a few weeks away. Sam seemed bummed about missing the haunted house last year. Why don't we invite her to help with the foster family party at the community center? Then, we just happen to mention that we need another adult to help out and suggest that Riley might like to come?"

"Good idea." Kim was curious to see Sam with Riley. She grinned, remembering what fun it had been participating in the haunted house. *Wonder if I'll still fit in that Dracula costume.* She sobered when she remembered the costume Jess had worn. "Are you going to ask Sam to lend you her uniform so you can go as a cop again?"

A shudder rippled through Jess. "No." She sank down next to Kim and pulled her close as if she needed the comfort. "I'll come up with something else."

Kim tried to keep her relief from showing. After what had happened to Sam, she couldn't bear to see Jess in Sam's uniform, even if it was only as a Halloween prop.

Without warning, her earlier fatigue settled over her, weighing her down. Kim yawned.

"Enough talk for tonight," Jess said. "We can work out the details tomorrow."

A second, bigger yawn hit Kim.

Jess snuggled against her.

As Kim started to drift off to sleep, a stray thought surfaced. *Will Riley even want anything to do with us?*

CHAPTER 34

The dim lighting muted the vibrant colors of the mural that decorated the hallway in pediatrics. Although the sun was several hours from rising, a time when most children would be sleeping, the ward was far from quiet. The sounds of children in distress tore at Riley. *I don't know how Carol does it. I could never be a pediatrician.* She wanted to take each one of them into her arms and soothe away their pain.

"I swear, from now on, I'm going to scrub down in the shower with Betadine before I touch Jeremy," Denny said as they made their way out of the pediatric ward. He smacked a fist into his palm. "Hell, maybe I'll just use bleach. I know he was sick because of me."

"Stop beating yourself up. You know as well as I do, with Jeremy being a preemie, his immune system just isn't what it should be. He could have picked up a virus anywhere." Riley patted his shoulder. "Jeremy's doing great. He's come a long way since last Saturday."

When they reached the elevators, she pressed the up button.

Denny's shoulders slumped. "I know. It's just," his voice caught, "if anything were to happen to him, I—" Tears filled his eyes.

Riley's insides clenched at the thought of Denny losing his son. She had held the little boy in her arms and been filled with longing. For the first time, she wondered what it would be like to have a child of her own.

The elevator dinged, and the doors slid open.

She tugged Denny into the elevator. Once the doors closed, she rubbed his back. "Jeremy is going to be fine. Didn't Carol say he was most likely going to be released tomorrow?"

"Yeah." He blotted his eyes on his shirtsleeve. "I don't know why it's hitting me so hard now, when he's doing so much better."

Riley's thoughts immediately went to the shooting. At the time, she had blocked out what Keith had done to her and focused only on saving Sam. It wasn't until after the surgery that it had hit her like a ton of bricks. "I'm not surprised. You've spent the last week so focused on getting Jeremy better, you didn't have time to think of anything else."

The elevator doors opened on the floor where their offices were located.

"Grab your stuff and head home. I'll cover for you." Denny motioned her out in front of him before joining her in the hall. "Enjoy the weekend. Otherwise, I'll never catch up on the days I owe you."

"You don't owe me anything. It's not like you asked because you wanted extra time off. This is about your son." She stuffed her hands in the pockets of her lab coat. "I'm off tomorrow and Monday, so don't worry about me. You spend your time with your wife and son."

Denny tugged her into a bear hug before she could react. "Thank you. You don't know what this means to Carol and me."

Riley allowed the close contact for a moment, then gently pushed against his chest. "You're squishing me. And you're welcome."

"Sorry." Dropping his arms, he stepped back.

They resumed their progress toward their offices.

"I don't know about you, but all of a sudden I'm starving." Denny glanced at his watch. "Cafeteria isn't open. I'm going to grab something from the vending machine. You want anything?" he asked as they rounded the corner.

Having been in the OR for several hours before stopping by to see Jeremy, Riley was hungry, but the thought of anything from the vending machines turned her stomach. She wrinkled her nose. "I have some protein shakes in my office. I'll just grab one of those."

He shuddered. "How can you stand to drink those things?"

About to retort, Riley stopped short when she spotted the large Styrofoam cooler in front of her office door.

"Expecting a delivery?" Denny asked.

"No." She took a step closer.

He put a restraining hand on her arm. "Maybe we should call security."

"Let me get a better look first. I won't touch it."

His hand tightened on her lab coat sleeve. "Wait."

Riley shook off his hand. "Stay here." When she moved closer, she spotted a white envelope with her name handwritten on it attached to the cooler by teddy bear stickers. Hand-drawn on the lid of the cooler, just below the envelope, was a police badge. Riley grinned. *Sam.*

She had no doubt the cooler contained food. Sam was always trying to feed her. It had been so long since anyone cared for her like this. Her throat grew tight, and she blinked away the sting of tears.

"Riley? You okay?"

"Fine." She turned and started, finding Denny right at her elbow. "Everything's all right. It's from a friend." Why hadn't Sam let her know she was here? Her pleasure at finding the gift dimmed a little.

Denny eyed the ice chest. "You sure?"

"Positive."

Riley dug her office key out of her lab coat pocket and then opened the door. She reached in and flipped on the lights, then stooped to pick up the cooler. It was heavier than she expected. *How much did you put in here, enough to feed an army?*

"Need a hand?"

"I've got it." Riley set the cooler on her desk. She reached for the envelope, then hesitated, not wanting to read the note in front of Denny.

He settled on the edge of her desk. "Aren't you going to see what's in the cooler?" He clasped his hands together as if trying to resist the temptation of opening the container.

"Sure." Riley slowly lifted the lid. *Wow. She went all out.*

The ice chest was filled to the brim. She lifted out a package of six huge muffins, each a different flavor. Resting below those was a large bowl with a plastic lid. She peeled back the cover and peeked inside. The scent of fresh cantaloupe drifted up to fill her senses. Unable to resist, she popped a piece of the succulent melon into her mouth. *Mmm. So good.*

"Must be some friend. There's enough in there for a herd of people."

Riley started. She had been so engrossed in investigating the contents of the care package, she had forgotten Denny was there. She smiled. "Yeah. She is."

"This wouldn't happen to be from your friend Sam, would it?" Grinning, he pointed at the police badge on the lid.

"Yes. She's always trying to feed me."

He tilted his head and peered at her. "Is it working?"

Heat rose up her neck. Denny was forever trying to get her to eat more, but she had always resisted his efforts. Riley shrugged. "Yeah. I guess."

"Good." He put on his most pathetic expression. "Any chance you might share with a poor, starving, long-time friend?"

"Oh, poor thing." Rummaging in the cooler, she came up with some small plastic bowls and disposable forks. She filled one with cantaloupe and offered him the bowl and a fork.

Denny eyed the bowl, then looked longingly at the muffins. "Don't suppose I could have a muffin instead?"

"Not only a mooch, but a picky mooch." She laughed and pushed the package of muffins across the desk toward him.

"That's more like it." He tore into the package and grabbed a muffin.

Riley snagged the rejected bowl and settled in her desk chair to savor the cantaloupe.

Denny scarfed the muffin in four huge bites and patted his stomach. "Much better. Thanks." When he pushed the muffins back in her direction, he scattered a stack of computer printouts on her desk. "Sorry."

Panic struck. Riley wasn't ready to face the questions he might ask. Almost dropping her bowl, she lunged for the papers. "I'll get them."

"It was my fault. I've got them." Oblivious to her distress, he gathered up the papers.

Riley slumped back into her chair.

As he set the papers back on the desk, his gaze went to the top sheet. "You looking for a new place? I know a good realtor—" His brow scrunched, and he looked up. "These are for condo rentals."

Trepidation welled in Riley. Firmly pushing the feeling away, she stood and faced him across the desk. No more hiding. She stroked her fingers over the police badge Sam had drawn on the cooler lid, taking strength from just the thought of her. "I'm not living at the condo anymore. My uncle threw me out."

Denny shot to his feet and smacked his palm against the desk. "He can't do that. You own that place."

Riley sighed, not looking forward to admitting what an idiot she had been. "That's what I thought too. Turns out I was wrong."

He strode around the end of her desk to stand in front of her, his hands clenched at his sides. "What the hell is going on, Riley?"

"It's a long story." She motioned toward the couch across the room. "Let's go sit down." She didn't want to ruin Sam's thoughtful gift before she got a chance to enjoy it, so she took a moment to put her bowl of fruit back in the cooler. As she set it inside, she noticed the juice bottles tucked amongst the ice and held one up. "Want some juice?"

He waved off the offer.

She pulled out a bottle for herself and then replaced the lid. After joining Denny, she opened her juice and took a drink, more for something to do than because she was thirsty. She struggled for a way to start the conversation.

Denny rested his hand on her shoulder.

She fixed her gaze on the bottle in her hands.

"Tell me what happened?" he asked, all the anger gone from his voice.

"I have something I want to say first." She gazed into his eyes. Her heart fluttered in her chest like a bird trying to escape its cage. "I'm gay," she said before she could change her mind.

He blinked owlishly.

The words hung in the air between them.

Riley's stomach sank. She had hoped he would be okay with it. *Say something.*

Denny pumped his fist and grinned. "About damn time."

What! You knew? But how? Her gob-smacked reaction must have shown on her face.

"Carol and I have known for a long time. Since med school." His expression darkened. "You told those heartless SOBs." It wasn't a question.

She nodded slowly, still trying to process the fact that Denny had known she was gay for years.

"And they freaked out. Big surprise." Denny snorted. "That doesn't explain your condo."

As succinctly as she could, Riley explained what had happened. Not wanting to add fuel to the anger burning in Denny's eyes, she left out the part about her aunt slapping her.

By the time she finished, his face was brick-red, and he punched the air. "I knew I was right about that bastard."

"It's over. Forget about them." Even as she said it, she acknowledged that it was easier said than done. However irrational, there would always be that inner child in her that wished for the love neither her aunt nor her uncle was capable of giving.

"How can you say that?" Denny knifed his fingers through his bushy hair. "Bastards."

"They've taken enough of my life. I'm not giving them any more."

"You're right." He flopped against the back cushion of the couch. "Would you be okay with me telling Carol?"

"Of course." She straightened and met his gaze. "I'm done hiding."

He sat up and gripped her forearm. "I'm proud of you for finally being true to who you are. That takes a lot of courage."

If only I had done it sooner. Riley pushed away the regret that tried to claim her. Sam would kick her butt if she could hear her thoughts. She smiled and gave Denny a quick one-armed hug. "That means a lot to me." *That wasn't so bad.* While she knew it wasn't always going to be so easy, it felt great to finally be honest with Denny.

Remembering what he had said earlier, she frowned. "But if you've known since med school, why didn't you say anything?" During med school, she had shared a house with Denny and Carol as well as several other medical students, including Linda, her ex, but she never suspected that anyone knew about her and Linda.

"I wanted to, especially after you finally walked away from that witch, Linda." He scowled. "And I could see how miserable you were with the men your aunt kept shoving at you. But Carol insisted it was up to you to decide when you were ready to tell us."

"How did you know about Linda and me?" Riley asked. "We were so careful and never even went out together."

In the beginning, she had been relieved that Linda understood her fear of her uncle and aunt's reaction. It wasn't until later that she learned Linda had used her fear and naiveté to manipulate her. Even after all these years, the realization still stung.

Denny leaned back against the couch and stretched out his long legs. "Yeah, she shunned you in public, but in the house you weren't as circumspect as you thought."

The tips of her ears burned. There had been a few times they had almost been caught kissing by other housemates, but she had been sure that they covered it well. *Apparently not.*

"Once we began to suspect, it didn't take more than one time of seeing Linda creeping out of your room in the middle of the night to put two and two together."

All those years of hiding, and they had been for nothing. "I'm sorry I didn't tell you sooner. It's not that I didn't trust you. It's just—" Her voice caught in her throat.

He waved away the apology. "I know what you've been through, especially with your bitch of an aunt. You told me, that's what's important. The when doesn't matter." His brow furrowed. "Oh, wait. Now I get it."

"What?"

He pointed at the cooler. "It makes sense now. Sam. She's your girlfriend. I have to admit I was surprised when you told me about becoming friends. But girlfriends? This soon? Are you sure?"

I wish. She shoved the thought away, remembering once again Linda's constant harping about Riley's lack of sexual appeal. *You could never be what Sam wants.*

"Hey, it's okay," Denny said. "I'm hardly one to talk about fast. You know Carol and I were only together two months before we got married."

"Sam's just a friend. I'm staying with her until I find a place to live."

"Damn. I'm sorry." He smacked himself on the head. "Some friend I am. I didn't even ask where you're staying. You could have come to Carol and me. We would have been happy to have you."

"I know that, Denny." But she also knew she would have never done it. That realization gave her pause. How could she be so comfortable living with Sam after knowing her for only a few months, when she wouldn't be with friends she'd known for years?

"Riley?" Denny's voice drew her out of her contemplations.

"Sorry." She rubbed her tight neck muscles. "Guess those hours in the OR are catching up with me." She rose from the couch and stretched. "I'm going to grab something to eat while I have the chance."

Denny trailed her over to the desk. "Go home. I'll take over."

"No." She shook her head adamantly. "Carol and Jeremy need you." She pulled the lid off the cooler. "Why don't you take Carol some juice and a muffin? I'm sure she could use a break."

"You don't need—"

"Don't make me get tough with you." She handed over the food. "Now get out of here and let me eat in peace."

"Yes, ma'am." Denny threw her a mock salute. "And thank you."

"Give Jeremy a kiss for me."

"Sure thing."

As soon as the door closed behind him, she pulled the envelope off the cooler's lid and tore it open.

Riley,
Just in case you're up late and the cafeteria is closed, I wanted to give you an option besides those protein shakes. No offense, but those just don't qualify as food in my book. Hope you find something to your liking in the cooler.
Sam

About to set the note aside, she noticed the P.S. written in a different color ink.

P.S. I tried to call you just in case you might be free when I got there. Your phone went straight to voice mail.

So Sam had tried to contact her. Riley's heart lifted. She grabbed her cell phone to let Sam know she'd gotten her care package. When the screen lit up, she caught the time. It was way too early for a call, so she put the phone back in its holder, took a bowl of fruit and a muffin with her to the couch, and sank into the soft cushions.

You're going to make someone a wonderful girlfriend. Riley sighed. *Too bad it won't be me.*

CHAPTER 35

Sam shifted in her sleep, something drawing her toward wakefulness. Rolling onto her back, she blinked open sleep-crusted eyes and rubbed her hands across her face. A glance at the clock confirmed what she already suspected—it was too early on a Sunday morning to be awake. She listened for any sound, but the apartment was quiet. Intent on returning to sleep, she turned over, but something niggled at the edge of her senses. When she yawned, she caught a tantalizing scent.

Bacon? Sam drew in a deep breath and sniffed again but couldn't place the other aroma. Smelled good, whatever it was. Her stomach rumbled. She would never get back to sleep now. Grumbling, she threw back the covers and headed for the bathroom. She took care of business, then stepped out into the hall. The scent of bacon and what she now recognized as cinnamon intensified. She couldn't remember cooking odors wafting so strongly from a neighboring apartment before.

Following her nose, she padded barefoot into the living room and stopped dead in her tracks at the sight of her dinette table set for two people. One of her oversized coffee mugs was serving as an impromptu vase for a small bunch of flowers. *What the...?*

Riley stuck her head out of the kitchen. "Good morning." Before Sam could muster a greeting, she disappeared back into the kitchen and returned with a cup of coffee.

Sam took the mug wordlessly, her sleepy brain trying to make sense of what was going on. Riley had spent the last forty-eight hours at the hospital, yet here she was, dressed in freshly pressed slacks and her signature silk blouse, looking bright-eyed and bushy-tailed, apparently making breakfast.

The smile dropped from Riley's face.

"Thanks," Sam said belatedly. She inhaled the steam rising from the mug. "This smells good. What is it?"

"Hazelnut. Hope you like it."

Sam tasted the coffee. "It's great." Taking her time, she took several more long sips, not only to enjoy the taste, but to give her brain a chance to process this unexpected development.

Because of the hours Riley worked, Sam had barely seen hide nor hair of her in the two weeks they had been roommates. This was the first time that Riley had acted as if she actually lived there. Although Sam had invited her to move in, she braced herself, determined to fight the feelings that were sure to come with this casual invasion of her space.

They never came. The only thing Sam's brain seemed interested in was the enticing aromas emanating from the kitchen.

"I, umm..." Riley fidgeted. "I hope you don't mind. I made breakfast." A brief smile flashed. "I'm celebrating."

Sam returned the smile and set her coffee cup down on the table. Unable to resist, she captured Riley's hand. "What's the occasion?"

"I came out to my friend Denny."

"Good for you. I take it things went well."

"It went great." Riley beamed, her smile fairly splitting her cheeks.

Before Sam realized what she was doing, she swept Riley into a tight embrace. "Congratulations. That's wonderful." The scent of Riley's shampoo teased her senses.

Riley wrapped her arms around Sam's waist. "Thanks." Her cheek pressed against Sam's braless breast.

Arousal singed through Sam. *Oh God.* She bit back a groan as her nipples hardened. A flush heating her face, she dropped her arms.

Riley held on for an interminable second or two longer, then stepped back.

Caught off guard by the strength of her own reaction, Sam glanced at Riley.

She stared wide-eyed up at Sam, the rapid rise and fall of her chest clearly visible.

Does she feel it too? Crossing her arms over her chest, Sam willed her body to behave. *It doesn't matter if she does. You're the last thing Riley needs. You'll just end up hurting her.*

"What're we having?" Sam asked in hopes of taking attention away from what was happening between them.

Riley didn't answer for a moment. Her expression closed off, then she roughly shook her head. Offering what looked like a forced smile, she said, "Cinnamon raisin pancakes with maple syrup, bacon, and fresh raspberries."

Sam's stomach growled loudly.

Riley laughed, and the tension between them dissipated. She motioned Sam over to the table. "Sit down. I'll bring everything out."

"Give me a minute to get dressed, then I'll help."

"No need for that. Sit." Riley turned on her heel and returned to the kitchen.

Sam chased the last traces of syrup on her plate with her final piece of pancake. She popped the bite into her mouth and smacked her lips. "Wow. That was really good. Thanks."

"Bet you didn't think I could cook."

Sam had thought exactly that but had kept the remark to herself. *The way she usually is around food, her freak aunt sure as hell didn't teach her to cook.*

Riley arched an eyebrow. "No comment, huh?"

Sam flushed.

It was apparently all the confirmation Riley needed. She laughed. "Well, honestly, for the most part I can't." Her gaze went distant for a moment, and her smile faltered. "I haven't made breakfast like this in more years than I can count."

"Well, out of practice or not, you did a wonderful job. You must've had a good teacher. That was delicious."

"Thanks. My mom always made a big Sunday breakfast, and I helped from the time I was old enough to sit on a stool at the kitchen counter." Riley ducked her head. "Although I did kind of have to look things up."

After seeing what a decisive, competent woman Riley was at work, Sam was always surprised to see her so unsure in private. She slid her fingers down Riley's arm. "Well, you can cook breakfast for me any time."

A stunning smile lit Riley's face.

There's the smile I wanted to see. Sam didn't quite understand why she got such enjoyment out of making Riley smile, but there was no denying that she did.

Riley turned away, trying to hide a yawn.

Sam rose from the table. "You cooked. I'll clean up. Why don't you lie down for a while?" She glanced at the clock on the wall. "You've got time for a short nap before we have to leave."

"You don't have to do that. I'm fine." Riley pushed back her chair. A yawn caught her, giving lie to her words, and she flushed.

Shooing her toward the living room, Sam said, "Go sit down. I've got this."

Riley shook her head and firmly held her ground.

And she thinks I'm stubborn. Sam ground her teeth together. "Come on. We'll do it together."

Riley had cleaned up as she prepared breakfast, so it only took a few minutes for the two of them to take care of the remaining dishes. They moved about the small kitchen together as if they had done it many times before.

As Sam was setting up the coffee maker, out of the corner of her eye, she caught Riley stifling another yawn. She turned and put her hands on Riley's shoulders. "Go sit down." When Riley didn't move, Sam guided her to the doorway. "I'll bring the coffee."

Riley looked over her shoulder, a protest forming on her lips.

Sam placed her finger on Riley's lips. She froze for a second, barely resisting the urge to stroke her finger across her soft lips. *What's wrong with you this morning?* She jerked back as if burned.

The light in Riley's eyes dimmed, and her shoulders slumped. "Okay. I'll be in the living room."

Sam stared at her retreating form for a few seconds, then shrugged and returned to the kitchen.

Several minutes later, she carried two cups of coffee into the living room.

Riley was slumped against the arm of the couch, her head resting at an unnatural angle.

Poor thing. She's exhausted. Sam set the cups down on the end table. She was hesitant to wake Riley, but she didn't want her to have a stiff neck from sleeping in such an awkward position. Keeping an eye on Riley to make sure she didn't wake, she moved the coffee table out of the way as quietly as she could. She knelt in front of the couch, slid one arm under Riley's neck and the other across her back, then eased her into a more supine position.

As she withdrew, Riley caught her arm and pulled it tightly against her chest. A sigh fluttered past her lips.

She must think I'm Annie. Sam gently extricated her arm from Riley's grasp.

Riley mewed in her sleep. "Sam," she breathed out on a whisper.

The sexy little sound kick-started Sam's libido. Her heart tripped double time. She stared at Riley.

Her brow furrowed, Riley shifted in her sleep and whimpered.

"Shh. Sleep now. I'm right here." Sam leaned down and placed a lingering kiss on Riley's forehead.

While her eyes remained closed, a smile blossomed on Riley's face. "Sam," she murmured again.

Sam moved away before she could give in to the temptation to take Riley in her arms. Settling on the loveseat, she tried to rub away the strange sensation in her chest. Her gaze lingered on Riley, and she sighed. No sense wishing for things that could never be.

CHAPTER 36

Riley glanced at the clock on the dash. It showed just before two in the afternoon. *I can't believe she let me sleep that long.* She scowled at Sam, then turned her gaze back to the road.

"You were exhausted and needed the rest," Sam said as if she had been privy to Riley's thoughts.

Riley flushed and kept her gaze focused out the windshield. She gripped the steering wheel, resisting the urge to argue, especially since she knew Sam was right.

"It was no big deal to reschedule for a later time. The property agent actually seemed relieved not to have to meet at nine o'clock on a Sunday morning." Sam raked her overly long bangs out of her eyes. "Look, I'm sorry if I overstepped my bounds. I just couldn't see where a couple of hours would hurt."

"No. I'm sorry. You're right. I was exhausted." Riley blindly reached across the console and patted Sam's leg. "It feels nice to be cared for. Just not something I'm used to." *That was officially pathetic.* Her ears burned, and she was sure her freckles must be glowing like fireflies in a jar. "Forgive me?"

"Nothing to forgive." Sam's hand covered Riley's before she could withdraw. "I'll always be there to look out for you," she said, her voice filled with conviction.

Riley's heart swelled with the realization that she hadn't messed up things between them. Sam had seemed a little distant when Riley woke up from her unplanned nap. She had worried that

Sam sensed her arousal during their impromptu hug that morning.

Suddenly aware of the tension in the muscled thigh beneath her hand, Riley tugged her hand free. She turned to smile at Sam, only to find her staring intently at her. Riley was caught by the swirling emotions in her silvery-blue eyes.

Sam quickly looked away.

Riley wrenched her gaze back to the road. Questions ricocheted through her mind. Did Sam feel something for her beyond friendship? Hope flared, then died a sudden death. *Don't kid yourself. You've seen Marina. You could never compete with someone like her.*

"Turn left in two hundred feet," the navigation system announced. A few moments later the unit beeped twice. "Arriving at destination."

Thankful for the interruption, Riley pulled into the complex. She stopped the car and glanced at Sam. All the emotion that had been so apparent in her eyes moments before was gone, making Riley wonder if she had imagined it.

"I don't see any open spaces," Sam said. "That's a problem with living downtown—parking is always going to be at a premium."

Forcing her mind back to the business at hand, Riley scanned the lot. Even the guest spaces were taken. She checked her watch and frowned, hating the idea of being late for an appointment.

"Does the condo come with a parking space as part of the rent?"

"I have no idea."

A horn honked behind them.

Riley pulled over to let the other car pass, then made a second loop around the complex parking lot. Luck was on her side, and a visitor spot opened up in front of the building.

Riley trailed after the property agent, Mr. Reynolds, her gaze sweeping the condo that was still furnished with the departing tenant's belongings. The modernistic furniture reminded her of her aunt and uncle's condo. After just two weeks at Sam's comfortable apartment, the stark furnishings turned her off. *Ignore them. You're interested in the condo, not the contents.* She glanced back at Sam and caught the look of distaste on her face.

Sam noticed her perusal, and her face immediately became an unreadable mask.

Ah, her cop face.

Riley forced her attention back to Mr. Reynolds, who was prattling on about the condo's many attributes. She tried to work up some enthusiasm for the place.

By the time they returned to the living room, she knew this wasn't the home for her. It stirred too many bad memories. She forced a polite smile and faced Mr. Reynolds. "If you'll excuse us for a moment." Tugging on Sam's sleeve, she guided her toward the balcony. "What do you think?" she asked, her voice low.

Sam glanced around, then down at Riley, her expression carefully neutral. "Do you like it?"

"No. Reminds me too much of—" Riley caught herself. "Where I used to live. No warmth."

Sam grinned. "Whew." She wiped imaginary sweat off her forehead. "Glad to hear you say that. I can't stand the place. I wasn't looking forward to visiting you here."

She elbowed Sam. "Why didn't you say something?"

"I'm just here to check that the building looks safe and the pipes don't leak." Sam's expression turned serious. "But no matter what I think, the decision is yours."

Riley smiled. "Then let's see what else he has to offer." She had a spring in her step as she headed for Mr. Reynolds. It felt wonderful not to have her opinion belittled, as her aunt was prone to do.

Sam leaned against the island that separated the kitchen from the main living area and let her gaze sweep the room. All the places they had seen so far looked alike. Stark white walls, a large expanse of glass, lots of chrome and marble, but not a trace of warmth. Even the hardwood floors appeared uninviting and cold. The wood was highly polished but without the richness she usually associated with wood floors.

It was more than just the condos, Sam acknowledged. As they had ridden the elevators and walked the halls of four different complexes around the downtown area, she had felt the assessing stares of the residents. Not one had offered more than a restrained nod, and most not even that. While her apartment complex was nowhere near as swanky as the places Riley was considering, at least most everyone was friendly, and there was a sense of community.

Gazing out onto the balcony, she watched Riley with Mr. Reynolds. He was gesturing expansively at the cityscape laid out as far as the eye could see. When Riley leaned against the balcony railing and smiled, appearing to enjoy the view, Sam sighed. *Guess this might be the one.* She renewed her vow to keep her mouth shut and support Riley's choice, whatever condo she picked.

"Knock. Knock," a woman called out.

Sam turned.

Two strangers stood in the open doorway of the condo. The woman was blond, well dressed, and quite beautiful while her male companion was dark-haired and boyishly handsome.

"We saw the door open and wanted to say hello," the woman said as they entered the condo. "We live next door."

Finally someone friendly. Maybe this place was okay after all.

The man smiled and took a slow perusal of Sam's body before finally making it to her face.

Or maybe not. Sam glared at him.

He smiled and had the audacity to wink at her.

Sam crossed her arms over her chest and straightened to her full height. She had dealt with her share of overzealous Lotharios, but the thought of Riley being exposed to his roving eyes sparked her ire.

"Are you the new tenant?" the woman asked, apparently oblivious to her companion's lustful gaze.

Mr. Reynolds and Riley came back in before Sam could answer.

Her protective instincts flaring, Sam strode up to Riley, draped an arm across her shoulders, and guided her across the room.

Riley's eyebrow arched, but she remained at Sam's side.

"These are the neighbors from next door," Sam said when they reached the couple. "Sorry. I didn't get your names."

The woman stared at Sam's arm where it rested across Riley's shoulders. Her mouth puckered as if she had bitten into a persimmon.

Aw crap. A homophobe. Then Sam caught the look on the man's face. An eager glint showed as he undressed her and Riley with his eyes. In trying to protect Riley, she had just made things much worse. *Damn it!*

Riley stiffened next to her.

Sam tightened her arm around Riley's shoulders and drew her closer.

"Sorry we bothered you." The woman's voice was wooden. She whipped around and took two steps toward the door. When her companion didn't immediately follow, she turned back and grabbed his arm. "Let's go."

The condo door slammed behind them.

Sam flinched and hastily pulled her arm from Riley's shoulders. It took her a moment to gather the nerve to look at Riley. She fully expected to see anger lurking in Riley's eyes.

Riley tilted her head and peered up at her. The only thing in her eyes was confusion.

"Please accept my apologies, Dr. Connolly," Mr. Reynolds said. "Not all the residents are like that." He threw a scowl at the door. "I hope you'll reconsider."

Riley shook her head. "It has nothing to do with the tenants. As I told you, it's just not what I'm looking for." She offered her hand. "I appreciate your time."

She doesn't want the place? While Sam was relieved, she knew it didn't get her off the hook.

Mr. Reynolds shook Riley's hand. "If you change your mind, please let me know. Rentals are limited, but there are several much nicer condos for sale in the complexes we visited today."

Riley nodded but made no comment.

Anxiety twisted Sam's stomach. The ride down in the elevator seemed interminable.

Mr. Reynolds droned on, trying to convince Riley what a good investment buying a condo would be with the current housing market.

Sam wished he would just shut up. She had bigger concerns, such as explaining to Riley what had happened and then apologizing.

When she felt Riley's hand on the small of her back, Sam looked down in surprise into Riley's smiling visage. The tension leaked out of her like pressure being released from an overinflated tire.

The elevator dinged, and the doors slid open. After saying good-bye to Mr. Reynolds, they made their way to the car.

Sam followed Riley to the driver side of the vehicle. When the lock clicked, Sam opened the door.

Riley smiled up at her. "You're the passenger. I thought I'm the one who's supposed to do that for you?"

Sam shrugged. It had been hard for her to turn over control and let Riley drive. She motioned for her to get in. "My pleasure."

"Thank you." Riley gave Sam's hand a brief squeeze before sliding into the driver's seat.

After closing the door, Sam walked around the car and got in on the passenger side. She turned in her seat as far as her long legs would allow and faced Riley. "I want to explain about what I did upstairs. I—" Riley's hand on her arm stopped her.

"You mean the part where you tried to keep me from ending up with a homophobic neighbor and her sleazy, womanizing, whatever he was to her?"

"Yeah. That. Well, I actually didn't know about the homophobic part, but the guy was blatantly ogling me when they first came in. I just figured if he thought we were together, he wouldn't bother you." Sam grimaced. "But it backfired."

Anger blazed across Riley's face. "That bastard. He's got a lot of nerve doing that to you." She turned and grabbed the door handle as if she planned to storm back into the building.

Sam put a restraining hand on Riley's arm and urged her back around. "Hey. It's okay. I've dealt with his type before."

Riley's eyes shone like living emeralds. "It is not okay. It will never be okay."

Never had a woman defended her with such passionate fervor. It was intoxicating. The intensity of Riley's gaze held Sam transfixed.

Unaware of having moved, Sam found herself face to face with Riley, so close that soft breath brushed over her lips, making her shiver.

Riley's gaze darted between Sam's lips and her eyes. With trembling fingers, she stroked Sam's face.

As Sam leaned into the touch, her eyes slid closed. Impossibly soft lips brushed hers as delicately as the touch of a butterfly's wings. A groan escaped her lips.

Riley kissed her again, deepening the contact.

The trill of a cell phone sounded as shrill as a fire alarm in the heated atmosphere.

Her heart pounding, Sam slumped back against her seat. Her body pulsed with arousal. *What the hell do you think you're doing?* She struggled to regain her composure.

Daring a glance at Riley, she found her staring straight ahead, her face a blank mask. She might have thought her totally unaffected by what had happened, if not for the flush on Riley's neck and face and the rapid rise and fall of her chest.

The insistent blare of Sam's cell phone refused to be ignored. As she jerked the phone from its holder, she wondered if she should thank the caller or curse them.

Riley's body thrummed with arousal. The sound of the phone grated on her nerves like a sour note across the strings of a violin.

Sam answered the call. "Hey, sis."

Of course it's her. Rarely moved to profanity, Riley mentally cursed Jess McKenna, long and colorfully. Her anger did little to rein in the desire singing through her. *God. I actually kissed her.*

Several times during the day, Riley thought she had detected a hint of interest lurking in Sam's gaze, but each time she had passed it off to her own wishful thinking. Then she had seen the unmistakable desire burning in Sam's silvery-blue eyes, and it had been her undoing. Just the memory of it was enough to kick her pulse into high gear again. She wanted to grab Sam by the shirt, pull her into a kiss, and satisfy the fiery need that had been painted across Sam's beautiful face. *And then what?* Reality hit like a dash of cold water in the face.

A memory from her past shattered the moment. Riley could hear Linda's voice as if she were right next to her: "I give up." Linda rolled away from her, leaving Riley aching. "If you want to get off, you'll have to do it yourself. Your body is about as exciting as a wooden plank."

"Riley?"

Torn from the painful memories, she realized Sam must have called to her several times. With Linda's words echoing in her head, she couldn't bring herself to meet Sam's gaze. "Uh, sorry." She started the car. "We should get going. I'll drop you at the apartment. I've got some other business that I need to take care of." The lie was bitter on her tongue.

As she pulled out of the parking spot, she caught a glimpse of the bewildered look on Sam's face. Guilt plucked at her. She cursed herself for kissing Sam. *Be glad you got interrupted before you humiliated yourself. Sam might think she wants you now, but if she saw you naked, that would change in an instant.*

By the time they reached Sam's apartment, the silence between them had grown oppressive. Riley pulled into the lot, but didn't park. "I'll...um...I'll see you later."

Sam turned in her seat. "Riley—"

"I have to go."

Sam slumped in her seat.

For a moment, Riley didn't think she was going to get out of the car.

Finally, Sam opened the door and got out, then leaned down to peer at Riley. "Will you be long?"

Riley shrugged. She didn't have any plans; she just needed to get away for a while.

Riley stared out unseeingly; the beauty of the ocean vista was lost to the turmoil of her thoughts. Things were no clearer now than they had been when she dropped Sam off several hours earlier. Linda's vicious words continued to reverberate through her mind.

It hadn't always been like that between them. In the early days of their relationship, Linda had seemed to enjoy touching her, bringing her to orgasm. *It was all a lie.* She had been so excited to be with a woman for the first time, it barely took a touch, and she went off like a rocket. During the latter part of their short relationship, things had changed. Linda was more than happy to have Riley please her but rarely reciprocated.

Riley shoved away the distressing memories. None of that mattered. She had to decide what to do about Sam. Though she had faith that Sam wouldn't be cruel, she couldn't help feeling Sam would react to her body the same as Linda. She clearly remembered Sam's words to Darcy: "I'm interested in women. I'm not into boys." Many times, Linda had told Riley that she had the body of a prepubescent boy.

No matter how many times she went over every scenario, there seemed to be only one solution. *I kissed her. I need to make this right.* The thought of seeing the desire in Sam's eyes die was more than she could bear. *You can never be what she wants.* Saddened by her decision, she made her way back to Sam's apartment and eased open the door, a part of her hoping that Sam had decided to go out.

Sam was sitting on the couch with a book in her lap. "Hi. Get everything taken care of?"

She nodded, unable to meet Sam's eyes. Her courage failed her. *I'll talk to her tomorrow.* "Well. Good night." She made a beeline for her room.

"Wait a second, Riley."

Riley reluctantly turned back.

"Did you get anything to eat? I was going to order a pizza."

"No, thank you. I'm not hungry." She fled to her room. After closing the door behind her, she leaned against it. *Coward.*

CHAPTER 37

Y ou've stalled long enough. Knowing that Riley had the day off, Sam had stopped after work to get a haircut and then pick up a few things at the grocery store. She transferred the bags to one hand so she could open the door. As hard as she tried to convince herself otherwise, she still felt the sting of Riley's rejection after their unexpected kiss the day before. *It's better this way. She's not even your type.* Sam imagined staring into Riley's vivid green eyes as she gave her the no-strings-attached speech. She cringed and rubbed at a dull ache behind her breastbone.

Sam scanned the living room. There was no sign of Riley. Her gaze happened on the small bouquet of flowers sticking out of one of the bags. Earlier, as she'd walked past the floral displays in the grocery store, the thought of Riley's smile at receiving flowers had made her reach for the bouquet.

She carried the grocery bags into the kitchen, tugged the flowers from the bag, and tossed them in the trash. She never should have bought the damn things. *Talk about sending mixed messages.*

After putting the groceries away, she headed for her bedroom to get changed and worked open the top buttons of her shirt.

The door to the bathroom swung open as she passed by.

The sight of Riley, wrapped in nothing but a towel, halted Sam in her tracks.

Riley stumbled back, her eyes going wide.

"Sorry, didn't mean to scare you."

Riley's gaze locked on Sam's chest, then her hair, and the color drained from her face. She clutched at the door frame with one hand; her other hand flew to the base of her throat.

Alarm shafted through Sam. *What the hell?* "Riley?"

Riley's mouth worked, but no sound escaped. Her eyes had a hazy, unfocused look.

One hand outstretched, Sam took a step toward her. "Easy. It's okay."

Whimpering, Riley clutched the towel to her chest. "No. God. Please." Her eyes rolled back in her head as her knees buckled.

Fuck! Sam dove forward. She managed to wrap her arms around Riley before she could hit the floor. As Sam fought to keep them both upright, she smacked her back on the edge of the door frame. Cursing, she looked down into Riley's slack face. Pale red lashes rested against bone-white skin. Even her freckles looked washed out. Panic held Sam frozen like an ice sculpture in a winter garden. *Get it together, McKenna. Freak out later.* She mentally shook herself as if to break away the encasing ice, slid her arm beneath Riley's knees, and easily lifted her limp body into her arms.

Cradling her precious cargo against her, she carried Riley into the bedroom and gently laid her on the bed. That was when she realized Riley's towel had come loose and gaped open. Heat crept up her neck. She jerked her gaze away from all the creamy skin on display. *Help. Don't ogle.* She quickly righted the towel, trying to ignore the feel of the silky skin under her fingertips. She pulled the comforter over Riley, then sat on the edge of the bed.

Riley groaned, her eyes fluttering open. She tried to sit up.

"No." Sam put a gently restraining hand on her bare shoulder. "Don't move."

"What happened?" Riley asked.

"That's what I was going to ask you. You fainted."

Riley's gaze went distant for a moment, then her mouth formed a silent "Oh." Emotion swirling in her eyes, she touched the sleeve of Sam's shirt. Her hand shook as it rose toward Sam's hair, but she shuddered and pulled her fingers away before making contact.

What's going on? Sam longed to take Riley into her arms but hesitated because of how strained things had been between them. "Riley? Talk to me."

Tears trembled at the corners of Riley's eyes.

"Please. Tell me what's wrong."

Riley swallowed heavily. "I...um... When I saw you standing there, dressed like that, with your hair..." She motioned toward Sam's head. "I had a flashback of the shooting."

Sam looked down at her police uniform, then ran her hand over her freshly shorn hair. Realization dawned. *Oh, damn.* This was the first time Riley had seen her in uniform since the shooting. To make matters worse, Sam had her hair cut into the style she had worn prior to the shooting. The one-two punch must have triggered the flashback.

"I'm so sorry. I didn't even think."

"You didn't do anything wrong." The comforter held tightly against her chest with one hand, Riley sat up, despite Sam's immediate protest. She stroked Sam's arm. "It just caught me off guard." She tugged on the short sleeve of Sam's uniform. "I need to get used to seeing you dressed like this."

I throw you into a flashback so bad you faint, and you comfort me. You are one amazing woman, Riley

Connolly. "I'll make sure I give you fair warning next time." Sam frowned. "But it will be a while before my hair grows out."

A bright smile lit Riley's face. "Actually, I really like your hair. It looks great."

"Thanks." An unaccustomed flush heated Sam's face, and she scolded herself for blushing like a teenager at a compliment from a woman.

Riley's smile faltered. "And I'll get used to the uniform...eventually."

Sam stood. "Well, you've seen more than enough of it today. But I do want to show you something." If she could alleviate even a small portion of Riley's fear, she was determined to do so. She turned away to unbutton her shirt, pulled it off, and turned back to show Riley the bulletproof vest underneath.

Riley wasn't looking at her. Instead, she kept her gaze fixed on the comforter that covered her. "This isn't my room," she said, confusion evident in her voice.

Sam looked around as if seeing the room for the first time. Without thought, she'd brought Riley into her bedroom—which meant that Riley was lying half-naked in Sam's bed. *Don't even think about it.* That command to her libido was about as successful as hoping she could ever get the image of Riley in only a towel out of her head. Arousal washed through her. She ruthlessly shoved it away and forced herself to meet Riley's gaze, praying none of her feelings showed. "No. It's mine. All I thought about was taking care of you."

Riley slid from the bed, her hands clutched around the top of her towel, holding it in place. The oversized towel that would have covered Sam to mid-thigh hung down past Riley's knees. She stepped close to Sam and peered up at her. "Thank you for keeping me safe. Again." She released one hand from the towel and touched the bulletproof vest just above her left breast. "You always wear this, right?"

Sam placed her hand on top of Riley's and pressed it to her vest-covered chest. "Always."

As it had in the car, the air between them became charged.

Riley pulled away first, breaking the spell. "I should get dressed." Her face pinking, she hitched her towel higher.

"Wait," Sam said before Riley could disappear into her own bedroom. After the fright they had both had, Sam wasn't ready to let her out of her sight for very long.

Riley turned back.

"I was going to make some dinner. You hungry?"

Riley hesitated, then smiled. "I could eat."

"Good. Just give me a few minutes to change, and I'll get dinner started."

"All right." Riley stepped into the hall.

As if drawn of its own accord, Sam's gaze went to Riley's towel-draped backside. Arousal flared. Sam growled under her breath and stomped toward her bathroom to take a shower. A very cold shower.

Riley tugged down the sleeves of her sweater as she stepped into the living room. It was comfortably warm in the apartment, but she was feeling exposed after ending up in Sam's bed in nothing but a towel. Heat flashed through her at the thought.

It had been easier when she thought her feelings were unrequited. Now that she knew Sam desired her, she had to remind herself over and over that it would never work. Even if Sam wanted her now, that would change the minute they got naked. Resolve filled Riley. She would set things right, no matter the cost to herself. She needed Sam in her life.

"Everything okay?" Sam asked.

Riley started at finding her so close.

Sam touched her arm. "Sorry. I seem to keep scaring you today."

Riley's gaze lingered on Sam's beautiful face. When Sam's eyes darkened, she took a step closer, longing to feel Sam's soft lips against hers again. *Stop it. Just stop it!* Taking a deep breath, she stepped back. "We need to talk."

Huh? Sam knew Riley had spoken, but the words weren't registering. She forced her gaze away from Riley's eyes and tried to shake off the trance she had fallen into. Even though she knew she shouldn't get involved with Riley, her body didn't listen to reason. "I'm sorry. What did you say?"

"We need to talk."

Sam grimaced. No good conversation ever started that way. Her heart rate picked up as another thought struck. *Is she going to move back to a hotel?* While a part of her realized it would probably be a good idea, a much larger part, despite the tension between them, wanted Riley to stay—period. That realization spiked her heartbeat into overdrive.

"Sam?"

She flushed. "Right. Um... You want to eat first?"

Riley shook her head.

"Okay," Sam said. "Let me grab a glass of wine." *Maybe a couple of them.* "Then we'll talk." She motioned toward the living room. "I'll be right there. Would you like some wine?"

"Sure. That would be good."

When Sam returned from the kitchen, she found Riley wedged in a corner of the couch, her knees drawn up to her chest. The sadness in her eyes tugged at Sam's heart. *This isn't going to be good.* She set the wine on the coffee table, then sat down on the opposite end of the couch. "So what did you want to talk about?"

"I wanted to apologize for how I acted yesterday." Riley swallowed visibly. "After I kissed you." She wrapped her arms around her knees, hugging them close to her chest. "You didn't deserve that. And I want you to know that it's not you, it's me."

Hearing the words she had said many times herself, Sam winced. *How can you think that? That's got to be your bitch of an aunt talking. You're a wonderful, special woman.* Sam bit her tongue to keep from saying the words. It would only make things harder. Whatever her reasons, it was better to let Riley be the one to do this.

"Your friendship means so much to me. I don't want to lose that." Riley's head dropped, and she stared at her knees. "It would be better if," her voice broke, "if we stayed just friends."

Just friends. No matter how much Sam knew this was how things had to be, the words still stung. She had never expected to find herself on the receiving end of this speech. Her thoughts went to the women she had said those exact words to, having convinced herself that they weren't hurtful and she was just being honest and clear in her intent. *You were delusional.*

"I understand." And Sam did. She had taken a chance with Christy, and as soon as they became exclusive, those same old feelings of being smothered had surfaced. *I won't do that to Riley. She deserves someone who can be totally committed to her.* She rubbed at an ache in her chest, sighing to herself, then reached across the couch and offered her hand. "Friends it is."

Riley took her hand.

When their gaze met, Sam swore she could see regret lurking in Riley's dull green eyes. *Wishful thinking.* She let go of Riley's hand and stood. "Well, I guess I should go start dinner."

"Nothing for me," Riley said. "I'm not hungry."

Sam shook her head. She forced a smile, determined to not make things any harder on Riley than they had to be. "No can do. As your friend, it's my job to see that you don't go hungry." She held out her hand. "Come on, my friend. I'll teach you how to make my famous spaghetti."

Riley put her hand in Sam's and allowed herself to be pulled from the couch. A tentative smile appeared on her face.

Sam smiled back, and the tightness in her chest eased. *I can do this. I can be her friend.* The alternative of not having Riley in her life at all wasn't acceptable, but that didn't stop the part of her, deep down, that wished she had more to offer Riley than friendship.

Riley kept her gaze firmly on her plate. *You can't tell her you want to just be friends and then ogle her.* Several times while they made dinner, she had caught herself staring at Sam's breasts. She needed to find an apartment soon.

"No good?"

"No." Her cheeks burned. "I mean, yes. It's good."

"Glad to hear it." Sam grinned. "You never know what you'll get when you're breaking in a new cook."

It hurt to realize that Sam was fine with just being friends, but Riley knew it was of her own doing. "Well, I was just following instructions. So if the instructions were bad..." She arched an eyebrow.

"Perish the thought." Sam laughed. "Any luck on the apartment front today?"

See, she wants you out of here too. Riley frowned. "No. Sorry. The places weren't much different than the ones we looked at yesterday."

"There's no rush. Take your time and find the right place."

Riley was taken aback by the wave of relief that washed through her.

"Would you consider someplace that's not downtown?"

"Um... Sure. I guess."

Sam shrugged. "If you prefer downtown, that's okay."

That's when it dawned on Riley that she had unconsciously considered only places her aunt would have found acceptable. Would she ever get away from that woman's influence? "No. What other areas would you suggest? I have to be able to reach the hospital in thirty minutes, no matter what time of day or night."

"Well, I was just thinking. After what happened at that last condo we looked at, maybe you'd prefer to live in a gay-friendly or gay-centric area of the city."

"I never thought of that. I didn't even know there were such places."

"You bet there are." Sam grinned. "You're living in one right now."

When she took a moment to think about it, Riley realized she had seen a lot of same-sex couples as she came and went from the apartment. "So where should I look?"

"Let me fire up the computer, and I'll show you."

For a moment, Riley wondered if there were any open apartments in Sam's complex, but she squashed the thought immediately. *Too close to temptation.*

CHAPTER 38

Riley leaned back against the couch and tried to catch her breath. Tears of laughter ran down her face. Each new story Sam regaled her with was more outrageous than the one before. "You're making that up."

"I'm not. I swear." Sam crossed her heart. "She was standing on her front porch, naked as the day she was born, holding out these huge breasts and shouting, 'who wouldn't love these?'" Laugh lines appeared at the corners of her eyes. "Did I mention she had bright red hair...at least on her head."

On her head? Oh! Heat shot up Riley's neck. She mock-scowled when Sam laughed.

"Anyway, the woman was really starting to draw a crowd of neighbors. It was one of my first patrols on my own after my probation period was over, and I was worried I'd have to call for backup. The last thing I wanted to do was have to call for help."

Riley couldn't blame her. She didn't like to ask for help either. After thinking about it for a moment, she realized that wasn't as true as it had been. She was finding it increasingly easy to ask Sam for help. As she turned more fully toward Sam, her knee bumped the empty popcorn bowl on the couch between them. She set it on the coffee table. "What did you do?"

"I headed for the porch, figuring the quicker I got her in the house the better. As I got close, I could smell the booze on her, like she'd bathed in it." Sam's nose wrinkled. "Anyway, she got quiet as I walked up. So I'm thinking, 'Great, this won't be so bad.'" She rolled her eyes. "Typical rookie naiveté."

"She didn't go quietly, huh?"

"No. I was being careful, keeping my eyes on her as I went up the porch steps. I was sure she didn't have a weapon... I was wrong."

Oh no. Riley's stomach sank. She grabbed Sam's arm.

The little half smirk on Sam's face should have warned her. "Yeah. She grabbed me by the front of my shirt and smashed my face into her huge breasts. She was an older woman, but she was strong. I almost smothered before I could get away."

"Oh. You scared me there for a minute." Riley shoved at Sam's shoulder. "Now I know you're making this up."

"I'm not." She held her hands out quite a distance from her own chest. "Those things were dangerous weapons."

"Did you arrest her for assaulting a police officer with her lethal breasts?"

Sam's eyes sparkled. She tipped back her head and laughed. "No. I finally managed to get her into the house and, thankfully, into a robe. I never did find out what set her off, but she promised to stay inside and not expose herself to the neighbors, so I let it go." She stood and brushed salt off her pants. "All that popcorn made me thirsty. You want some water?"

"No, thanks. You go ahead."

A cell phone rang.

Dang. That was the end of a fun evening. Riley was on back-up call. She leaned over the arm of the couch and reached for her phone where it rested next to Sam's on the end table. At the next ring, she realized it wasn't her phone that was lit up.

"Sam. That's your phone."

Sam popped out of the kitchen and grabbed her phone. "Hey, sis." She flopped down on the couch.

Riley rose, intending to give her some privacy. When Sam looked up and caught her gaze, Riley mouthed, "Good night."

Sam shook her head and held up one finger.

Riley sank back onto the couch.

Sam listened for several moments, then a bright smile spread across her face. "Of course I would. That would be great. Do you need my uniform and gear again?"

What was that all about? Riley caught herself leaning a little closer.

"I have no idea." Sam's gaze cut to Riley. "I don't know, Jess. I—" She shook her head as if Jess could see her. "No. Don't." Sam sighed. "Hey, Kim." She scowled at the phone but listened to whatever Kim was saying. "Okay. I will. I'll let you know. Love you too. Bye." She thumbed the screen of her phone and turned to Riley. "How would you like to go to a Halloween party with me? It's—"

Riley shook her head. "I don't think that's a good idea. Sorry."

"Wait. I know you're not a big fan of Halloween, but before you say no, let me explain."

Sam knew only half of it. Meeting Keith at a Halloween party wasn't Riley's worst memory associated with the October holiday. The only other time she had attended a Halloween party, she had gotten drunk and lost her virginity in a bathroom at a haunted house while in college.

"Riley?" Sam scooted across the cushions and put her hand on Riley's arm.

Sam's touch grounded her, and she shook away the unpleasant memories. "I'm sorry, but I don't think there's anything you can say that will change my mind. I let myself get talked into a party last year." A lump formed in her throat. "We both know how well that turned out. And to be honest, even if I put aside meeting Keith, I really don't enjoy being around a bunch of people drinking and acting out."

"That's what I wanted to explain. This isn't an adult party. Kim and Jess donate their time at a group foster home for teenagers. Every year, the local community center sponsors a haunted house and Halloween party for the foster kids and their families. And there are a lot of them." Sam's eyes grew shadowed. "And most of them are so grateful when someone does something for them or takes an interest in them. The group homes do their best, but special things like this party mean the world to these kids."

The thought of all those children removed from their families and living with strangers tugged at Riley's heart. She knew firsthand what it was like to want for attention as a child. "It's just for the kids?"

Sam nodded. "Last year, Jess and Kim worked in the haunted house. I wish I could have been there, but I was on duty. Jess asked me if I'd help out this year. They're short on volunteers, so Kim wanted me to ask if you'd consider helping out. What do you say? Will you help?"

Riley gazed into Sam's shining silvery-blue eyes and found herself nodding.

"Great."

"Oh, wait."

Sam's expression fell.

"When exactly is this party? I have to check my schedule."

"Halloween night. It falls on a Friday this year."

After pulling her phone from the charger, Riley called up her schedule. "I'm due to work during the day, but I don't have call. It's in the evening, right?"

"Starts early, at six, because of the younger children. Could you maybe get off early?" Sam asked, a wistfulness in her voice.

Riley hesitated. She had never asked anyone to cover for her.

Sam waited, not saying anything to pressure her.

She couldn't bring herself to disappoint Sam. "I'll ask Denny if he could cover for a couple of hours."

The brilliant smile that lit Sam's face made Riley's heart thump in her chest. She looked away before Sam could see the desire in her eyes.

Sam whooped. "All right. Now all we have to do is decide what our costumes will be."

"No way." Riley shook her head. "You never said anything about a costume."

"I didn't?" Sam was the picture of innocence.

Riley elbowed her in the ribs. "I'll gladly help, but I draw the line at wearing a costume. Not going to happen."

"Come on. Please?" Sam batted her eyes and worked her puppy-dog expression for all it was worth.

Riley crossed her arms over her chest. "No costume."

Ignoring her, Sam picked up her phone and scrolled through several screens. She grinned and held out the phone.

Riley gingerly took the phone as if it might grow teeth and bite her.

Sam burst out laughing.

Scowling, Riley looked at the screen. At first glance, she thought it was a picture of Sam with a woman dressed as Dracula but then realized it was Jess and most likely Kim dressed as Dracula. They were surrounded by smiling children. The kids' faces shone with exuberance.

The corners of Sam's mouth drooped as if pulled by weights. "You wouldn't want to disappoint all those children, would you?"

"That's...that's..." Riley waved her hands in the air, searching for the perfect word. Her hands dropped to her lap. "That's so not fair."

"Yeah. Yeah. But did it work?"

Riley threw her a narrow-eyed look and slumped back against the couch. "Yes." She tried to hold on to her pique but couldn't do it. She looked down at the picture again. The thought of making Halloween special for those kids appealed to her.

Sam grinned. "So what do you want to be for Halloween?"

Riley groaned. *Wonder if my personal shopper does Halloween costumes?* "Someone not in a costume?"

"Come on." Sam nudged Riley's leg with her knee. "Let out your inner child. I know she's in there somewhere."

Is she? Or had she been ground to dust during all the years beneath her aunt's heel? Riley's thoughts went to the baseball game she had attended with Sam several weeks ago. A glimpse of that little girl had appeared that day. Then, just a few days ago, when she had made breakfast for Sam, memories of that happy little girl had surfaced after being repressed for years. Riley called to that child now, releasing that part of herself from the rigid restraint she normally maintained. It was as if a weight lifted off her shoulders, leaving her feeling more lighthearted than she had in years.

After the last time they had talked about Halloween, Sam sensed that there was more to

Riley's dislike of the holiday than the bad memories attached to meeting Keith. Sam wanted to change that. She was determined to make Halloween fun for Riley. *Come on, Riley. I know you can do this.*

Riley pulled her legs up onto the couch. She sat cross-legged, scooted around to face Sam, and grinned up at her. "Okay. Let's figure this out. What should I be for Halloween?"

Relief flowed through Sam; for a moment, she'd thought she had pushed Riley too hard. "How about Wonder Woman?" *I think you're pretty wonderful.* An image of Riley in a Wonder Woman costume flashed through her mind, followed by a strong pulse of arousal. *On second thought, maybe not. I'd never survive it.*

Riley shook her head and laughed. "Ah, definitely no. I don't do skimpy."

"Okay. Something less revealing." Strong female movie characters paraded through her mind. "Let's see, how about Rion from *Lomax's Revenge*?"

"That's a definite no too." Riley crossed her arms over her chest. "It's just exchanging skimpy for skintight."

Sam grinned. *It was worth a try.* "All right, then, what about...?" She named several other possibilities.

Riley shook her head at each one. She worried her bottom lip with her teeth. "Um...what about something simple like a cowboy?" She slashed her hand in negation as if she could wipe away the idea. "Never mind. That's a dumb suggestion."

"No it's not." Sam touched Riley's knee. "It could be really great." She pictured Riley in a close-fitting shirt and vest, tight jeans, and a full-length leather duster. Her cowboy hat was pulled down to shade her eyes. And maybe a pair of chaps. Sam groaned to herself. *Oh yeah, her ass would look incredible framed by a pair of chaps.*

"You really think so?"

Riley's voice drew Sam from her lustful thoughts. *Down,* she commanded her wayward libido. "Oh, yeah. Definitely." Sam flushed. Her voice had come out much huskier than she had expected.

Color flooded Riley's face. "A... great. Yeah. That's great," she stammered. She cleared her throat. "What about you? What are you going as?"

"That's a good question. Maybe one of the characters I mentioned before." Sam went through them again, but none of them jumped out at her as the perfect character. She huffed out a breath. "Any suggestions?"

"Well..." Riley's complexion that had just returned to normal glowed with color. "Never mind."

Sam swore she could almost feel the heat of Riley's blush. "Tell me. Please."

Riley muttered something under her breath.

"I didn't get that. Who?"

She peeked at Sam from beneath half-lidded eyes. "You could go as Deven Masters."

"Oh. So you liked that movie, huh?" Sam smirked. Earlier, when looking for a movie to watch, she had discovered that Riley knew who Colleen Bryce was, but she had never seen one of her Deven Masters movies. Sam had chosen one of her favorites to introduce her to the character but had ended up spending more time watching Riley than the movie.

As impossible as it seemed, Riley's blush deepened. "What can I say? Who wouldn't like a take-charge kind of woman who can kick ass? It's enticing." Her eyes darkened. "But add a hidden, vulnerable side that needs to be protected," she locked gazes with Sam, "that's compelling."

The intensity of Riley's gaze drew Sam in. She struggled not to lose herself in the depths of Riley's emerald green eyes. Sam wrenched her gaze away before she could drown. *Whoa. Talk about compelling.* She grabbed her water bottle off the table and chugged half its contents. It still took her two tries to get her voice to work. "So you think I should go as Deven Masters?"

"Huh?" Riley shook her head as if breaking free from a trance. She scrubbed her hands over her face and firmly planted her feet on the floor. "Sure. That could work."

"See. That wasn't so hard."

Riley smiled. "So where should we go to get the stuff we need? One of those Halloween superstores?"

"I know just the place," Sam said. "It's not your run-of-the-mill Halloween store. This place specializes in quality costumes and props. They're located in this huge warehouse and furnish costumes and props to the movie industry and TV shows. You have to see this place to believe it."

"Sounds like fun. When do we go?"

"Store's an hour drive away, so it would probably be best if we went on your next day off, since you work later than I do."

Riley rose from the couch. "All right, pardner." She tipped an imaginary hat. "I'll be ready. But for now, I need to mosey on to bed. Five a.m. comes early for us cowboys."

"Good night." Sam couldn't help being charmed by Riley's enthusiasm. *Guess I won her over to Halloween.*

CHAPTER 39

Marina stepped out of the bathroom. As she headed back to the kitchen, where she had left Sam, she heard voices. *Riley must be home.*

She had not seen her since the night at the bar after the softball game, but she had heard plenty about her. Riley was all Sam talked about these days, though she seemed totally unaware of it.

Marina still wasn't over the shock of learning that Sam had invited Riley to move in. Even during the few short weeks that she and Sam were lovers, Sam had been much more comfortable staying at Marina's place. Marina remembered only a single time she had stayed the night here at Sam's apartment.

"No. I'm not taking it."

Sam's insistent tone stopped Marina just outside the kitchen doorway.

Sam and Riley stood facing off across the small room. Riley had a slip of paper in her hand.

"Yes, you are." Riley took a step closer. "I agreed when I thought it would only be for a week or so, but I've been here almost a month."

Sam's jaw tightened as she crossed her arms over her chest. "It's not necessary."

Marina knew too well that determined jut of Sam's chin. *You're fighting a losing battle there, Doc.*

"You either take my half of the rent money, or I go start packing."

"But—"

"Sam." The warning was evident in Riley's tone.

Sam's arms dropped to her sides. With an audible sigh, she took the check.

Marina grinned. *I'll be damned.*

"This is too much."

"No, it's not," Riley said.

"You don't even know how much my rent is."

"Actually, I do. I called to see if there were any apartments for rent in your complex."

Sam frowned, then a little half smirk twitched at the corners of her lips. "Okay. I'll keep the check." She folded the check in half and stuffed it into her pocket.

Ah. Keep, not cash. Sometimes Sam was too stubborn for her own good. But Marina gave Riley credit for giving it a good try.

Riley stalked toward Sam, a fierce scowl darkening her face.

Marina struggled not to laugh as Sam, who towered over Riley by almost a foot, retreated as if faced with an advancing tiger. She backpedaled until her back hit the refrigerator.

Riley went toe to toe with her. "And don't even think about not cashing it."

Sam held up her hands in surrender. "Okay. I'll cash it." She looked down into Riley's eyes and gulped. "Uh...right away."

You've definitely met your match. Laughing to herself, Marina stepped back before her presence became known. She cursed when the floor squeaked.

Riley's head swung around. Fiery green eyes pinned her in place.

Whoa. "Sorry. I didn't mean to intrude."

Riley's face flushed. "I didn't realize you had company." She moved to the kitchen doorway. "Excuse me," she said to Marina as she slipped past her.

As soon as Riley had disappeared from sight, Marina went into the kitchen. Grinning at a blushing Sam, she fanned herself. "Wow. That's one feisty lady you've got there."

Sam scowled. "I told you, we're just friends."

Get a clue. "Oh. That's right. Not your type." Marina nudged her in the ribs. "Too bad she doesn't have a few more curves, huh?" *Come on, Sam. Take the bait.*

"Marina." Sam's eyebrows lowered. "Knock it off. It's got nothing to do with that. Not everything has to be about getting laid."

Since when? "Yeah. You're right. I was just thinking. Since you're not interested, Elisabeth has several friends that are single. A woman like Riley...cute, a doctor, and she obviously has a very passionate nature." She struggled not to laugh at the gathering storm on Sam's face. "I know they'd be all over her. I think I'll ask Riley for her number so I can pass it along."

Sam rammed her hands into the pockets of her jeans and glowered. "Riley can find all the dates she wants on her own. She doesn't need your help."

Marina shrugged. "I'm just trying to help." She bit the inside of her cheek.

"We should get moving. I'll let Riley know we're ready to go." Sam stomped away.

Oh yeah. Bagged and tagged. You just don't know it yet.

Riley sat slumped on the side of the bed. What was Marina doing in Sam's apartment? Were they getting back together? Although she knew she could never be what Sam wanted, the thought of them together made her heart ache. She couldn't stand to stay in Sam's apartment, even for a single day, while Sam and Marina renewed their relationship.

A knock sounded.

Riley eyed the door. She knew there was no getting out of it, but she dreaded facing Sam.

"Riley?" Sam knocked again.

Just get it over with. Riley shuffled to the door and opened it a few inches. "I'm sorry. I had no idea Marina was here."

Sam waved away the apology. "I should have told you she was here as soon as you came in. You about ready to go?"

Go? Riley frowned. Then she remembered—the Halloween costumes. She shook her head. "We can do it another time. I don't want to intrude on your time with Marina."

"Marina?" Sam's brow furrowed. "Could you open the door, please, so I can talk to you?"

Riley was tempted to say they were talking but bit her tongue on the childish comment. She slowly opened the door the rest of the way.

"Look, I'm sorry." Sam leaned against the door frame. "I should've asked you if you minded Marina tagging along before agreeing. Marina asked me if she could go with us, and I thought it would be okay." She sighed. "Just give me a minute, and I'll tell her that I'll take her another time." Sam turned away.

"Wait. Marina wants to go with us to the costume store? That's why she's here?"

"Yeah. Elisabeth talked her into going to a charity costume ball for Halloween. They're supposed to attend as famous characters from literature. Elisabeth suggested they go as Odysseus and Penelope or maybe Scheherazade and King Shahryar. Not the kind of costume you'll find in your average Halloween store." Sam laughed. "I think Marina was hoping more for Robin Hood and Maid Marian or even Sherlock Holmes and Dr. Watson."

"If you don't mind me asking, who's Elisabeth?"

Sam smacked her forehead. "Oh. I thought I'd said. She's Marina's girlfriend."

It just postponed the inevitable. She had to face the fact that Sam would have a girlfriend eventually. It was surprising that she didn't have one already. "Just let me grab my jacket, and I'm ready."

Sam put a hand on Riley's arm. "You're sure you don't mind Marina coming with us?"

"It's fine." Now that she knew that Marina had a girlfriend, she would be more comfortable around her. "I'm looking forward to seeing this place and finding the perfect costume."

"Great. Let's go."

CHAPTER 40

Sam turned down a street that led to an area filled with warehouses. She made several turns as she wove her way deeper into the industrial complex.

Riley glanced back to make sure Marina's car was still behind them. How did customers ever find the place?

Finally, Sam pulled up in front of a huge two-story building. The sign on the side of the building read *Fisher Film Services.* "This is it."

Marina pulled into the parking spot next to them.

After getting out of the car, Sam led the way to an unmarked side-door of the building.

"This doesn't look like a store," Marina said.

"Because it's not. Normally, they only rent costumes and props for film, TV, and the occasional large special event. But I know the owner, and he's making an exception for us." Sam pressed the small buzzer next to the door.

Nothing happened for several moments, then the door swung open. A plump, middle-aged man with hanging jowls and a rotund belly motioned them inside.

"Hi, Melvin," Sam said.

The door clanged shut behind them. Riley's eyes widened as she took in long aisles filled with costumes and shelves loaded down with props.

"Samantha. It's good to see you." Melvin grabbed Sam's hand and pumped it vigorously. His smile faded. "I saw on the news what happened." His gaze swept her from head to toe. "Are you really okay?"

"I'm fine. How's Teddy doing?"

Melvin beamed, making his eyes disappear in the folds of fat on his face. "Wonderful. Just wonderful. He made the dean's list the last two semesters."

"Glad to hear it. He's a good kid."

"He is. But if it wasn't for you," his voice choked with emotion, "I would have lost him."

Sam patted his shoulder. "I'm glad it all worked out."

Riley thought back to the owners of their favorite Chinese restaurant. How like Sam not to mention helping out another family. How many more were there?

"As I told you on the phone, I brought some friends with me." Sam introduced them. "Think you can set us up?"

"Of course, of course. Any friend of yours is a friend of mine." Melvin turned to Riley and Marina and made a courtly bow—or at least as much of a bow as his large belly would allow. "Ladies, what's your pleasure?"

Riley glanced at Marina, who gave her a go-ahead motion. "I was thinking something simple... like a cowboy outfit?"

"Pish Posh. Too ordinary." His gaze swept Riley, and he beamed at her. "I've got a much better idea."

Riley clipped a heavy, black sack to her belt and grinned at her reflection in the dressing room mirror. She straightened the collar of her long-sleeved western shirt, then checked the tuck line at the waist of her button-fly jeans. A short, braided leather whip hung from her belt and trailed down alongside the seam of her pant leg. She wiggled her toes in the pointed cowboy boots. A full-length leather duster and black Stetson completed the look. She tested the effects on her costume to make sure she could unobtrusively trigger them. *Definitely not ordinary.* She tugged her hat down low so it shaded her eyes and then strode out of the dressing room.

Marina was waiting outside. A rich, dark green tunic that hung to mid-thigh stretched taut across her ample chest. Close-fitting tights clung to her strong legs. Her hat tilted at a jaunty angle, and bow and arrow slung over her shoulder, she made a striking Robin Hood.

An uncomfortable stab of envy pricked Riley. No matter what she did, she would never look like that. She smoothed her hands down the soft leather of her duster.

"You look great," Marina said.

"Thanks. You too." Riley peered toward the dressing rooms, eager to show Sam her costume.

"She's not in there. Melvin decided he wasn't happy with the Deven Masters outfit. He said it was too common, so he took her to try on some special costume that he insisted would be perfect for her."

Too bad. Riley had been looking forward to seeing Sam in those leather pants.

Silence stretched between them.

Trying not to fidget, Riley walked over and checked out some of the props on the wall. As she turned back, she spotted a beautiful gown that was hanging outside the dressing room.

"I can't wait for Elisabeth to see it," Marina said.

Riley moved closer to get a better look at the dress. It was lovely. The pale green gown was embroidered with tendrils of ivy surrounding the bodice and trailing down onto the skirt. "Maid Marian?"

A glowing smile lit Marina's face. "Yes. Elisabeth is going to look fantastic in it."

At the obvious look of adoration on Marina's face, Riley's discomfort with her slipped another notch.

"Ah. Ladies, let's see how you look." Melvin trundled toward them. When he reached them, he motioned for Marina, then Riley to turn in a circle in front of him. "Nice. Very nice." He checked the sleeve of Riley's jacket. "Everything working?"

Riley nodded.

"Then it's time to meet the last member of your group." He clapped his hands. "Come join us," he called out.

Heavy footfalls sounded on the concrete floor. A stunning, white-haired figure appeared from between the aisles and marched toward them.

Unbelievable! Riley knew her mouth was hanging open but was helpless to do anything about it. Even Riley, who wasn't a fan of science fiction movies, recognized Baylin. The mega-hit *Rescue from Zebturion Prime* had smashed box-office records all over the world.

Dark blue pants clung to Baylin like a second skin, her powerful thighs flexing with every step. Heavy, knee-high paratrooper boots encased her feet and calves. Her vest, studded with silver discs, molded to her upper body. A wide metal band around each bicep highlighted the sleek muscles beneath. Bracers with flashing circuitry covered her forearms. Short, spiky white hair added to her intimidating look. She stopped directly in front of Riley.

Riley gazed into Baylin's stony face. Deep amethyst eyes held her captive. She stood frozen like prey in front of a predator.

"Hot damn," Marina said, breaking the spell. "You look incredible."

You've got that right. It was the perfect costume for Sam. Who better than the rescuer of abandoned children?

Sam grinned. "It is pretty cool."

Riley couldn't take her eyes off her. The enticing cleavage on display was doing a number on her libido. *Great, now I'm channeling a horny teenager.*

Sam tugged on the sleeve of Riley's jacket.

When Riley's gaze darted to her face, Sam winked.

A blush made the tips of Riley's ears burn. At the sound of Marina's and Melvin's chuckles, she tugged her hat down in an attempt to cover her flaming face.

"Hey, we haven't checked out Riley's costume yet," Marina said.

Grateful for the rescue from an unexpected quarter, Riley pushed her hat back and smiled at Marina.

"So, what kind of cowboy are you?" Sam asked.

Riley curled her hands around her belt and braced her feet wide apart. "I'm a ghost wrangler." She pulled the short, stiff whip from her belt. "Stand back and give me some room."

Once everyone had moved away, she waved the whip slowly back and forth in front of her. It began to hum and glow a dim red. She moved to her right; the hum became louder and the glow increased. The whip coiled like a snake around its prey. "I've got one."

She flipped back her jacket and tugged open the black bag at her waist with one hand as she struggled to hold on to the whip with the other. She guided the tip of the tightly coiled whip into the bag. As soon as it touched, sparks erupted. Flashes of electricity raced up the sleeve of her duster. She jerked the whip free and slammed the bag closed.

The contents of the bag writhed for a moment, then went still. "Got 'im!"

Sam and Marina clapped.

"Well done," Melvin said.

Riley took a bow.

"That was great," Sam said. "The kids are going to love you."

Riley smiled. "Thanks." She couldn't wait to try out her act on the kids. "But I bet Baylin's going to be the hit of the party."

"Well, ladies, I think you're all set," Melvin said. "Let's get these costumes boxed up."

As Riley made her way into the dressing room, she shook her head. She hadn't expected to find herself dressing up in any sort of costume, but it had been fun. *Guess Halloween isn't so bad after all.*

CHAPTER 41

Riley hurried toward the entrance of the community center. Taking a moment, she checked her reflection in the glass door. *You look fine. Quit stalling.* Considering Jess's attitude after the shooting, she couldn't help being a bit leery of seeing her again. She ran damp palms down the front of her jeans, straightened her hat, and pulled open the door.

Black and orange streamers hung from the ceiling. A large cauldron, surrounded by cobwebs and spiders, formed the centerpiece of a row of tables along the back wall. Colorful cardboard cutouts of pumpkins, witches, bats, and skeletons covered the walls. Pumpkins with painted faces were scattered throughout the room. *Looks great.* She scanned the room, looking for Sam.

Across the room, dressed in a blood-red vest and cape and a black tuxedo, Dracula stood in conversation with a witch and a pirate.

Remembering the picture from Sam's phone, Riley smiled. *That must be Kim.* There was no sign of Sam in her Baylin costume.

Dracula caught sight of her and headed in her direction. "Good evening," Dracula said with his classic accent. He spread his cape wide and bowed.

Riley stared at the slicked-back raven hair, deathly pale face, and blood-red lips, trying to find some resemblance between the person standing before her and the woman she had met months ago. "Kim?"

Kim smiled, displaying a set of fangs. "Hi, Riley. Glad you could make it. Thanks for being willing to help out." She eyed Riley's costume. "So that's what a ghost wrangler looks like, huh? I can't wait to see you in action. Sam's been bragging about you since she got here."

Heat flooded Riley's face. She ducked her head, silently bemoaning her fair complexion. She glanced around again, hoping to spot Sam.

"Sam's in the haunted house with Jess," Kim said. "They were having some last minute issues with the runner lights on the floor."

As much as Riley wanted to go to Sam, she resisted. *You're here to help. So, help.* "Umm...what do you need me to do?"

"There are still a few treat bags to fill. Would you mind helping with that?"

"Just point me in the right direction." A prickling awareness nudged at the edge of Riley's senses.

Kim looked at something behind Riley, and a bright smile blossomed.

Riley turned, and then she smiled too.

Sam strode toward them with Jess, dressed in military fatigues, at her side. With Sam in her Baylin costume, their striking facial resemblance was muted, but the tall, broad-shouldered build and long-legged, confident stride they shared was readily evident.

As Jess reached them, she wrapped her arm around Kim's shoulders and pulled her close. "You doing okay? Not standing too much?"

"I'm fine." Kim cupped Jess's cheek for a moment, then inclined her head in Riley's direction. "Our ghost wrangler is here."

"Drive up okay?" Sam asked.

Very aware of Jess and Kim nearby, Riley kept her gaze on Sam's face. "Traffic was really light. I got hung up at the hospital and ended up leaving later than I planned."

"We know how that goes, don't we, Kim?" Jess said with a smile. "Thanks for coming to help out."

Riley peered at Jess and saw only friendliness in her eyes. "I'm happy to."

"Did you guys get the light problem solved?" Kim asked.

"All set," Jess said. "One of the spider's feet got caught and pulled a connection loose."

"Spider?" Riley shuddered. *Great. Just had to be a spider.*

"Oh, yeah. A huge, hairy one." Sam smirked. "Mutant size. Want to see?"

Riley adamantly shook her head. "Sorry, no can do. I'm going to help fill treat bags."

"Come on, I'll protect you." Laughing, Sam draped her arm across Riley's shoulders. "Or I'm sure I could find you a big book around here."

Narrowing her eyes at Sam, Riley said, "Are you sure there aren't any mannequins in there that need saving?"

Sam threw back her head and laughed. "Touché."

"Would one of you like to clue us in?" Kim asked.

Riley and Sam exchanged a look and then shook their heads in unison.

"Long story," Sam said and winked at Riley.

"Baylin. Jed." A dark-haired little girl waved as her foster mother tried to corral her toward the door of the community center.

Riley laughed to herself, remembering how panicked she'd been the first time one of the kids had asked her name. She thought she'd done a pretty good job coming up with a cowboy name on the spur of the moment.

The girl darted away from the woman and ran to Riley. "Jed. You got the ghosts?" She reached into Riley's open jacket and touched the black bag hanging at her waist. The bag writhed beneath her fingers, making her squeal.

"Careful. Don't let them loose." Riley smiled at the little girl. *Wish I could remember her name.* She had met so many children and foster parents tonight that the names had all blurred together.

The little girl grinned at Riley. "You catch some more?"

Riley shook her head. "Not tonight. I think I got them all."

"Darla." Her foster mother smiled at Sam and Riley as she reached for the girl's hand. "It's time to go."

"No." Darla pulled away, her lips set in a stubborn line. She tipped her head back and peered up at Sam, her dark eyes brimming with tears. "Don't go, Baylin." She flung her arms around Sam's thigh.

Sam patted her back. "I have to, sweetie—"

"No. Please." Darla buried her face against Sam's thigh and clung to her.

"The party's over," Darla's foster mother said. "Baylin has to go, honey."

"No. Baylin stay." Darla's voice was muffled by Sam's pants. She locked her arms around Sam's thigh.

Panic flashed across Sam's face. She looked helplessly at Darla's foster mother.

"No, Darla. Baylin has to leave. Come on now, it's time for us to go home." The woman reached for Darla's hand.

Riley forestalled her with a "one minute" gesture. She knelt down next to Darla. "Baylin stopped by tonight because she really wanted to see all of you and make sure that you were safe and taken care of. But now she needs to go, so she can save some more children and make sure they're safe too." She ran a gentle hand up and down Darla's back. "You want her to do that, right?"

Darla lifted her head and looked at Riley. Her face was streaked with tears. She gazed up at Sam. "You save them?"

The look of hope and too many disappointments on her face nearly broke Riley's heart.

Sam nodded. "Yes. I will. I promise."

"'Kay." Darla released her.

Her foster mother scooped up Darla. "Thank you," she mouthed before carrying Darla away.

"Thanks for the save," Sam said as soon as the pair was out of earshot. "My God, did you see the look on her face? Made me want to cry. I don't know how these foster families do it, day in and day out."

Riley stepped close and rubbed Sam's back. "Just remember all the joy you brought these kids tonight. Even if it was only for a little while, you made them feel special." She shook her head. "Sure gave me some perspective. Compared to what some of these kids have been through, my time with my aunt and uncle was a walk in the park."

"Hey, you two," Kim said as she came up. "I want to thank you both. You did a wonderful job tonight." She gave Sam a hug, then smiled at Riley and pressed her hand. "I bet the kids are going to be ghost hunting for days. And they were just over the moon about Baylin being here. Everyone has been raving that this was the best Halloween party ever. Is it too soon to ask if you'll both help next year?"

Sam laughed. "I'm in. How about you, Riley?"

Guess my Halloween jinx is over. She couldn't wait until next year. "Count me in. Although I don't know how we can top this year."

"I'm sure Melvin will come up with something," Sam said.

"You need to introduce Jess and me to Melvin. I thought my Dracula was good, but with you two around, the kids barely looked at me." Kim smiled. "Don't get me wrong, I don't mind, but it would be fun to see what he could come up with for the four of us."

"No problem," Sam said. "I'm sure Melvin will set us all up next year."

Riley smiled. It felt surprisingly good to be included in the group.

"Last of the kids are gone, so we're done here," Kim said. "The clean-up crew will take care of the rest. Are we still on to meet for a bite to eat?"

Glad she suggested a restaurant. While Riley was more comfortable with them than she had expected, she still wasn't ready to go to their home.

"What do you think?" Sam asked. "It's been a long day. You too tired?"

Riley glanced at Kim, then back at Sam. She appreciated Sam giving her an out if she wanted one. "I'm okay. I could use a bite to eat."

"Great." Kim smiled. "I got to thinking, though, a lot of places may be pretty busy. What do you think of meeting at the restaurant in your hotel?"

"That's probably a good idea," Sam said.

Jess strode up, her combat boots ringing against the tile beneath her feet. "What's the verdict? We going to eat? I'm starving."

"Yeah," Sam said. "You guys going home to change first?"

"Definitely," Kim said. "We need to let Thor out. And I want to get this makeup off. I wouldn't want to ruin Dracula's image by being seen eating a burger or something."

"It could be a bloody raw burger," Sam said.

Kim shuddered. Her hand went to her stomach.

Jess glared at Sam and wrapped her arm around Kim's shoulders.

Sam grimaced. "Sorry."

Riley frowned and looked between them.

"Sam didn't tell you?" Kim asked.

"Tell me what?"

"You told me not to tell anyone," Sam said.

"It's okay. You can now. We told the folks." Kim turned to Riley. "I'm pregnant."

Oh. Wow. Riley smiled. "Congratulations. That's wonderful." She elbowed Sam in the ribs. "How could you even mention," she caught herself, "that kind of burger."

"Yeah!" Jess said.

Sam laughed. "Oh. Now we're having a gang-up-on-Sam night?"

"Yes," three voices answered in unison.

"Fine. Be like that." Sam crossed her arms over her chest.

Laughing, Riley tugged at her arm. "Come on. I'll follow you back to the hotel. I know you must want to get out of that outfit." She allowed her gaze to sweep Sam, lingering for just a moment on her enticing cleavage. *I'm going to be sad to see Baylin go.* Watching Sam in the skintight outfit all night had been a guilty pleasure. She forced her attention off Sam and back to Kim and Jess.

Kim arched an eyebrow at her and winked.

Riley's face burned with the heat of her blush. *Busted.* Her gazed darted to Jess. A very familiar little half smirk made an appearance. "So...um... we'll meet you in the hotel restaurant."

"See you there," Kim said.

CHAPTER 42

Jess tossed her socks on the bed and then padded barefoot into the bathroom to see what was taking Kim so long.

Kim stood beneath one of the double heads of the large walk-in shower, her hands braced on the tile. Eyes closed, she tilted her head back as she rinsed shampoo from her hair. Water and suds cascaded down her back and over the cheeks of her ass.

Mesmerized, Jess found herself shucking her clothes before even being aware of making the decision to join her. Steam wafted out as she tugged open the shower door and stepped inside. "Need some help?"

Kim's head jerked down. She moved out of the direct spray. "I forgot what a pain it was to get this black gel out of blond hair." She slicked back her wet hair. "I thought you weren't going to take a shower."

"I changed my mind."

Just the sight of Kim's body ripening with their child was enough to make Jess ache for her. She wrapped her arms around Kim's waist and pressed against her back. Trailing her hands over Kim's belly, she longed for the day that she would feel their baby stir beneath her fingers. Jess slid her hands up until she reached Kim's breasts. Smiling, she gently cupped the abundant flesh. "Hmm...not that you were lacking to start with, but I love how your breasts have filled out." Her thumbs softly stroked Kim's nipples, bringing them to stiff points.

Kim whimpered and pushed her ass into Jess's groin.

"And you're so sensitive now, I bet I could make you come just by caressing your breasts."

"As much as I'd love that," Kim said, her voice gone husky, "Sam and Riley are waiting for us." Despite her words, she made no attempt to move out of Jess's embrace.

"Then maybe I should just help you with your hair?" Jess reached around her and put a dollop of shampoo in her hands. She rubbed her hands together, then slid one hand down Kim's abdomen.

"That's not the hair that needs washing."

Jess nuzzled the slim column of Kim's throat, interspersing open-mouth kisses with tiny bites. "I'm just being thorough." She massaged the shampoo into the curly hair at the apex of Kim's thighs.

Groaning, Kim shifted, spreading her feet wider apart.

Jess smiled and allowed her hand to slip lower. She found Kim's clit and stroked it in a circular motion, increasing the pressure with each pass. "Come for me," she whispered close to Kim's ear.

Kim bucked in her arms as she climaxed. "Jess." Her thighs clamped shut on Jess's hand.

Jess tightened her hold around Kim's ribcage, careful not to put too much pressure on her sensitive breasts. Once she was sure Kim's legs were going to hold her, she loosened her grip and guided her to the bench seat inset in the wall of the shower.

Kim looked up, her eyes still hazy with passion. "I love you." She kissed Jess's belly. "Please don't take this wrong. I'd like to return the favor, but I'm starving and need to eat before I get faint."

Jess smiled. "I love you too. And don't worry about it." After having to stand by helplessly while Kim was plagued by recurring bouts of nausea during the first three months of her pregnancy, she was more than happy to hear Kim say she was hungry. She dispensed a generous amount of shampoo into the palm of her hand. "Let's get this black gel out of your hair before the hot water runs out, then I'll get you a snack to hold you until the restaurant." She worked the shampoo into Kim's shoulder-length curls. "I still can't believe that Sam got her hair cut off like that again. I just about fell over when she came in."

"Hmm..." Kim's eyes slipped shut for a moment, then opened. "I know what you mean. I mentioned it to Riley, and she said she'd been shocked at first too. Sam and Riley sure were the hit of the party." She stroked Jess's thighs and peered up at her. "So, what did you think of Riley?"

Jess knew exactly what Kim was asking, but she wasn't ready to admit she'd judged Riley unfairly. "That costume and her whole ghost-wrangling act were great."

"That's not what I was talking about." Kim slid her hand across Jess's ass and pinched it. "And you know it."

"Ow!" Caught, Jess grinned. "Okay. I wasn't around her too much, but Riley seemed really nice. She was wonderful with the kids." She tipped Kim's chin up and turned her head from side to side. Dark remnants of the gel tinted the skin around her hairline. "And you were right about Sam. She couldn't keep her eyes off Riley."

"And you're okay with that?" Kim asked.

"Close your eyes." Jess carefully scrubbed the skin at Kim's hairline. "Yeah. I talked with Sam quite a bit while we were between groups in the haunted house. All she talked about was Riley. She doesn't seem to have a clue that she's even doing it." Jess couldn't help comparing Sam's behavior to her own when she became friends with Kim. *You were just as clueless.* She urged Kim to her feet. "Rinse."

Kim washed the shampoo out of her hair, then shut off the water. She pushed open the shower door, stepped out, grabbed a thick towel, and passed it to Jess. After snagging a second towel for herself, she dried off.

"You spent time with Riley," Jess said as she wiped the water from her body. "What did you think? Is she interested in Sam?"

"No doubt about it in my mind. She watched Sam like a hawk all night. I thought I was going to have to offer her a drool bib."

"Right. I almost forgot. Riley's face was so red when we spotted her eyeing Sam's cleavage, I thought she was going to spontaneously combust." Jess laughed, then sobered. "You don't think a fling is all Riley is interested in, do you?"

Kim wrapped her towel around herself. "Let's talk while we get dressed." She walked into the bedroom.

Jess followed in her wake.

"No. I didn't get that impression," Kim said. "Like Sam talking about Riley, all Riley could talk about was Sam. It's clear to me that they care deeply for each other. I don't know why they haven't acted on their feelings yet."

"Makes me wonder what we don't know." Jess sat down on the side of the bed with a sigh. "I don't want to see Sam get hurt again and decide to go back to meaningless affairs."

"All we can do is be as supportive of her relationship with Riley as we can." Kim's stomach growled loudly.

Laughing, Jess hurriedly buttoned her shirt. "We better get you fed."

CHAPTER 43

As Jess began to regale them with another work story, Sam pushed her empty plate away and glanced over at Kim.

Kim smiled and sent her an unobtrusive wink.

She had been quieter than usual during dinner. Earlier, she had ushered Jess into the seat opposite Riley, giving them ample opportunity to connect.

Now I know she's doing it on purpose.

Riley laughed, drawing Sam's attention back to Jess's story.

"Ah. The bane of senior residents, I-know-it-all-itis," Riley said. "Infects them all at some point."

"Exactly. So I presented a case of a male patient with severe hip pain," Jess said. "The residents were moaning and groaning, not paying attention to the fact that I hadn't given them the patient's age or any other history. 'Cause how boring, right, hip pain?" She laughed. "So I cued up the AP film of my dog's hips."

"Your dog?" Riley asked. "Wouldn't that be pretty obvious?"

"To a vet, sure." Jess grinned. "But not a resident, not when the dog is a two-hundred-pound Great Dane."

Riley gulped. "Wow."

Sam reached over and patted her leg. "No worries. He's really a gentle giant. You'll love him."

At Riley's skeptical look, Kim said, "Sam's right. Thor really is incredibly gentle. Although I will admit I was a bit taken aback the first time I met him."

Sam still remembered the look of confusion on Jess's face as she described Kim and Thor's first meeting. Thor had, in his own way, acknowledged what a special woman Kim was to become to both of them.

Riley turned back to Jess. "So what did your residents make of Thor's films?"

"Their guesses were all over the place—congenital deformities, bone dysplasia, endocrine imbalance."

"Did anyone ever figure it out?" Riley asked.

"Believe it or not, yes." Jess laughed. "But he had an unfair advantage. His parents used to raise Great Danes." Her expression turned serious. "It was all in fun, but it's also an important lesson for the residents. I'm sure I don't have to tell you, medicine is all about attention to details. Never assume anything."

Riley nodded. "Not just residents. All physicians would do well to remember that."

"I think that's true of any profession," Sam said. "You get complacent, and that's when you start making mistakes."

"All right, you three," Kim said. "This is getting way too serious. It's Halloween. How about some ghost stories or something?"

The waiter arrived at the table. "Excuse me, ladies. Could I interest you in some dessert? Our special tonight is graveyard chocolate fudge cake topped with ghost meringue."

"Oh yeah, I'll have that," Sam said. "Kim, you in?" There was no point in asking Jess. Her sister didn't share her and Kim's love affair with chocolate.

Kim rubbed her hands together. "You bet."

Although Sam was sure she knew the answer, she asked Riley, "How about you?"

"I'll pass."

"Not a chocolate addict?" Jess asked.

"No." Riley grinned at Sam. "Not like someone I know."

"Your loss," Sam said, bumping shoulders with her.

"Finally, someone else who doesn't worship chocolate." Jess reached across the table and gave Riley's arm a quick pat. "Now these two can't make me feel like a heathen because I don't share their obsession."

Kim leaned out of her chair and elbowed her in the ribs. "It's not an obsession. It's one of life's necessities."

"Would you like to see the dessert menu?" the waiter asked, glancing between Riley and Jess.

"Do you have any sorbet?" Riley asked.

Sam feigned a shudder. *Not even ice cream.*

Riley shot her a quelling look.

Jess snickered, earning a glare from Sam.

The waiter smiled. "Yes. What flavor would you like?"

"Raspberry."

"That sounds good," Jess said. "I'll have the same."

A few minutes later, the waiter returned with their desserts.

Kim lifted her dessert directly from the server's tray, ignoring Jess's chuckles.

The waiter set down an individual-sized chocolate cake dripping with thick chocolate fudge icing in front of Sam. A meringue ghost with chocolate chips for its eyes and mouth topped the cake.

Taking a deep, appreciative sniff, Sam groaned, her senses filling with the aroma of rich, dark chocolate. "Oh yeah. This is going to be good." She glanced over at Riley. "Sure you don't want to try a bite?"

Riley shook her head and smiled. "Enjoy it." She dipped her spoon into her sorbet.

Sam dug her fork into the cake and took a large bite of the sinfully sweet treat. Her eyes fluttered closed, and she hummed as the mingled chocolate flavors inundated her taste buds. She opened her eyes to find Riley staring at her with an intensity that made her flush. "Your dessert okay?"

"Excellent." Riley took another spoonful of the sorbet.

Sam watched Riley's lips close around the spoon. The flash of arousal was instantaneous. She tore her gaze away and kept it glued to her own dessert, which had lost some of its appeal.

"We were so busy earlier I didn't get a chance to ask you," Jess said. "How did your appointment go this morning?"

Oh shit! Sam stared at her sister and tried to subtly shake her head. *Shut up, Jess.*

A furrow appeared between Jess's brows. "Was there a problem? Didn't the department doctor clear you to return to full duty next week?"

Riley gasped. Her spoon crashed onto the table, leaving a red smear across the white tablecloth.

Sam dared a glance in her direction.

The color had drained from Riley's face. Looking as if she'd been sucker-punched, she pushed her chair back, stood, and stared down at Sam. "When were you going to tell me?"

"I...I'm sorry," Sam stammered. She had planned on telling Riley before Monday, but knowing how she would react, Sam had convinced herself it was okay to put it off. She tried to get the words out to explain, but they refused to come.

Riley gripped the edge of the table so tightly her knuckles blanched. "Were you even going to tell me?" She shook her head roughly. Glancing toward Kim and Jess, she said, "Excuse me. I need to get some air."

With that, she spun on her heel and walked away, but not before Sam caught a glimpse of the tears in her eyes.

Sam jumped up. "Riley. Wait."

Riley's head dropped, but her gait never faltered. *Fuck.*

"How could you not tell her?" Kim asked.

Sam's head whipped back around. She'd forgotten Kim and Jess were there. "I was going to."

Kim arched an eyebrow.

Jess shook her head and threw in her own skeptical look.

"I swear. I just...it was Halloween, and I didn't want to put a damper on it." Sam squeezed the back of her neck hard, using the pain to help her to focus. "And I'm an idiot." She reached into her back pocket for her wallet. "I've got to find Riley and explain."

"Go," Jess said. "I'll take care of this."

"Thanks. I'll call you tomorrow," Sam said, her mind already on what she was going to say to Riley. She looked toward the exit.

Riley had disappeared from sight.

Dammit. Dodging tables and waiters, Sam went after her. *I have to fix this.*

CHAPTER 44

A large crowd of costumed teenagers milled about the hotel lobby. Sam scanned the room, hoping to catch a glimpse of Riley. A flash of green, the same shade as the sweater Riley was wearing, caused Sam to veer off to her right, but it was just another kid.

Using her height to its full advantage, she worked her way through the crowd. There was no sign of Riley. Maybe she had gone up to her room. Sam changed direction and headed for the elevators.

The area adjacent to the bank of elevators was crammed with laughing, rowdy teenagers, who seemed in no hurry to go anywhere.

Groaning, she waded into the group. "Excuse me. Excuse me." She worked her way deeper into the crowd and closer to the elevators. "Excuse me."

A teenage boy, dressed as a gang banger, refused to budge.

Sam took a closer look at his outfit. It wasn't a costume. *Oh great.* "Excuse me." She sidestepped him.

Moving directly into her path, the boy swept his gaze over her and sneered. "Get yo dyke ass out of here." He puffed out his scrawny chest.

Sam dealt with his kind every day. She glanced to either side of the thug. His buddies, dressed in the same colors, were engrossed with the girls hanging on their arms. She needed to end the encounter quickly, before his homies took notice. Straightening to her full height, she donned her cop face, wrapped her hands around her leather belt, and widened her arms to make herself look broader. She leaned close to him, making sure he could hear her above the raucous crowd. "Move. Now." She locked gazes with him in a silent test of wills.

He broke first. With a vicious curse, he turned away.

An elevator dinged.

Sam stood on her toes to see over the crowd. The herd of teenagers shifted, and she got a glimpse of the open elevator. *Riley!* She spotted her stepping into the packed elevator. The crowd closed around Sam again. Still a good six feet from the elevators, she growled under her breath when the elevator doors slid shut. After the look Riley had given her in the restaurant, she feared Riley might not let her into her hotel room, so she needed to catch her before she got back to her room.

Another elevator car arrived.

Sam barely resisted the urge to shove through the crowd to reach the elevator. A strange compulsion made her turn around and look to the right of the elevators. It took a moment for the sign hanging there to register. *The stairs!*

As if by magic, a gap opened in the crowd, clearing her way to the stairs. Sam didn't know if she could beat the elevator to the third floor, but she was damn well going to try. She shoved open the door to the stairway and sprinted up the stairs.

By the time she hit the last half flight of stairs, she was panting. Pushing forward, she reached the third-floor landing.

The door burst open. Two laughing teenaged girls barreled toward her.

Sam reared back. She immediately realized her mistake, but it was too late to stop the instinctive reaction. Her foot slipped off the landing. She teetered backwards, frantically grabbing for the railing.

Strong hands clamped onto her upper arms from behind and levered her back onto the landing, out of harm's way.

The two teenagers shared a panicked look, then turned and bolted back the way they had come.

Sam's rescuer joined her on the landing. "Are you all right?" he asked.

Sam nodded, her heart pounding in her chest after her near tumble. "Thanks to you." *Where did he come from?* Wherever it was, Sam was grateful for his sudden appearance. "Thank you."

The man smiled, and deep laugh lines appeared at the corners of his eyes. "Glad to be of service."

Sam stared at him. He was a few inches shorter than she was, with sandy brown hair and twinkling green eyes. There was something familiar about him, especially his eyes, but she couldn't place where she had seen him.

"If you're sure you're all right...?"

"I'm fine."

He held the door open for her.

"Thanks again," Sam said as she stepped out into the hallway.

"Go after your lady," he said from behind her. "Sometimes, you only get one chance." The stairwell door closed.

How could he know that? Sam turned back and peered into the window set in the door. *What the—?* She pulled open the door and glanced up and down the stairwell. There was no trace of the man. *People don't disappear into thin air.* Sam had witnessed some strange things on Halloween but nothing like this. *Did I just have my own ghostly encounter?* She shook her head. *Nah.*

She started to head down the stairs to search for him when a voice whispered in the back of her mind, "Riley."

Sam froze. It was probably too late. The delay had surely given Riley time to get to her room. Pushing away thoughts of the strange encounter, she returned to the hallway and headed around the corner at a fast trot.

Riley scowled at the card reader. It had worked earlier, but now of all times it refused to cooperate. She slid the key card into the slot again, but the light remained aggravatingly red.

"Riley," Sam called. "Wait up. Please."

She doubled her efforts to get the door open, not ready to face Sam. Rapid footsteps heading her way drew her attention back to the hallway. The sight of Sam's long-legged strides as she raced toward her easily brought to mind Sam chasing down a criminal. *I have to do this—for both of us.*

"I'm sorry," Sam said as soon as she reached her side. "I should've told you right away."

Riley gazed up at her. Her anger and hurt had drained away, leaving sadness and resignation in their wake. A deep sigh escaped her. "I think it would be best if I returned to San Diego." She bit her lower lip. "And moved back into a hotel."

"What?" Sam clutched Riley's arm. "No, don't do that. I'm sorry I didn't tell you."

"It's not about that." The worry and guilt on Sam's face strengthened her determination. *I can't do this anymore.* It wasn't fair to Sam. She was a police officer and would never give up her job, no matter how often it put her in the path of danger. Riley wasn't sure she would ever be able to accept that. Her fear was like a living thing inside of her, just waiting to ambush her with the image of Sam sprawled on the ER floor in a pool of blood.

"If it's not because I didn't tell you about work, then what is it?" Sam asked. "Give me a chance to fix it."

As difficult as it was to talk about, she owed Sam an explanation.

Laughter drifted down the hallway from the direction of the elevators.

Riley gave the key card one final try. The light instantly turned green, and the door lock clicked. After a puzzled shake of her head, she pushed open the door. "Come inside." She turned on several lights and walked to the mini-fridge. "Want some water?"

"Sure. Thanks."

Riley carried the water to the small table in the corner, pulled out one of the chairs, and dropped onto it.

Sam trailed in her wake. She settled into the other chair and picked up a bottle. "Let me apologize again. I'm very sorry that I didn't tell you right away." She rubbed her neck. "That was wrong. I realize that now. It's just...it was Halloween, and I really wanted it to be special for you. So I wasn't going to tell you until tomorrow." Her hand tightened around the bottle, making the plastic crackle. "But I swear, I was going to tell you."

Although it had hurt at first, Riley understood why Sam had not told her. "I believe you."

Sam's breath left her in an audible whoosh.

"But finding out that you're returning to the streets made me realize something." Riley's hands clenched into fists. "I can't stand the fact that I might lose you."

"You won't." Sam reached across the table and covered Riley's hands. "Nothing is going to happen to me."

Her fear spiking, Riley pulled away and stood. "You can't know that." A vision of Sam on the ER floor flashed through her mind. She felt as if she couldn't get enough air into her lungs. "You don't understand. I have to leave. I can't live with the thought of losing someone again, someone I..." *Love.*

The word caught in Riley's throat. Realization struck with the force of a lightning bolt to her heart. *I'm in love with her.*

Sam rocketed from her chair and clasped Riley's shoulders. "Don't leave." Her hands tightened until her grip became almost painful. "Please."

The emotions swirling in Sam's silvery-blue eyes held Riley captive. Her fear vanished like a footprint obliterated by the shifting sands of a desert. The crippling doubts that had haunted her since their brief kiss were, for the moment, mercifully silent. There was no past, no worries of the future; there was only here and now with Sam. She clutched the front of Sam's shirt, rose up on her toes, and pulled her down. A second later, their lips met.

Sam wrapped her arms around Riley's back, crushing their bodies together.

Riley licked at Sam's bottom lip, urging her to open to her. When Sam readily accepted her inside, Riley moaned into her mouth. Filled with an aching need stronger than she had ever experienced, she released Sam's shirt and slid her hands down to cup her breasts. She squeezed the pliant globes, massaging Sam's already hard nipples through her shirt.

Sam groaned and pressed herself into the touch. Her hands moved down Riley's back to cup her ass.

Their kiss grew torrid as their tongues battled for dominance.

Wrenching her lips from Sam's was an exercise in sheer willpower. Riley struggled to get her breath as Sam's passion-glazed eyes bore into hers. *I need to touch her bare skin. Now.* When she tried to work the buttons of Sam's shirt open, her usually rock-steady hands were shaking, and her fingers felt like blunt sticks of wood.

Sam attempted to help but wasn't any more successful than Riley. "Damn it," she muttered, fumbling with the buttons.

Growling in frustration, Riley pushed Sam's hands away and wrapped her fingers around the edges of the shirt. The rapid beat of Sam's heart thumped against the backs of her fingers. She locked gazes with Sam.

A growl rumbled up from Sam's chest. "Do it."

Emboldened by the encouragement, Riley ripped the shirt open, sending buttons flying. A groan was torn from her throat at the sight of Sam's bra-clad breasts and finely muscled abdomen.

Sam shoved the ruined shirt off her shoulders, letting it drop to the floor. She pulled her sports bra over her head and stood before Riley bare to the waist.

So beautiful. Long-repressed desire burned through Riley, overwhelming her. Her hand closed on one of Sam's breasts. The sight of Sam's nipples, at the perfect height to take into her mouth, was impossible to resist. Leaning forward, she licked Sam's breast like an ice cream cone, then latched on to a taut nipple.

"Oh." The breath hissed from between Sam's lips. "Yes." As her knees started to buckle, she grabbed Riley's hips. "I'm going to fall." She whimpered when Riley pulled her mouth away.

Seeing Sam made weak by her touch thrilled Riley beyond measure. Her own body pulsed with arousal. "Get on the bed."

Sam pulled off her shoes and socks. Her hands went to her belt.

"No," Riley said. "I'll do that." She followed her to the side of the bed. Where was the confidence to take control coming from? She had never been the aggressor in a sexual situation. Linda had always remained firmly in command, telling her when, where, and how to touch her. But with Sam, taking the lead felt completely natural. It was as if her recognition of her love for Sam had freed a previously unknown power inside Riley.

Sam stood passively, her hands at her sides, while Riley opened her belt. The sound of the zipper being lowered seemed loud in the quiet room. When Riley slipped her hands into the top of Sam's pants, the muscles under her fingers contracted. Sam's willingness to relinquish control further buoyed her self-assurance.

With one strong tug, she pulled Sam's pants and underwear past her hips. She followed the garments to the floor and knelt. Her gaze landed on the raised, pink scars on Sam's thigh, marring her otherwise flawless skin. Riley's throat grew tight at the reminder that she had almost lost Sam before ever getting the chance to love her. She traced the scars gently with her fingertips. Goosebumps erupted in the wake of her touch. She placed a lingering kiss on the most prominent scar.

Sam stroked Riley's hair. "Come up here."

Her gaze swept Sam's nude body as she rose to her feet. *Exquisite.* She brushed her fingers across Sam's abdomen. "You're gorgeous."

A flush worked its way down Sam's chest to her hard nipples. She stepped out of her pants and underwear.

Riley jerked the comforter to the foot of the bed. After pulling the sheet and blanket back, she motioned for Sam to lie down.

Still keeping eye contact, Sam lay on the bed. "Your turn. I want to see you."

Arousal skittered down Riley's spine at the sexy timbre of Sam's voice. She removed her flats, then her knee-high stockings. Her hands went to the bottom of her sweater and then froze. Now that the focus was on her, the first bite of insecurity nipped at her.

"Please." Sam reached out and trailed her fingers across the front of Riley's sweater but stopped short of touching her breasts. "For me."

The heat of Sam's gaze overrode Riley's trepidation. She tugged her sweater over her head, opened her slacks, and allowed them to drop to the floor, leaving her clad in a silk camisole and matching panties. She looked down at her tiny breasts. *Wish all you want. They aren't going to get any bigger.* Leaving the camisole and panties in place, Riley knelt next to Sam on the bed, facing her.

Sam smiled, the warmth of her gaze like a physical caress. She laid a hand on Riley's knee and stroked up her leg. When she reached the edge of the camisole, she ran the silky material between her fingers before releasing it and starting to slip her hand underneath the camisole.

Riley intercepted Sam's hand and placed it back on the bed. Before Sam could protest, she leaned forward and took her lips in a deep kiss. She brought her hands into play, stroking Sam's breasts as she continued to kiss her.

By the time the kiss broke, Sam was panting and her eyes were once again glazed with passion.

Riley clenched her thighs together, trying to stem the tide of her own rising arousal. Touching Sam, seeing her growing excitement, was fueling her own.

Sam wrapped her arms around Riley's back and tried to urge her down against her.

Riley put her hand on the center of Sam's chest and shook her head. "Not yet. Let me touch you." She stared deeply into Sam's eyes, willing her to comply. "I need to touch you."

A shudder rippled through Sam's body. Her eyes darkened to a striking bluish-silver. She held Riley's gaze hostage for several long moments, then spread her arms out on the bed, palms up as if offering herself to Riley.

Oh. My. God. Riley's clit twitched warningly, and she bit back a groan. She rose up on her knees and straddled Sam's thighs, careful to keep their bodies from touching. Her panties were soaked through, and she knew if their sexes rubbed, she would lose it. She took her time, immersing herself in the delights of Sam's body, exploring every dip and curve, first with her fingers and then with her mouth. Every sound of pleasure she coaxed from Sam's lips pushed her own arousal higher. She licked the beads of sweat between Sam's breasts, then sucked one of her nipples into her mouth.

"Riley." Sam writhed beneath the onslaught, her eyes clamped shut. "Please."

Riley reluctantly released the rock-hard nipple and moved off to her side, giving Sam room to spread her legs. Her fingers shook as she slid her hand down Sam's firm abdomen; she moaned when her fingers slipped into the slick heat between Sam's thighs.

Sam's hips bucked. "Yes. Please." Her thighs trembled. She clutched at the bedding as if trying to anchor herself.

Riley looked back and forth between Sam's face and her own hand stroking between Sam's thighs. The sight of Sam on the verge of orgasm was the most amazing thing she ever hoped to see. *I never believed it would actually happen.* She moved her fingers down and then hesitated, hovering outside Sam's entrance. Not everyone enjoyed penetration. She didn't.

When Sam's eyes flew open, the raw need in them drove the breath from Riley's body.

"Go inside." Sam growled. "Deep."

Riley shivered, and her hips thrust. She could no more deny her than she could stop the frantic beating of her heart. Riley thrust inside with a single deep stroke.

Sam groaned, and her body coiled tight.

Riley thrust again, as deeply as she could.

With an inarticulate yell, Sam's body arched, her thighs clamping shut on Riley's hand.

The feel of Sam's internal muscles pulsing around her fingers triggered Riley's climax. Her hips surged against Sam's side, and she groaned. When Sam's legs relaxed and the pulsations around her fingers ceased, Riley gently eased out.

Sam moaned, her muscles twitching. "What did you do to me?" Her voice was hoarse. "My muscles feel like they've turned to jelly." She lifted a hand a few inches off the bed and let it flop back down. "I can't move."

Riley smiled at the dazed expression on Sam's face. "You liked that, huh?" After tugging the sheet up to cover them, she moved up so she could put her head on Sam's shoulder.

"That's the understatement of the year. That was incredible." Sam yawned. "Sorry." She blinked several times, clearly struggling to keep her eyes open. She wrapped her arm around Riley's back and drew her closer. "Just give me a couple of minutes, then it's my turn. I'll take care of you."

Riley stiffened. Those were the words Linda always used as if it was an obligation she had to fulfill. *That's not what Sam means.* Still, now that the words had been uttered, Riley's insecurities about her body came roaring back.

Sam's arm tightened across her back. "What's wrong?"

"Nothing." The night had been amazing; Riley didn't want anything to ruin it. She caressed Sam's belly, trailing her fingers up and down in long, languid strokes.

Sam laid her hand on top of Riley's and stilled the movement. "You'll put me to sleep like that."

That's the idea. Riley raised up and placed a soft kiss on Sam's lips, meant to soothe, not arouse. She tugged her hand free and resumed stroking Sam's belly. "Just relax."

"If I was any more relaxed, I'd be comatose," Sam murmured, her voice growing thick with approaching sleep.

Riley smiled when she felt Sam's body go lax and her breathing even out into the rhythm of sleep. Making love to Sam had been an incredible experience. She'd deal with everything else in the morning. Laying her arm over Sam's stomach, she snuggled against her side and let sleep take her.

CHAPTER 45

Riley woke. After years of being on-call, she was either awake or asleep, never in between. Memories of last night flooded her mind. She glanced over her shoulder.

Sam was right behind her, lying on her side, with her back to Riley.

She eased away and sat up on her side of the bed. When she glanced at the bedside clock, she was surprised to find it was a quarter to eight. She had grown so used to rising early that she rarely slept in, even on her day off.

Sam grumbled in her sleep, rolled onto her back, threw an arm over her eyes, and kicked off the sheet. The pale morning sun, shining in through the partially open drapes, painted her body with a golden glow.

Riley's gaze lingered on Sam's nude form. The memory of caressing every inch of Sam's beautiful body sent arousal surging through her. She pressed her thighs together. As if drawn by an irresistible force, she scooted closer to Sam and reached out to stroke her silky skin. *And then what?* Her hand froze in mid-air.

How are you going to put her off this time? She had no doubt that Sam would want to touch her. *That will change fast once she sees you naked.*

Looking down at her chest, Riley sighed. Her breasts were barely perceptible beneath the silk camisole. She surveyed the rest of her body, then gazed over at Sam in all her naked glory. Compared to her, she looked like a stick figure. Sam's words to Darcy rang in her head. "I'm interested in women. I'm not into boys."

Linda's voice rose up to join the clamor. "One look at that body and no woman would want you."

Riley's insecurities descended with the power of a tsunami and threatened to drown her. Seeing the desire in Sam's eyes disappear, or worse yet, see her try to fake being excited was more than she could bear. *I'm the one who told her I just wanted to be friends. I should have stuck with that.* Tears closed her throat. *Now I've ruined everything.*

Careful not to jostle the bed, she inched toward the edge, then stood. She picked up her clothes from the floor and slipped them on, keeping a close eye on Sam to make sure she didn't awaken. Quietly gathering the rest of her belongings, she prepared to leave. Her shoes in one hand and her suitcase in the other, she stopped just shy of the door. Sam would feel like some one-night stand if she woke up and she was gone without even leaving a note. Riley couldn't to that to her. She went to the desk and penned a note, then crept over to the bed and left it on her empty pillow. As she gazed down at Sam, tears trailed down her cheeks. *I love you.* She wished with all her heart that things could be different. *I'm sorry I can't be what you want.*

Chilled, Sam groped blindly for the sheet. The light from the partially open drapes shone in her eyes. She rolled over to escape the brightness. More awake now, she was stuck by the realization that it was morning. She blushed. *Oh great. I fell asleep on her. That's smooth.* She opened her eyes and reached for Riley. Her hand encountered empty, cold sheets. She sat up and looked around the room.

There was no sign of Riley.

Sam rose naked from the bed and padded around the room. Riley's belongings, including her suitcase, were gone. *What the hell?*

The chill in the air sent her back to the bed to grab the sheet. That's when she spotted the piece of hotel stationery on Riley's pillow. Her stomach sank. She gingerly picked up the paper as if expecting it to explode in her face.

Sam,
I care deeply for you. But I can't do this. I'm sorry.
Riley

Can't do what? Be my lover? That couldn't be the problem. Last night had been incredible. Then she remembered Riley wanting to move out and end their friendship because of her fear of Sam's job. *So she makes love to me like that, changes her mind, and just walks away? No fucking way.*

She grabbed her underwear off the floor and jerked it on. She would go after Riley and do whatever it took to make her see reason. As she shrugged into her ruined shirt, another thought intruded. *Maybe this is for the best. You'll just end up hurting her later.*

Doubts began to assail her. She recalled her failed relationship with Christy and the tragic end of her relationship with Leslie.

Conflicting needs tore at her. As much as she was afraid of losing Riley, she couldn't stand the thought that she might hurt her in the end because of her own inadequacy. Her breath came in short pants as she paced the room.

Finally, she forced herself to stop pacing. She needed help. It was a hard admission for her. She would call her sister. Sam knew there had been issues between Jess and Kim when they first got together. Obviously, they had worked things out between them, so maybe Jess would have some idea of how to fix things with Riley. Despite her fears, there was one thing Sam could not deny. She needed Riley in her life. She snagged her jeans from the floor and then pulled her phone out of the pocket.

Jess's phone went straight to voice mail.

Sam cursed a blue streak when she remembered Jess was working today. She paced the hotel room. *Now what?*

Plagued by the thought that every minute she delayed, Riley was that much closer to San Diego, she debated between heading for her own apartment and trying to catch Jess at the hospital. Then her thoughts turned to Kim. She'd know how to handle this. Still, Sam hesitated to call her, reluctant to add any stress to her life now that Kim was pregnant.

Her fear of losing Riley won out. Kim was still working, so she must be okay dealing with these types of issues. Resolutely, Sam made the call.

CHAPTER 46

Sam glanced at her watch as she hurried toward the house. *Dammit.* The clock was ticking, but catching up to Riley wouldn't do her any good if she didn't know what to say. Thor's booming bark announced her arrival. When Kim opened the door, he rushed toward Sam.

She took a moment to love on the big dog before turning to Kim, who tugged her into a hug.

"We'll figure this out."

She let herself sink into Kim's caring embrace for a few moments before drawing back. "I'm sorry to drop this in your lap."

"I told you over the phone, it's fine," Kim said. "Let's go into the family room."

After motioning Sam toward the couch, she settled into the recliner opposite the couch. Thor lay down at her feet.

Sam took Riley's note from her pocket and handed it over before plopping on the couch. "What the hell do I do?"

Kim read the note. "What do you want to happen here?"

"I want this fixed. I want Riley to stay. I want us to be..." *Lovers? Girlfriends?* Neither of those things were possible. She threw up her hands. "I want things to be like they were."

"So you want to be friends? And forget what happened last night?"

Sam hesitated. Heat rushed through her at the memory of Riley's commanding touch. She had never given herself to someone like that. *Hell, I even insisted on being on top the night I lost my virginity in high school.* Could she live without that, without Riley ever touching her again or getting the chance to touch her? Old fears battled with new longings.

"Yes." She fisted the hair at her temples. "No. But I don't want to hurt her."

Kim leaned forward. "Why would you being lovers and in a relationship hurt Riley?"

"I always screw it up. You saw how things were with Christy. I tried, but I just couldn't be what she needed. Just the thought of committing to a woman, letting her take over my life, makes me break out in a sweat. That's what happened with Christy. The minute we became exclusive, I started feeling smothered and trapped."

"That doesn't mean it will be the same with Riley," Kim said, her voice soothing and calm.

Memories of Leslie rose up in Sam's mind, threatening to overwhelm her. "It happened before. There's something wrong with me in here." She thumped her chest over her heart. "I'm just not capable of that kind of deep, committed love."

"No, Sam," Kim said. "That's not true. You—"

"It is true. You don't understand. It's even worse than you know." Sam wrapped her arms around her churning stomach and rocked back and forth.

"Then tell me."

Sam gazed at Kim. Caring blue eyes regarded her. *Tell her about Leslie.*

"Help me understand."

Kim's neutral expression and non-judgmental tone gave Sam the courage to share the burden she had carried alone for so many years.

Kim tried to remain objective as Sam fought with her fears, but it was a losing battle. Sam was her sister-in-law, after all, not a patient. She rose from the recliner and sat down next to her on the couch.

Thor moved to Sam's other side and settled on the floor at her feet. He put his big head on her knee, offering his own brand of comfort.

Sam stroked the big dog's head and neck. "Thanks, boy," she said, a catch in her voice.

Kim ran her hand up and down Sam's back. She had never seen her so distraught and emotionally vulnerable.

Sam leaned into the touch. Finally, she straightened, leaving one hand on Thor's head. "We met my second year in college. Leslie transferred in from a local community college. We ended up in several classes together and really hit it off. When she admitted to me one night that she was gay, I was thrilled. I was out and proud." She smiled. "Did Jess ever tell you that I came out to our parents first?"

"Yes. She did." *And you're avoidance coping.* "But Leslie wasn't out, was she?"

"No. She said her folks would never accept her being gay." Sam's expression darkened. "We should have just stayed friends." Tension radiated from her.

When the silence lengthened, Kim said, "But you didn't."

"No. She was beautiful and funny, and I couldn't resist. I didn't find out she had never been with a woman," Sam scrubbed her hands over her face, "with anyone until the first time we were together.

I should've stopped as soon as I realized." She flushed. "But I didn't."

"And afterwards?"

"After that first night, she slowly took over my life. If I was five minutes late calling her, she freaked out, convinced something had happened to me. If I went out with my friends, I knew I'd have to face her tears when I got back to the dorm. She begged me to move off campus, away from everyone. She wanted me to be her everything: best friend, lover, confessor, you name it. Every day that went by, I felt more trapped." Sam sent Kim a pleading look. "Please understand; I cared about Leslie." Tears glistened at the corners of her eyes. "I couldn't be what she needed. That's what I mean. There's something wrong with me." Sam pressed her palm against her chest over her heart.

Oh, Sam. That's not true. There was more to this story. Kim was sure of it. Many people had been through a relationship where one person's feelings were stronger than the other's, and they broke up. It normally didn't cause this level of commitment phobia. "So you broke it off."

"I tried to. Several times. But Leslie always got so hysterical I would give in and come back." Sam hung her head. "Then it just... It was just too much. I couldn't do it anymore." She pressed her arms to her belly and rocked.

Kim scooted closer, draped her arm across Sam's back, and clasped her shoulder. "What happened?"

"I was determined to end it. So I demanded the one thing I knew she would never do." Sam's shoulders shook. "I told her if she wanted to be with me, she had to tell her parents about us. I thought it was finally over."

"But it wasn't?"

"No. It took her two weeks, but she went home and told them." Tears streamed down Sam's face. "Her sister called me the next day."

Kim braced herself, knowing that something very bad was coming.

"Her father," Sam's voice broke, "Leslie told her father and—" Her chest hitched. "He beat her to death."

Kim pulled Sam into her arms and stroked her hair. Her eyes stung with repressed tears, not only for Sam, but also for the young life that had been so brutally cut short. "What happened to Leslie was horrible but it wasn't your fault."

"She died because I couldn't commit to her."

"No, Sam." Kim tipped Sam's chin up and made her look her in the eyes. "That's not true. How Leslie acted when you were together wasn't normal. That's not how you treat someone you love. But this wasn't about being committed to her. What happened to Leslie wasn't your fault. Or even hers for that matter. Her father would have found out eventually. There's nothing you could have done to change that. He murdered her. This is all on him." She stroked Sam's back, trying to soothe her. "What happened to Leslie is why you became a cop, isn't it?"

Sam nodded. "If I can save just one person from what happened to Leslie, it's worth it."

No wonder she was so drawn to Riley after the shooting.

She doubted Sam had done it consciously, but that must have been the driving force when she stepped into the line of fire and saved Riley. It was her atonement for not being able to save Leslie.

"And that brings us back to Riley. What happened with Leslie and Christy, that's why you think you'll end up hurting Riley? That those feelings of being trapped will come again?"

Sam nodded and hung her head.

Now that Sam seemed a bit calmer, Kim was determined to help her realize what she was trying so hard to hide, even from herself. "How long has Riley been living with you?"

Sam's brow furrowed, and she moved out of Kim's embrace. "Huh?"

"How long has Riley been living with you?" Kim watched Sam's body language closely.

Sam turned her shoulder and tilted her body slightly away from Kim. "I don't know. A couple of weeks, I guess."

Ah. You know exactly how long. "Hmm...I thought it was longer than that."

"Maybe it has been. Why? What does that have to do with anything?"

Ignoring the question, Kim said, "Help me out here. Just answer the questions, okay?"

Sam frowned, then nodded.

"Do you spend a lot of time together after work and such?"

"Riley works long hours," Sam shrugged, "but yeah, we hang out when she's home."

Kim smiled to herself. *Home.* "And do you feel smothered with her being there? Like she's invading your space?" She already knew the answer, of course, but wanted Sam to verbalize it.

"No." There was no hesitation in Sam's voice. "It's kind of nice to have someone to share dinner with," a soft smile graced her face, "or just hang out and watch a movie."

"Let me make sure I have this right. You care about Riley. You've been living with her for over a month and enjoying it. Correct?" When Sam nodded, Kim allowed her smile to show. "So you're already in a relationship with Riley. And none of those feelings you're worried about have surfaced?"

Sam's eyebrows shot up. "I am?" Her leg began to bounce. "No. It's not the same thing. We're just friends."

"Not after last night," Kim said. "Unless it didn't mean anything to you and you were just in it for the sex."

"No. I would never do that to Riley."

Kim smothered a smile at the vehement denial. "Does being Riley's lover change how you feel about her living with you? Think about it and picture being together for the next month. Does that make you feel smothered or wanting her out of your space?"

Sam's eyes went distant for several moments. She turned toward Kim and smiled. "No. It doesn't." Her amazement was clearly evident in her tone.

"And why do you think that is? Why can't you stand the thought of losing Riley?"

Sam sucked in a breath, then froze. Her eyes lost focus.

Kim held perfectly still, afraid of breaking the moment. She prayed Sam would have the courage to admit the truth.

Sam's breath burst from her in a whoosh, and she began to pant.

"Take it easy. Slow breaths." Kim rubbed her hand slowly up and down Sam's back as she regained control of her breathing.

Wide-eyed, Sam stared at her. "I'm in love with her," she whispered, awe in her voice. "I have to tell her." She jumped up from the couch. "I've got to go after her." She glanced at her watch. "Damn it. I'll never catch her. She'll already be gone."

"If Riley's already gone, find her." Kim nudged her in the ribs and smiled. "You are a cop after all."

"Right. I'll find her." Sam straightened. The defeated slump of her shoulders was gone as if a huge weight had been lifted. "I have to tell her how I feel about her."

Kim locked gazes with her. "One thing I know, beyond a shadow of a doubt: love is worth whatever risks you need to take." She touched Sam's cheek. "It's okay to be scared. But I promise you, it's worth it." Her hand went to her belly.

Sam pulled her into a hug, lifted her feet off the floor, and twirled her in a circle. "Thank you. You're the best."

Thor jumped up and woofed at Sam.

Kim's stomach lurched. "The best is going to hurl on you if you don't put me down."

Sam froze. "Shit. I'm sorry. I didn't think." Keeping her arm loosely wrapped around Kim, she put her hand over Kim's where it rested on her slightly rounded belly. "Are you okay? Is the baby okay?"

"We're both fine." Kim stepped out of Sam's embrace and smiled at her. "Now go get Riley." She put a restraining hand on Sam's arm before she could bolt away. "Please be careful. You won't do either of you any good if you have an accident speeding down to San Diego."

"I'll be careful. I promise." Sam placed a soft kiss on Kim's cheek. "Thank you." She turned and sprinted for the front door.

CHAPTER 47

Sam rapped her hands on the steering wheel, willing the light to turn green. *Come on!*

As she had feared, Riley had already been gone by the time she reached her apartment. A number of Riley's things were left with a note on them that she would be sending someone by for them.

Like hell. She would find Riley if she had to go to every hotel in the city, starting with the hotel Riley had retreated to after her uncle threw her out of the condo. When the light changed, Sam resisted the urge to punch it. A few minutes later, she pulled into the hotel parking lot. When she spotted Riley's car, the tight band that had constricted her chest since waking that morning and finding her gone eased a notch.

She pulled her car up to the valet parking, jumped out, and tossed her keys to the attendant before marching across the lobby and up to the front desk.

The clerk looked up from the computer screen. "May I help you?"

"Yes. What room is Dr. Connolly in?"

"I'm sorry, ma'am, but I can't give out information on a guest."

Sam ground her teeth. She reached into her back pocket, pulled out her police credentials, and flipped them open. "What room is Dr. Connolly in?"

The clerk's gaze darted from the black leather wallet in Sam's hand to her face. He gulped. "Just a moment." He accessed the computer. "Four-oh-seven."

"Thank you." Sam spun on her heel and headed for the elevator.

Sam stood outside the door to Riley's hotel room. All she had been focused on was finding her. Now that she was here, about to face Riley, she was shaking. She wiped her sweaty palms on her jeans. *She cares deeply for you. You just have to make her see reason.*

Fueled by the realization that she was in love with Riley, Sam felt as if a weight she had carried for so long had been lifted. She held on to the hope that Riley was in love with her as well. *Remember the look in her eyes as she made love to you.*

Thus fortified, she knocked on the door.

After a moment of silence, a gasp came from inside the room.

She knocked again. "Riley? Please, let me in."

"Oh, Sam. What are you doing here?" Riley's voice came through the door. "Why didn't you stay in LA?"

"I came after you. How could you just leave like that?" Sam's pain leaked into her voice. "Please let me in. We have to talk."

"It's better this way." Riley's voice broke. "Just go."

Tension, as thick as the door that separated them, filled the air.

"I'm not going away," Sam said. "Not until you talk to me. You owe me that much." She breathed a sigh of relief when she heard the chain being removed.

The door slowly opened.

Sam's heart clenched at her first sight of Riley. Her normally vibrant green eyes were red-rimmed and dull.

Riley turned away and walked back into the hotel room.

Sam followed.

An open suitcase, filled to overflowing, lay on the bed. Riley moved as if the weight of the world rested on her shoulders. Sadness dripped from her like drops of rain from a weeping willow.

Oh, Riley. Why are you doing this?

Riley walked over to the bed, grabbed several shirts from the suitcase, and threw them into the dresser drawer, apparently not caring how they landed. "You shouldn't have come. Please don't make this harder than it already is." She went to get more clothes out of the suitcase.

"Why does it have to be hard at all? Come back home." Sam couldn't miss the irony of the situation, having had her share of women asking her not to leave. She stepped into Riley's path.

Riley tried to step around her, but Sam moved with her, blocking her escape.

"Please don't." A wounded sound escaped Riley's throat.

"Talk to me." Sam took a chance and put her hands on Riley's shoulders. Her own fears had almost ruined things; she wouldn't let Riley's fear destroy their relationship before it even got started. "Tell me why you're doing this? Especially after what happened last night."

Clutching the clothes in her arms tightly to her chest, Riley refused to look at her.

Just say it. Her heart pounding in her chest like a bass drum, Sam said, "Please don't do this. I love you."

Riley's head whipped up. "Oh, Sam. I love you too."

Euphoria filled Sam.

Riley gazed at her with pain-filled eyes. "That's why I had to leave before—" Her voice caught in her throat.

Sam's heart plummeted like a boulder thrown from a cliff. She tightened her grip on Riley's shoulders. "Before what, Riley? I get hurt? You don't know that's going to happen. You can't live your life worrying about what might happen."

Riley jerked away. "It's not just that. You don't understand. I can't... I'm not..." She tossed the clothes toward her suitcase. Half of them landed on the floor. She grabbed them and threw them back into the suitcase.

The hell with this. Sam moved behind Riley and turned her around to face her. "What are you afraid of?" When Riley tried to pull away, she refused to let go. She didn't want to hurt Riley, but she wasn't going to let her run either. "Please. I'm begging you. Tell me why you're doing this."

All the fight went out of Riley, and she slumped against Sam, who cradled her against her body. Finally, Riley lifted her head. Tears trailed down her face.

Pierced by the pain in Riley's eyes, Sam leaned down. She feathered butterfly-soft kisses across her tear-streaked cheeks.

Riley's eyes fluttered closed.

Sam kissed her eyelids, her temples, her cheeks, and finally her lips.

With a low moan, Riley wrapped her arms around Sam's waist.

The sound went straight to Sam's center. She licked at Riley's bottom lip. When Riley opened to accept her, she groaned and pressed her tongue into Riley's mouth, deepening the kiss. Her hands slid down to cup Riley's sweet ass. *Just perfect.*

Riley's hips thrust against her thigh.

Sam needed more, she needed to finally touch Riley—all of her.

With a throaty growl that made Sam shiver, Riley took control of the kiss, her tongue chasing Sam's back into Sam's mouth. She brought her hands up and cupped Sam's breasts.

Sam groaned, a warning pulse throbbing in her clit. *Oh no, you don't, not this time. It's my turn.*

She reluctantly released Riley's ass and tugged Riley's hands off her breasts and onto her shoulders. At the look of confusion in Riley's passion-glazed eyes, she smiled and kissed her forehead. She dipped her head and captured Riley's lips in a searing kiss. She slipped her hands underneath Riley's sweater and caressed the silky smooth skin of her back before moving around to the front and stroking her soft belly.

After wrenching away from the torrid kiss, Riley backed away, breaking the contact between them. Tears overflowed her eyes. "This is a mistake. I can't be what you want."

Not again. Was this some kind of game? The pain in Riley's eyes deflated Sam's anger. "Why? That doesn't make sense. You're exactly what I want."

Riley brushed away her tears, her expression going distant. "You said it yourself. You're into women, not boys."

Sam struggled to get air into her lungs. It felt as if someone had sucker-punched her. *I caused this?* She knew Riley had body-image issues but had no idea she had taken her words to heart. "I was drunk and trying to get rid of Darcy. What I said has nothing to do with you."

"Doesn't it?" Riley looked down at herself. "I know what I am." She crossed her arms over her chest. "I know you care about me. And you may think you want me now, but once you see me..."

She slowly closed the distance between them, praying Riley wouldn't reject her touch. "Please listen to me." She cupped Riley's cheek. "I know what you are too. You're the woman I'm in love with."

A small gasp escaped Riley's lips as her knees buckled.

Sam pulled Riley into her arms and held her close. "I've been in love with you for weeks. I've just been too afraid to admit it, even to myself." All she wanted to do was kiss her senseless, but there were things that still needed to be said. She stroked her thumb across Riley's soft lips. "I've loved you for weeks, but I've wanted you for a lot longer than that." Sam tightened her embrace. She had to make Riley understand. She cradled Riley's face between her palms and held her gaze, willing her to believe. "I know what I want. I want you. Just the thought of touching you makes me tremble."

Riley studied Sam's face, then stared deeply into her eyes as if trying to look into her very soul. Her expression crumbled. "I'm sorry. I was scared. And—" She buried her face against Sam's chest and cried.

Sam held her tightly and soothed her as best she could.

After several long moments, Riley pulled out of the embrace and blotted her face on her sleeve. Her emotions darkened her eyes to a deep emerald. "This wasn't your doing. I let my insecurities get the best of me, and I ended up hurting you. Hurting us. I'm sorry."

"I understand." Looking for a place to sit so that they could be close, Sam bypassed the clothes-strewn bed and guided Riley to the straight-backed chair in front of a small desk. Before Riley could protest, she pulled her into her lap and slipped her arms around Riley's waist. "I know what your aunt put you through. How she made you feel about yourself."

"No. It wasn't my aunt. She was just fixated on my weight. To her, the thinner I was, the better." A bright flush covered her already blotchy face, making her freckles stand out. "Remember I mentioned that I had been with a woman in medical school?"

Sam nodded. She knew nothing about the woman but disliked her already.

Riley blew out a breath. "This is even harder than I thought." She ducked her head.

No matter how much Sam wanted to know, she wouldn't pressure her. Sam softly stroked Riley's back, waiting for her to make up her mind.

"Her name was Linda." Riley rested her head against Sam's shoulder. "We shared a large house with several other medical students. That's also where I met my friend Denny and his wife, Carol. Anyway, Linda was three years ahead of me in school. I'd never had a woman look at me like she did. I didn't understand why I reacted so strongly to her," she pressed her face to Sam's shirt as if to hide her blush, "but later when she kissed me, I finally figured it out. At first things were great between us. Or so I thought..."

Sam struggled to keep her expression neutral. Just the thought of what this woman must have done to Riley to make her so unsure of herself was enough to spark Sam's ire.

"Linda even claimed to understand my fear of my aunt and uncle finding out about us. I didn't realize until later that it made things all the more convenient for her." Bitterness filled Riley's voice. "That way she had the perfect excuse not to have anything to do with me outside the bedroom."

The more Sam heard about the woman, the more she despised her. She mentally braced herself for what was coming.

Riley took several deep breaths like a diver preparing to jump into the deep end. "We had only been together two months when she started making comments about my body. Just little snide remarks when we were in bed, about how boyish I looked, how nonexistent my breasts were. Finally it reached the point where she expected me to take care of her, but she never touched me anymore. I can't tell you how many times she compared my body to a prepubescent boy."

Dammit! Sam bit her lip. No wonder what she'd said to Darcy had struck so close to home.

"I remember the night I broke it off with her like it was yesterday. I can still hear Linda's voice." Riley's eyes went distant as if she were in another time and place. "Good. At least now I don't have to pretend anymore. Do us all a favor and go back to men. Plenty of them don't care about the rest of your body as long as there's a warm hole for them to shove their dick in. No dyke in her right mind would want you." Riley buried her face against Sam's neck.

"What a fucking bitch!" Then it hit her. Pain as sharp as a spear to the heart stabbed Sam. She reared back as far as she could from Riley with her sitting in her lap. "And you thought I'd treat you like that? Like she did?"

Riley clutched Sam's shirt. "God, Sam. No. Never! I know you'd never treat me like that. It was just after what you said to Darcy and seeing Marina, knowing she was the kind of woman you'd been with…" A tear trickled down her face. "I let my fears run away with me. I'm so sorry."

She cradled Riley against her chest. "I understand. I've let my own fears rule me for too long."

Riley sniffed. "I wish we could go back to bed and start this day over."

"That's a good idea." Sam stood up with Riley in her arms.

"What are you doing?" Riley wrapped her arms around Sam's neck.

"Just what you said. We're going back to bed and starting this day over." Sam gently set Riley down next to the bed. She gathered up the clothes on the bed, shoved them into the suitcase, flipped the lid down, and carried the overflowing case over to the luggage rack by the door. Smiling, she walked back to the bed.

Riley was standing exactly where she had left her, her hands worrying the bottom of her sweater.

Sam leaned down and whispered close to her ear, "Relax. We're just going to sleep. I would never pressure you to let me touch you." She nipped Riley's earlobe and smiled to herself when Riley shivered. "No matter how much I want to touch you."

Under Riley's watchful eyes, she stripped out of her clothes, leaving just her sports bra and underwear. *Don't even think about how she's looking at you, or you'll never survive this.* She pulled the comforter to the end of the bed, turned back the sheet and blanket, and slipped into the bed. "Your turn."

Riley smiled hesitantly. Her hands trembled as she reached for the bottom of her sweater. She pulled it over her head, then removed the rest of her clothes, except for her undergarments.

Sam held her gaze until she saw some of her trepidation ease, then allowed her gaze to travel over Riley's silk camisole, down to her panties, and back to her face. "You're beautiful."

Riley flushed, and her gaze darted away.

I'll convince you of that. No matter how long it takes. Sam longed to touch her. Holding up her arm in invitation, she said, "Join me."

Riley climbed into the bed, slipped under Sam's arm, and snuggled against her side.

Sam pulled her close and let out a contented sigh. The press of Riley's body against her excited and soothed her at the same time. "Are you comfortable?"

Riley nodded against her shoulder. She put her arm over Sam's belly.

Sam placed a soft kiss on her forehead. "This is just what we needed."

CHAPTER 48

Riley woke with her cheek pressed against bare skin. *Now this how the day should have started.* She was lying behind Sam, spooned against her, with her arm around Sam's waist and one hand resting on her belly. She lifted up enough to peer over Sam's shoulder. Sam's eyes were closed, and her chest rose and fell with the rhythm of sleep.

She still found it hard to believe Sam had come after her. Not only that, but Sam was in love with her. Not in her wildest dreams had Riley dared hope for that. *And she wants me. Just like I am.* That realization had been as exhilarating as finding out Sam loved her.

Her euphoria dimmed at the pain she had caused Sam. No matter how long it took, she would make it up to her. She tried to go back to sleep but couldn't resist the feel of Sam's silky skin beneath her fingers. She stroked Sam's abdomen, from the bottom of her bra to the top of her underwear. Needing to feel more skin, she bunched her camisole up to expose her chest and cuddled closer. Her bare breasts pressed against Sam's back, and Riley bit back a groan. She resumed caressing Sam's belly.

Sam closed her fingers around Riley's wrist, startling her, and tugged her hand up to cover Sam's breast. "I dreamed about this."

"About us?" Riley asked.

Sam pulled up her sports bra and guided Riley's hand to her bare breast. "About waking up with your naked breasts pressed against my back." Her breathing sped up. "You squeezed my breast, then rolled my nipple between your fingers."

Riley's thighs clenched as arousal shot straight to her center. She squeezed Sam's breast.

Sam pressed back against her.

After taking Sam's nipple between her fingers, she rolled it until it became a tight, hard bud. "Then what did I do?"

"You. You... God I can't think with you doing that."

She grinned and increased the pressure on her nipple. "Want me to stop?"

Sam whimpered.

I'll take that as a no. "What did I do then?"

"You didn't do anything. I took your hand off my breast," Sam said, matching her actions to her words. "And..." She lifted her leg and guided Riley's hand into her underwear and between her thighs.

Riley groaned when her fingers were engulfed in slick, wet heat. She sought out Sam's clit and began to stroke her. "Then what happened?"

Having Sam relating her dream was unexpectedly erotic. She wondered how long she could keep her talking.

"Then...then the freaking phone rang, and I woke up."

Riley burst out laughing and shifted as if she were going to remove her hand. *Like that would ever happen.* She could touch her forever and never tire of it.

Sam grabbed her wrist. "Please."

Allowing Sam to set the pace, Riley stroked her. When she felt Sam was close, she pushed inside and thrust hard and deep.

Sam's body went taut. "Riley."

Riley thrilled to the sound of her name wrenched from Sam's lips. She kept her fingers in place until the contractions around them had stopped, then gently eased out. She pressed against Sam's back, stroking her belly as she recovered.

Sam put her hand on top of Riley's and startled Riley by rolling over and facing her.

She quickly pulled her camisole down to cover her breasts.

"Please don't do that." Sam ran her fingers across the bottom edge of the camisole. "Will you let me touch you?"

A spark of apprehension flared. Riley firmly smothered it. *You don't have to be afraid with Sam.* "I'd like that."

Sam sat up, removed her sports bra, then tugged her underwear off. She slid back down in the bed so they were face to face.

Unable to resist the temptation, Riley cupped one of Sam's breasts.

"Ah. Not this time." Sam gently removed her hand. "It's my turn." Her striking silvery-blue eyes glowed with passion. "Please. I need to touch you."

Riley shivered as renewed arousal swept through her.

Taking her time, Sam trailed her fingers over Riley's silk-covered belly, down her thighs, and back up toward her breasts.

Every touch ratcheted Riley's breathing up another notch. By the time Sam reached her breasts, she was panting. Sam caressed her breasts through the camisole, repeatedly brushing her thumbs over her aching nipples. When she withdrew her hand, Riley whimpered.

Sam captured her gaze and held her hostage. "I want you. Only you." She slipped her hand under the camisole and stroked her bare belly. "Please. Take this off." Her voice dropped to a husky purr. "And the panties too."

Riley clenched her thighs, sure she was going to climax from just the sexy timbre of Sam's voice. She sat up. Her fingers trembled as she removed the camisole and her panties under Sam's watchful eyes. Despite her arousal, as she lay back down facing Sam, she swallowed heavily at baring herself fully.

Sam's gaze swept her body like a physical caress.

When Sam looked back up, the raw passion on her face took Riley's breath away.

"You're beautiful."

And Riley believed her. No one had ever looked at her like that before. "Please, Sam. Touch me."

Sam growled. "I thought you'd never ask."

Oh. God. Riley's hips thrust before she even touched her. Her body surged forward and pressed against Sam's, desperate for the contact.

Sam wrapped her arm around Riley's back and pulled their bodies together as if trying to merge them into one being.

She moaned at the feel of Sam's bare breasts against hers.

Dipping her head, Sam took Riley's lips in a searing kiss. She stroked up and down her back before cupping her ass.

Riley struggled to contain the rising tide that threatened to obliterate her tenuous control. *Not yet.* She needed to feel Sam touching her, loving her.

"Relax. Just let go. There will be lots more times to go slow," Sam whispered close to her ear as if she could read Riley's thoughts. She lowered her head and captured Riley's breast in her mouth.

Fire coiled in Riley's belly.

Sam slid her hand down Riley's abdomen and delved into the heat between her thighs.

The world shrank down to the exquisite point of pleasure between her legs. A single stroke across her clit and she shattered. A climax unlike any Riley had experienced roared through her.

When she regained her equilibrium, she was cradled in Sam's strong arms, face pillowed on her breast. She lifted her head and gazed into Sam's loving blue eyes. "I love you." Emotion choked her voice.

Sam hugged her almost painfully tight. "I love you too."

Riley's stomach growled loudly. Heat shot up her neck.

Sam grinned. "Have you eaten at all today?"

Riley was loath to admit she hadn't. She didn't want Sam to move, but her traitorous stomach growled again, answering for her.

Sam laughed, threw back the covers, and got out of bed. "Me neither, and I'm suddenly starving."

Already missing her warmth, Riley pulled the sheet up to cover her chest.

Sam found the room service menu. She smiled as she settled back into the bed with Riley. "What do you say we order some breakfast, then after we've eaten, we'll gather all this stuff up and go home?"

A home with Sam. No words had ever sounded so right. "Sounds perfect to me."

Sam leaned over and nibbled on Riley's neck. "Well, maybe there might be a couple of other things we need to do before we go home."

Riley shivered as Sam's lips dipped lower, taking the sheet with her. *Even better.*

EPILOGUE

T hanks for the help putting the grill together."
Marina slid open the glass patio door.

Sam followed her into the house. "No problem.
How's your finger? Has it stopped bleeding?"

She had refused to let Sam look at her finger
after she cut it while fitting the heating element
into place.

"It's fine." Marina scowled at the blood-soaked
paper towel wrapped around her index finger.

"You should let Riley take a look at it." She
glanced at her watch. "They should be back soon."

Marina waved away the suggestion. "It's just a
scratch, not a traumatic amputation. I'll go rinse it
out. Want another beer?"

"No thanks. Two's my limit."

"Geez, how the mighty have fallen." Marina
smirked. "What's the matter, little woman won't let
you have more than two beers?"

Sam laughed, refusing to take the bait.
"Look who's talking." She swept her arm wide
encompassing the whole area. "I'm not the old,
married lady living with the little woman in a house
with a real picket fence."

"You've got me there." Marina arched an
eyebrow. "You know, it's not like it used to be. You
could marry your woman too."

Just the thought of Riley made Sam's smile
widen. The last six months with Riley had been
amazing. She fell more in love with her every day.

"I knew it. You are going to ask her."

Sam had never thought she would find herself totally in love and looking forward to spending the rest of her life with anyone. She was going to propose; she was just waiting until she could create the perfect moment. But she wasn't ready to admit that to Marina. She gave Marina her most innocent look. "Who me? You think I'd do something like that?"

Marina laughed. "Who do you think you're kidding?" She bumped shoulders with Sam. "I'm so happy for you, mi amiga."

The front door opened, and Elisabeth and Riley came in.

"How was the meeting?" Sam was so glad Elisabeth had talked Riley into joining the women's support group for partners of police officers.

Riley smiled and rose up on her toes for a kiss. "It was good. We had some newcomers tonight. It felt great to give something back to the group. They've helped me so much."

Sam gave her a one-armed hug. "That's—"

"What happened to your hand?" Elisabeth cut in.

Marina tucked her hand behind her back. "Nothing. Just a little scratch."

Elisabeth stood toe to toe with her. "Let me see your hand."

"Really it's—" Marina winced at the look she was getting and held out her hand.

Sam grinned at her over Elisabeth's shoulder and mouthed, "Pussy-whipped."

Riley elbowed her in the ribs.

When Sam glanced down at her, the expression on Riley's face wiped the smirk off Sam's.

Marina shot her a serves-you-right look.

Riley moved to Elisabeth's side and examined Marina's hand. "Doesn't look too bad. Clean it up with peroxide or Betadine if you have it, then a couple of steri-strips. Make sure she keeps it clean, and it'll be fine."

Elisabeth nodded. "Thanks, Riley."

"Yeah, thanks, Doc," Marina said. "Everyone hungry? I've got the grill heating. Should be ready to put the burgers on by now."

Sam's phone rang. She glanced at the screen. The name displayed sent her pulse into overdrive. They had been on baby watch for almost two weeks. "It's Jess." She thumbed the screen. "Hey, Jess."

"Kim's in labor. We're leaving for LA Metro now. Meet us at the birthing center."

Sam couldn't remember ever hearing her always calm and in-control sister sounding so anxious. She heard Kim in the background. Her voice sounded stressed, but Sam couldn't make out what she was saying. *I hope she's okay.*

"I have to go. Get here." Jess hung up before Sam could reply.

"Well?" Riley asked.

"Kim's in labor."

"How long has she been in labor? Did she say how far effaced and dilated she was?" Riley stared at Sam's phone as if she could make it give her the answers she wanted.

Sam shook her head. "I have no idea. Jess didn't give any details, just said to get up there."

"Right." Riley nodded. "Jess has a lot more pressing things on her mind at the moment than reassuring us." She tugged Sam's arm and took a step toward the door. "Let's go. I promised Kim we'd be there. I'll call Denny on the way and get him to cover for me tomorrow." She frowned and turned back to Marina and Elisabeth. "Sorry about dinner."

"Don't worry about that," Elizabeth said. "Get out of here. Be sure to call us when the baby is born."

"We will," Sam said.

Sam strode toward the nurses' station, still grumbling about the temporary shutdown of the freeway that had delayed them. When she realized Riley had to trot to keep up with her, she shortened her strides.

"Can I help you?" a nurse asked.

"We're here to see Kim Donov—" Sam caught herself. "I mean Kim McKenna. I'm her sister-in-law. What room is she in?" She glanced at Riley, wondering if she'd be willing to change her name someday too.

The nurse consulted her computer. "Dr. McKenna is in three-twelve."

"Thanks," Sam said.

The closer they got to Kim's room, the more Sam's anxiety rose. She had dealt with women in labor while on the job. The thought of seeing Kim like that, bathed in sweat with her face contorted in pain, made her stomach burn.

"What's the matter?"

She started at the sound of Riley's voice. "Just worried about Kim."

"I'm sure she and the baby will be fine." Riley put her hand on Sam's arm. "She's had an uncomplicated pregnancy."

They stopped outside the room marked three-twelve.

Unlike most of the other rooms they had passed, this door was closed. Sam's anxiety spiked. She hesitated to knock.

Riley had no such qualms. She knocked on the door.

There was no response for several moments, then a nurse in scrubs pulled the door open just enough to stick her head out. "McKenna family?"

Fear held Sam's voice hostage.

"Yes, we're her family," Riley said.

"You'll need to give us a few minutes to finish up with Dr. McKenna." The nurse ducked back into the room and shut the door.

"We missed it? The baby was born?" While Sam was sorry they had missed the birth, she couldn't repress the relief that washed over her at not having to see Kim in pain.

"Kim and Jess will understand. They know what traffic can be like between San Diego and LA." Riley glanced at her watch. "Though I admit I'm kind of surprised. I don't know how long they waited before coming in, but Jess only called us three and a half hours ago. That's pretty fast for a first delivery."

Sam stared at the closed door. "But you think Kim's okay, right? The nurse would have said something, wouldn't she?"

Riley stepped close and wrapped her arm around Sam's waist. "Kim and the baby are fine. I'm sure of it."

Gazing down into Riley's calm, loving green eyes, Sam felt her tension ease.

It wasn't long before the door swung open.

A nurse exited, pushing an IV stand. Kim's obstetrician was right behind her. "Congratulations again, you two. Sorry I have to run." She waved, offered Sam and Riley a smile, then hurried down the hall.

The same nurse as before greeted them with a smile. "Come in and meet the newest member of the family."

Sam entwined her fingers with Riley's as they entered. The lights were turned low, bathing the room in a gentle glow. The head of the bed was raised, and Jess sat on the far side, her arm wrapped protectively around Kim and their child. She looked up when Sam and Riley reached the bed.

Sam's breath caught at the open, emotion-filled look in her sister's eyes. She had never seen her look so vulnerable—or so happy. "Hey, sis. Congratulations. Sorry we couldn't get here in time." Sam's voice cracked.

Riley leaned in and hugged Kim, then kissed her cheek, being careful of the baby. "I'm so sorry I wasn't here for you."

"You're here now," Kim said. "That's what matters."

Sam smiled when she noticed the pink hat on the baby. *Oh wow. A little girl.* Kim had been adamant about not knowing the gender of the baby in advance. She leaned down and placed a kiss on Kim's cheek.

Riley wiped tears from her eyes. "Congratulations to both of you." She reached across Kim and pressed Jess's hand.

The strains of the labor and delivery were etched on Kim's face, but her eyes glowed with happiness. She motioned to Jess, who eagerly took the baby from her arms. "Please meet Erin Marie McKenna."

Jess carried Erin around the end of the bed and over to Sam and Riley so they could get a closer look. She carefully opened the blanket swaddling Erin.

Thick black hair peeked out from beneath the stocking cap.

Riley ran a gentle finger across Erin's cheek. "She's a big girl."

"She weighed in at eight pounds, five ounces." Cuddling her close to her chest, Jess pulled the blanket closed.

"She looks just like pictures of Jess as a baby." Sam grinned when Jess's chest puffed with pride.

Erin emitted a whimper and opened her eyes.

Sam knew the color of her eyes might change with time, but right now they were the same sky blue as Kim's. "She's beautiful." Tears traced down Sam's cheeks.

Riley wrapped one arm around her waist.

Sam pulled Riley against her side, wrapped her arms around her, and held her close.

Erin let out a lusty yell.

Jess smiled at her daughter. "I think someone's hungry." She took Erin to Kim, who lowered her gown.

It took several minutes, but she finally got Erin situated at her breast.

Riley and Sam shared a quiet moment of joy with Jess and Kim as Erin nursed.

When Riley looked up at her with love shining in her eyes, Sam felt as if her heart would burst with love. That's when she realized she'd had it all wrong. It wasn't about creating the perfect moment to ask Riley. *No more waiting.* She glanced at Jess and Kim. "Hey you guys, we'll be back in a little while."

Jess waved without looking away from Erin. Kim gave Sam a quick smile and a nod.

"Come with me, please." Sam urged Riley out of the room.

"What's wrong?"

"Nothing." Sam took her hand. "Trust me."

Smiling, Riley squeezed Sam's hand. "Lead on."

Sam led her to a small, secluded courtyard Jess had shown her. It didn't compare to the hidden garden where they'd first had lunch, but it was beautiful nonetheless.

Riley looked around, then stared up at Sam with a bemused expression. "What's so important here?"

Sam dropped to one knee and took both of Riley's hands in hers.

Riley's eyes went wide.

"I've been trying to think of how to create the perfect moment to ask you, but what I never realized, until now, is that the perfect moment comes when you say yes."

Riley's hands trembled in Sam's.

"Riley, will you marry me?"

"Yes!" Riley threw herself into Sam's arms, almost taking them both to the ground. "Yes."

Sam's heart soared. *My wife.*

# # #

ABOUT RJ NOLAN

RJ Nolan lives in the United States with her spouse and their Great Dane. She makes frequent visits to the California coast near her home. The sight and sound of the surf always stir her muse. When not writing, she enjoys reading, camping, and the occasional trip to Disneyland.

E-Mail: rjnolan@gmail.com
Website: http://www.rjnolan.com

EXCERPT FROM *L.A. METRO*

BY RJ NOLAN

Entering the park, Kim followed the signs that lead to the dog run area. Jess had really managed to shock her yesterday. Having Jess ask her to meet with her outside the hospital was the last thing she had expected. While it was what she had been hoping for, Kim was still nervous. She wasn't sure what to expect. *I can do this.* Finally spotting what she was looking for, she headed for the large fenced-in area.

Dogs of all shapes and sizes were playing in the bright fall sunshine. She easily spotted Jess leaning against the fence just inside the dog run, near the gate. Kim stopped for a minute to admire the woman. Instead of the Dockers and button-down shirt or scrubs she was used to seeing Jess wear, she was dressed in Lycra shorts and a T-shirt. Kim's gaze ran appreciatively over her well-muscled body. Broad muscular shoulders, well defined biceps, and a flat stomach with trim hips led down to heavily muscled legs. Kim knew that Jess was a beautiful woman, but now, dressed like this... Kim shivered as a wash of arousal cascaded down her body. The strength of her response surprised her. *Friends,* she sternly reminded her wayward libido.

I'm going to be her friend. She forced the distracting feelings away before heading over to Jess.

"Hey, Jess. Good morning."

Jess offered a tentative smile. "Hi, Kim. Glad you could make it." She opened the gate for Kim and motioned her inside the dog run.

The realization that Jess was a bit anxious made Kim feel better about her own nervousness. To give them both a chance to get used to being together in a non-work situation, Kim took the time to look around. Excited dogs chased each other, nimbly dodging the park benches scattered throughout the area. A black lab was splashing in one of the large water bowls strategically placed around the run.

Several small dogs ran up. Their exuberant yipping pierced the crisp morning air. Kim knelt down and held out her hand to be sniffed. Once assured of their friendliness, she petted them. She smiled at Jess when she squatted down next to her and offered her own gentle ear rubs to the canine trio.

Kim stood as the small dogs scampered off. A lot of her tension had eased. Dogs were great stress relievers. She looked at Jess, pleased to see she appeared more relaxed as well. "They were cute, but I still like big dogs best."

"Well, luckily I can help you out there," Jess said. "Ready to meet my boy?"

Knowing Jess had a big dog, Kim checked out the dogs nearby. The only two dogs she saw that she considered big dogs were a German Shepard and a very large Doberman. "Which one is he?"

Jess quickly scanned the area, glancing right past both dogs Kim had spotted. "He must be down at the other end. See where those trees are? He'll come when I call."

That's when Kim noticed just how large the fenced area really was. "Great. I'm looking forward to meeting him." Kim glanced over at Jess. *Uh-oh. Never saw that look before.* Jess had a little half smirk on her face. The look screamed—look out; here comes trouble. Kim tried to brace herself for whatever was coming. At the same time, she was delighted to see Jess relaxing the tight control of her emotions she maintained at work.

Jess led them over toward a group of benches. Just as they reached the seats, Jess let out a piercing whistle, causing Kim to jump. "Sorry about that. I should've warned you." She pointed off to the left. "Here he comes." Jess slapped her palms against the tops of her thighs. "Come on, Thor. Come here, boy!"

Kim turned toward where Jess had pointed and nearly fainted. Charging straight at them was the biggest dog Kim had ever seen.

"Oh my God, Jess, that's not a dog. That's a horse!" Kim took a step back and moved slightly behind Jess.

Jess grinned as the big dog skidded to a halt in front of her. "I thought you said you liked big dogs."

Embarrassed that her bravado had slipped so badly, Kim mock-scowled at Jess. "Yeah, big dogs. You didn't say anything about a Clydesdale."

"Don't worry," Jess said, trying hard to control her laughter. Reaching out and stroking the big dog, Jess reassured Kim. "He's big, but he's harmless." Jess took Kim's hand and urged her to stand next to her. "Kim, this is my Great Dane, Thor."

Kim offered her hand to be sniffed.

"Thor, this is Kim. Be nice," Jess said.

Thor took a step forward to check her out. Kim swallowed a bit nervously when she realized the dog's head was almost chest height. And she was tall for a woman, she only missed by a couple of inches matching Jess's almost six-foot stature. He wagged his tail and proceeded to give her a thorough sniff. She smiled as her trepidation eased. Kim quickly saw what a gentle giant the big dog truly was and began to stroke his head and ears.

Thor made his approval known. He gazed into her eyes, and then laid his head against her breasts.

"I don't believe it," Jess muttered. She shook her head and stared.

"What?" Kim asked as she continued to pet Thor.

"I've never seen him do that with anyone except myself or my sister. He's not unfriendly, but he tends to be standoffish about offering affection to strangers. Usually he sniffs someone and then just walks away."

Thor suddenly leaned harder into Kim, forcing her to step back as his weight against her increased.

"Thor." Jess grabbed his collar. "Back up." She urged Thor back several steps. "Sorry."

Kim laughed. "It's okay. He's not bothering me." Pointing to the bench next to her, she said, "Why don't we sit down and you can tell me about this handsome boy."

Jess sat down, but kept a firm grip on Thor's collar.

"He's fine, really. Let him go," Kim said as she moved to a spot on the bench near Jess.

As soon as Jess let go of Thor's collar he headed for Kim.

Kim was a little taken aback when Thor stepped close. The huge dog's head was now level with hers. She met his eyes and was surprised by the intelligence that shone in his dark brown eyes.

Thor gently laid his head in Kim's lap. When she began to stroke his head, he closed his eyes and sighed in contentment.

"Come on, you big moose. Kim is not a cuddly toy." Jess reached for Thor's collar, intent on pulling the big dog off of Kim's lap.

Kim laughed. "Honestly, he's fine. Leave him." She stroked her hand down his shining black coat. "I've never seen a Great Dane that looked like this before." His black head and body shone in sharp contrast to his white neck and chest. "He looks like he's dressed in a top hat and tuxedo." Kim slid her hand down one of his strong front legs. "He even has the white spats to go along with his formal attire."

"He's what's called a Mantle Great Dane," Jess said. "Most people are more familiar with Fawn or Brindle Great Danes."

"I knew Great Danes were big," Kim reached down and tried to close her hand around Thor's front leg but couldn't, "but I never realized they were this huge," she said.

"They can get pretty big. Thor is larger than average. He's thirty-nine inches tall at the withers and just shy of two hundred pounds."

Kim gulped. It appeared to her that most of that two hundred pounds was solid muscle. "Good thing he's so docile."

"Yeah, they're big babies for the most part. But under the right circumstances they can be very protective of their owners." Jess stretched, arching her back.

Kim struggled to keep her eyes on Jess's face where they belonged. "Ready to go jogging?" *Either that or I'm going to need a cold shower.*

"Sure. Let's go." Jess snapped Thor's leash onto his collar.

Jess guided them back to where they had started before slowing down to a walk. Knowing Kim had not jogged in a few months, Jess had offered the one-mile route. Kim had opted for the two-mile trail. *Bet she's regretting that decision about now.* Kim was bent over at the waist with her hands resting on the top of her thighs as she tried to catch her breath.

Allowing her eyes to run over Kim's body for the first time, she took in the tall, slender figure before her. She had been so nervous earlier she had not really paid that much attention to Kim's attire. Kim had on short nylon running shorts and a T-shirt. Jess had suspected a gorgeous body lurked beneath the professionally tailored slacks and silk blouses she wore at work. The reality was much more than she had anticipated. *Your imagination sucks.* Drops of sweat trailed down Kim's well-defined arms and legs that seemed to go on forever. Her tight, sweat-soaked T-shirt clung to a flat stomach and hugged her breasts. Jess's libido immediately flared to life, and she pushed it down with difficulty. *Friends. Just friends*, she repeated what was becoming a mantra.

"You okay?" Jess asked.

Kim straightened up and started to shake out her arms and legs. "I'm fine. I know I'll probably be sore tomorrow, but it still felt good to get out and run. I need to get back to regular workouts."

"You're welcome to join Thor and me anytime on our runs." *What are you doing? This was supposed to be a one-time thing until you saw how she acted at work afterward.* Jess couldn't bring herself to retract the spontaneous offer. It felt right.

A quick glance at Kim proved she was just as stunned by the invitation as Jess was at having made it. A smile tugged at Jess's lips as Kim tried to regain her composure.

"I wouldn't want to intrude. I know you don't get to spend a lot of time with Thor," Kim said.

Beautiful and incredibly thoughtful. Jess knew Kim was offering her a graceful way out. "Thor really likes you." *And so do I.* "It's not an intrusion. We enjoy your company."

That beautiful, sun out from behind the clouds smile that Jess was coming to adore, blazed across Kim's face. "That would be great, Jess."

Thor bumped Jess's hip.

"Sorry, boy." She had been so distracted by Kim she had forgotten what she was supposed to be doing. "I need to get him some water. Walk over to my truck with us?"

"Sure."

On the way to the truck Jess couldn't help noticing the occasional sour look Kim was throwing at Thor. She looked him over but couldn't see any reason for Kim's apparent ire. Nothing untoward had happened on their run.

"Is something wrong?" *Oh I bet I know what the problem is.* Jess was so used to his drool she forgot that most people didn't appreciate being covered in Thor's slobber. Jess pulled the small white towel she had tucked in her waistband and wiped Thor's muzzle. "Sorry. Did he slime you?"

"No, he's fine." Kim glanced down at Thor, and a slight scowl once again marred her face.

Jess was getting a bit worried. Had Kim decided she didn't like Thor after all?

Kim looked up at Jess and laughed. "Don't mind me. I'm just jealous."

Huh? "Of what?"

Kim pointed at Thor.

"Of Thor? Why?" Jess asked. She looked back and forth between Kim and Thor, totally confused by this turn of the conversation.

"We just ran two miles and he wasn't even winded. He looks like he could go another two miles, easy, if not more. I'm jealous. I used to do five miles at a time and now look at me."

Jess did as instructed. Kim's hair was windblown and damp with sweat; her T-shirt was wet with perspiration, and her face was still flushed from exertion. *You're beautiful.* While undoubtedly true, Jess figured it was best to keep that observation to herself.

Pulling on her own damp T-shirt, Jess made a show of checking herself out. "I look pretty much the same. I can't keep up with him either. I kept him by my side today. Normally he runs in front of me and zigzags back and forth to get some extra mileage. I think he runs twice as far as I do, and he's still not tired." She reached over Thor's back and patted Kim's shoulder. "Don't feel bad. He's a lot younger than we are."

Kim snorted. "Great. Thanks. I feel much better now." She looked down at Thor. "You just wait. Once I get back in shape then we'll see who gives out first."

Thor let out a deep-throated woof as if accepting the challenge.

Kim jumped and then laughed. She gently bumped Thor with her leg. "No comments from the peanut gallery."

Kim is so good with him. No wonder he likes her. She talks to him like Sam and I do. Watching the two interact, Jess had a feeling her quiet, solitary life was about to change. Her heart felt light at the prospect.

Thor's pace quickened, and he began to tug on the leash at the sight of Jess's vehicle.

L.A. Metro is available as a paperback and in various e-book formats at many online bookstores.

OTHER BOOKS FROM
YLVA PUBLISHING

http://www.ylva-publishing.com

L.A. METRO
(second edition)

RJ Nolan

ISBN: 978-3-95533-041-5
Length: 349 pages

Dr. Kimberly Donovan's life is in shambles. After her medical ethics are questioned, first her family, then her closeted lover, the Chief of the ER, betray her. Determined to make a fresh start, she flees to California and L.A. Metropolitan Hospital.

Dr. Jess McKenna, L.A. Metro's Chief of the ER, gives new meaning to the phrase emotionally guarded, but she has her reasons.

When Kim and Jess meet, the attraction is immediate. Emotions Jess has tried to repress for years surface. But her interest in Kim also stirs dark memories. They settle for friendship, determined not to repeat past mistakes, but secretly they both wish things could be different.

Will the demons from Jess's past destroy their future before it can even get started? Or will L.A. Metro be a place to not only heal the sick, but to mend wounded hearts?

CONFLICT OF INTEREST
(revised edition)

Jae

ISBN: 978-3-95533-109-2
Length: 502 pages

Workaholic Detective Aiden Carlisle isn't looking for love—and certainly not at the law enforcement seminar she reluctantly agreed to attend. But the first lecturer is not at all what she expected.

Psychologist Dawn Kinsley has just found her place in life. After a failed relationship with a police officer, she has sworn never to get involved with another cop again, but she feels a connection to Aiden from the very first moment.

Can Aiden keep from crossing the line when a brutal crime threatens to keep them apart before they've even gotten together?

COMING HOME
(revised edition)

Lois Cloarec Hart

ISBN: 978-3-95533-064-4
Length: 371 pages

A triangle with a twist, *Coming Home* is the story of three good people caught up in an impossible situation.

Rob, a charismatic ex-fighter pilot severely disabled with MS, has been steadfastly cared for by his wife, Jan, for many years. Quite by accident one day, Terry, a young writer/postal carrier, enters their lives and turns it upside down.

Injecting joy and turbulence into their quiet existence, Terry draws Rob and Jan into her lively circle of family and friends until the growing attachment between the two women begins to strain the bonds of love and loyalty, to Rob and each other.

HEARTS AND FLOWERS BORDER
(revised edition)

L.T. Smith

ISBN: 978-3-95533-179-5
Length: 318 pages

A visitor from her past jolts Laura Stewart into memories—some funny, some heart-wrenching. Thirteen years ago, Laura buried those memories so deeply she never believed they would resurface. Still, the pain of first love mars Laura's present life and might even destroy her chance of happiness with the beautiful, yet seemingly unobtainable Emma Jenkins.

Can Laura let go of the past, or will she make the same mistakes all over again?

Hearts and Flowers Border is a simple tale of the uncertainty of youth and the first flush of love—love that may have a chance after all.

COMING FROM YLVA
PUBLISHING IN 2014

http://www.ylva-publishing.com

HEART'S SURRENDER

Emma Weimann

Neither Samantha Freedman nor Gillian Jennings are looking for a relationship when they begin a no-strings-attached affair. But soon simple attraction turns into something more.

What happens when the worlds of a handywoman and a pampered housewife collide? Can nights of hot, erotic fun lead to love, or will these two very different women go their separate ways?

DEPARTURE FROM THE SCRIPT

Jae

Aspiring actress Amanda Clark and photographer Michelle Osinski are two women burned by love and not looking to test the fire again. Even if they were, it certainly wouldn't be with each other.

Amanda has never been attracted to a butch woman before, and Michelle personifies the term butch. Having just landed a role on a hot new TV show, Amanda is determined to focus on her career and to stay away from complicated relationships.

After a turbulent breakup with her starlet ex, Michelle swore she would never get involved with an actress again. But after a date that is not a date and some meddling from Amanda's grandmother, they both begin to wonder if it's not time for a departure from their usual dating scripts.

In a Heartbeat
© by RJ Nolan

ISBN: 978-3-95533-159-7

Also available as ebook.

Published by Ylva Publishing, legal entity of Ylva Verlag, e.Kfr.

Ylva Verlag, e.Kfr.
Owner: Astrid Ohletz
Am Kirschgarten 2
65830 Kriftel
Germany

http://www.ylva-publishing.com

First edition: May 2014 (Ylva Publishing)

Credits
Edited by Sandra Gerth and Day Petersen
Cover Design by Streetlight Graphics